JOHN CARPENTER PRESENTS

STORM KIDS

Series created by
JOHN CARPENTER and SANDY KING

JOHN CARPENTER PRESENTS

STORM KIDS

THE GRIMMS TOWN TERROR TALES:
RISE OF THE CANDY CREEPER

Written by NEO EDMUND
Art by RENAE DELIZ
Lettering by JANICE CHIANG
Edited by SANDY KING
Cover art by RENAE DELIZ

Book Design by SEAN SOBCZAK
Title Treatment by JOHN GALATI

Publishers: John Carpenter & Sandy King
Managing Editor: Sean Sobczak
Storm King Office Coordinator: Antwan Johnson
Publicity by Sphinx PR - Elysabeth Fulda

John Carpenter Presents Storm Kids: THE GRIMMS TOWN TERROR TALES: RISE OF THE CANDY CREEPER,
February 2021.
Published by Storm King Comics, a division of Storm King Productions, Inc.

AGES 8 AND UP
STORMKINGCOMICS.COM

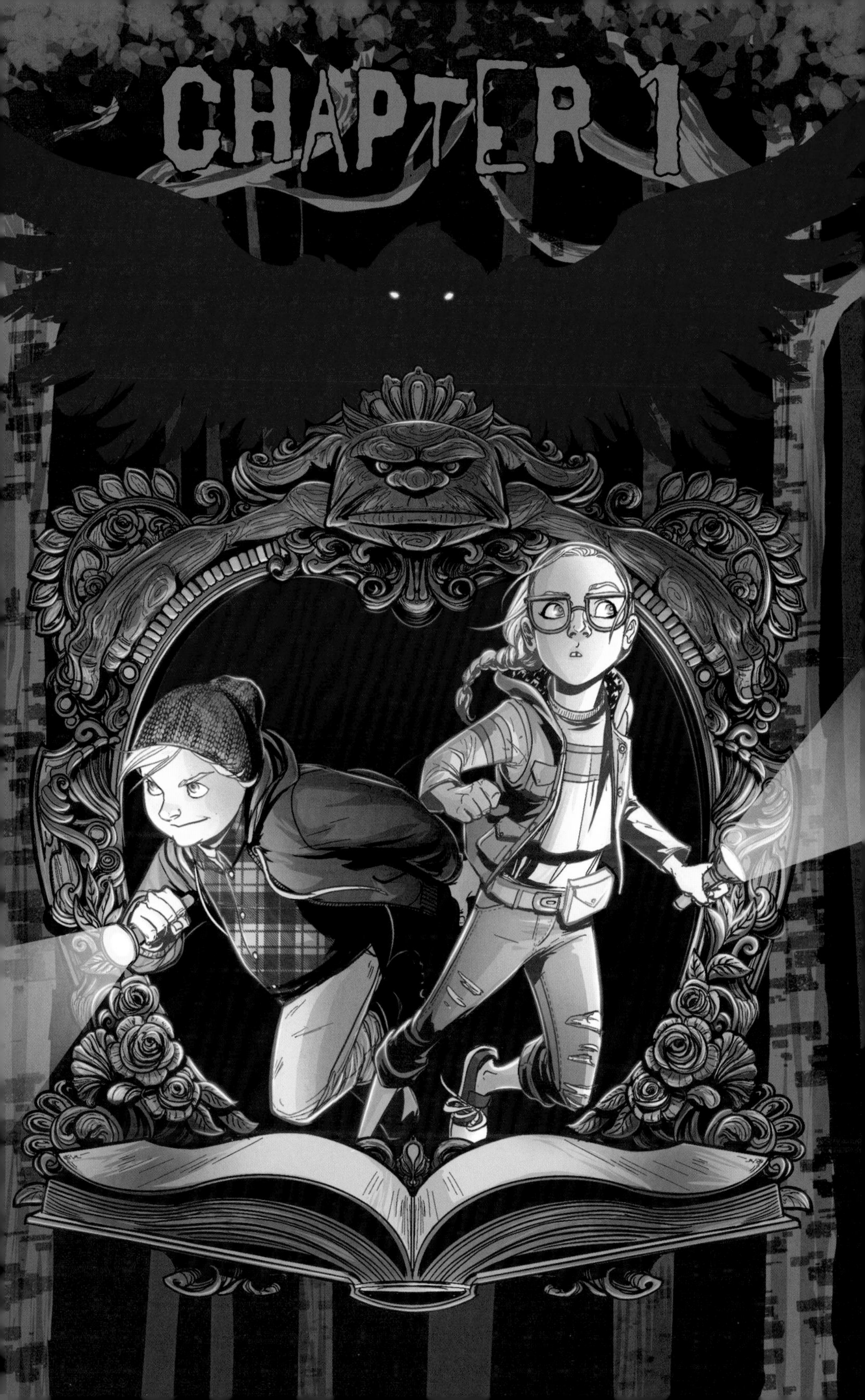
CHAPTER 1

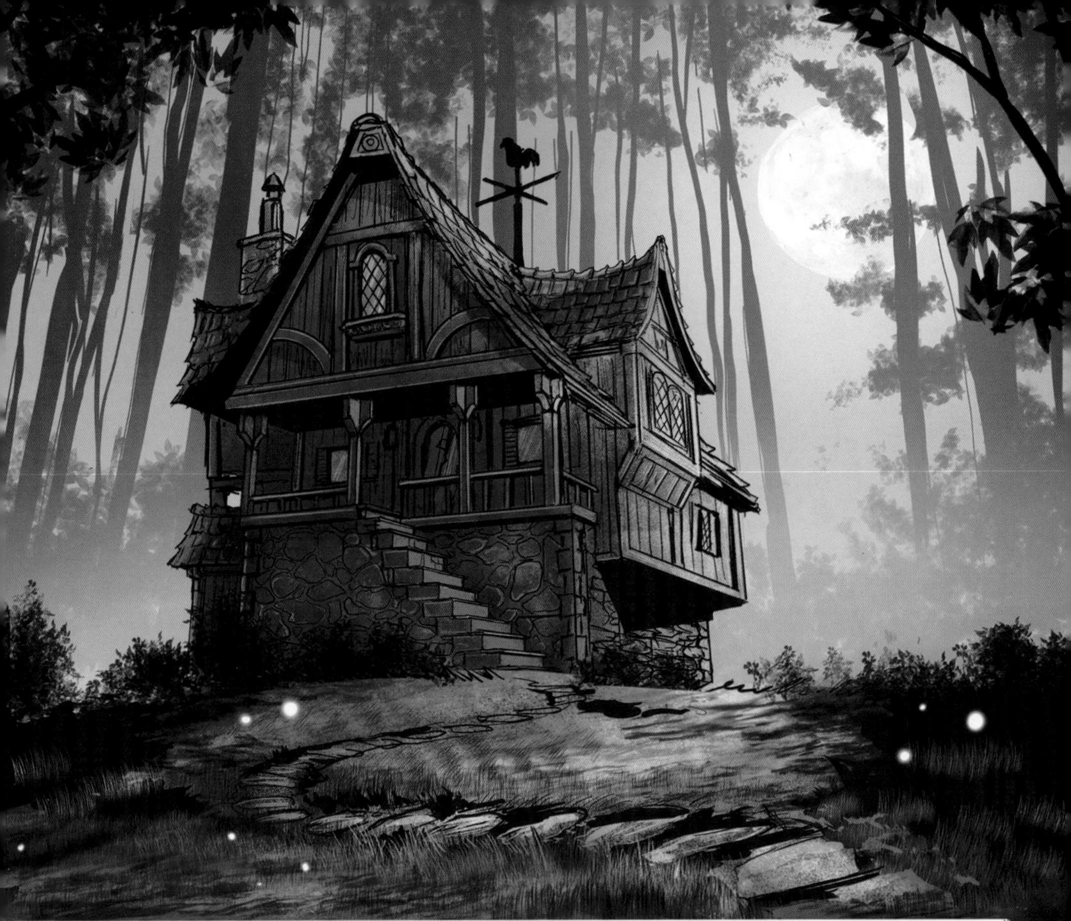

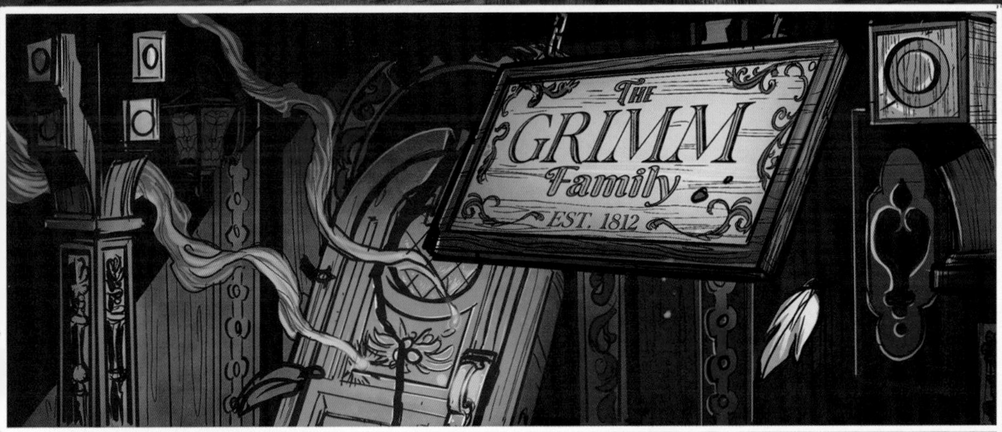
THE
GRIMM
Family
EST. 1812

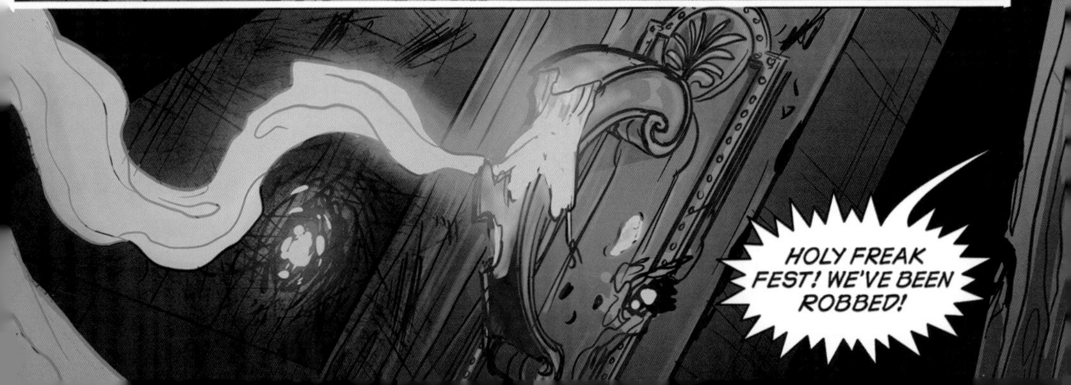
HOLY FREAK FEST! WE'VE BEEN ROBBED!

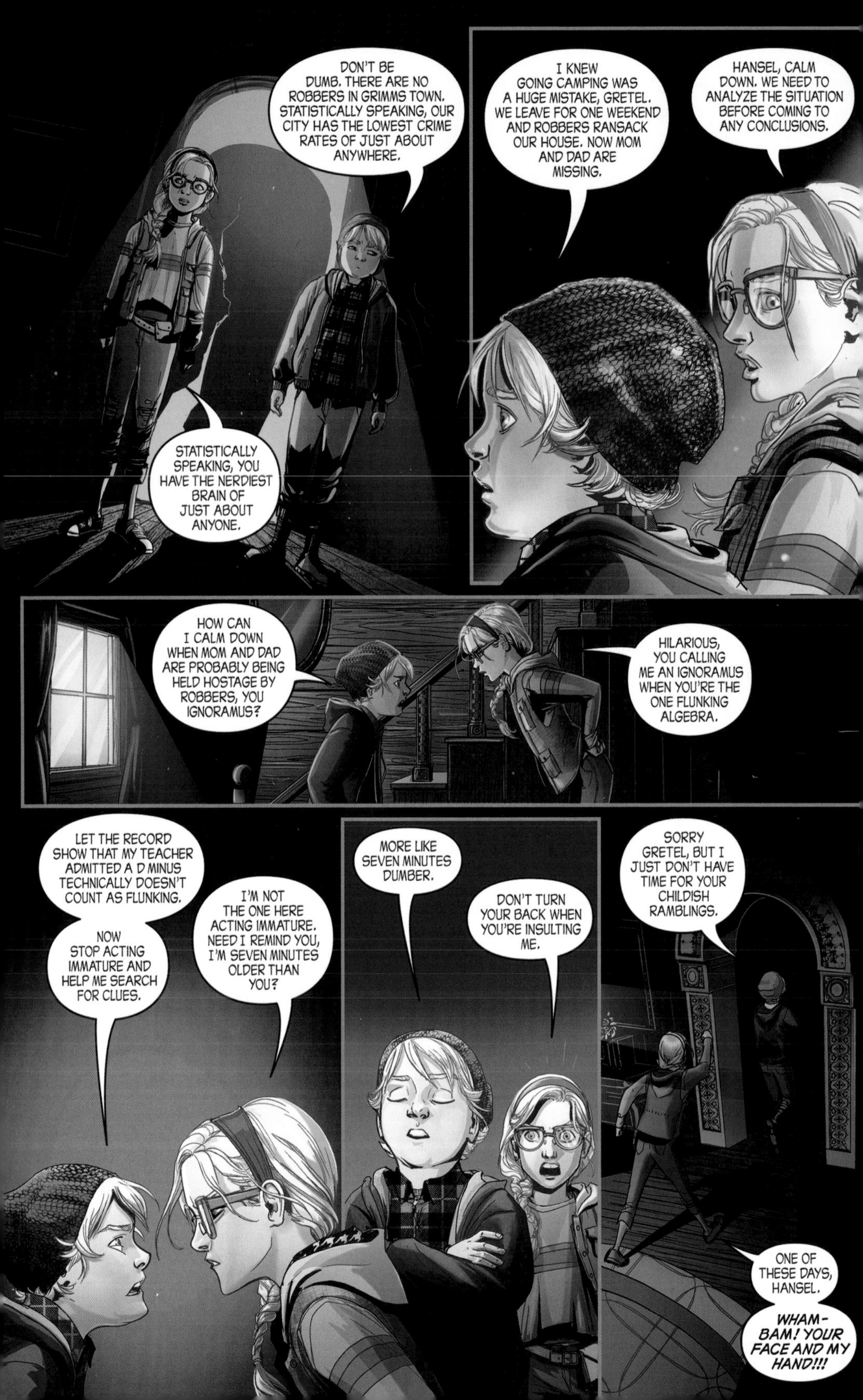
DON'T BE DUMB. THERE ARE NO ROBBERS IN GRIMMS TOWN. STATISTICALLY SPEAKING, OUR CITY HAS THE LOWEST CRIME RATES OF JUST ABOUT ANYWHERE.
STATISTICALLY SPEAKING, YOU HAVE THE NERDIEST BRAIN OF JUST ABOUT ANYONE.
I KNEW GOING CAMPING WAS A HUGE MISTAKE, GRETEL. WE LEAVE FOR ONE WEEKEND AND ROBBERS RANSACK OUR HOUSE. NOW MOM AND DAD ARE MISSING.
HANSEL, CALM DOWN. WE NEED TO ANALYZE THE SITUATION BEFORE COMING TO ANY CONCLUSIONS.
HOW CAN I CALM DOWN WHEN MOM AND DAD ARE PROBABLY BEING HELD HOSTAGE BY ROBBERS, YOU IGNORAMUS?
HILARIOUS, YOU CALLING ME AN IGNORAMUS WHEN YOU'RE THE ONE FLUNKING ALGEBRA.
LET THE RECORD SHOW THAT MY TEACHER ADMITTED A D MINUS TECHNICALLY DOESN'T COUNT AS FLUNKING.
NOW STOP ACTING IMMATURE AND HELP ME SEARCH FOR CLUES.
I'M NOT THE ONE HERE ACTING IMMATURE. NEED I REMIND YOU, I'M SEVEN MINUTES OLDER THAN YOU?
MORE LIKE SEVEN MINUTES DUMBER.
DON'T TURN YOUR BACK WHEN YOU'RE INSULTING ME.
SORRY GRETEL, BUT I JUST DON'T HAVE TIME FOR YOUR CHILDISH RAMBLINGS.
ONE OF THESE DAYS, HANSEL.
WHAM-BAM! YOUR FACE AND MY HAND!!!

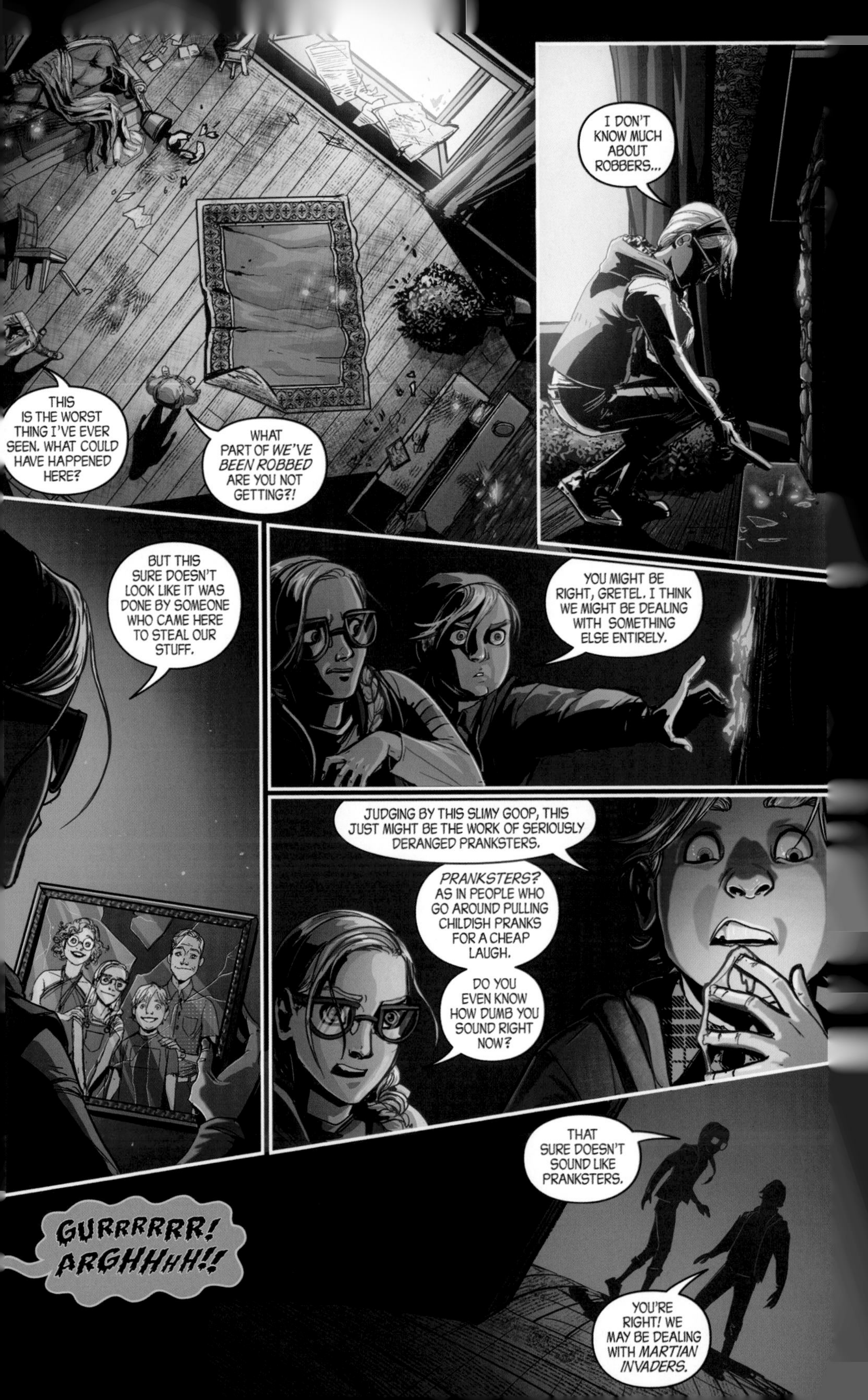
THIS IS THE WORST THING I'VE EVER SEEN. WHAT COULD HAVE HAPPENED HERE?
WHAT PART OF *WE'VE BEEN ROBBED* ARE YOU NOT GETTING?!
I DON'T KNOW MUCH ABOUT ROBBERS...
BUT THIS SURE DOESN'T LOOK LIKE IT WAS DONE BY SOMEONE WHO CAME HERE TO STEAL OUR STUFF.
YOU MIGHT BE RIGHT, GRETEL. I THINK WE MIGHT BE DEALING WITH SOMETHING ELSE ENTIRELY.
JUDGING BY THIS SLIMY GOOP, THIS JUST MIGHT BE THE WORK OF SERIOUSLY DERANGED PRANKSTERS.
PRANKSTERS? AS IN PEOPLE WHO GO AROUND PULLING CHILDISH PRANKS FOR A CHEAP LAUGH.
DO YOU EVEN KNOW HOW DUMB YOU SOUND RIGHT NOW?
GURRRRRR! ARGHHHH!!
THAT SURE DOESN'T SOUND LIKE PRANKSTERS.
YOU'RE RIGHT! WE MAY BE DEALING WITH *MARTIAN INVADERS.*

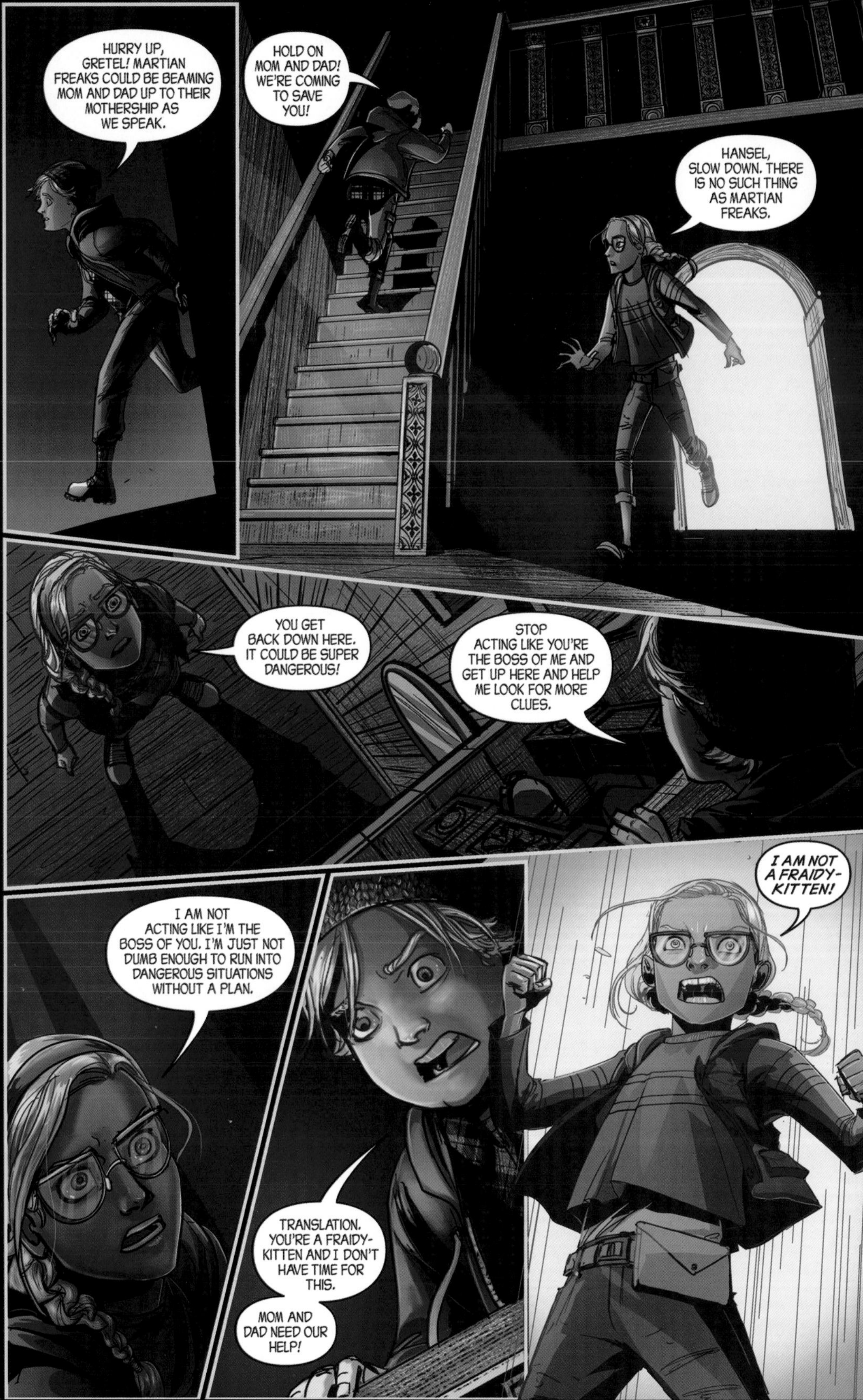
HURRY UP, GRETEL! MARTIAN FREAKS COULD BE BEAMING MOM AND DAD UP TO THEIR MOTHERSHIP AS WE SPEAK.
HOLD ON MOM AND DAD! WE'RE COMING TO SAVE YOU!
HANSEL, SLOW DOWN. THERE IS NO SUCH THING AS MARTIAN FREAKS.
YOU GET BACK DOWN HERE. IT COULD BE SUPER DANGEROUS!
STOP ACTING LIKE YOU'RE THE BOSS OF ME AND GET UP HERE AND HELP ME LOOK FOR MORE CLUES.
I AM NOT ACTING LIKE I'M THE BOSS OF YOU. I'M JUST NOT DUMB ENOUGH TO RUN INTO DANGEROUS SITUATIONS WITHOUT A PLAN.
TRANSLATION. YOU'RE A FRAIDY-KITTEN AND I DON'T HAVE TIME FOR THIS.
MOM AND DAD NEED OUR HELP!
I AM NOT A FRAIDY-KITTEN!

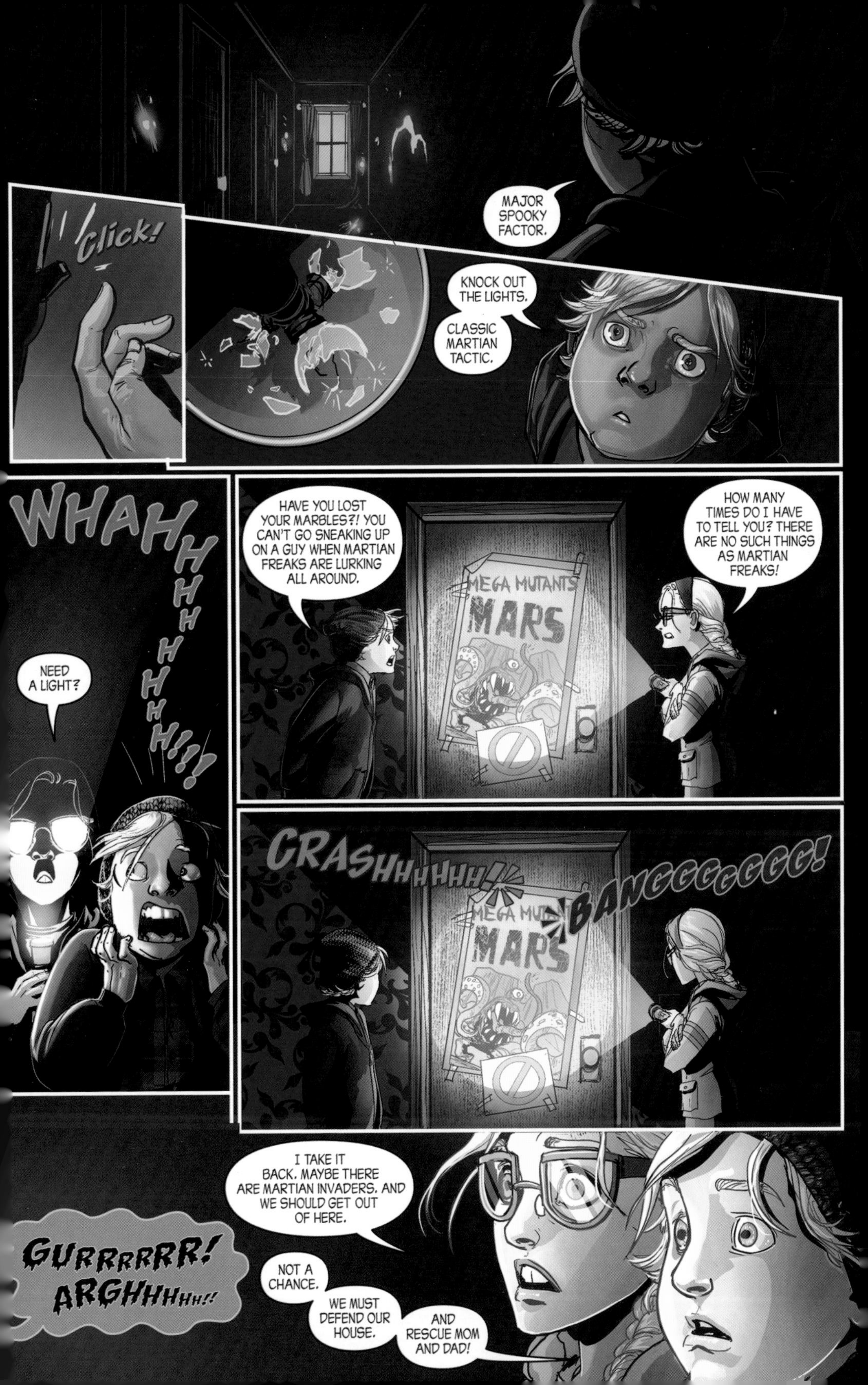
MAJOR SPOOKY FACTOR.
CLICK!
KNOCK OUT THE LIGHTS.
CLASSIC MARTIAN TACTIC.
NEED A LIGHT?
WHAHHHHHHHHHH!!!
HAVE YOU LOST YOUR MARBLES?! YOU CAN'T GO SNEAKING UP ON A GUY WHEN MARTIAN FREAKS ARE LURKING ALL AROUND.
HOW MANY TIMES DO I HAVE TO TELL YOU? THERE ARE NO SUCH THINGS AS MARTIAN FREAKS!
MEGA MUTANTS MARS
CRASHHHHHHH!
BANGGGGGGGG!
MEGA MUTANTS MARS
I TAKE IT BACK. MAYBE THERE ARE MARTIAN INVADERS. AND WE SHOULD GET OUT OF HERE.
GURRRRRRR! ARGHHHHH!!
NOT A CHANCE.
WE MUST DEFEND OUR HOUSE.
AND RESCUE MOM AND DAD!

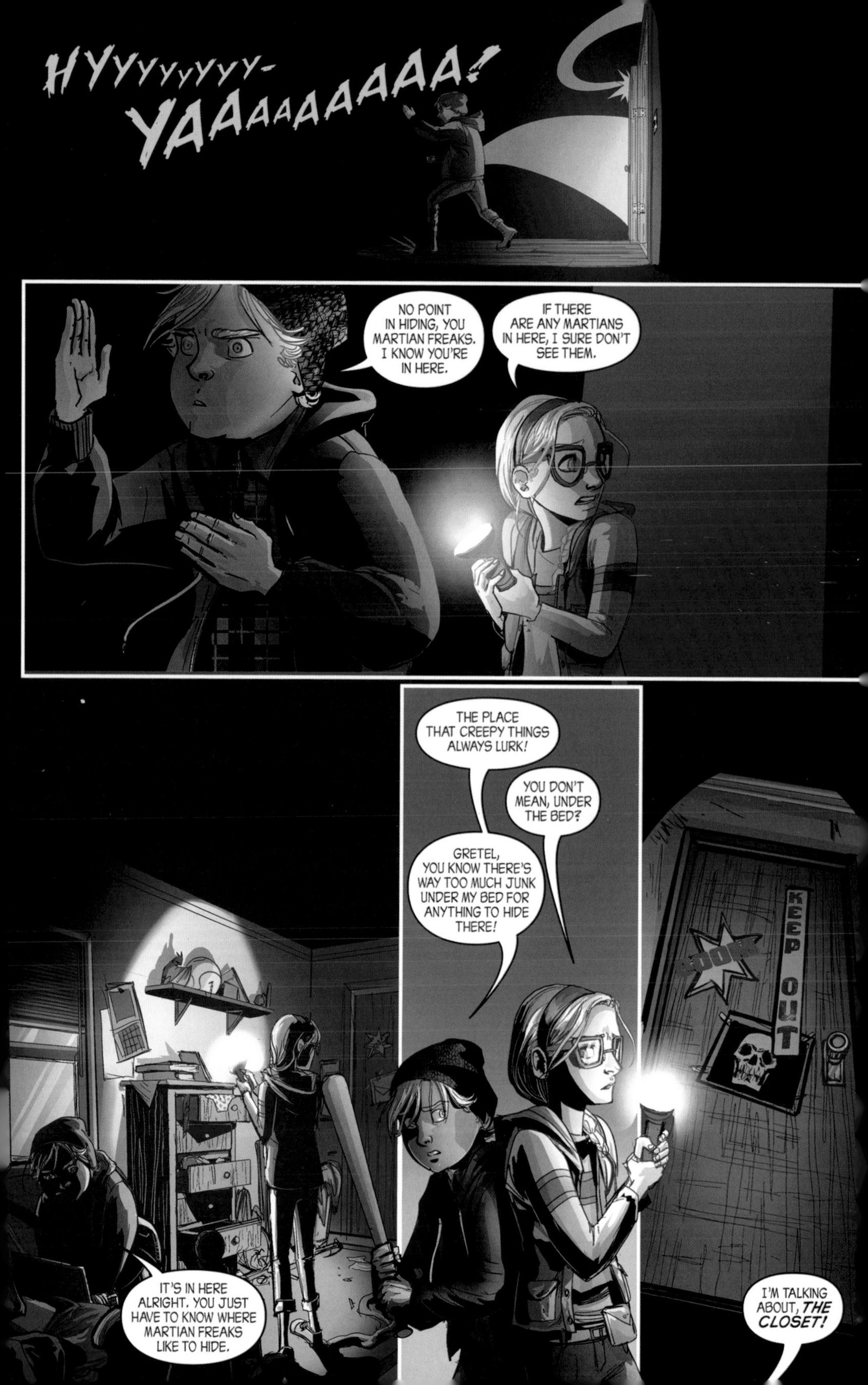
HYYYYYYYY-
YAAAAAAAAA!
NO POINT IN HIDING, YOU MARTIAN FREAKS. I KNOW YOU'RE IN HERE.
IF THERE ARE ANY MARTIANS IN HERE, I SURE DON'T SEE THEM.
IT'S IN HERE ALRIGHT. YOU JUST HAVE TO KNOW WHERE MARTIAN FREAKS LIKE TO HIDE.
THE PLACE THAT CREEPY THINGS ALWAYS LURK!
YOU DON'T MEAN, UNDER THE BED?
GRETEL, YOU KNOW THERE'S WAY TOO MUCH JUNK UNDER MY BED FOR ANYTHING TO HIDE THERE!
KEEP OUT
I'M TALKING ABOUT, THE CLOSET!

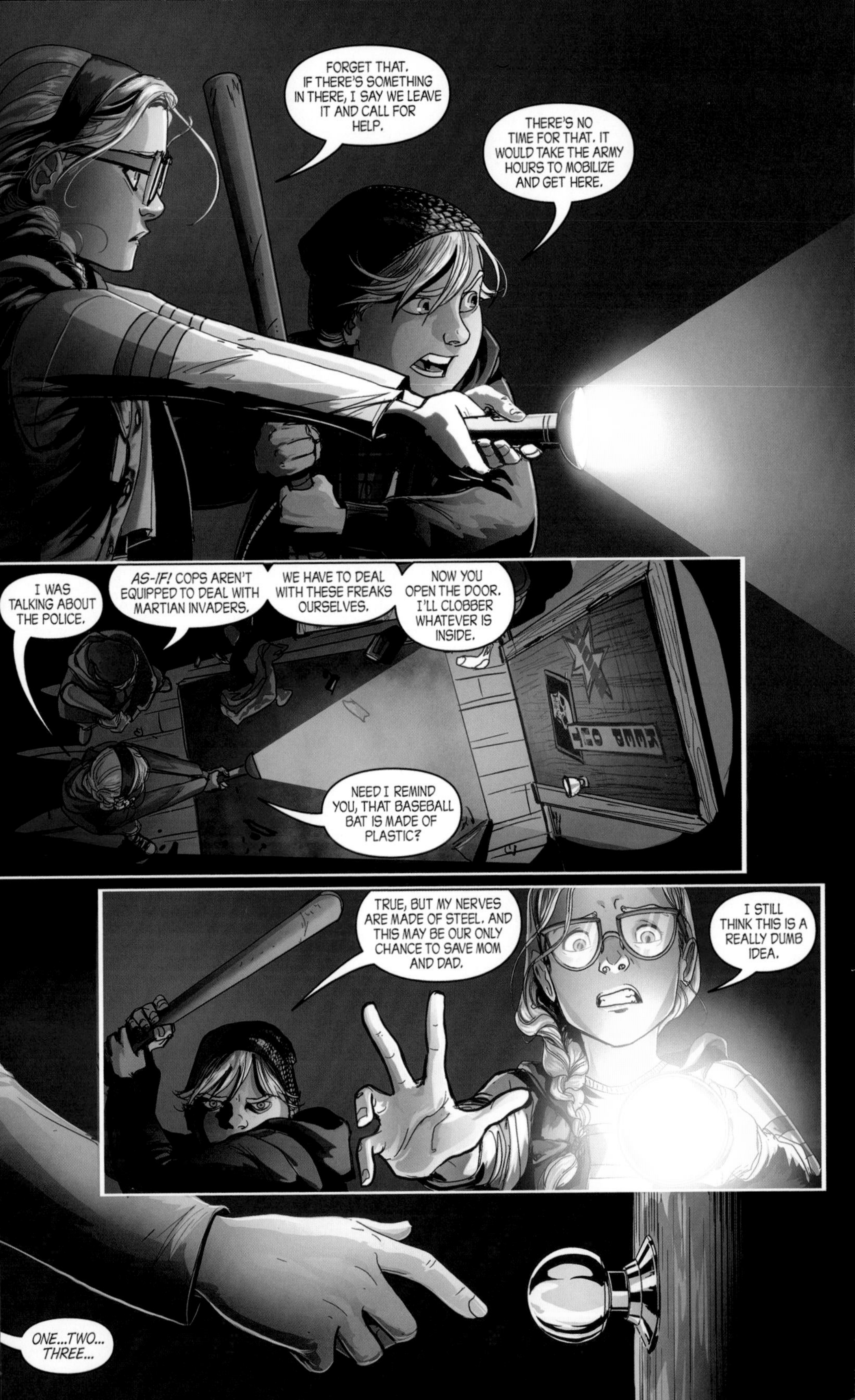
FORGET THAT. IF THERE'S SOMETHING IN THERE, I SAY WE LEAVE IT AND CALL FOR HELP.
THERE'S NO TIME FOR THAT. IT WOULD TAKE THE ARMY HOURS TO MOBILIZE AND GET HERE.
I WAS TALKING ABOUT THE POLICE.
AS-IF! COPS AREN'T EQUIPPED TO DEAL WITH MARTIAN INVADERS.
WE HAVE TO DEAL WITH THESE FREAKS OURSELVES.
NOW YOU OPEN THE DOOR. I'LL CLOBBER WHATEVER IS INSIDE.
NEED I REMIND YOU, THAT BASEBALL BAT IS MADE OF PLASTIC?
TRUE, BUT MY NERVES ARE MADE OF STEEL. AND THIS MAY BE OUR ONLY CHANCE TO SAVE MOM AND DAD.
I STILL THINK THIS IS A REALLY DUMB IDEA.
ONE...TWO... THREE...

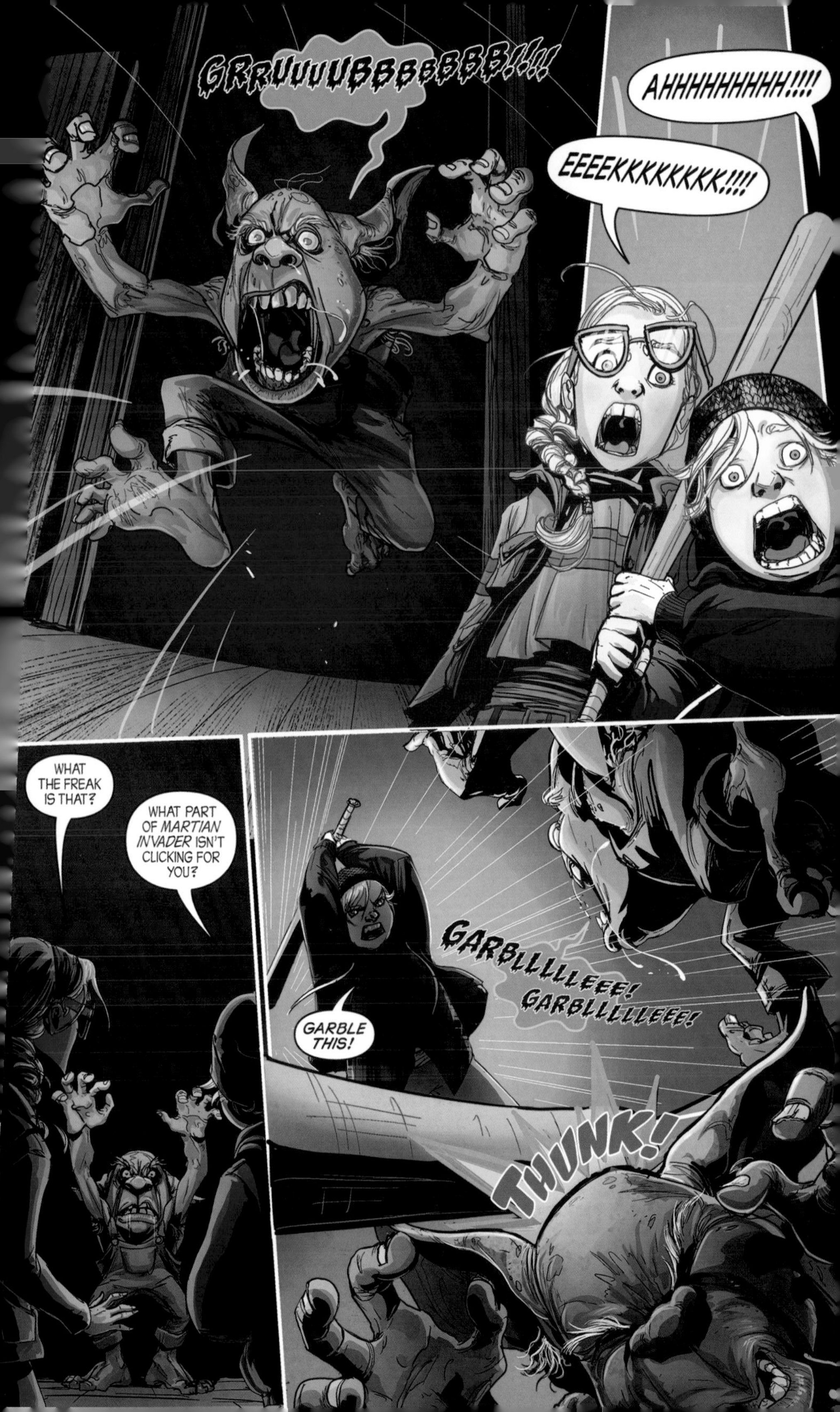
GRRUUUUBBBBBBB!!!!
AHHHHHHHHH!!!!
EEEEKKKKKKKK!!!!
WHAT THE FREAK IS THAT?
WHAT PART OF *MARTIAN INVADER* ISN'T CLICKING FOR YOU?
GARBLLLLLEEE! GARBLLLLLLEEE!
GARBLE THIS!
THUNK!

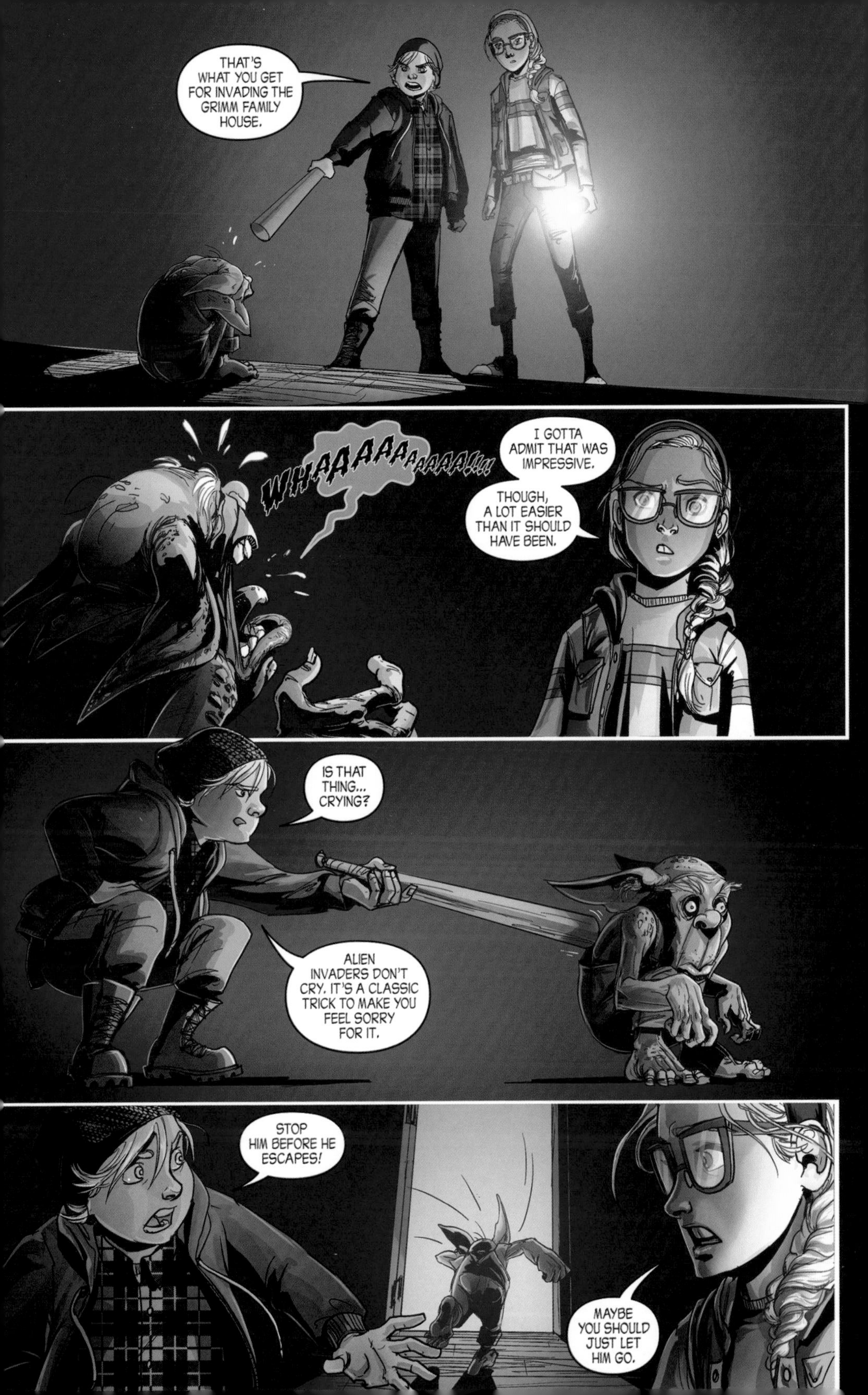
THAT'S WHAT YOU GET FOR INVADING THE GRIMM FAMILY HOUSE.
WHAAAAAAAAAAA!!!
I GOTTA ADMIT THAT WAS IMPRESSIVE.
THOUGH, A LOT EASIER THAN IT SHOULD HAVE BEEN.
IS THAT THING... CRYING?
ALIEN INVADERS DON'T CRY. IT'S A CLASSIC TRICK TO MAKE YOU FEEL SORRY FOR IT.
STOP HIM BEFORE HE ESCAPES!
MAYBE YOU SHOULD JUST LET HIM GO.

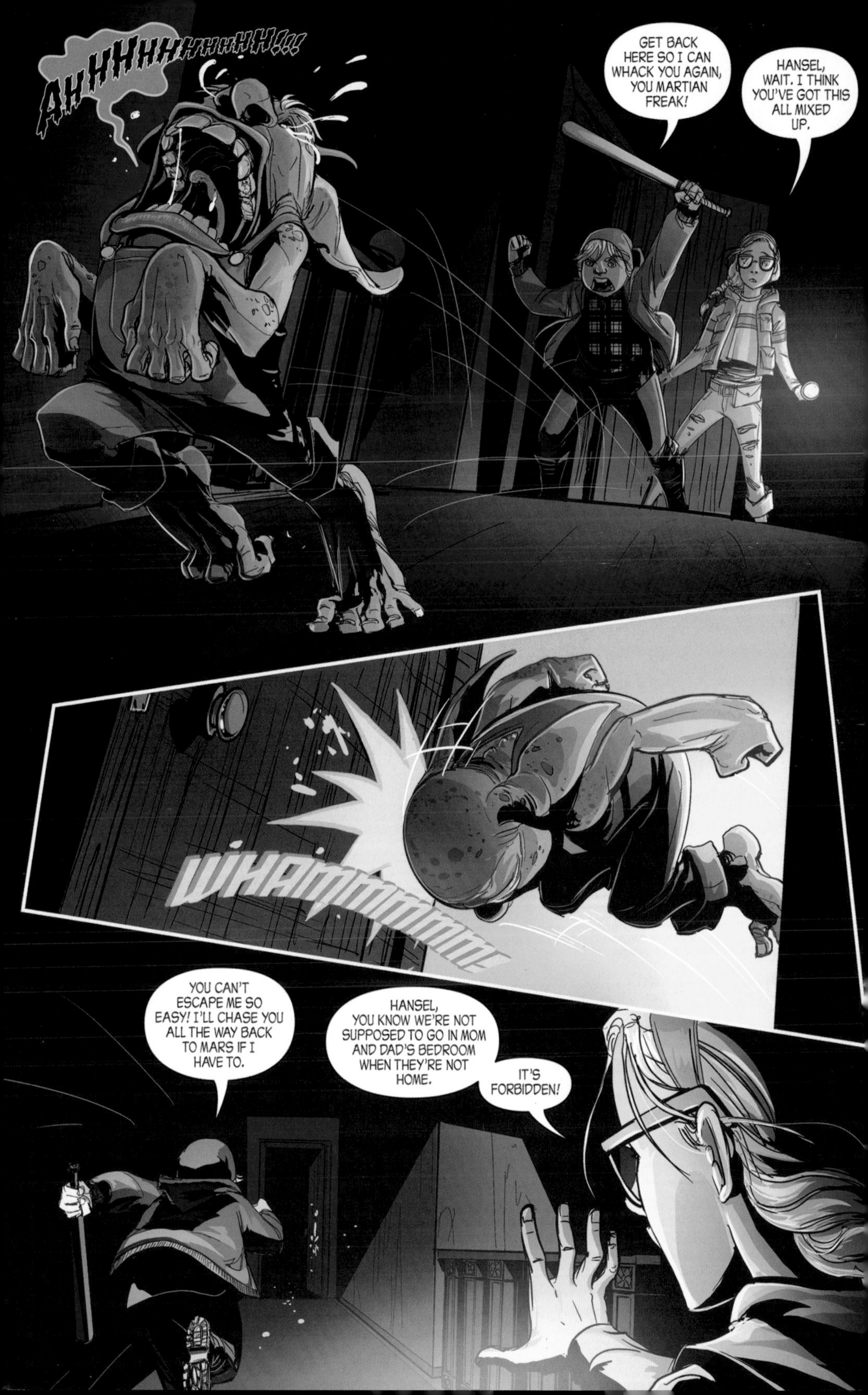
AHHHHHHHHHHH!!!
GET BACK HERE SO I CAN WHACK YOU AGAIN, YOU MARTIAN FREAK!
HANSEL, WAIT. I THINK YOU'VE GOT THIS ALL MIXED UP.
WHAMMMMM!
YOU CAN'T ESCAPE ME SO EASY! I'LL CHASE YOU ALL THE WAY BACK TO MARS IF I HAVE TO.
HANSEL, YOU KNOW WE'RE NOT SUPPOSED TO GO IN MOM AND DAD'S BEDROOM WHEN THEY'RE NOT HOME.
IT'S FORBIDDEN!

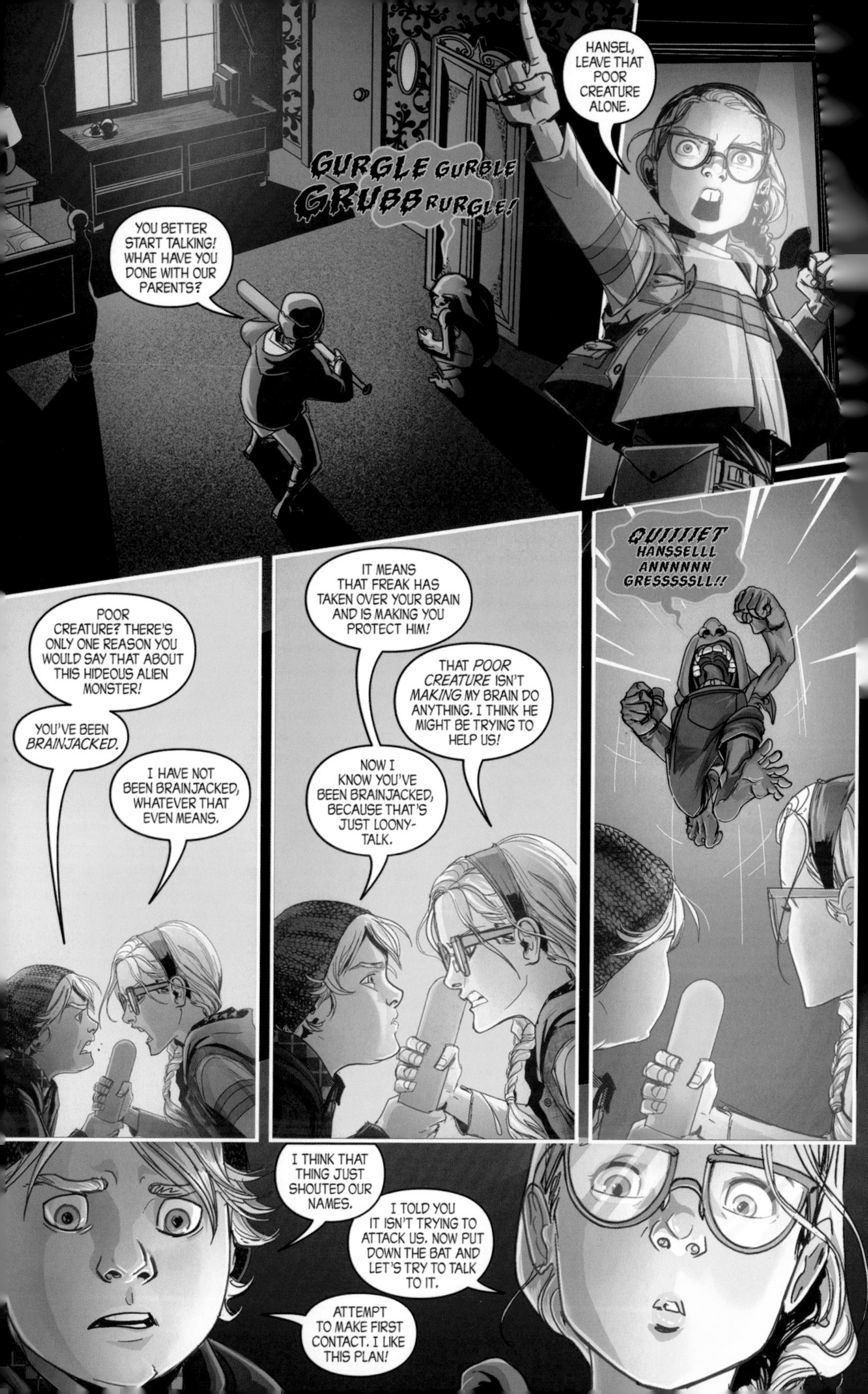
HANSEL, LEAVE THAT POOR CREATURE ALONE.
GURGLE GURBLE GRUBB RURGLE!
YOU BETTER START TALKING! WHAT HAVE YOU DONE WITH OUR PARENTS?
POOR CREATURE? THERE'S ONLY ONE REASON YOU WOULD SAY THAT ABOUT THIS HIDEOUS ALIEN MONSTER!
YOU'VE BEEN *BRAINJACKED.*
I HAVE NOT BEEN BRAINJACKED, WHATEVER THAT EVEN MEANS.
IT MEANS THAT FREAK HAS TAKEN OVER YOUR BRAIN AND IS MAKING YOU PROTECT HIM!
THAT *POOR CREATURE* ISN'T *MAKING* MY BRAIN DO ANYTHING. I THINK HE MIGHT BE TRYING TO HELP US!
NOW I KNOW YOU'VE BEEN BRAINJACKED, BECAUSE THAT'S JUST LOONY-TALK.
QUIIIIET HANSSELLL ANNNNNN GRESSSSSLL!!
I THINK THAT THING JUST SHOUTED OUR NAMES.
I TOLD YOU IT ISN'T TRYING TO ATTACK US. NOW PUT DOWN THE BAT AND LET'S TRY TO TALK TO IT.
ATTEMPT TO MAKE FIRST CONTACT. I LIKE THIS PLAN!

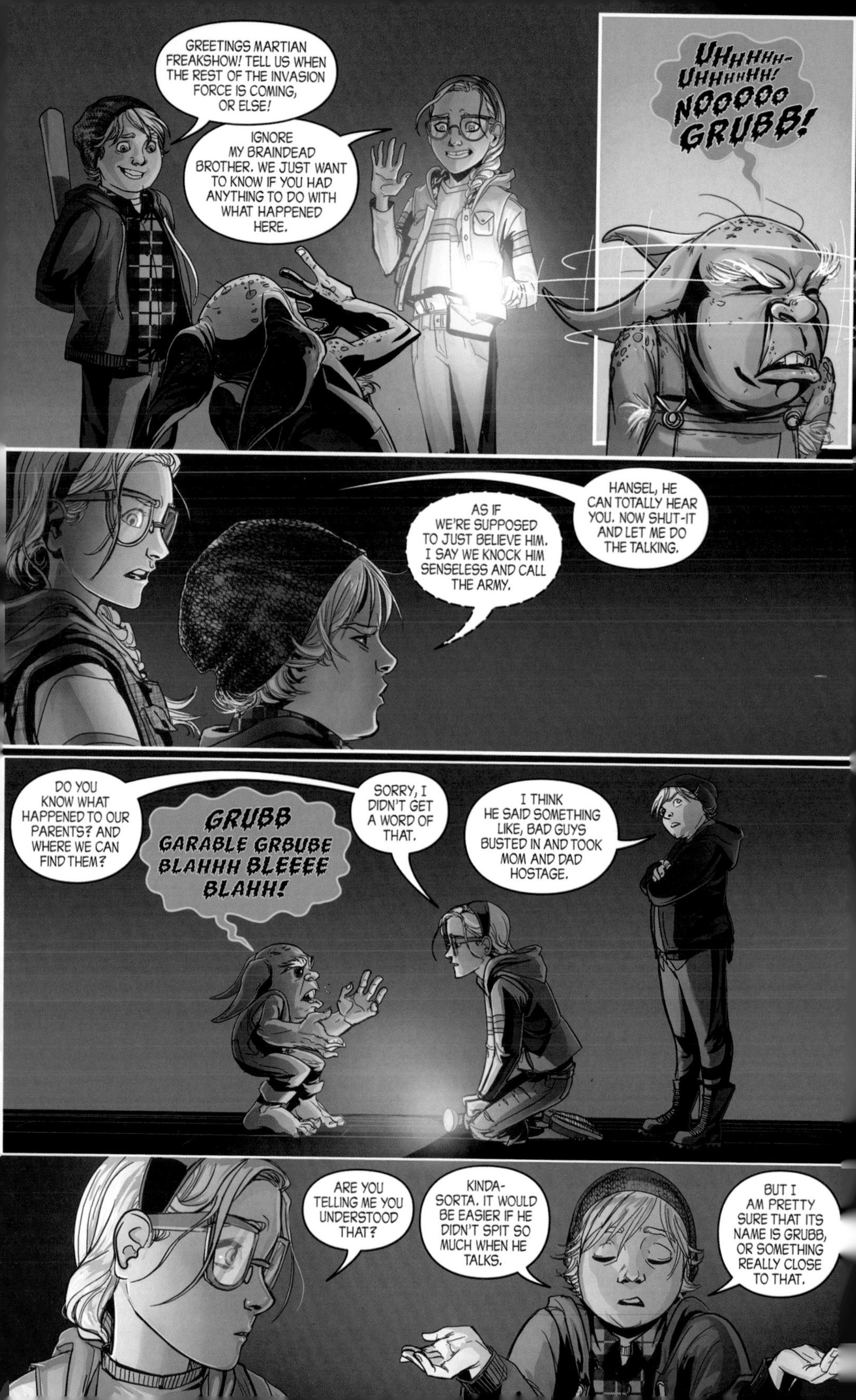
GREETINGS MARTIAN FREAKSHOW! TELL US WHEN THE REST OF THE INVASION FORCE IS COMING, OR ELSE!
IGNORE MY BRAINDEAD BROTHER. WE JUST WANT TO KNOW IF YOU HAD ANYTHING TO DO WITH WHAT HAPPENED HERE.
UHHHHH-UHHHHHH! NOOOOO GRUBB!
AS IF WE'RE SUPPOSED TO JUST BELIEVE HIM. I SAY WE KNOCK HIM SENSELESS AND CALL THE ARMY.
HANSEL, HE CAN TOTALLY HEAR YOU. NOW SHUT-IT AND LET ME DO THE TALKING.
DO YOU KNOW WHAT HAPPENED TO OUR PARENTS? AND WHERE WE CAN FIND THEM?
GRUBB GARABLE GRBUBE BLAHHH BLEEEE BLAHH!
SORRY, I DIDN'T GET A WORD OF THAT.
I THINK HE SAID SOMETHING LIKE, BAD GUYS BUSTED IN AND TOOK MOM AND DAD HOSTAGE.
ARE YOU TELLING ME YOU UNDERSTOOD THAT?
KINDA-SORTA. IT WOULD BE EASIER IF HE DIDN'T SPIT SO MUCH WHEN HE TALKS.
BUT I AM PRETTY SURE THAT ITS NAME IS GRUBB, OR SOMETHING REALLY CLOSE TO THAT.

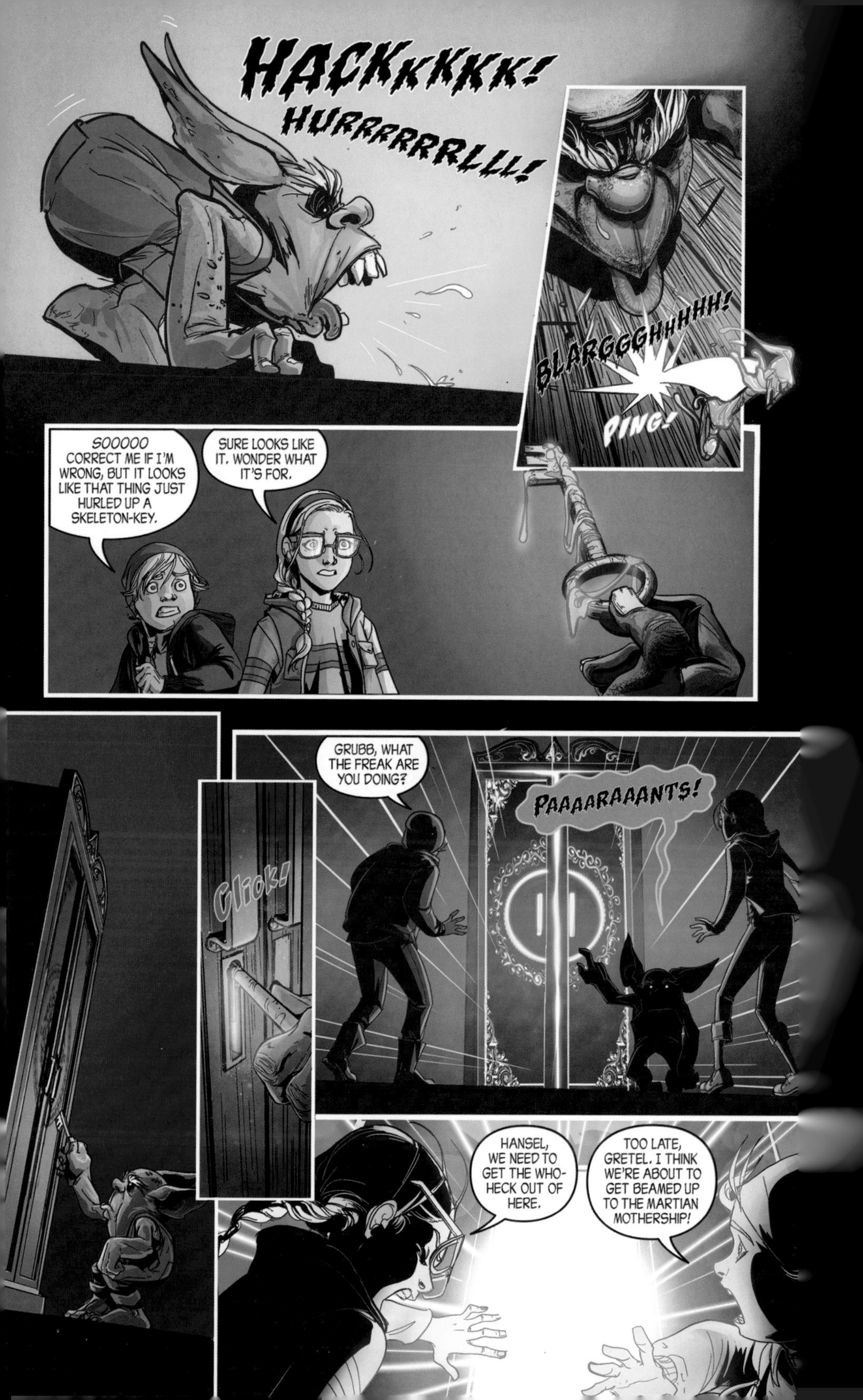
HACKkkkk!
HURRRRRRRLLL!
BLARGGGHHHHH!
PING!
SOOOOO CORRECT ME IF I'M WRONG, BUT IT LOOKS LIKE THAT THING JUST HURLED UP A SKELETON-KEY.
SURE LOOKS LIKE IT. WONDER WHAT IT'S FOR.
CLICK!
GRUBB, WHAT THE FREAK ARE YOU DOING?
PAAAARAAANTS!
HANSEL, WE NEED TO GET THE WHO-HECK OUT OF HERE.
TOO LATE, GRETEL. I THINK WE'RE ABOUT TO GET BEAMED UP TO THE MARTIAN MOTHERSHIP!

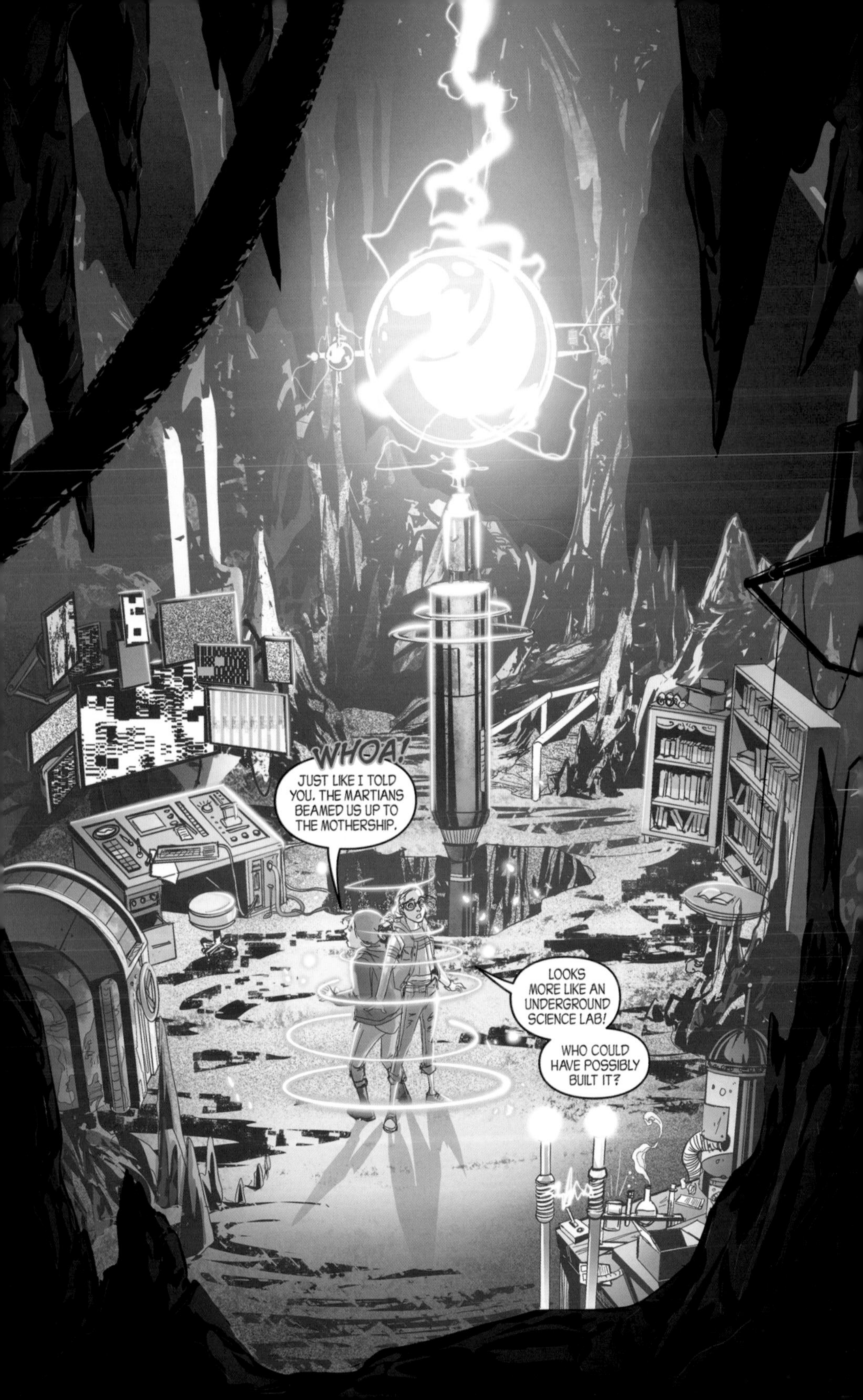
WHOA!
JUST LIKE I TOLD YOU. THE MARTIANS BEAMED US UP TO THE MOTHERSHIP.
LOOKS MORE LIKE AN UNDERGROUND SCIENCE LAB!
WHO COULD HAVE POSSIBLY BUILT IT?

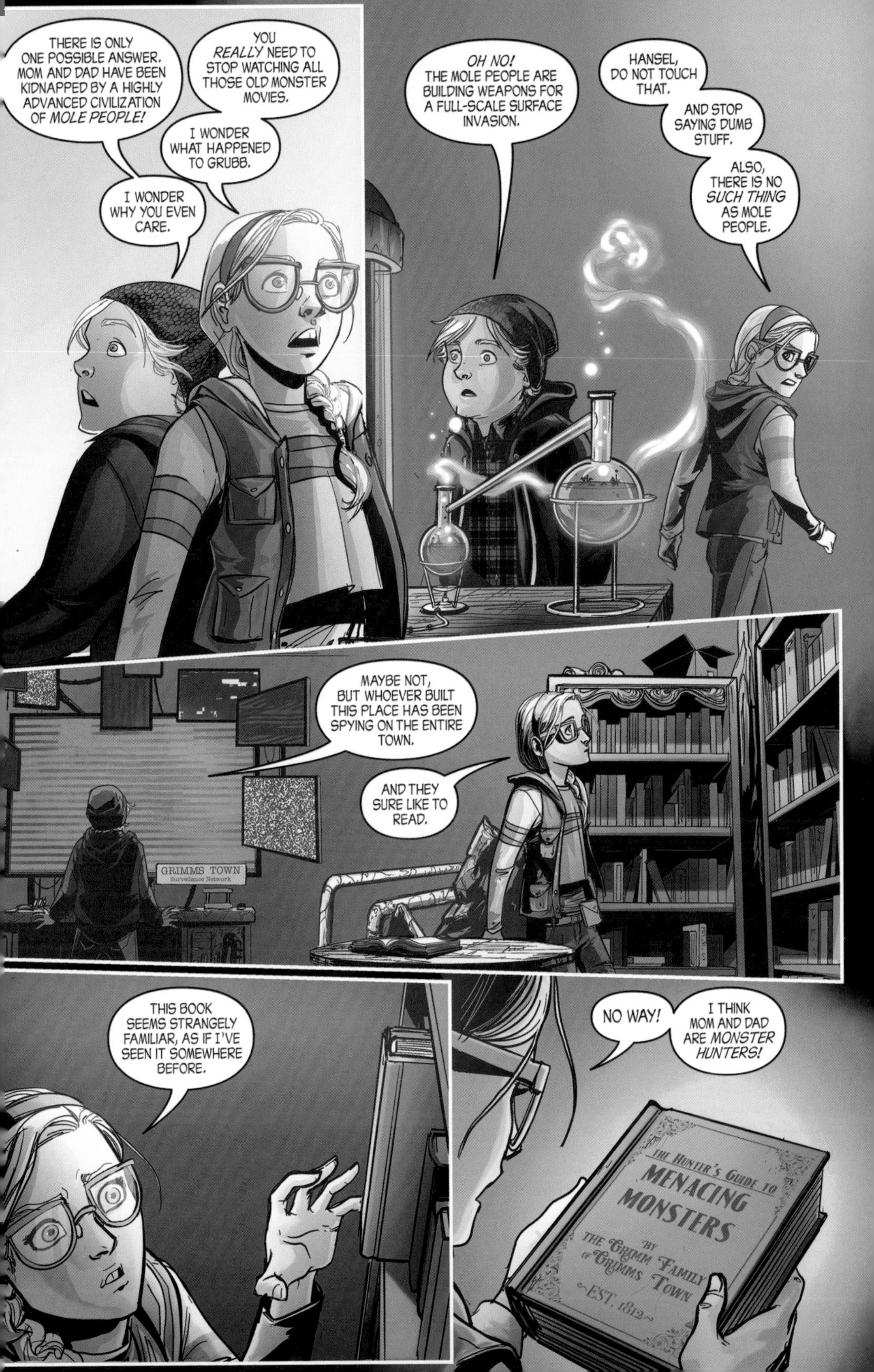
THERE IS ONLY ONE POSSIBLE ANSWER. MOM AND DAD HAVE BEEN KIDNAPPED BY A HIGHLY ADVANCED CIVILIZATION OF *MOLE PEOPLE!*
YOU *REALLY* NEED TO STOP WATCHING ALL THOSE OLD MONSTER MOVIES.
I WONDER WHAT HAPPENED TO GRUBB.
I WONDER WHY YOU EVEN CARE.
OH NO! THE MOLE PEOPLE ARE BUILDING WEAPONS FOR A FULL-SCALE SURFACE INVASION.
HANSEL, DO NOT TOUCH THAT.
AND STOP SAYING DUMB STUFF.
ALSO, THERE IS NO *SUCH THING* AS MOLE PEOPLE.
GRIMMS TOWN
Survellance Network
MAYBE NOT, BUT WHOEVER BUILT THIS PLACE HAS BEEN SPYING ON THE ENTIRE TOWN.
AND THEY SURE LIKE TO READ.
THIS BOOK SEEMS STRANGELY FAMILIAR, AS IF I'VE SEEN IT SOMEWHERE BEFORE.
NO WAY!
I THINK MOM AND DAD ARE *MONSTER HUNTERS!*
THE HUNTER'S GUIDE TO
MENACING MONSTERS
BY
THE GRIMM FAMILY of GRIMMS TOWN
~EST. 1812~

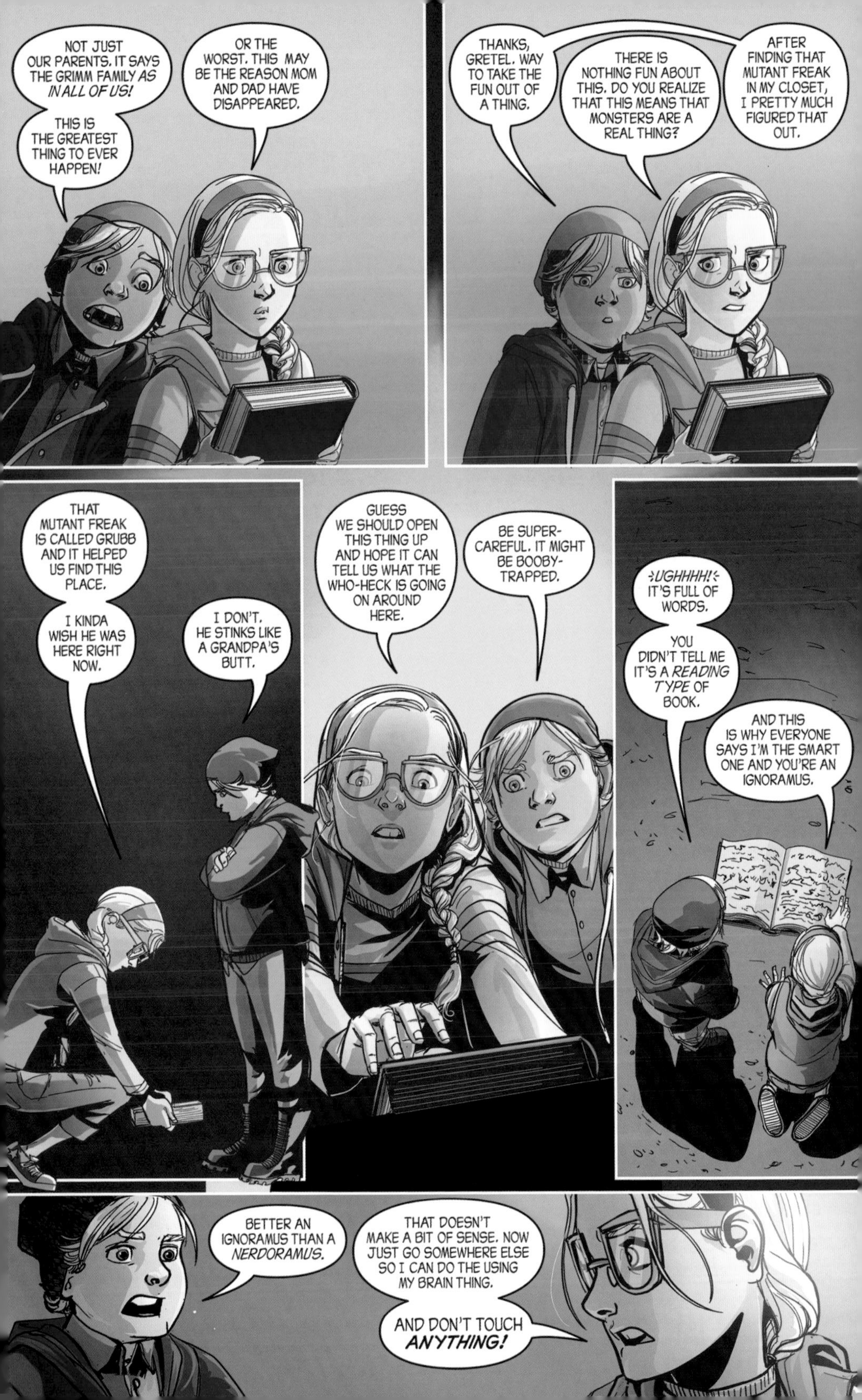
NOT JUST OUR PARENTS. IT SAYS THE GRIMM FAMILY *AS IN ALL OF US!*
THIS IS THE GREATEST THING TO EVER HAPPEN!
OR THE WORST. THIS MAY BE THE REASON MOM AND DAD HAVE DISAPPEARED.
THANKS, GRETEL. WAY TO TAKE THE FUN OUT OF A THING.
THERE IS NOTHING FUN ABOUT THIS. DO YOU REALIZE THAT THIS MEANS THAT MONSTERS ARE A REAL THING?
AFTER FINDING THAT MUTANT FREAK IN MY CLOSET, I PRETTY MUCH FIGURED THAT OUT.
THAT MUTANT FREAK IS CALLED GRUBB AND IT HELPED US FIND THIS PLACE.
I KINDA WISH HE WAS HERE RIGHT NOW.
I DON'T. HE STINKS LIKE A GRANDPA'S BUTT.
GUESS WE SHOULD OPEN THIS THING UP AND HOPE IT CAN TELL US WHAT THE WHO-HECK IS GOING ON AROUND HERE.
BE SUPER-CAREFUL. IT MIGHT BE BOOBY-TRAPPED.
UGHHHH! IT'S FULL OF WORDS.
YOU DIDN'T TELL ME IT'S A *READING TYPE* OF BOOK.
AND THIS IS WHY EVERYONE SAYS I'M THE SMART ONE AND YOU'RE AN IGNORAMUS.
BETTER AN IGNORAMUS THAN A *NERDORAMUS*.
THAT DOESN'T MAKE A BIT OF SENSE. NOW JUST GO SOMEWHERE ELSE SO I CAN DO THE USING MY BRAIN THING.
AND DON'T TOUCH ***ANYTHING!***

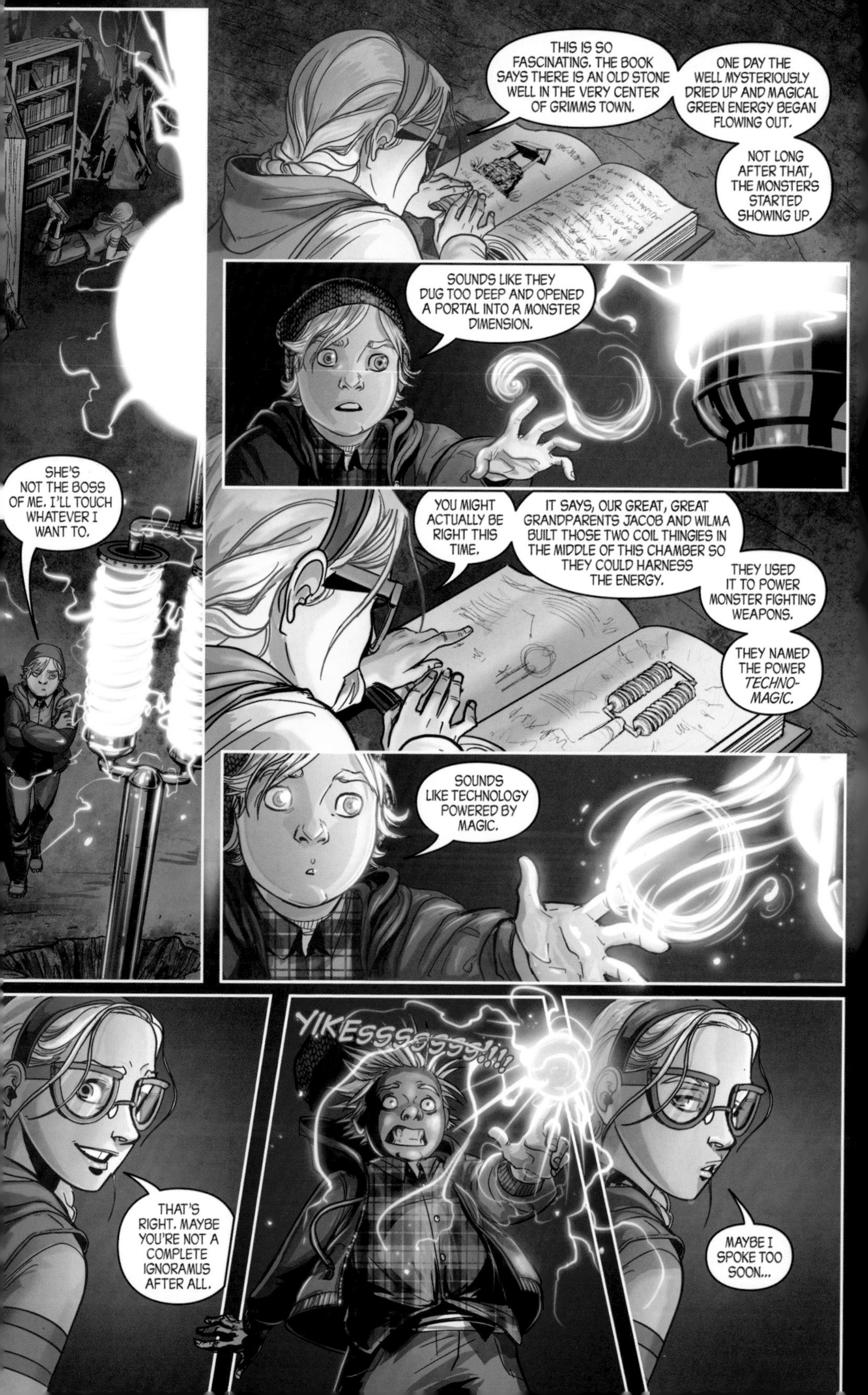
SHE'S NOT THE BOSS OF ME. I'LL TOUCH WHATEVER I WANT TO.
THIS IS SO FASCINATING. THE BOOK SAYS THERE IS AN OLD STONE WELL IN THE VERY CENTER OF GRIMMS TOWN.
ONE DAY THE WELL MYSTERIOUSLY DRIED UP AND MAGICAL GREEN ENERGY BEGAN FLOWING OUT.
NOT LONG AFTER THAT, THE MONSTERS STARTED SHOWING UP.
SOUNDS LIKE THEY DUG TOO DEEP AND OPENED A PORTAL INTO A MONSTER DIMENSION.
YOU MIGHT ACTUALLY BE RIGHT THIS TIME.
IT SAYS, OUR GREAT, GREAT GRANDPARENTS JACOB AND WILMA BUILT THOSE TWO COIL THINGIES IN THE MIDDLE OF THIS CHAMBER SO THEY COULD HARNESS THE ENERGY.
THEY USED IT TO POWER MONSTER FIGHTING WEAPONS.
THEY NAMED THE POWER *TECHNO-MAGIC.*
SOUNDS LIKE TECHNOLOGY POWERED BY MAGIC.
THAT'S RIGHT. MAYBE YOU'RE NOT A COMPLETE IGNORAMUS AFTER ALL.
YIKESSSSSSS!!!
MAYBE I SPOKE TOO SOON...

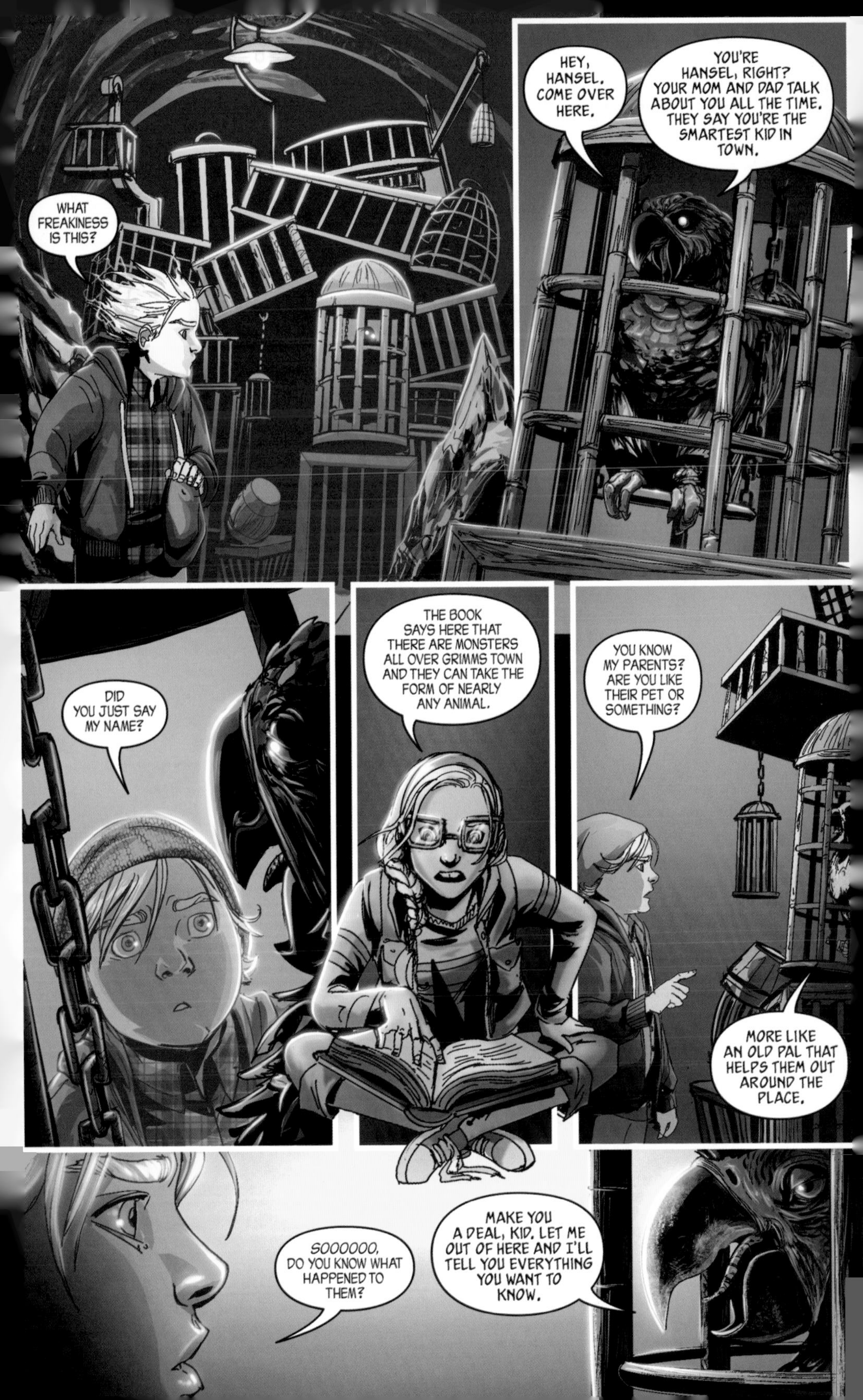
WHAT FREAKINESS IS THIS?
HEY, HANSEL. COME OVER HERE.
YOU'RE HANSEL, RIGHT? YOUR MOM AND DAD TALK ABOUT YOU ALL THE TIME. THEY SAY YOU'RE THE SMARTEST KID IN TOWN.
DID YOU JUST SAY MY NAME?
THE BOOK SAYS HERE THAT THERE ARE MONSTERS ALL OVER GRIMMS TOWN AND THEY CAN TAKE THE FORM OF NEARLY ANY ANIMAL.
YOU KNOW MY PARENTS? ARE YOU LIKE THEIR PET OR SOMETHING?
MORE LIKE AN OLD PAL THAT HELPS THEM OUT AROUND THE PLACE.
SOOOOOO, DO YOU KNOW WHAT HAPPENED TO THEM?
MAKE YOU A DEAL, KID. LET ME OUT OF HERE AND I'LL TELL YOU EVERYTHING YOU WANT TO KNOW.

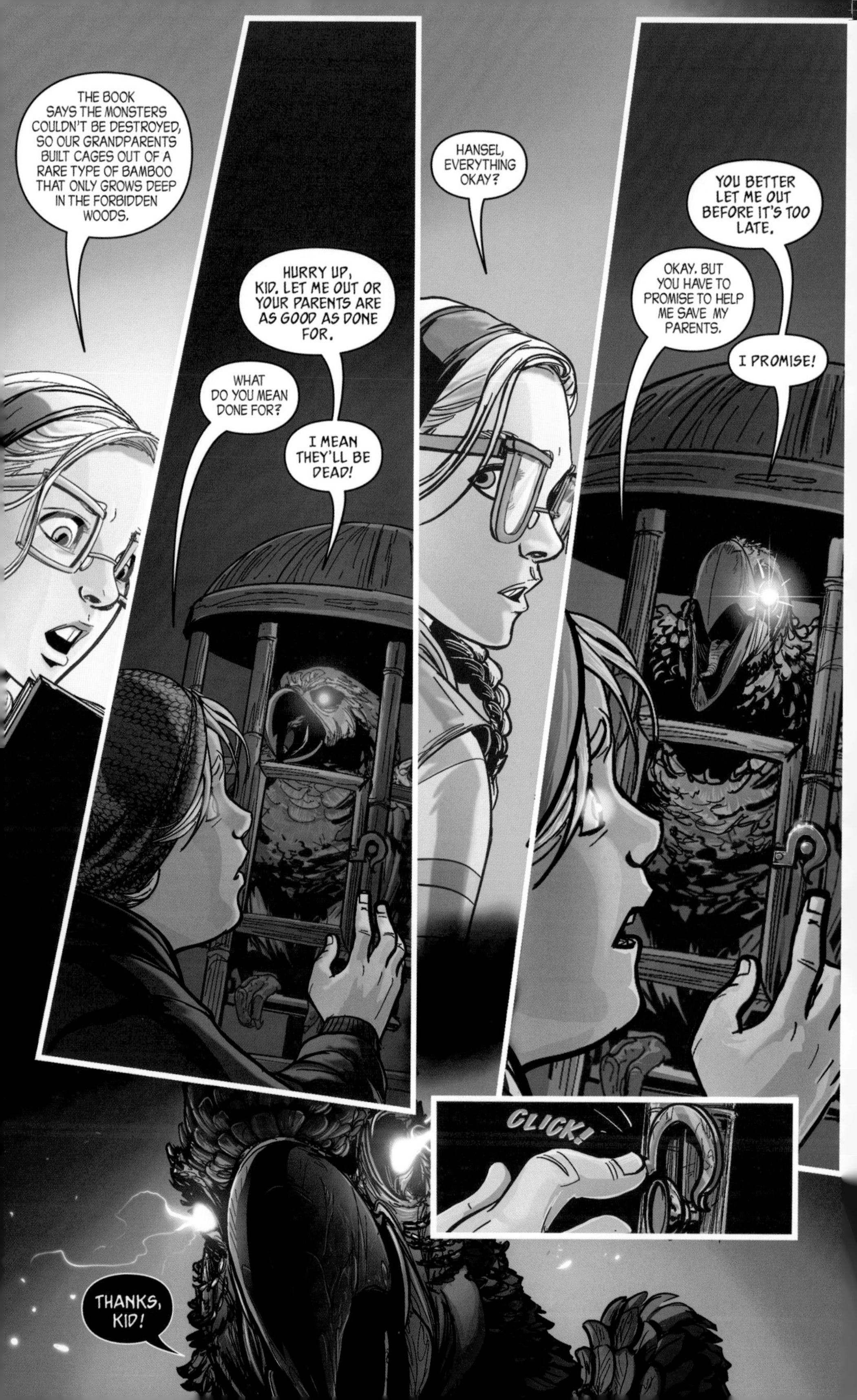
THE BOOK SAYS THE MONSTERS COULDN'T BE DESTROYED, SO OUR GRANDPARENTS BUILT CAGES OUT OF A RARE TYPE OF BAMBOO THAT ONLY GROWS DEEP IN THE FORBIDDEN WOODS.
HURRY UP, KID. LET ME OUT OR YOUR PARENTS ARE AS GOOD AS DONE FOR.
WHAT DO YOU MEAN DONE FOR?
I MEAN THEY'LL BE DEAD!
HANSEL, EVERYTHING OKAY?
YOU BETTER LET ME OUT BEFORE IT'S TOO LATE.
OKAY. BUT YOU HAVE TO PROMISE TO HELP ME SAVE MY PARENTS.
I PROMISE!
CLICK!
THANKS, KID!

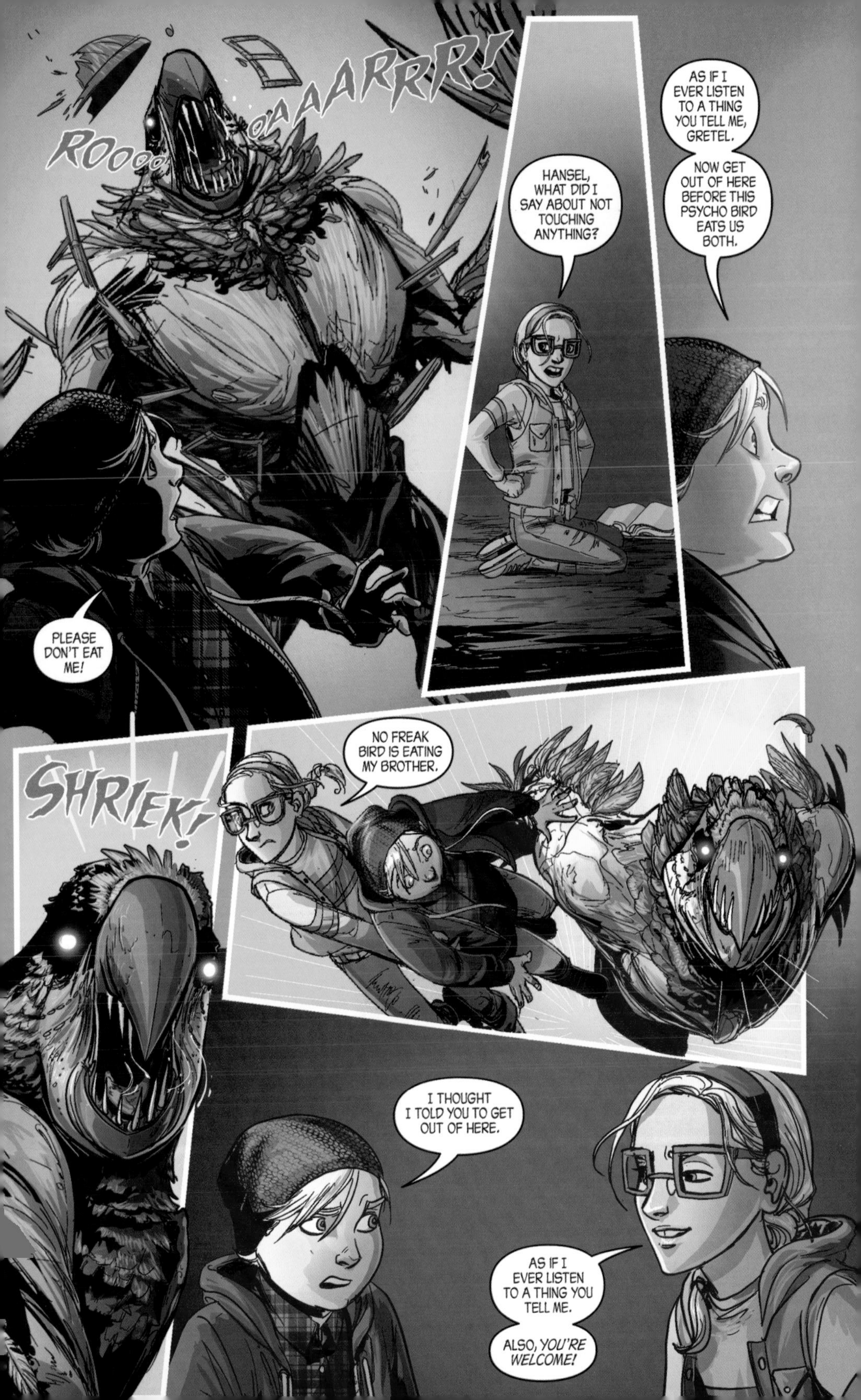
ROOOOO OAAAARRRR!
PLEASE DON'T EAT ME!
HANSEL, WHAT DID I SAY ABOUT NOT TOUCHING ANYTHING?
AS IF I EVER LISTEN TO A THING YOU TELL ME, GRETEL.
NOW GET OUT OF HERE BEFORE THIS PSYCHO BIRD EATS US BOTH.
SHRIEK!
NO FREAK BIRD IS EATING MY BROTHER.
I THOUGHT I TOLD YOU TO GET OUT OF HERE.
AS IF I EVER LISTEN TO A THING YOU TELL ME.
ALSO, *YOU'RE WELCOME!*

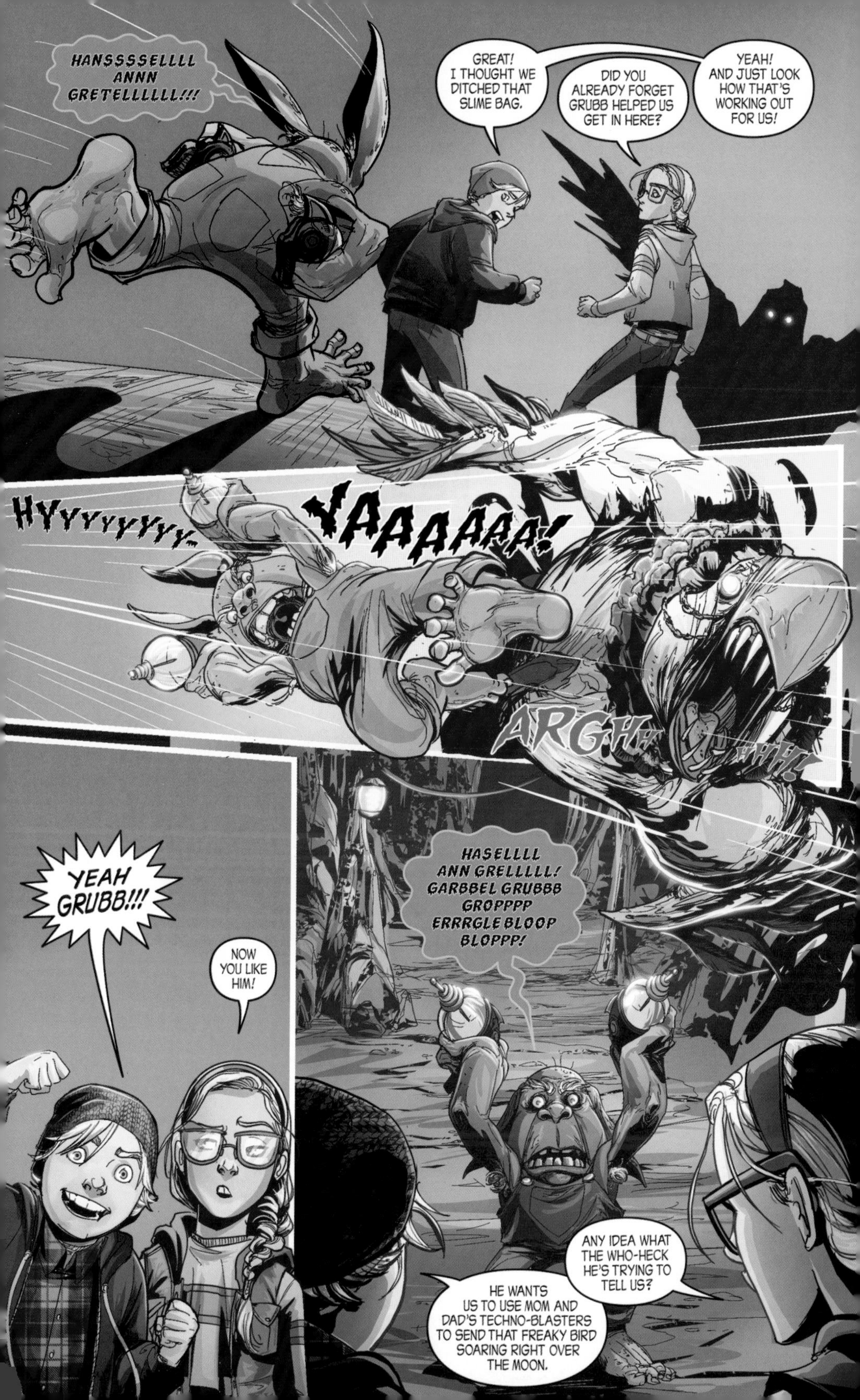

HANSSSSELLLL ANNN GRETELLLLLLL!!!
GREAT! I THOUGHT WE DITCHED THAT SLIME BAG.
DID YOU ALREADY FORGET GRUBB HELPED US GET IN HERE?
YEAH! AND JUST LOOK HOW THAT'S WORKING OUT FOR US!
HYYYYYYYY-
YAAAAAA!
ARGH
YEAH GRUBB!!!
NOW YOU LIKE HIM!
HASELLLL ANN GRELLLLLL! GARBBEL GRUBBB GROPPPP ERRRGLE BLOOP BLOPPP!
ANY IDEA WHAT THE WHO-HECK HE'S TRYING TO TELL US?
HE WANTS US TO USE MOM AND DAD'S TECHNO-BLASTERS TO SEND THAT FREAKY BIRD SOARING RIGHT OVER THE MOON.

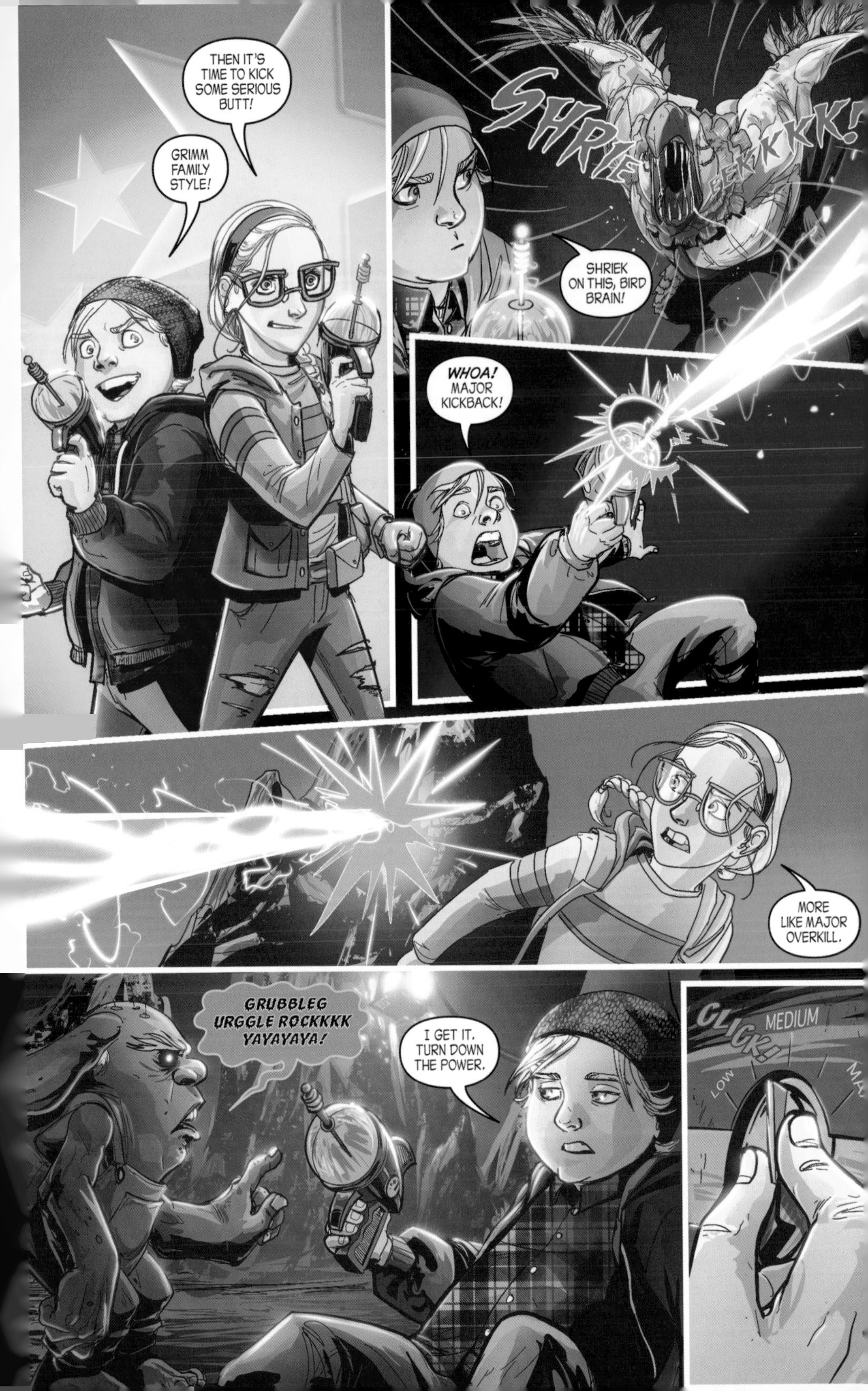
THEN IT'S TIME TO KICK SOME SERIOUS BUTT!
GRIMM FAMILY STYLE!
SHRIEEEKKKK!
SHRIEK ON THIS, BIRD BRAIN!
WHOA! MAJOR KICKBACK!
MORE LIKE MAJOR OVERKILL.
GRUBBLEG URGGLE ROCKKKK YAYAYAYA!
I GET IT. TURN DOWN THE POWER.
CLICK!
LOW
MEDIUM

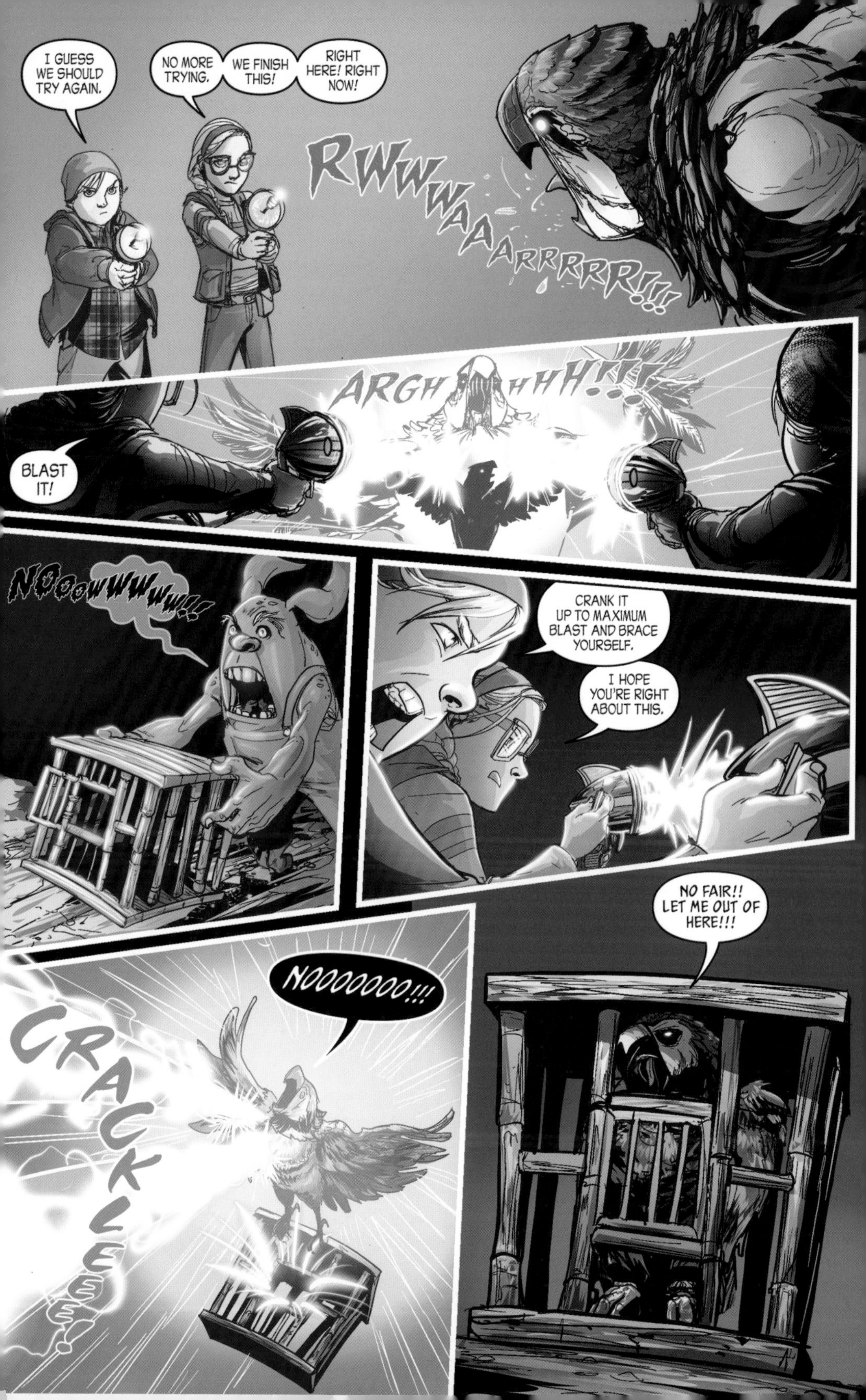
I GUESS WE SHOULD TRY AGAIN.
NO MORE TRYING.
WE FINISH THIS!
RIGHT HERE! RIGHT NOW!
RWWWAAARRRRRR!!!
ARGHHHHH!!!!
BLAST IT!
NOooWWWWW!!!
CRANK IT UP TO MAXIMUM BLAST AND BRACE YOURSELF.
I HOPE YOU'RE RIGHT ABOUT THIS.
NOOOOOOO!!!
CRACKLEEE!
NO FAIR!! LET ME OUT OF HERE!!!

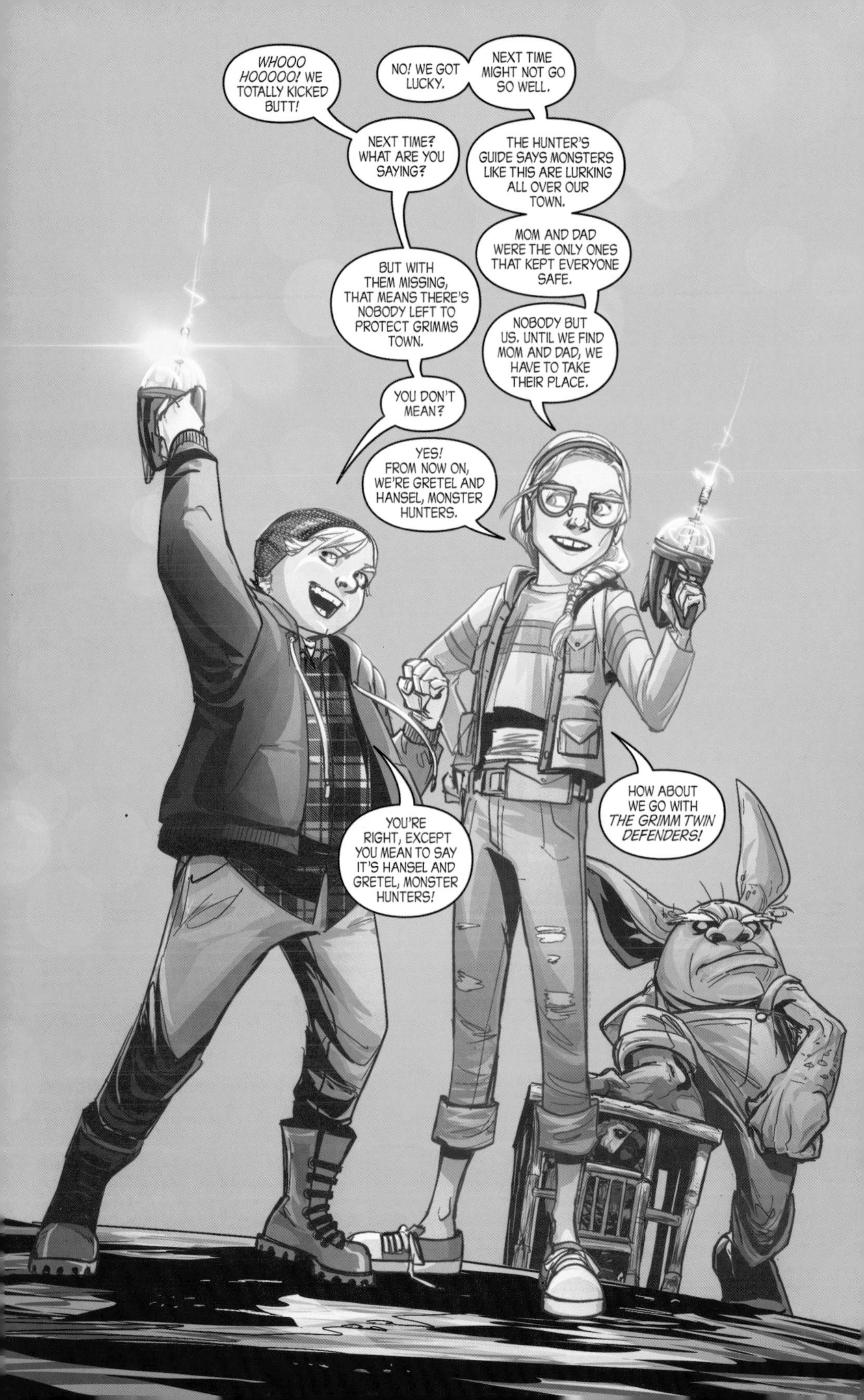

WHOOO HOOOOO! WE TOTALLY KICKED BUTT!
NO*!* WE GOT LUCKY.
NEXT TIME MIGHT NOT GO SO WELL.
NEXT TIME? WHAT ARE YOU SAYING?
THE HUNTER'S GUIDE SAYS MONSTERS LIKE THIS ARE LURKING ALL OVER OUR TOWN.
MOM AND DAD WERE THE ONLY ONES THAT KEPT EVERYONE SAFE.
BUT WITH THEM MISSING, THAT MEANS THERE'S NOBODY LEFT TO PROTECT GRIMMS TOWN.
NOBODY BUT US. UNTIL WE FIND MOM AND DAD, WE HAVE TO TAKE THEIR PLACE.
YOU DON'T MEAN?
YES! FROM NOW ON, WE'RE GRETEL AND HANSEL, MONSTER HUNTERS.
YOU'RE RIGHT, EXCEPT YOU MEAN TO SAY IT'S HANSEL AND GRETEL, MONSTER HUNTERS!
HOW ABOUT WE GO WITH *THE GRIMM TWIN DEFENDERS!*

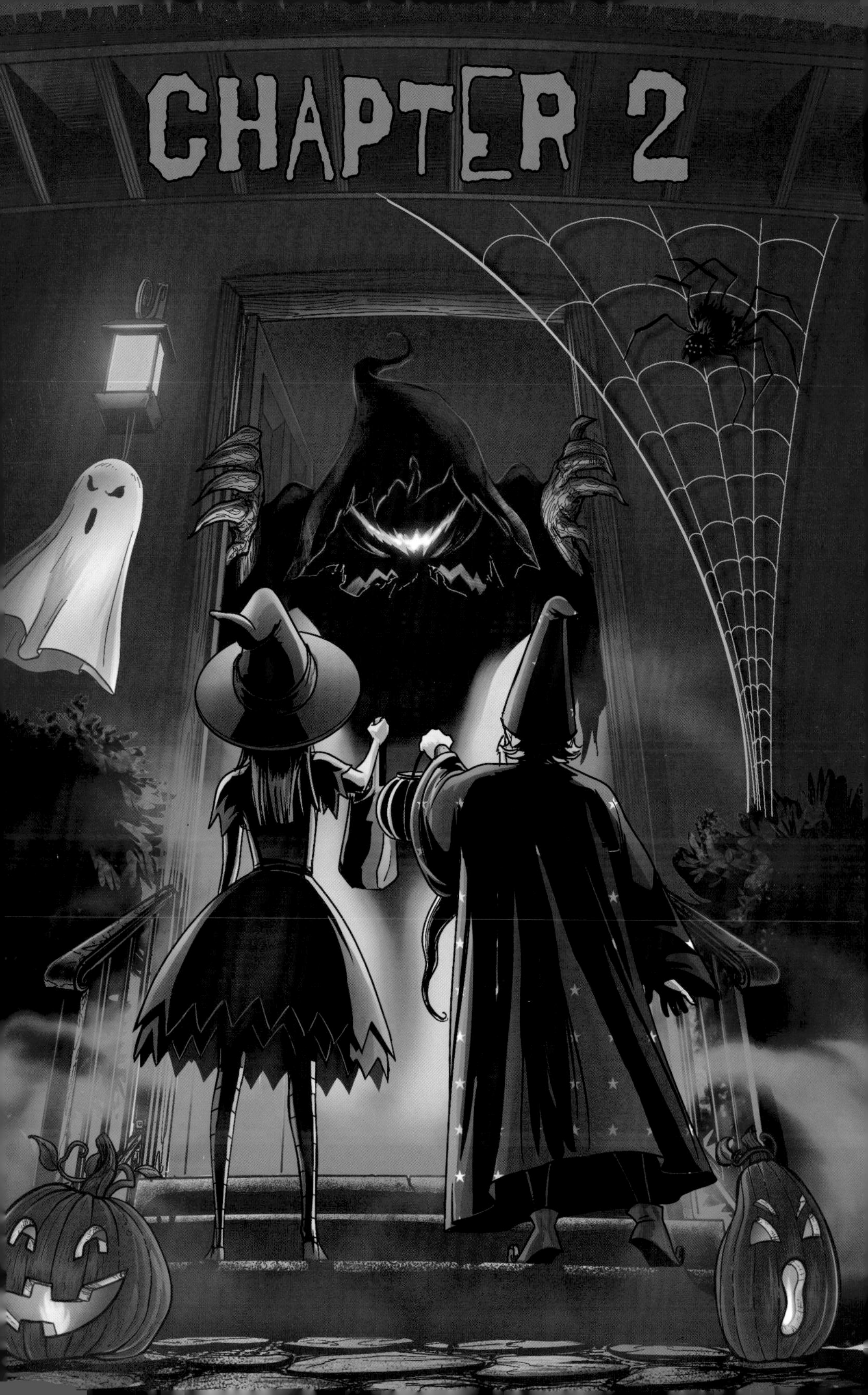
CHAPTER 2

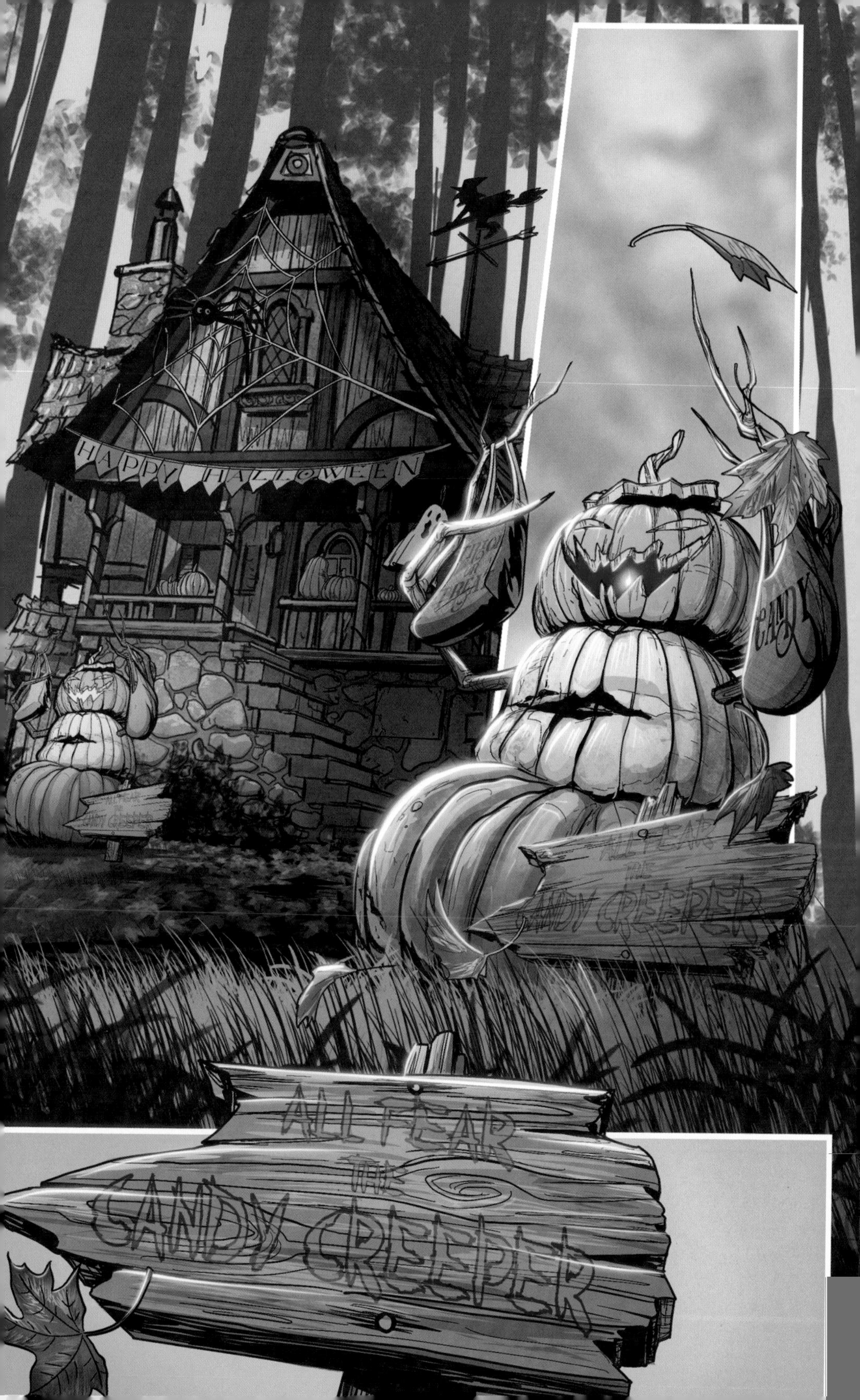
HAPPY HALLOWEEN
CANDY
ALL FEAR THE CANDY CREEPER
ALL FEAR THE CANDY CREEPER

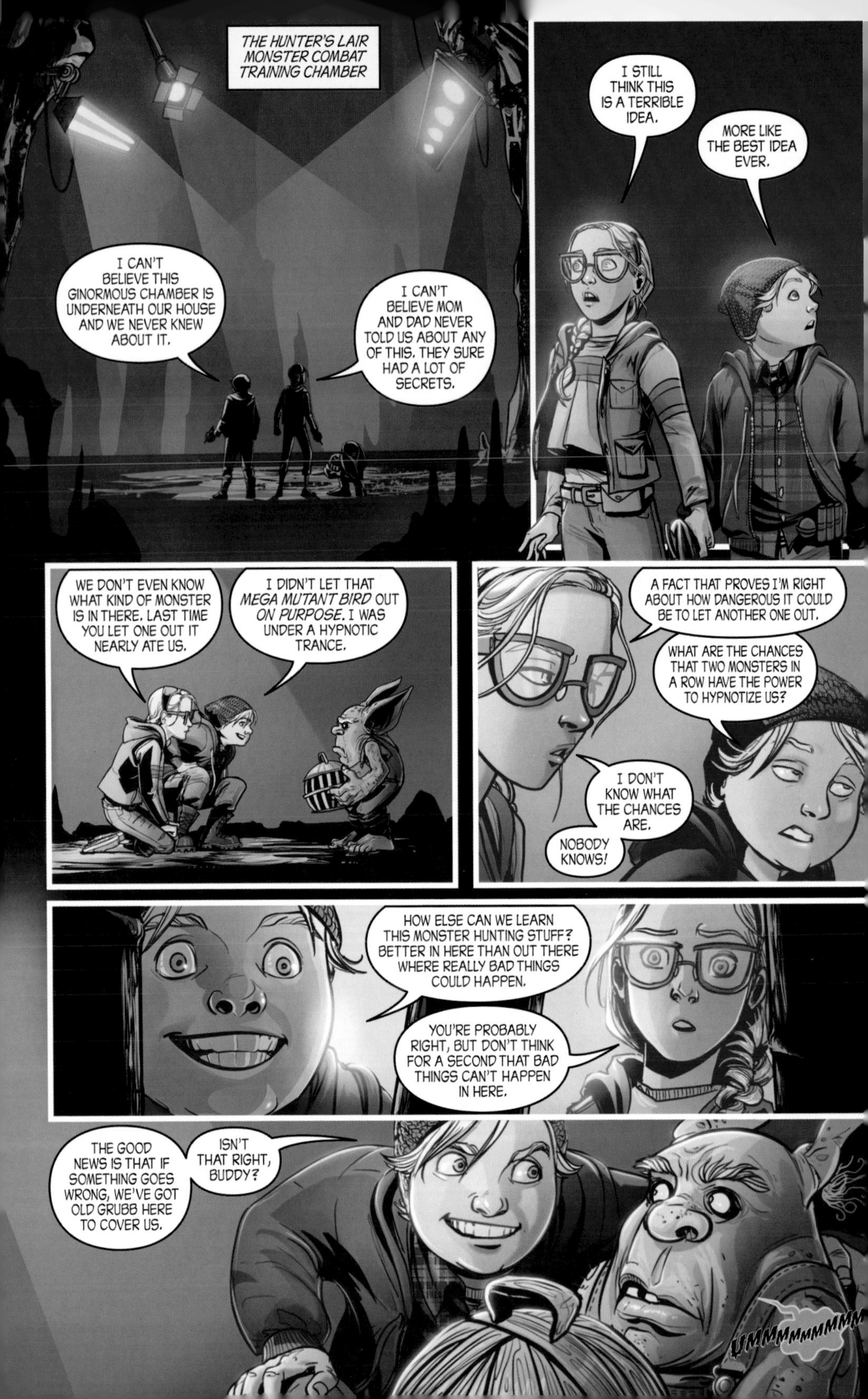
THE HUNTER'S LAIR MONSTER COMBAT TRAINING CHAMBER
I CAN'T BELIEVE THIS GINORMOUS CHAMBER IS UNDERNEATH OUR HOUSE AND WE NEVER KNEW ABOUT IT.
I CAN'T BELIEVE MOM AND DAD NEVER TOLD US ABOUT ANY OF THIS. THEY SURE HAD A LOT OF SECRETS.
I STILL THINK THIS IS A TERRIBLE IDEA.
MORE LIKE THE BEST IDEA EVER.
WE DON'T EVEN KNOW WHAT KIND OF MONSTER IS IN THERE. LAST TIME YOU LET ONE OUT IT NEARLY ATE US.
I DIDN'T LET THAT *MEGA MUTANT BIRD* OUT *ON PURPOSE*. I WAS UNDER A HYPNOTIC TRANCE.
A FACT THAT PROVES I'M RIGHT ABOUT HOW DANGEROUS IT COULD BE TO LET ANOTHER ONE OUT.
WHAT ARE THE CHANCES THAT TWO MONSTERS IN A ROW HAVE THE POWER TO HYPNOTIZE US?
I DON'T KNOW WHAT THE CHANCES ARE.
NOBODY KNOWS!
HOW ELSE CAN WE LEARN THIS MONSTER HUNTING STUFF? BETTER IN HERE THAN OUT THERE WHERE REALLY BAD THINGS COULD HAPPEN.
YOU'RE PROBABLY RIGHT, BUT DON'T THINK FOR A SECOND THAT BAD THINGS CAN'T HAPPEN IN HERE.
THE GOOD NEWS IS THAT IF SOMETHING GOES WRONG, WE'VE GOT OLD GRUBB HERE TO COVER US.
ISN'T THAT RIGHT, BUDDY?
UMMMMMMMMM

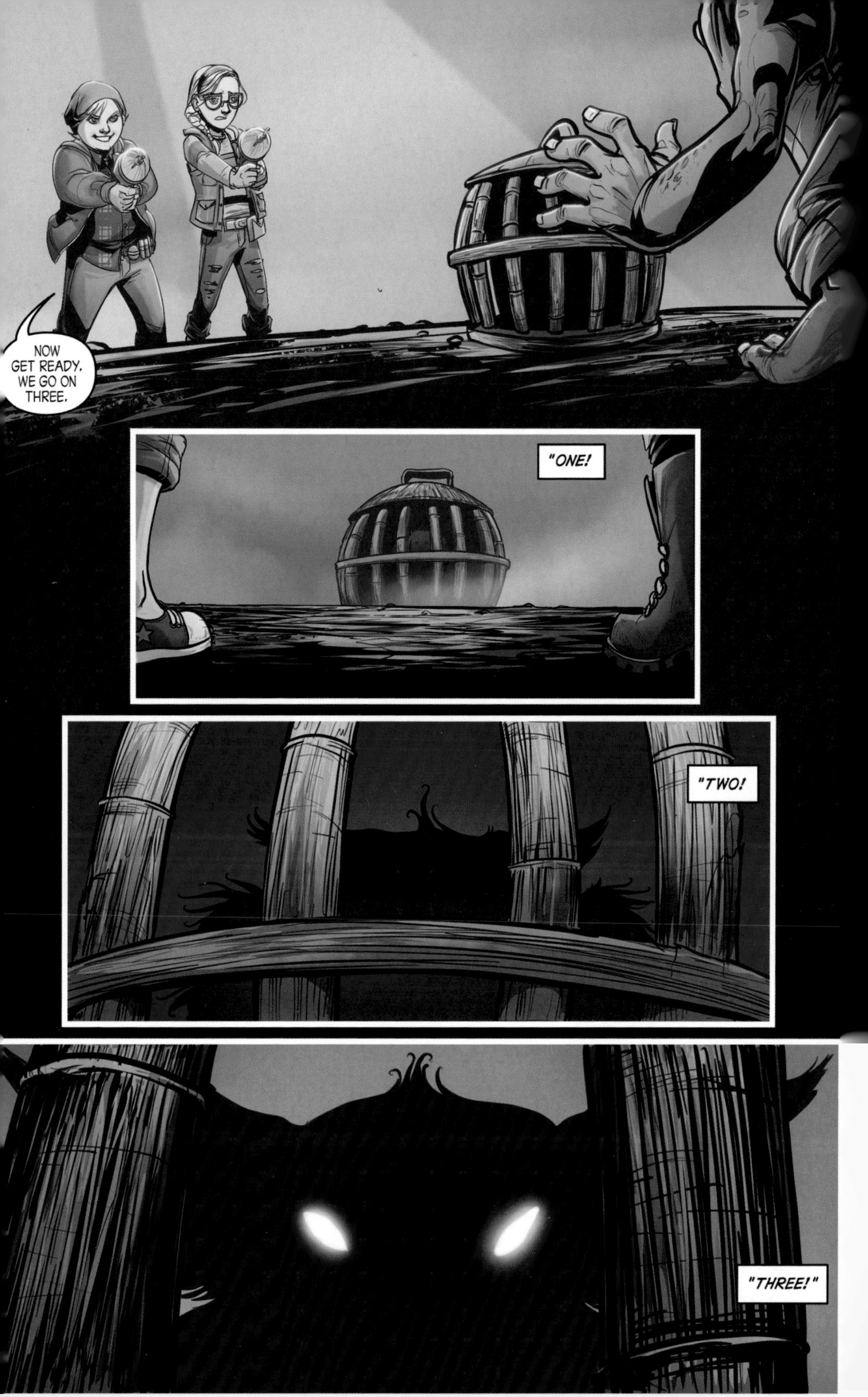
NOW GET READY. WE GO ON THREE.
"ONE!
"TWO!
"THREE!"

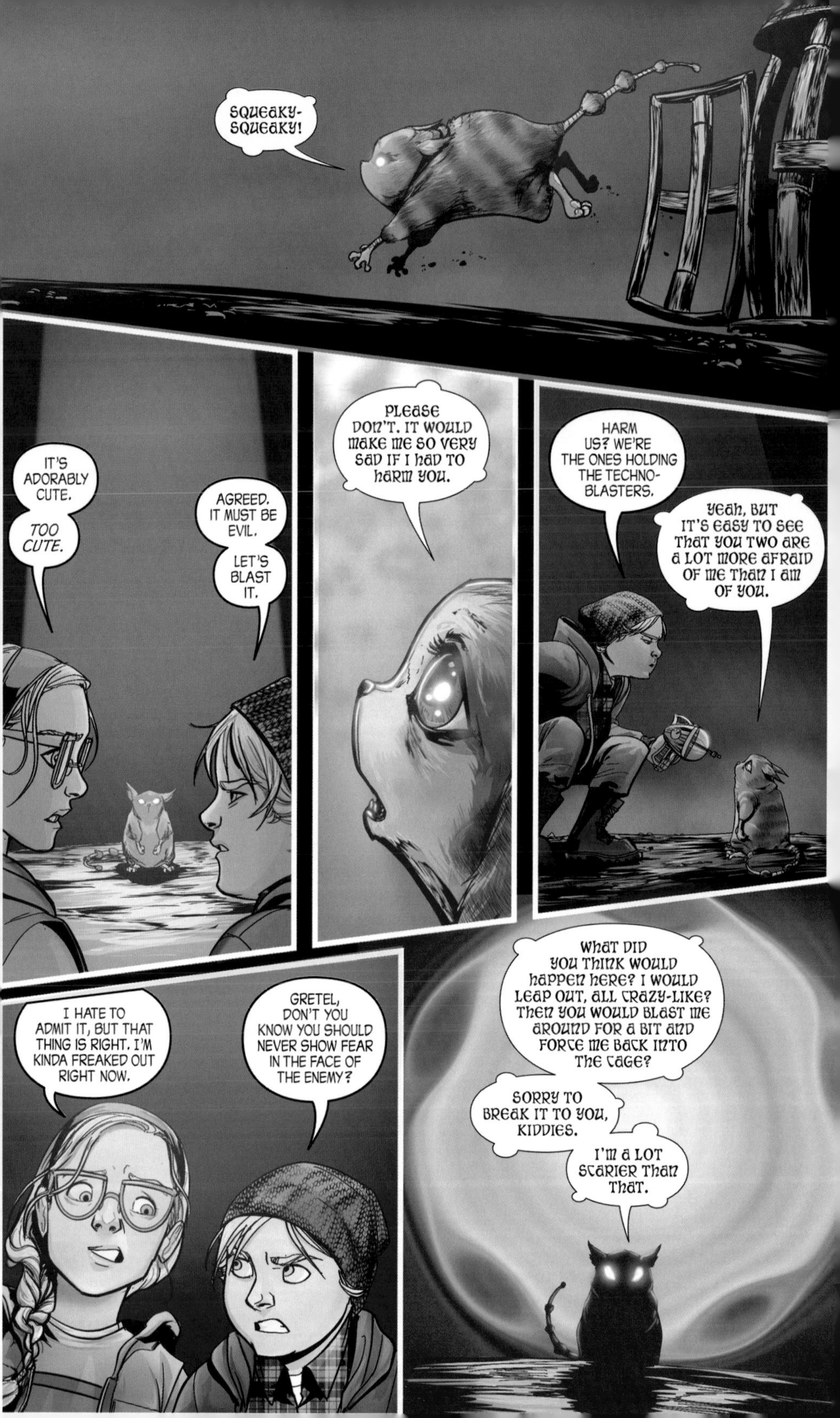
SQUEAKY-SQUEAKY!
IT'S ADORABLY CUTE.
TOO CUTE.
AGREED. IT MUST BE EVIL.
LET'S BLAST IT.
PLEASE DON'T. IT WOULD MAKE ME SO VERY SAD IF I HAD TO HARM YOU.
HARM US? WE'RE THE ONES HOLDING THE TECHNO-BLASTERS.
YEAH, BUT IT'S EASY TO SEE THAT YOU TWO ARE A LOT MORE AFRAID OF ME THAN I AM OF YOU.
I HATE TO ADMIT IT, BUT THAT THING IS RIGHT. I'M KINDA FREAKED OUT RIGHT NOW.
GRETEL, DON'T YOU KNOW YOU SHOULD NEVER SHOW FEAR IN THE FACE OF THE ENEMY?
WHAT DID YOU THINK WOULD HAPPEN HERE? I WOULD LEAP OUT, ALL CRAZY-LIKE? THEN YOU WOULD BLAST ME AROUND FOR A BIT AND FORCE ME BACK INTO THE CAGE?
SORRY TO BREAK IT TO YOU, KIDDIES.
I'M A LOT SCARIER THAN THAT.

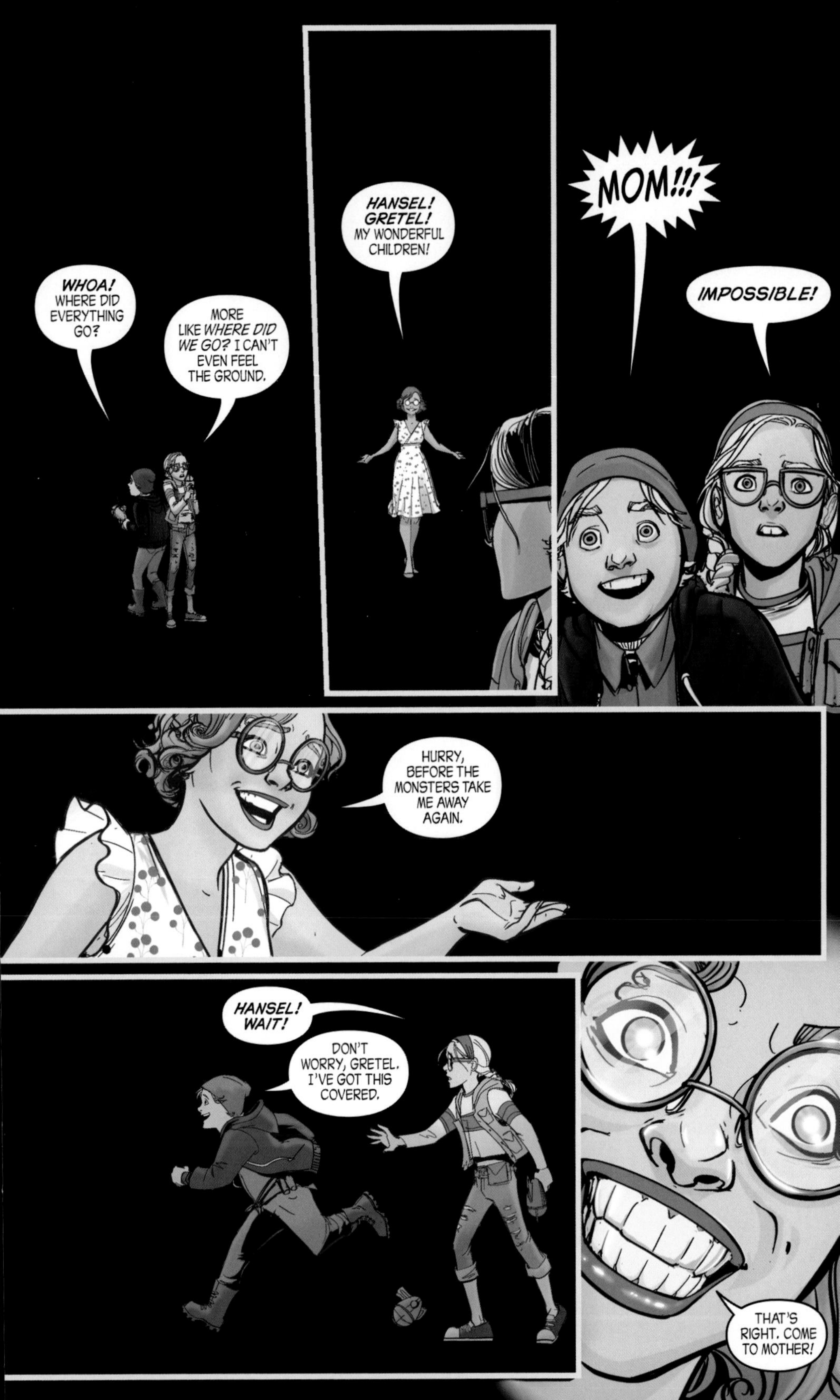
WHOA! WHERE DID EVERYTHING GO?
MORE LIKE WHERE DID WE GO? I CAN'T EVEN FEEL THE GROUND.
HANSEL! GRETEL! MY WONDERFUL CHILDREN!
MOM!!!
IMPOSSIBLE!
HURRY, BEFORE THE MONSTERS TAKE ME AWAY AGAIN.
HANSEL! WAIT!
DON'T WORRY, GRETEL. I'VE GOT THIS COVERED.
THAT'S RIGHT. COME TO MOTHER!

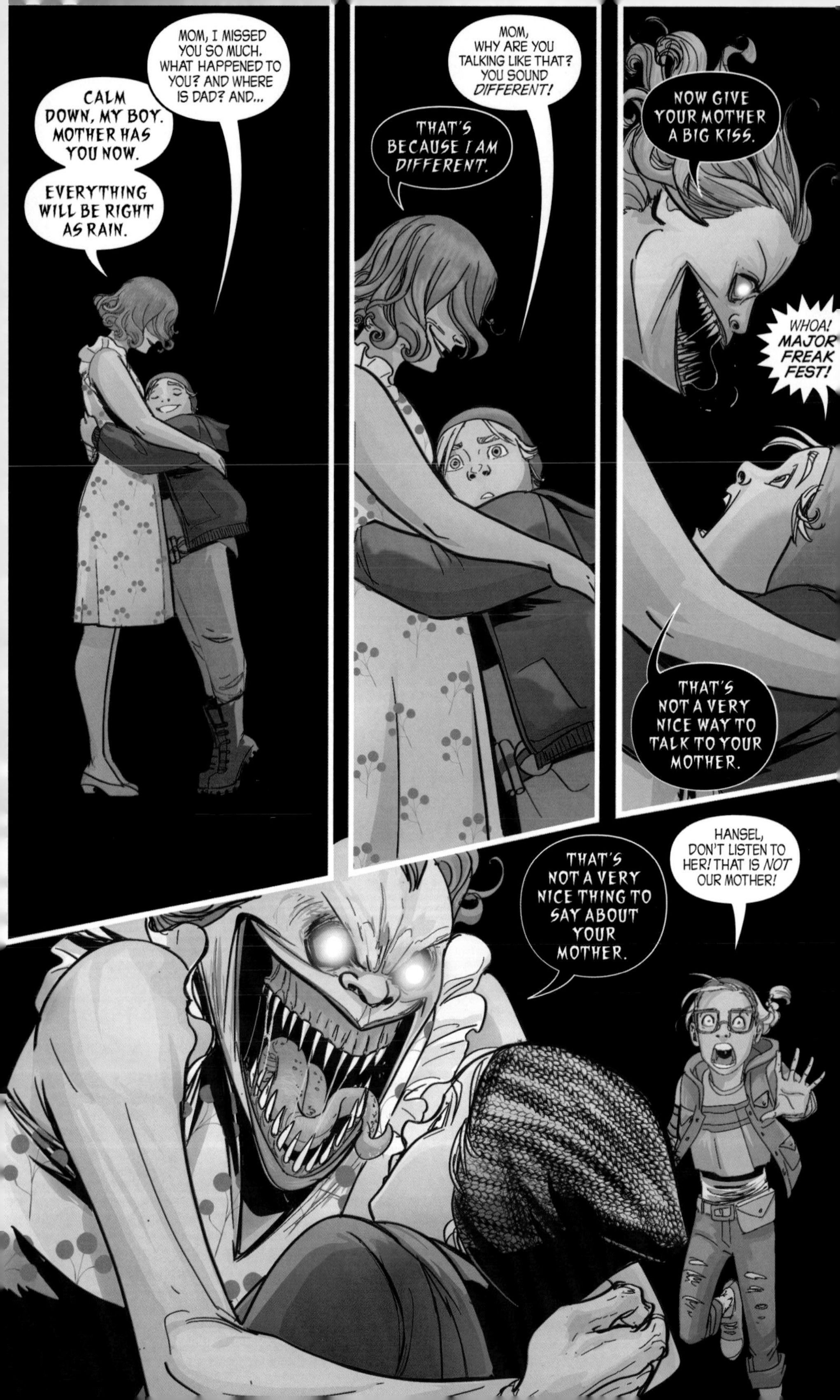
MOM, I MISSED YOU SO MUCH. WHAT HAPPENED TO YOU? AND WHERE IS DAD? AND...
CALM DOWN, MY BOY. MOTHER HAS YOU NOW.
EVERYTHING WILL BE RIGHT AS RAIN.
MOM, WHY ARE YOU TALKING LIKE THAT? YOU SOUND *DIFFERENT!*
THAT'S BECAUSE *I AM DIFFERENT.*
NOW GIVE YOUR MOTHER A BIG KISS.
WHOA! **MAJOR FREAK FEST!**
THAT'S NOT A VERY NICE WAY TO TALK TO YOUR MOTHER.
THAT'S NOT A VERY NICE THING TO SAY ABOUT YOUR MOTHER.
HANSEL, DON'T LISTEN TO HER! THAT IS *NOT* OUR MOTHER!

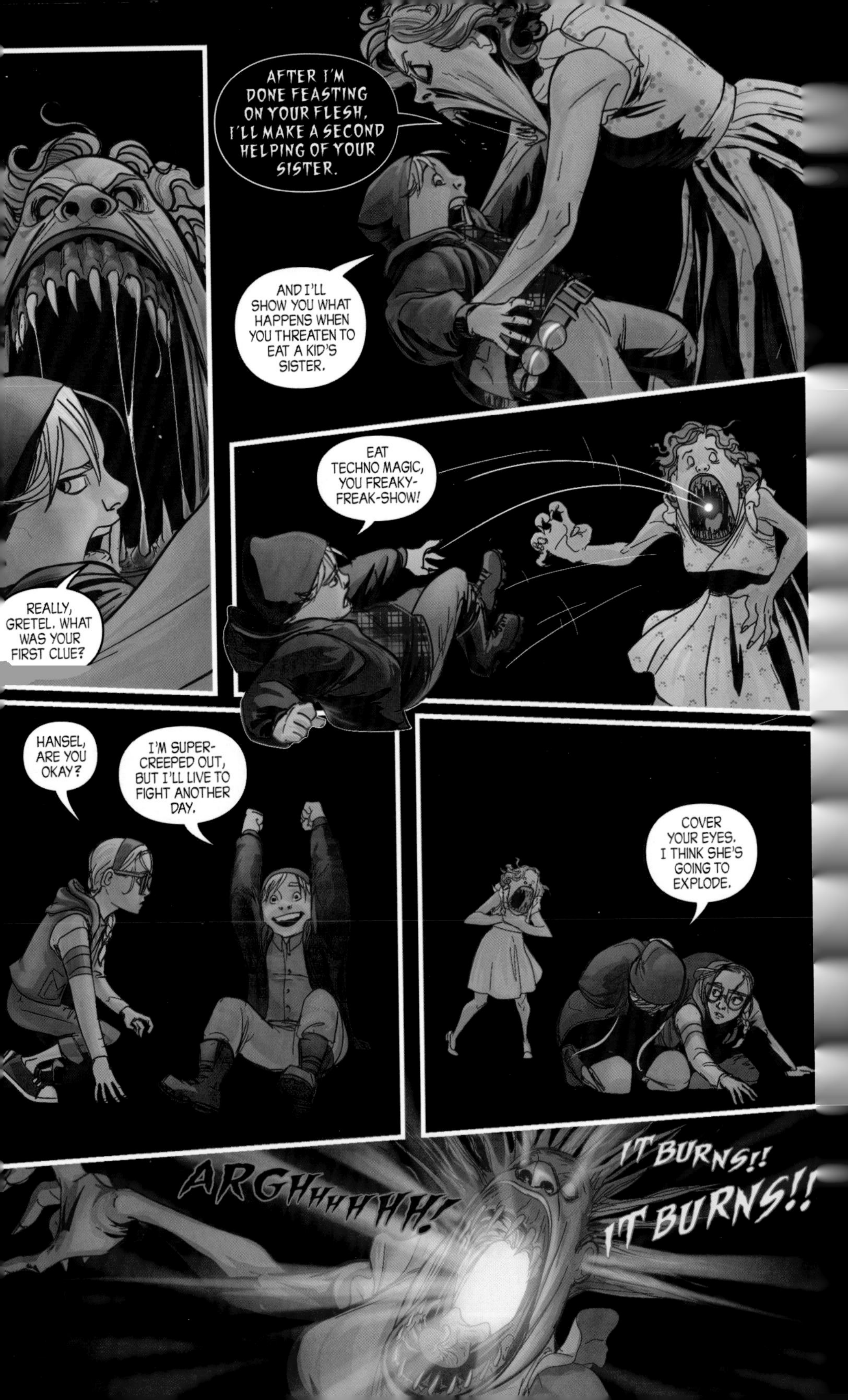
REALLY, GRETEL. WHAT WAS YOUR FIRST CLUE?
AFTER I'M DONE FEASTING ON YOUR FLESH, I'LL MAKE A SECOND HELPING OF YOUR SISTER.
AND I'LL SHOW YOU WHAT HAPPENS WHEN YOU THREATEN TO EAT A KID'S SISTER.
EAT TECHNO MAGIC, YOU FREAKY-FREAK-SHOW!
HANSEL, ARE YOU OKAY?
I'M SUPER-CREEPED OUT, BUT I'LL LIVE TO FIGHT ANOTHER DAY.
COVER YOUR EYES. I THINK SHE'S GOING TO EXPLODE.
ARGHHHHHHH!
IT BURNS!!
IT BURNS!!

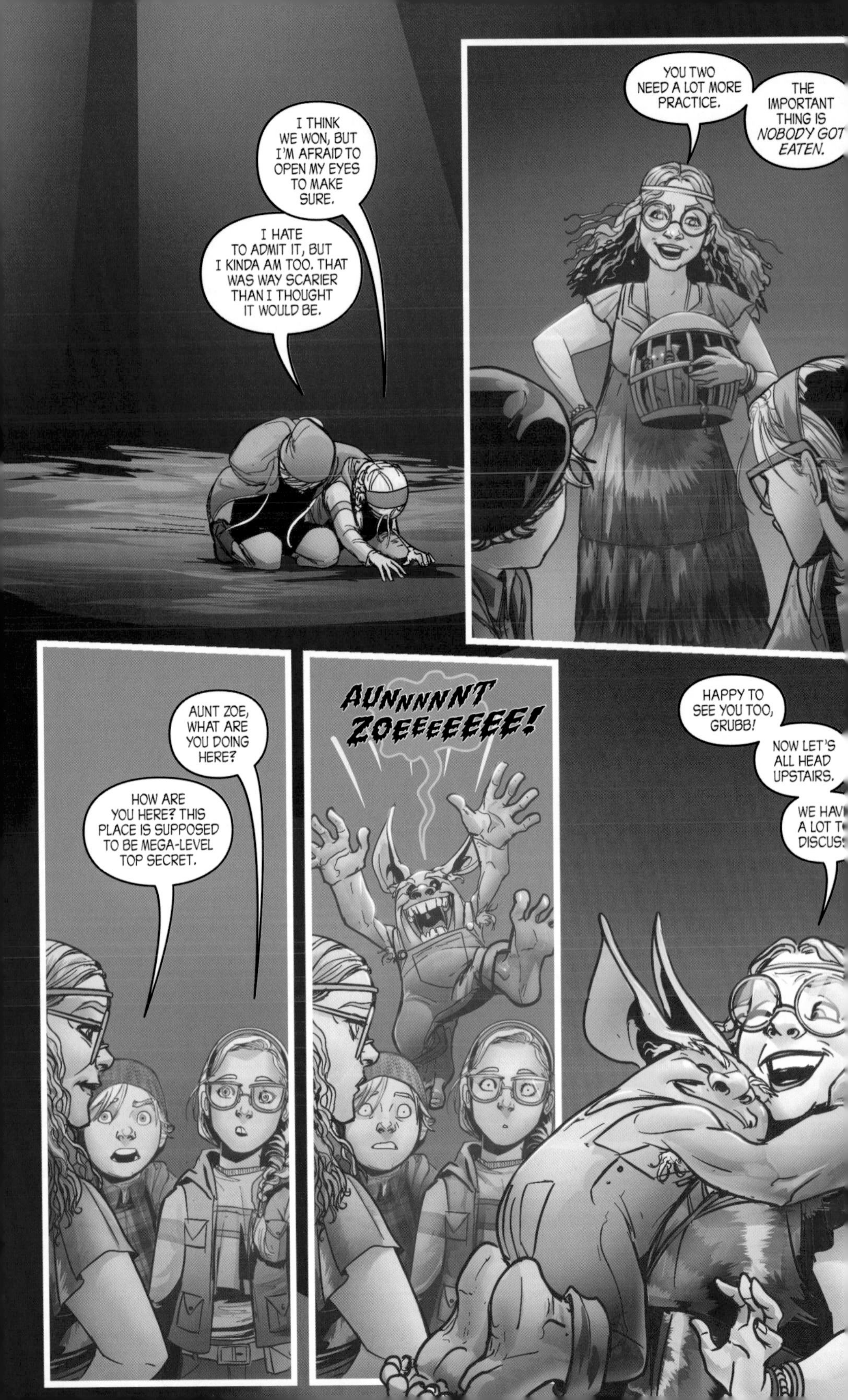
I THINK WE WON, BUT I'M AFRAID TO OPEN MY EYES TO MAKE SURE.
I HATE TO ADMIT IT, BUT I KINDA AM TOO. THAT WAS WAY SCARIER THAN I THOUGHT IT WOULD BE.
YOU TWO NEED A LOT MORE PRACTICE.
THE IMPORTANT THING IS *NOBODY GOT EATEN.*
AUNT ZOE, WHAT ARE YOU DOING HERE?
HOW ARE YOU HERE? THIS PLACE IS SUPPOSED TO BE MEGA-LEVEL TOP SECRET.
AUNnnnNT ZOEeeeEEEE!
HAPPY TO SEE YOU TOO, GRUBB!
NOW LET'S ALL HEAD UPSTAIRS.

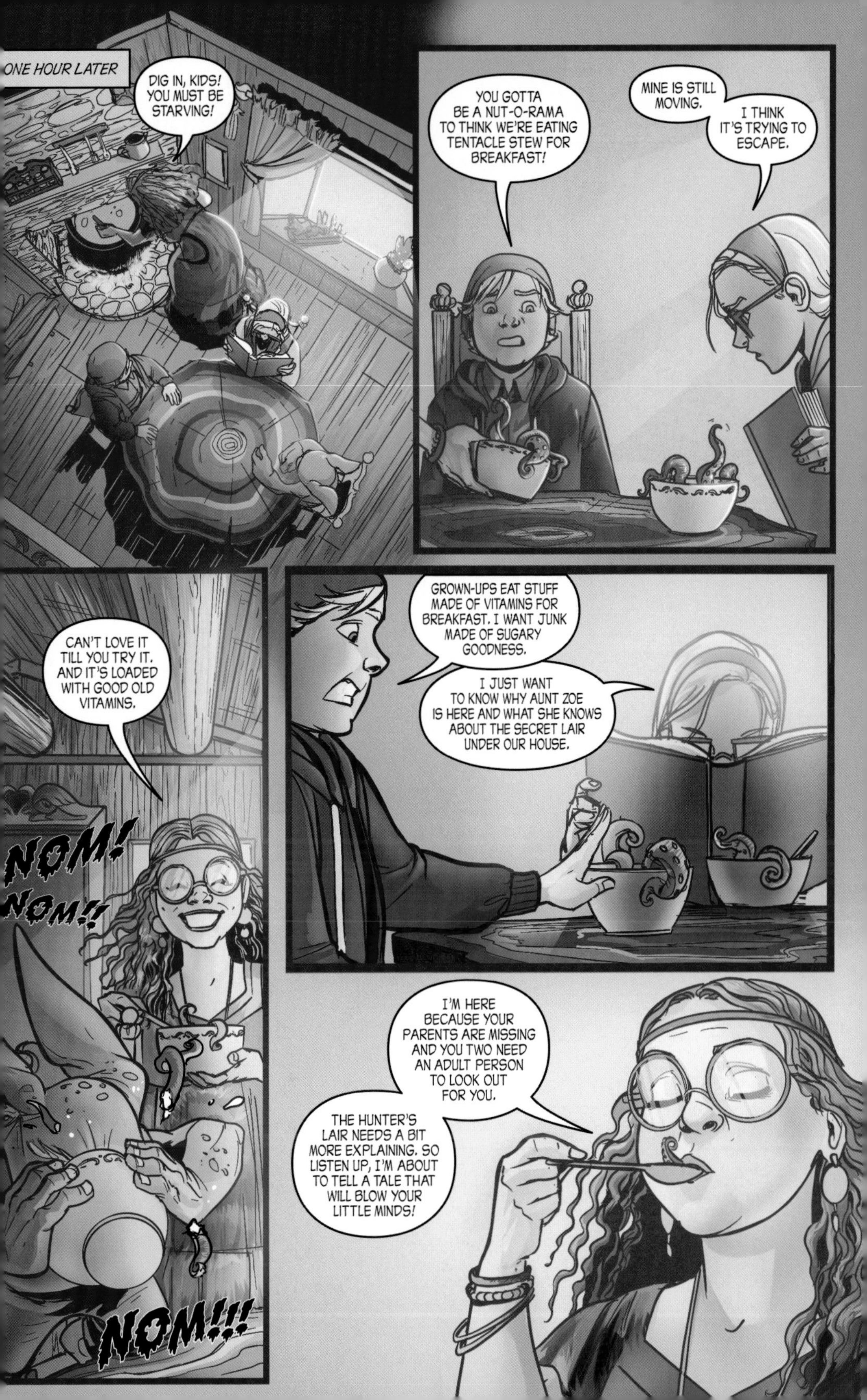
ONE HOUR LATER
DIG IN, KIDS! YOU MUST BE STARVING!
YOU GOTTA BE A NUT-O-RAMA TO THINK WE'RE EATING TENTACLE STEW FOR BREAKFAST!
MINE IS STILL MOVING.
I THINK IT'S TRYING TO ESCAPE.
CAN'T LOVE IT TILL YOU TRY IT. AND IT'S LOADED WITH GOOD OLD VITAMINS.
NOM! NOM!! NOM!!!
GROWN-UPS EAT STUFF MADE OF VITAMINS FOR BREAKFAST. I WANT JUNK MADE OF SUGARY GOODNESS.
I JUST WANT TO KNOW WHY AUNT ZOE IS HERE AND WHAT SHE KNOWS ABOUT THE SECRET LAIR UNDER OUR HOUSE.
I'M HERE BECAUSE YOUR PARENTS ARE MISSING AND YOU TWO NEED AN ADULT PERSON TO LOOK OUT FOR YOU.
THE HUNTER'S LAIR NEEDS A BIT MORE EXPLAINING. SO LISTEN UP, I'M ABOUT TO TELL A TALE THAT WILL BLOW YOUR LITTLE MINDS!

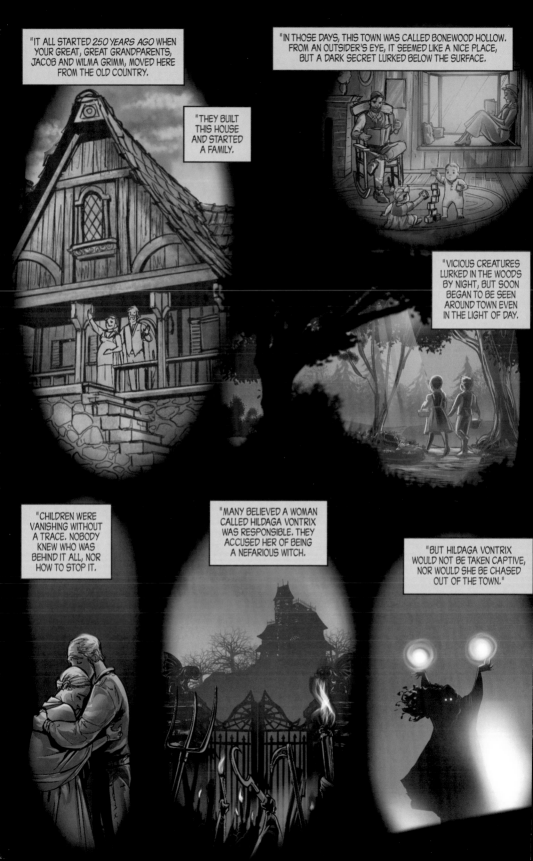

"IT ALL STARTED *250 YEARS AGO* WHEN YOUR GREAT, GREAT GRANDPARENTS, JACOB AND WILMA GRIMM, MOVED HERE FROM THE OLD COUNTRY.

"THEY BUILT THIS HOUSE AND STARTED A FAMILY.

"IN THOSE DAYS, THIS TOWN WAS CALLED BONEWOOD HOLLOW. FROM AN OUTSIDER'S EYE, IT SEEMED LIKE A NICE PLACE, BUT A DARK SECRET LURKED BELOW THE SURFACE.

"VICIOUS CREATURES LURKED IN THE WOODS BY NIGHT, BUT SOON BEGAN TO BE SEEN AROUND TOWN EVEN IN THE LIGHT OF DAY.

"CHILDREN WERE VANISHING WITHOUT A TRACE. NOBODY KNEW WHO WAS BEHIND IT ALL, NOR HOW TO STOP IT.

"MANY BELIEVED A WOMAN CALLED HILDAGA VONTRIX WAS RESPONSIBLE. THEY ACCUSED HER OF BEING A NEFARIOUS WITCH.

"BUT HILDAGA VONTRIX WOULD NOT BE TAKEN CAPTIVE, NOR WOULD SHE BE CHASED OUT OF THE TOWN."

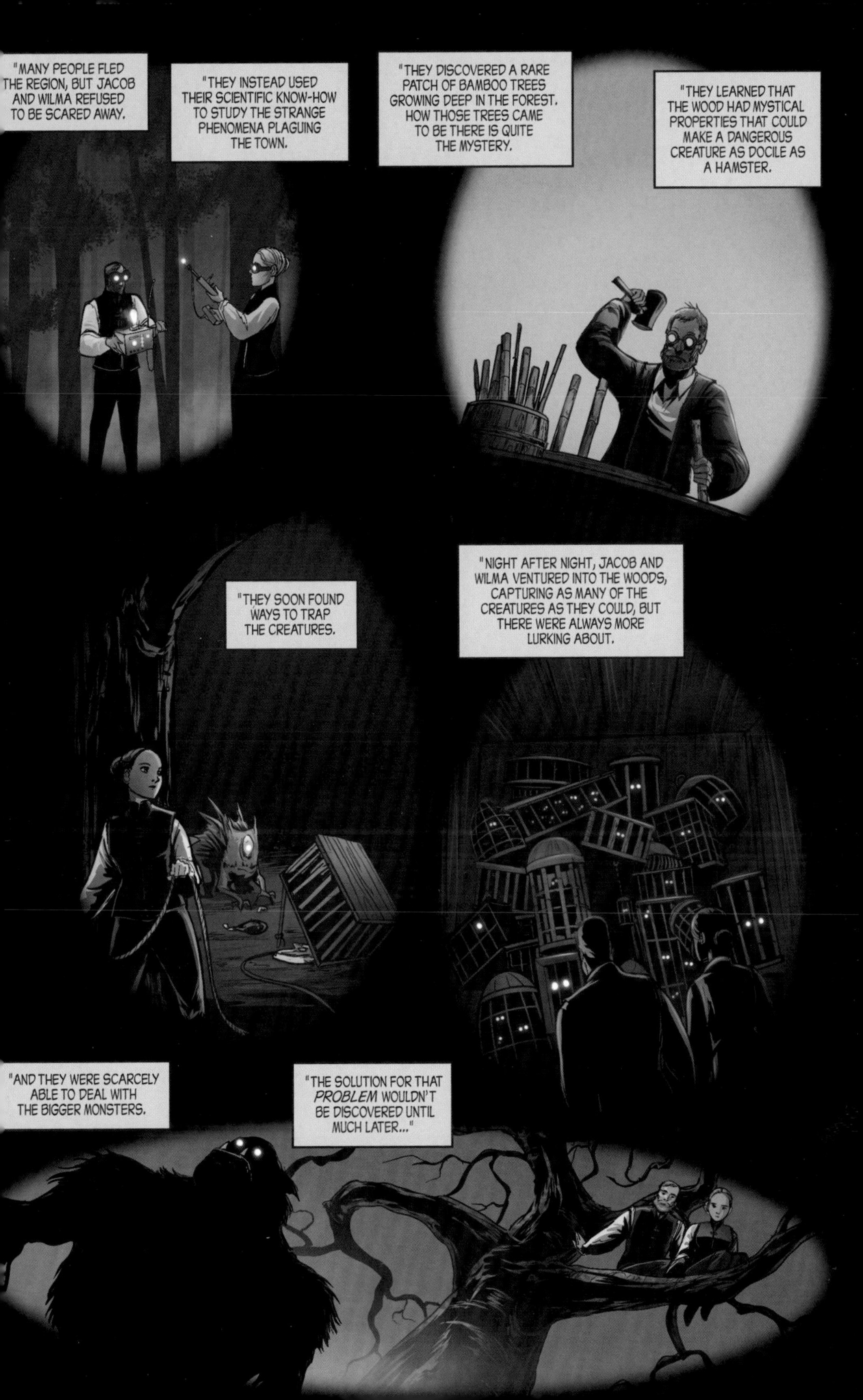
"MANY PEOPLE FLED THE REGION, BUT JACOB AND WILMA REFUSED TO BE SCARED AWAY.
"THEY INSTEAD USED THEIR SCIENTIFIC KNOW-HOW TO STUDY THE STRANGE PHENOMENA PLAGUING THE TOWN.
"THEY DISCOVERED A RARE PATCH OF BAMBOO TREES GROWING DEEP IN THE FOREST. HOW THOSE TREES CAME TO BE THERE IS QUITE THE MYSTERY.
"THEY LEARNED THAT THE WOOD HAD MYSTICAL PROPERTIES THAT COULD MAKE A DANGEROUS CREATURE AS DOCILE AS A HAMSTER.
"THEY SOON FOUND WAYS TO TRAP THE CREATURES.
"NIGHT AFTER NIGHT, JACOB AND WILMA VENTURED INTO THE WOODS, CAPTURING AS MANY OF THE CREATURES AS THEY COULD, BUT THERE WERE ALWAYS MORE LURKING ABOUT.
"AND THEY WERE SCARCELY ABLE TO DEAL WITH THE BIGGER MONSTERS.
"THE SOLUTION FOR THAT *PROBLEM* WOULDN'T BE DISCOVERED UNTIL MUCH LATER..."

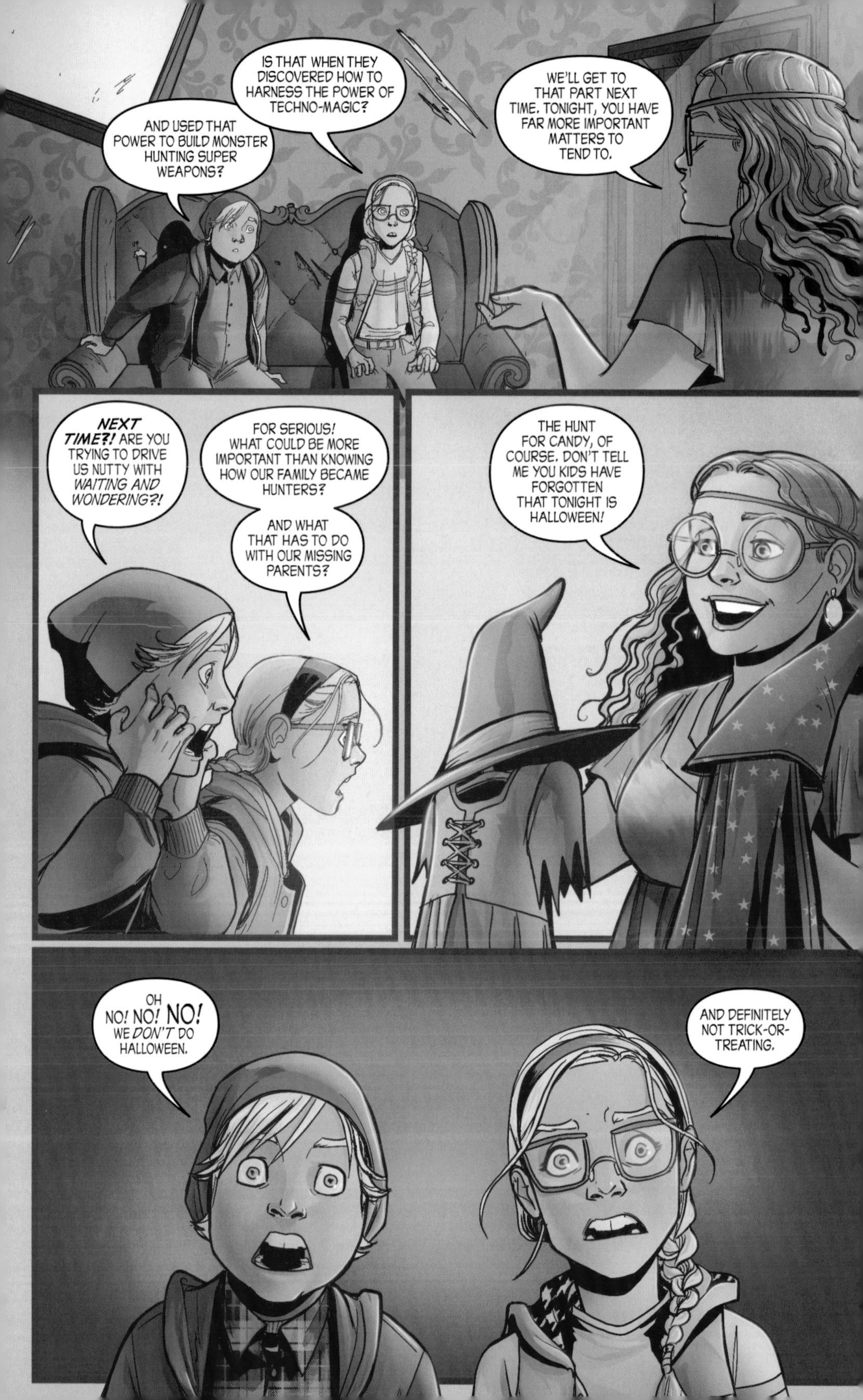
AND USED THAT POWER TO BUILD MONSTER HUNTING SUPER WEAPONS?
IS THAT WHEN THEY DISCOVERED HOW TO HARNESS THE POWER OF TECHNO-MAGIC?
WE'LL GET TO THAT PART NEXT TIME. TONIGHT, YOU HAVE FAR MORE IMPORTANT MATTERS TO TEND TO.
NEXT TIME?! ARE YOU TRYING TO DRIVE US NUTTY WITH WAITING AND WONDERING?!
FOR SERIOUS! WHAT COULD BE MORE IMPORTANT THAN KNOWING HOW OUR FAMILY BECAME HUNTERS?
AND WHAT THAT HAS TO DO WITH OUR MISSING PARENTS?
THE HUNT FOR CANDY, OF COURSE. DON'T TELL ME YOU KIDS HAVE FORGOTTEN THAT TONIGHT IS HALLOWEEN!
OH NO! NO! NO! WE DON'T DO HALLOWEEN.
AND DEFINITELY NOT TRICK-OR-TREATING.

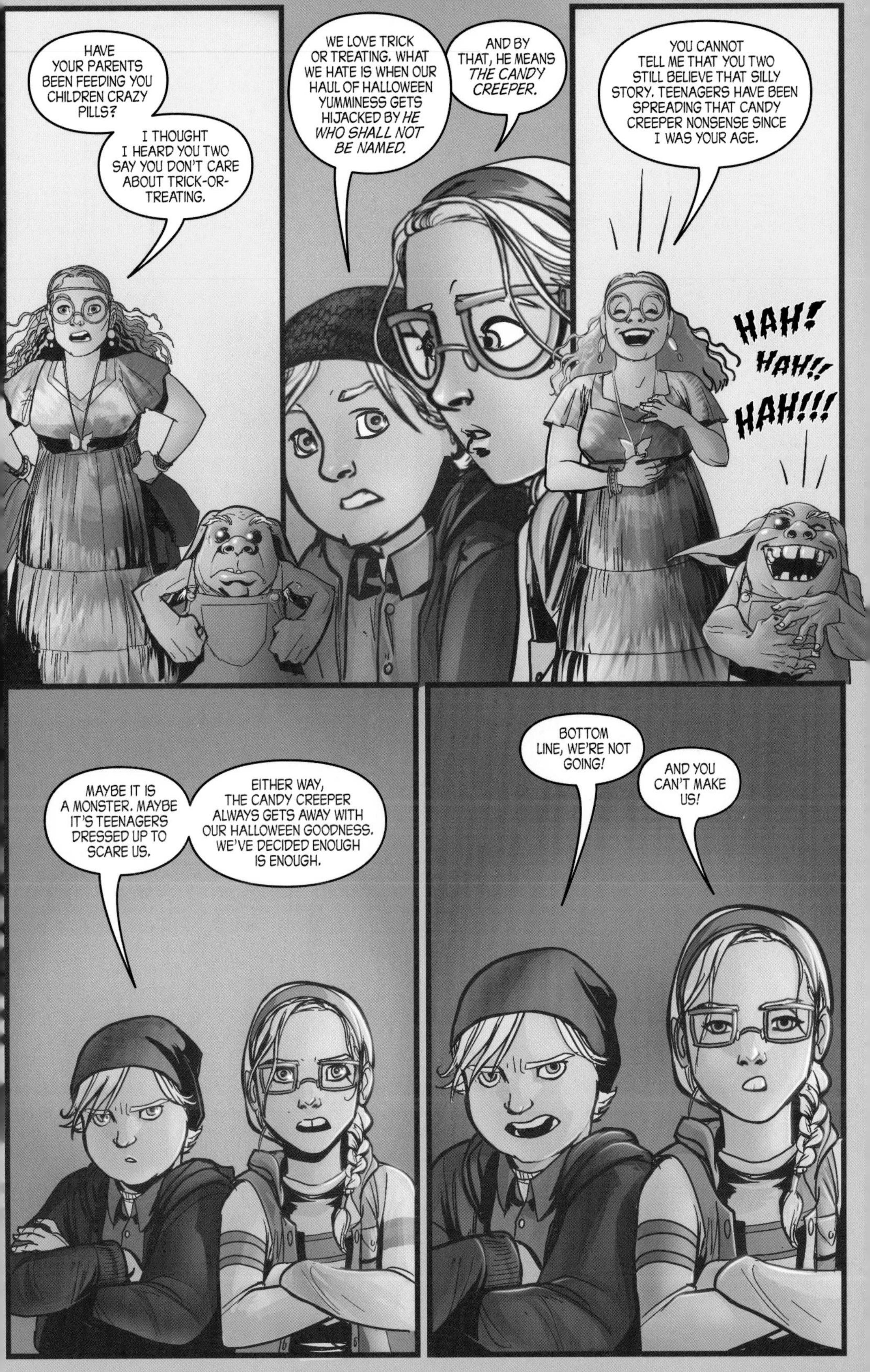
HAVE YOUR PARENTS BEEN FEEDING YOU CHILDREN CRAZY PILLS?
I THOUGHT I HEARD YOU TWO SAY YOU DON'T CARE ABOUT TRICK-OR-TREATING.
WE LOVE TRICK OR TREATING. WHAT WE HATE IS WHEN OUR HAUL OF HALLOWEEN YUMMINESS GETS HIJACKED BY *HE WHO SHALL NOT BE NAMED.*
AND BY THAT, HE MEANS *THE CANDY CREEPER.*
YOU CANNOT TELL ME THAT YOU TWO STILL BELIEVE THAT SILLY STORY. TEENAGERS HAVE BEEN SPREADING THAT CANDY CREEPER NONSENSE SINCE I WAS YOUR AGE.
HAH! HAH!! HAH!!!
MAYBE IT IS A MONSTER. MAYBE IT'S TEENAGERS DRESSED UP TO SCARE US.
EITHER WAY, THE CANDY CREEPER ALWAYS GETS AWAY WITH OUR HALLOWEEN GOODNESS. WE'VE DECIDED ENOUGH IS ENOUGH.
BOTTOM LINE, WE'RE NOT GOING!
AND YOU CAN'T MAKE US!

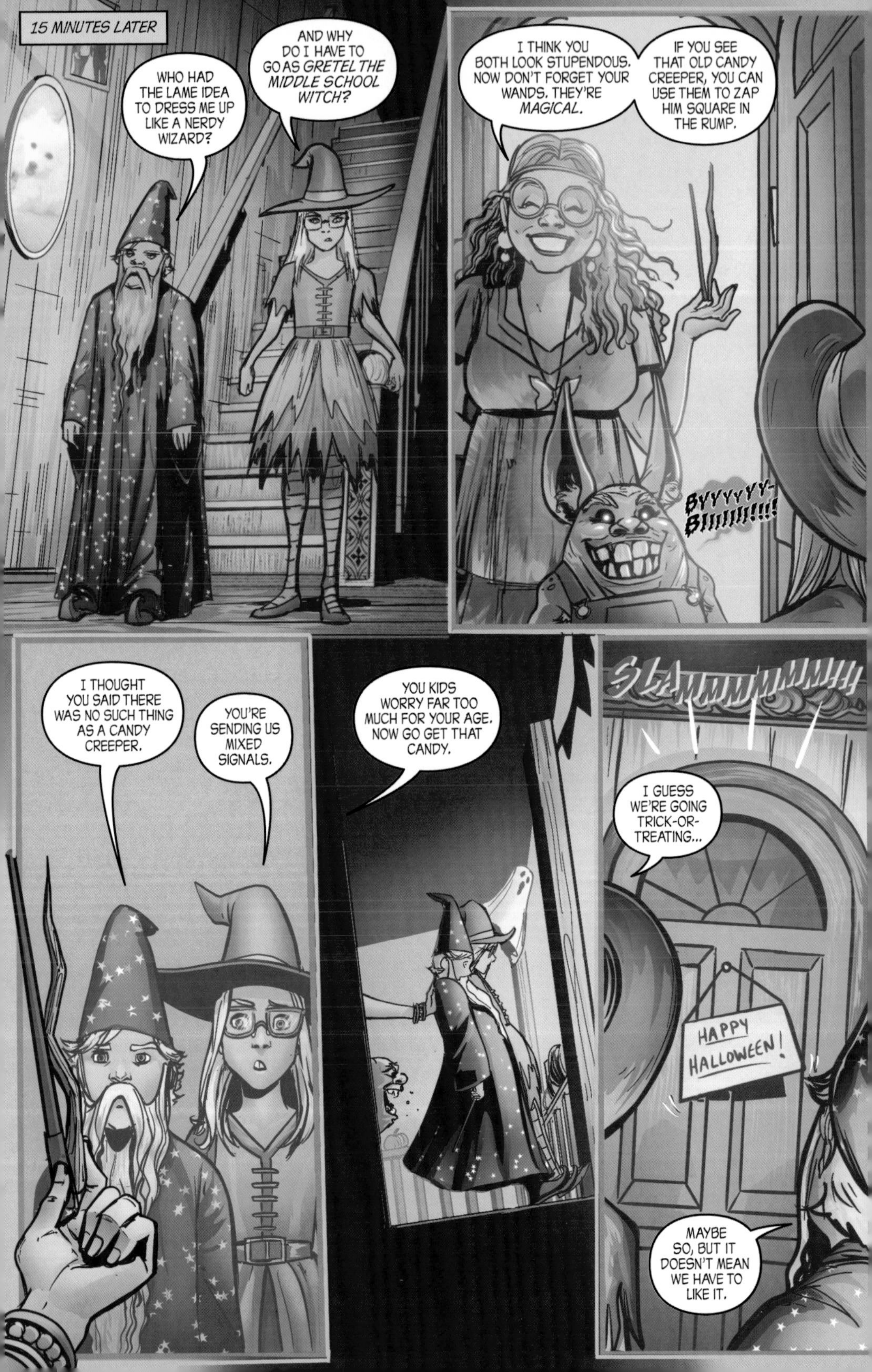
15 MINUTES LATER
WHO HAD THE LAME IDEA TO DRESS ME UP LIKE A NERDY WIZARD?
AND WHY DO I HAVE TO GO AS *GRETEL THE MIDDLE SCHOOL WITCH?*
I THINK YOU BOTH LOOK STUPENDOUS. NOW DON'T FORGET YOUR WANDS. THEY'RE *MAGICAL.*
IF YOU SEE THAT OLD CANDY CREEPER, YOU CAN USE THEM TO ZAP HIM SQUARE IN THE RUMP.
BYYYYYY-BIIIIIII!!!!
I THOUGHT YOU SAID THERE WAS NO SUCH THING AS A CANDY CREEPER.
YOU'RE SENDING US MIXED SIGNALS.
YOU KIDS WORRY FAR TOO MUCH FOR YOUR AGE. NOW GO GET THAT CANDY.
SLAMMMMMMMH!
I GUESS WE'RE GOING TRICK-OR-TREATING...
HAPPY HALLOWEEN!
MAYBE SO, BUT IT DOESN'T MEAN WE HAVE TO LIKE IT.

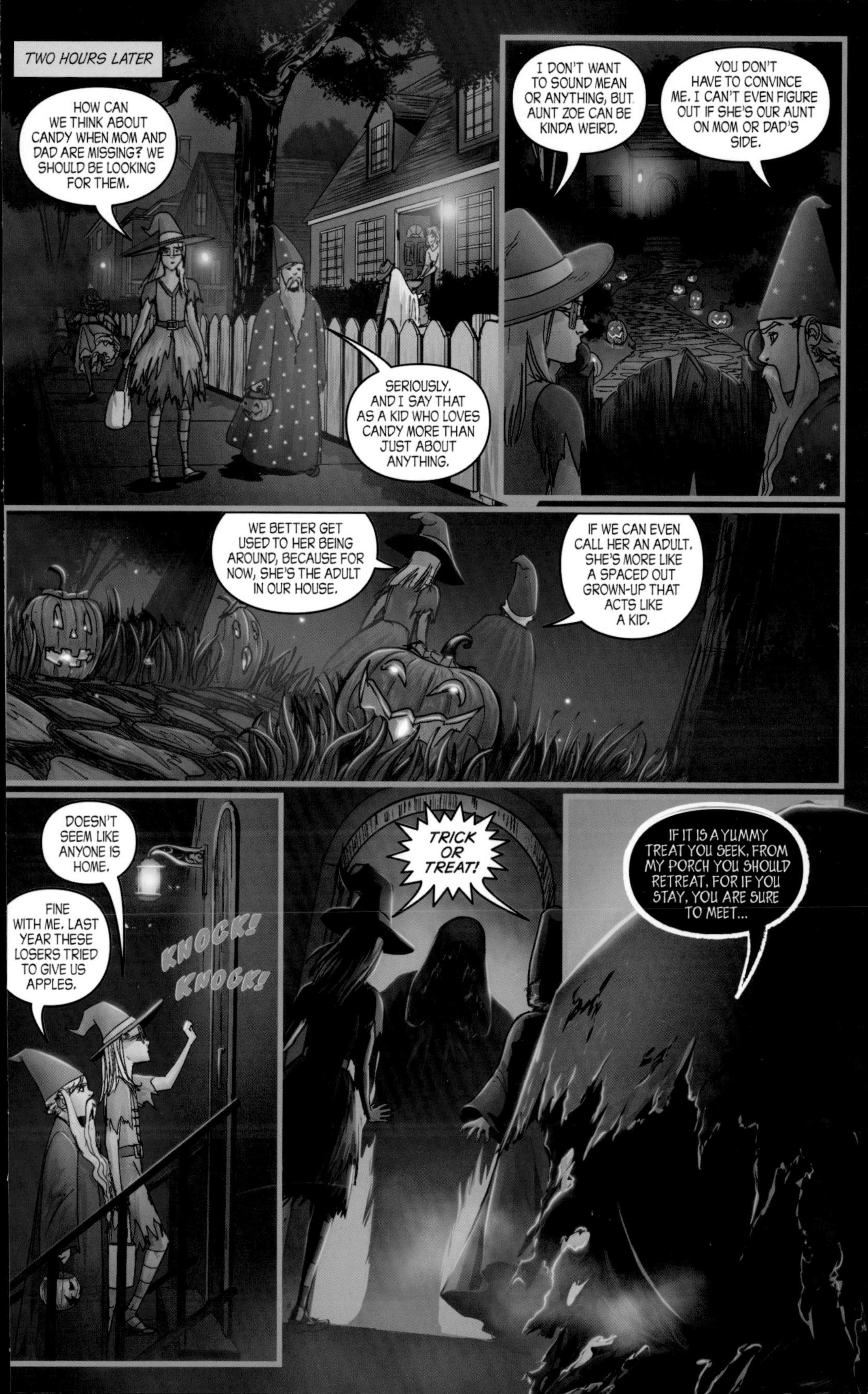
TWO HOURS LATER
HOW CAN WE THINK ABOUT CANDY WHEN MOM AND DAD ARE MISSING? WE SHOULD BE LOOKING FOR THEM.
SERIOUSLY. AND I SAY THAT AS A KID WHO LOVES CANDY MORE THAN JUST ABOUT ANYTHING.
I DON'T WANT TO SOUND MEAN OR ANYTHING, BUT AUNT ZOE CAN BE KINDA WEIRD.
YOU DON'T HAVE TO CONVINCE ME. I CAN'T EVEN FIGURE OUT IF SHE'S OUR AUNT ON MOM OR DAD'S SIDE.
WE BETTER GET USED TO HER BEING AROUND, BECAUSE FOR NOW, SHE'S THE ADULT IN OUR HOUSE.
IF WE CAN EVEN CALL HER AN ADULT. SHE'S MORE LIKE A SPACED OUT GROWN-UP THAT ACTS LIKE A KID.
DOESN'T SEEM LIKE ANYONE IS HOME.
FINE WITH ME. LAST YEAR THESE LOSERS TRIED TO GIVE US APPLES.
KNOCK! KNOCK!
TRICK OR TREAT!
IF IT IS A YUMMY TREAT YOU SEEK, FROM MY PORCH YOU SHOULD RETREAT, FOR IF YOU STAY, YOU ARE SURE TO MEET...

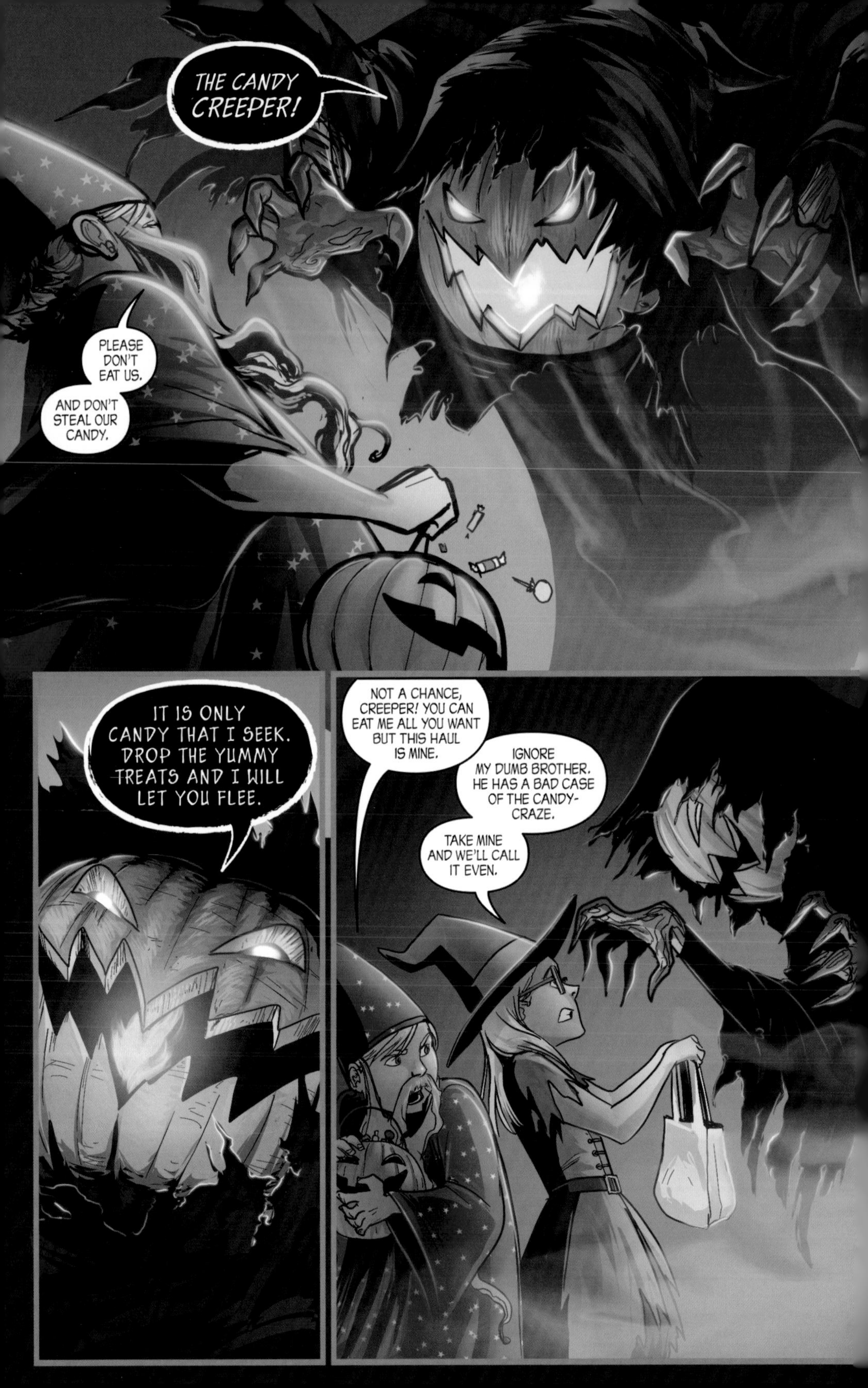
THE CANDY CREEPER!
PLEASE DON'T EAT US.
AND DON'T STEAL OUR CANDY.
IT IS ONLY CANDY THAT I SEEK. DROP THE YUMMY TREATS AND I WILL LET YOU FLEE.
NOT A CHANCE, CREEPER! YOU CAN EAT ME ALL YOU WANT BUT THIS HAUL IS MINE.
IGNORE MY DUMB BROTHER. HE HAS A BAD CASE OF THE CANDY-CRAZE.
TAKE MINE AND WE'LL CALL IT EVEN.

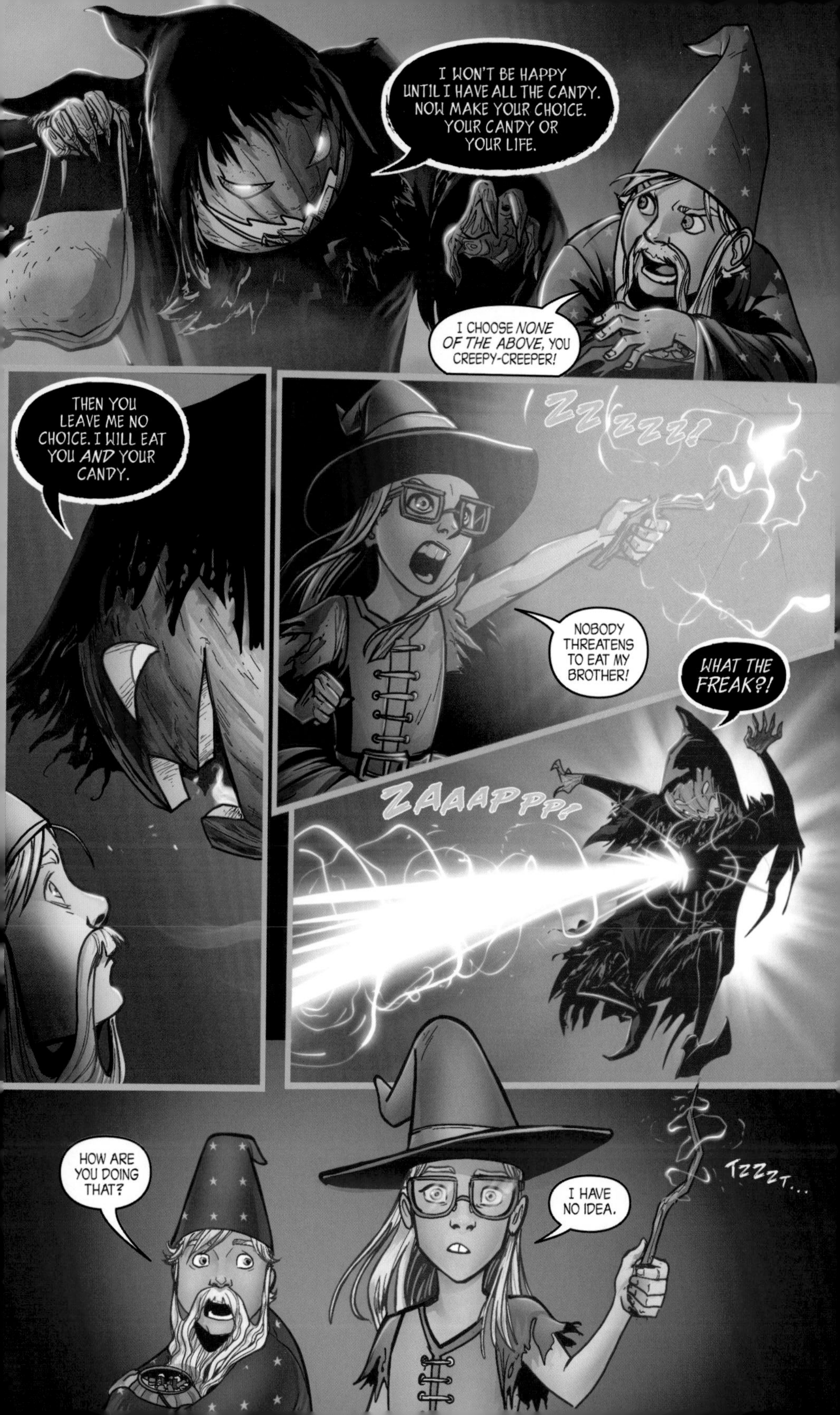
I WON'T BE HAPPY UNTIL I HAVE ALL THE CANDY. NOW MAKE YOUR CHOICE. YOUR CANDY OR YOUR LIFE.
I CHOOSE *NONE OF THE ABOVE*, YOU CREEPY-CREEPER!
THEN YOU LEAVE ME NO CHOICE. I WILL EAT YOU *AND* YOUR CANDY.
ZZZZZZ!
NOBODY THREATENS TO EAT MY BROTHER!
WHAT THE FREAK?!
ZAAAPPP!
HOW ARE YOU DOING THAT?
I HAVE NO IDEA.
TZZZT...

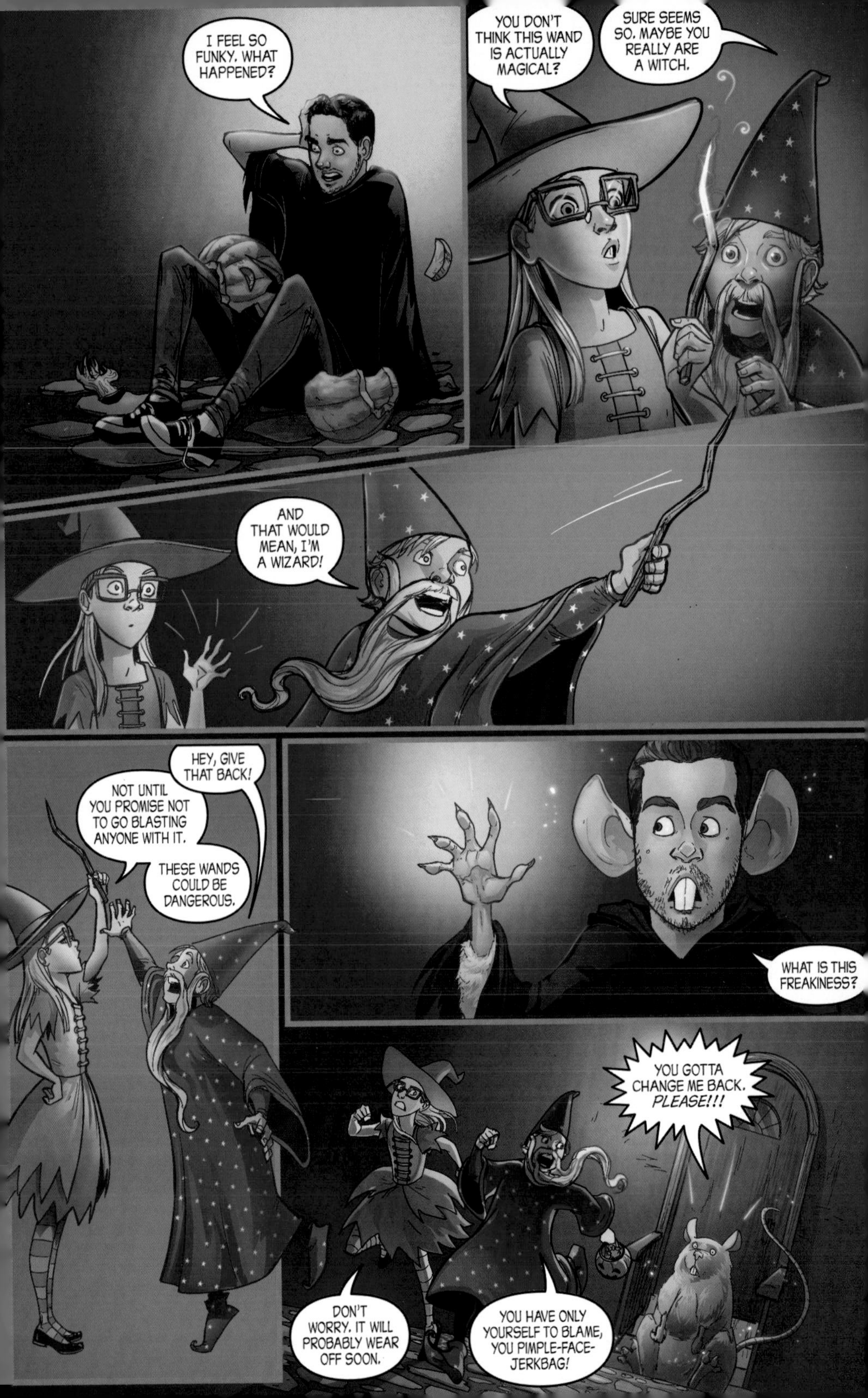

I FEEL SO FUNKY. WHAT HAPPENED?
YOU DON'T THINK THIS WAND IS ACTUALLY MAGICAL?
SURE SEEMS SO. MAYBE YOU REALLY ARE A WITCH.
AND THAT WOULD MEAN, I'M A WIZARD!
HEY, GIVE THAT BACK!
NOT UNTIL YOU PROMISE NOT TO GO BLASTING ANYONE WITH IT.
THESE WANDS COULD BE DANGEROUS.
WHAT IS THIS FREAKINESS?
YOU GOTTA CHANGE ME BACK. *PLEASE!!!*
DON'T WORRY. IT WILL PROBABLY WEAR OFF SOON.
YOU HAVE ONLY YOURSELF TO BLAME, YOU PIMPLE-FACE-JERKBAG!

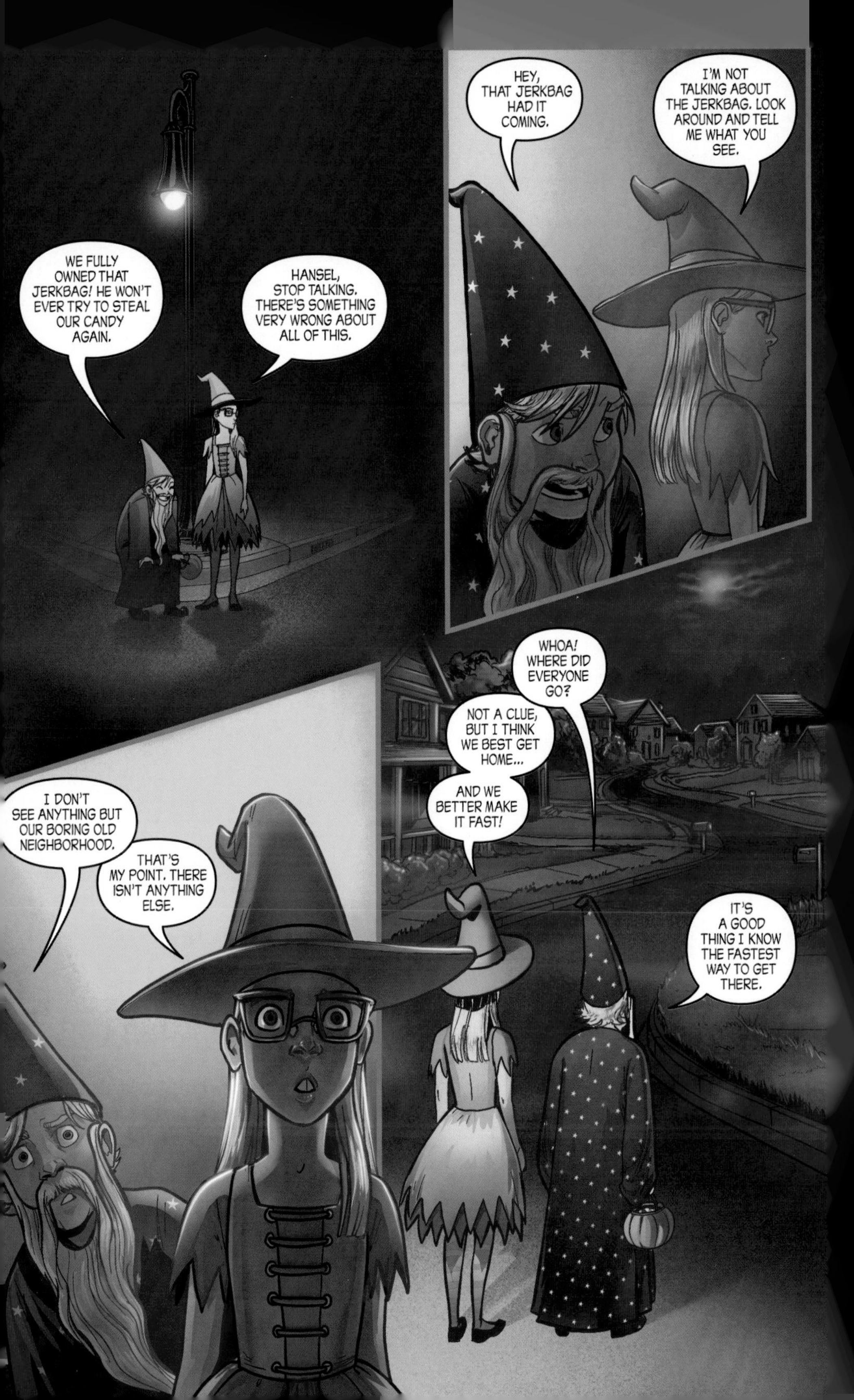
WE FULLY OWNED THAT JERKBAG! HE WON'T EVER TRY TO STEAL OUR CANDY AGAIN.
HANSEL, STOP TALKING. THERE'S SOMETHING VERY WRONG ABOUT ALL OF THIS.
HEY, THAT JERKBAG HAD IT COMING.
I'M NOT TALKING ABOUT THE JERKBAG. LOOK AROUND AND TELL ME WHAT YOU SEE.
I DON'T SEE ANYTHING BUT OUR BORING OLD NEIGHBORHOOD.
THAT'S MY POINT. THERE ISN'T ANYTHING ELSE.
WHOA! WHERE DID EVERYONE GO?
NOT A CLUE, BUT I THINK WE BEST GET HOME...
AND WE BETTER MAKE IT FAST!
IT'S A GOOD THING I KNOW THE FASTEST WAY TO GET THERE.

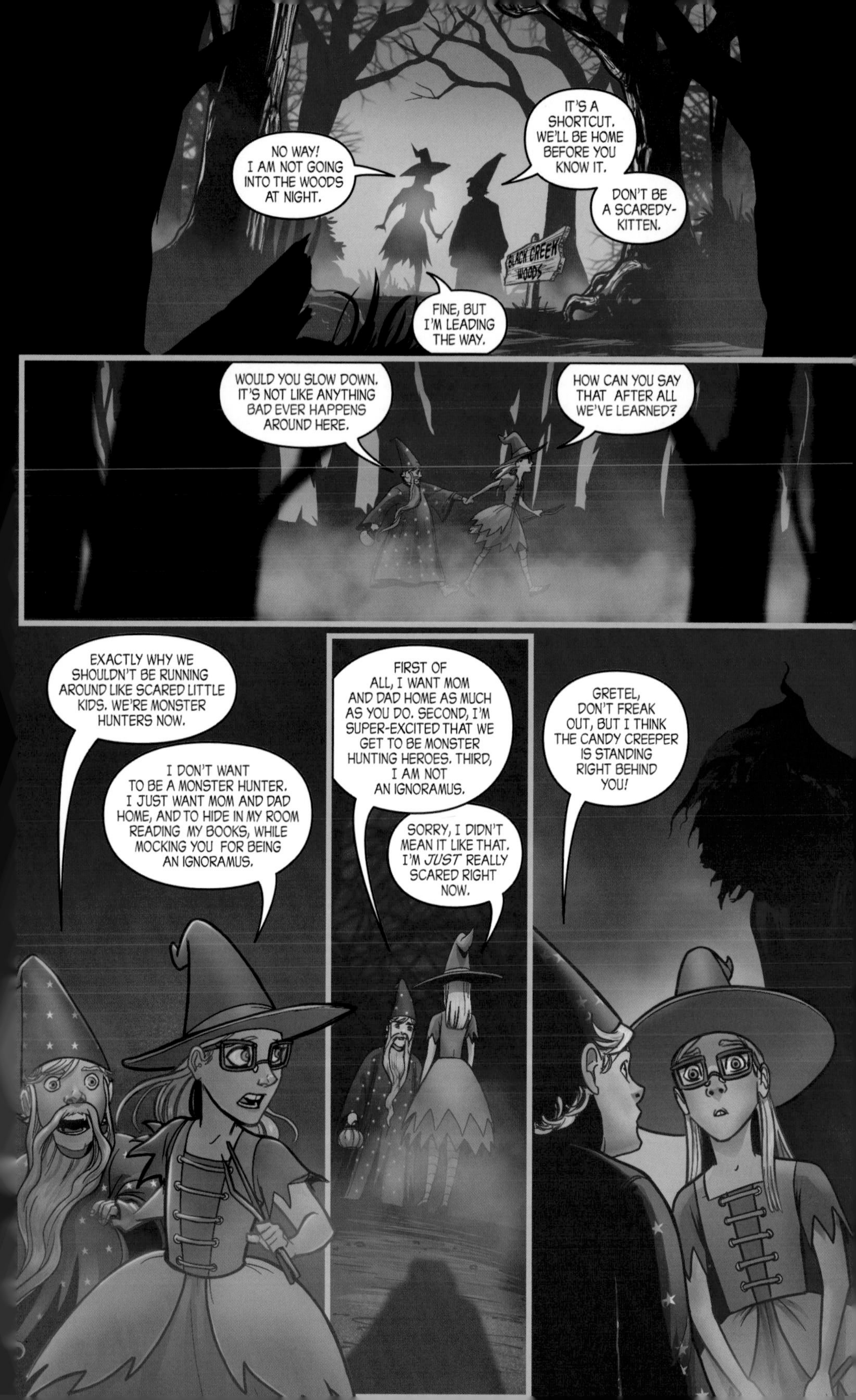
NO WAY! I AM NOT GOING INTO THE WOODS AT NIGHT.
IT'S A SHORTCUT. WE'LL BE HOME BEFORE YOU KNOW IT.
DON'T BE A SCAREDY-KITTEN.
BLACK CREEK WOODS
FINE, BUT I'M LEADING THE WAY.
WOULD YOU SLOW DOWN. IT'S NOT LIKE ANYTHING BAD EVER HAPPENS AROUND HERE.
HOW CAN YOU SAY THAT AFTER ALL WE'VE LEARNED?
EXACTLY WHY WE SHOULDN'T BE RUNNING AROUND LIKE SCARED LITTLE KIDS. WE'RE MONSTER HUNTERS NOW.
I DON'T WANT TO BE A MONSTER HUNTER. I JUST WANT MOM AND DAD HOME, AND TO HIDE IN MY ROOM READING MY BOOKS, WHILE MOCKING YOU FOR BEING AN IGNORAMUS.
FIRST OF ALL, I WANT MOM AND DAD HOME AS MUCH AS YOU DO. SECOND, I'M SUPER-EXCITED THAT WE GET TO BE MONSTER HUNTING HEROES. THIRD, I AM NOT AN IGNORAMUS.
SORRY, I DIDN'T MEAN IT LIKE THAT. I'M *JUST* REALLY SCARED RIGHT NOW.
GRETEL, DON'T FREAK OUT, BUT I THINK THE CANDY CREEPER IS STANDING RIGHT BEHIND YOU!

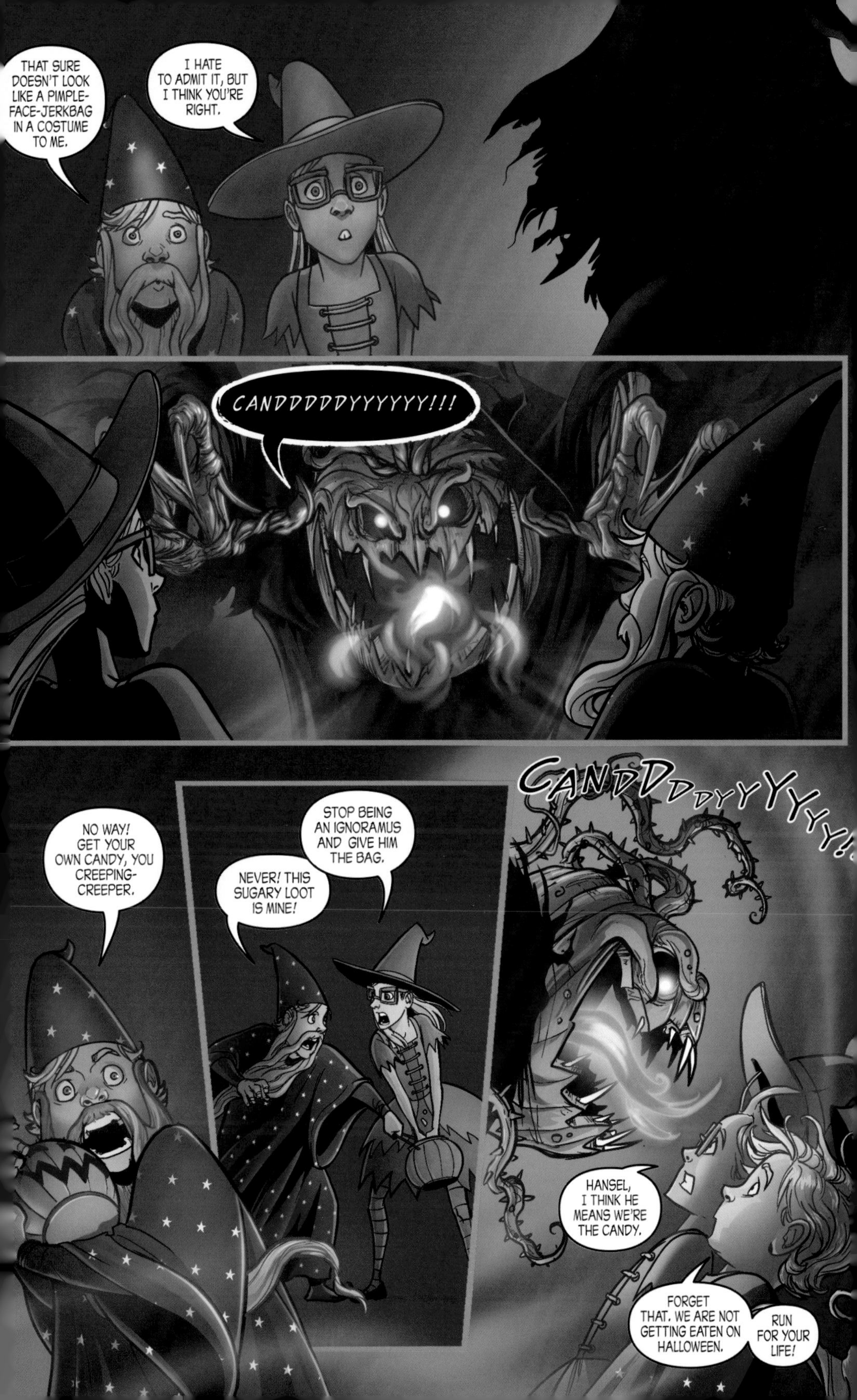
THAT SURE DOESN'T LOOK LIKE A PIMPLE-FACE-JERKBAG IN A COSTUME TO ME.
I HATE TO ADMIT IT, BUT I THINK YOU'RE RIGHT.
CANDDDDDYYYYYY!!!
NO WAY! GET YOUR OWN CANDY, YOU CREEPING-CREEPER.
STOP BEING AN IGNORAMUS AND GIVE HIM THE BAG.
NEVER! THIS SUGARY LOOT IS MINE!
CANDDDDYYYYYY!!
HANSEL, I THINK HE MEANS WE'RE THE CANDY.
FORGET THAT. WE ARE NOT GETTING EATEN ON HALLOWEEN.
RUN FOR YOUR LIFE!

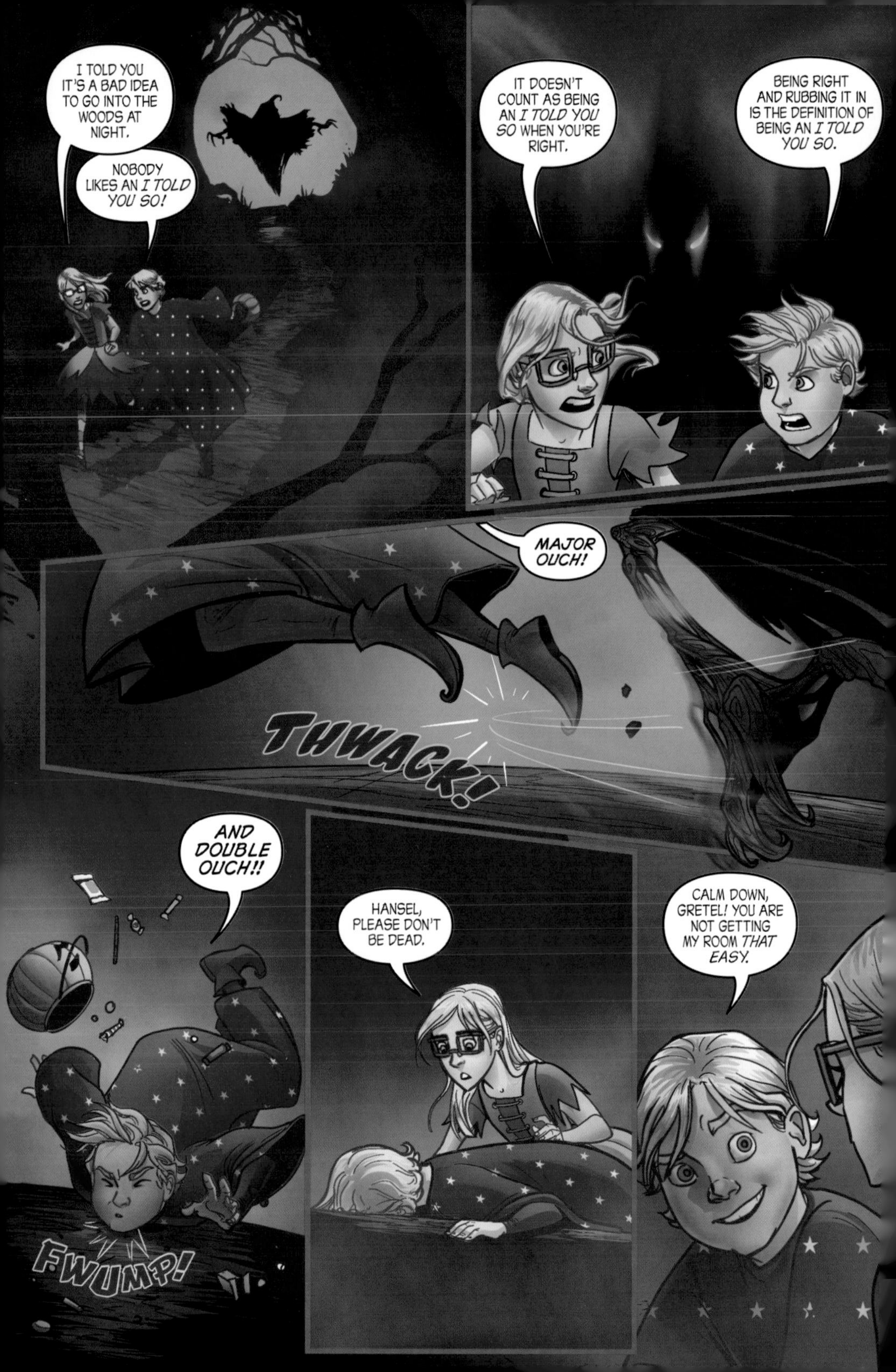
I TOLD YOU IT'S A BAD IDEA TO GO INTO THE WOODS AT NIGHT.
NOBODY LIKES AN *I TOLD YOU SO!*
IT DOESN'T COUNT AS BEING AN *I TOLD YOU SO* WHEN YOU'RE RIGHT.
BEING RIGHT AND RUBBING IT IN IS THE DEFINITION OF BEING AN *I TOLD YOU SO.*
MAJOR OUCH!
THWACK!
AND DOUBLE OUCH!!
FWUMP!
HANSEL, PLEASE DON'T BE DEAD.
CALM DOWN, GRETEL! YOU ARE NOT GETTING MY ROOM *THAT EASY.*

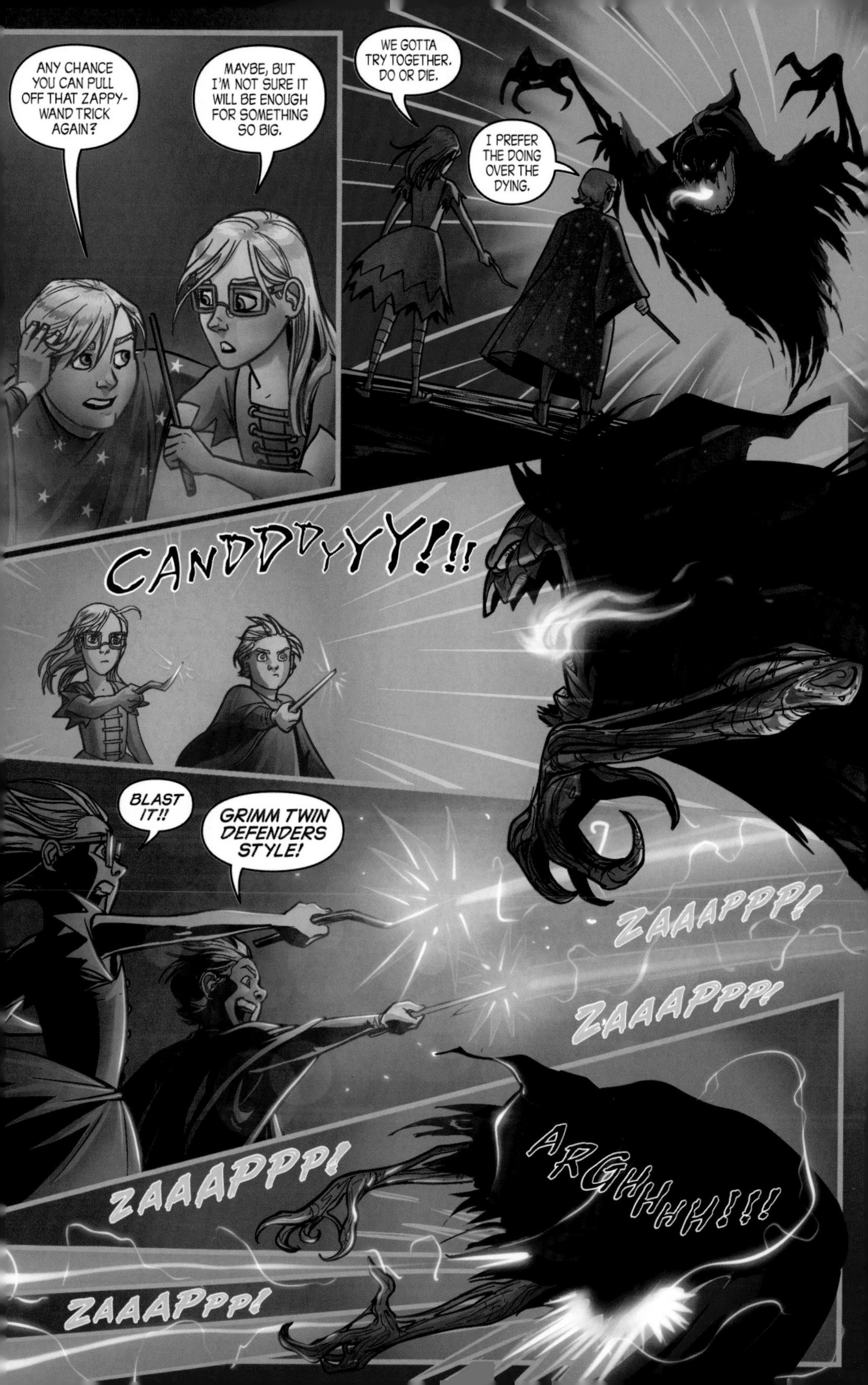
ANY CHANCE YOU CAN PULL OFF THAT ZAPPY-WAND TRICK AGAIN?
MAYBE, BUT I'M NOT SURE IT WILL BE ENOUGH FOR SOMETHING SO BIG.
WE GOTTA TRY TOGETHER. DO OR DIE.
I PREFER THE DOING OVER THE DYING.
CANDDDYYY!!!
BLAST IT!!
GRIMM TWIN DEFENDERS STYLE!
ZAAAPPP!
ZAAAPPP!
ZAAAPPP!
ARGHHHH!!!
ZAAAPPP!

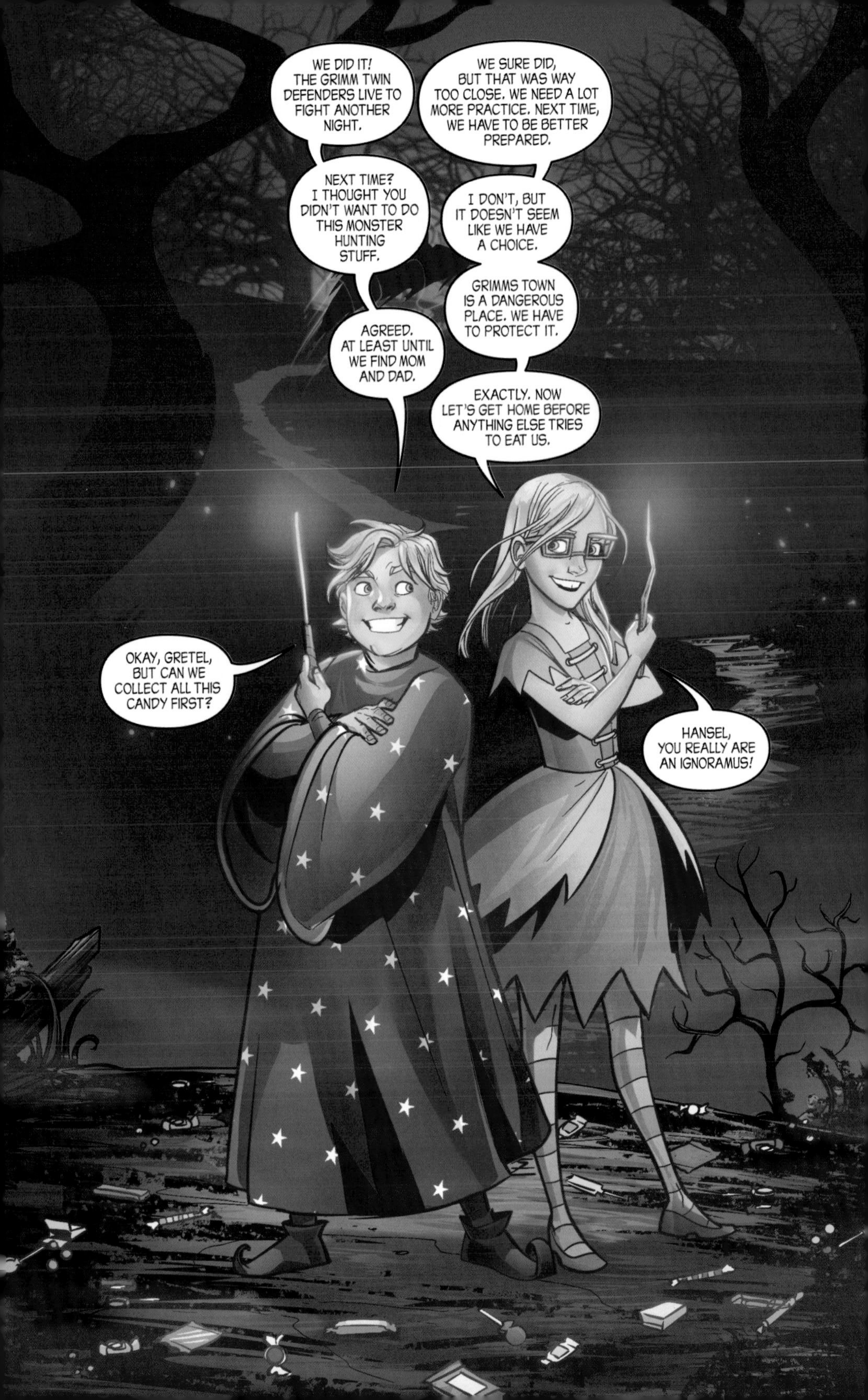
WE DID IT! THE GRIMM TWIN DEFENDERS LIVE TO FIGHT ANOTHER NIGHT.
WE SURE DID, BUT THAT WAS WAY TOO CLOSE. WE NEED A LOT MORE PRACTICE. NEXT TIME, WE HAVE TO BE BETTER PREPARED.
NEXT TIME? I THOUGHT YOU DIDN'T WANT TO DO THIS MONSTER HUNTING STUFF.
I DON'T, BUT IT DOESN'T SEEM LIKE WE HAVE A CHOICE.
GRIMMS TOWN IS A DANGEROUS PLACE. WE HAVE TO PROTECT IT.
AGREED. AT LEAST UNTIL WE FIND MOM AND DAD.
EXACTLY. NOW LET'S GET HOME BEFORE ANYTHING ELSE TRIES TO EAT US.
OKAY, GRETEL, BUT CAN WE COLLECT ALL THIS CANDY FIRST?
HANSEL, YOU REALLY ARE AN IGNORAMUS!

CHAPTER 3

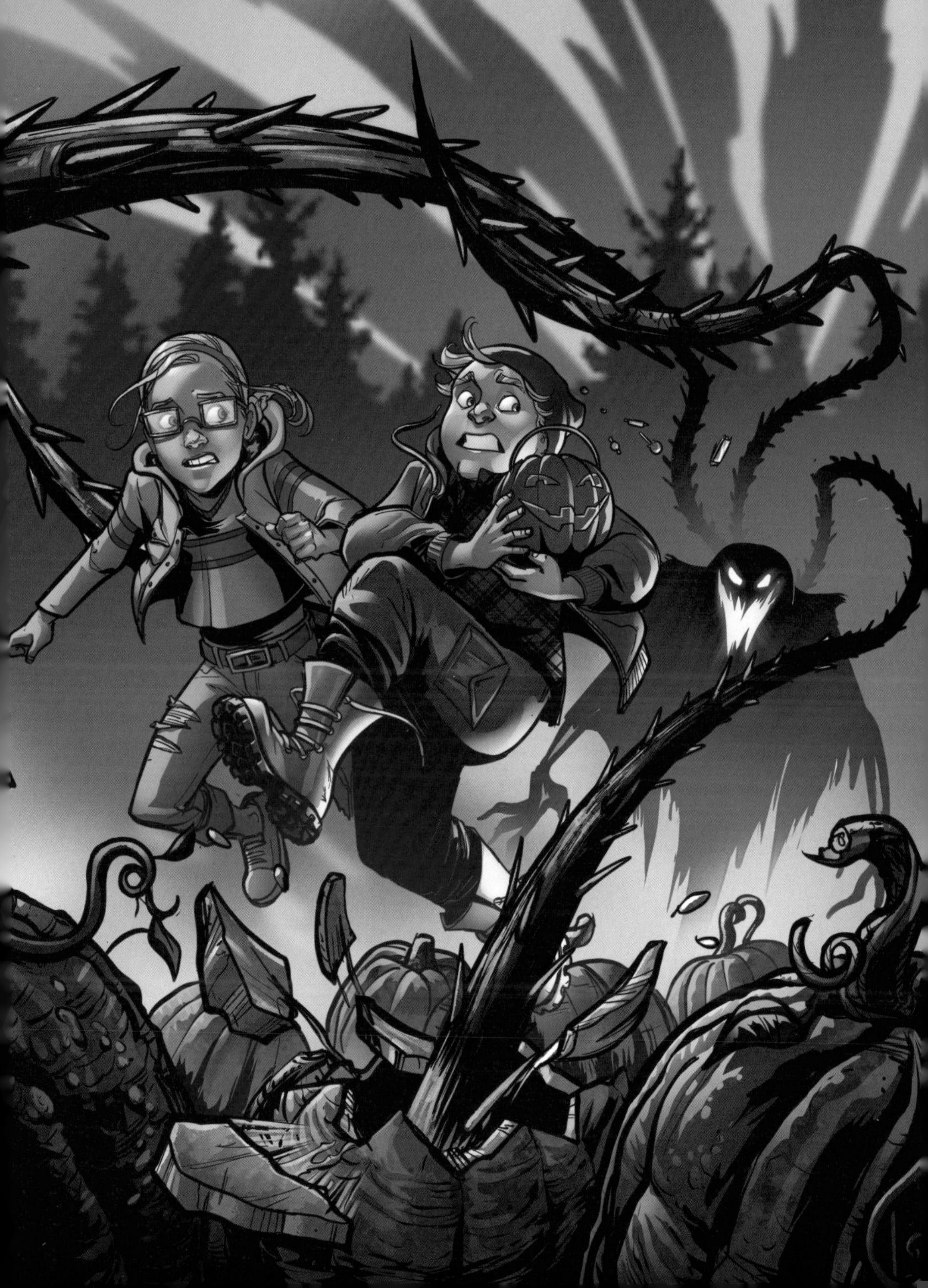

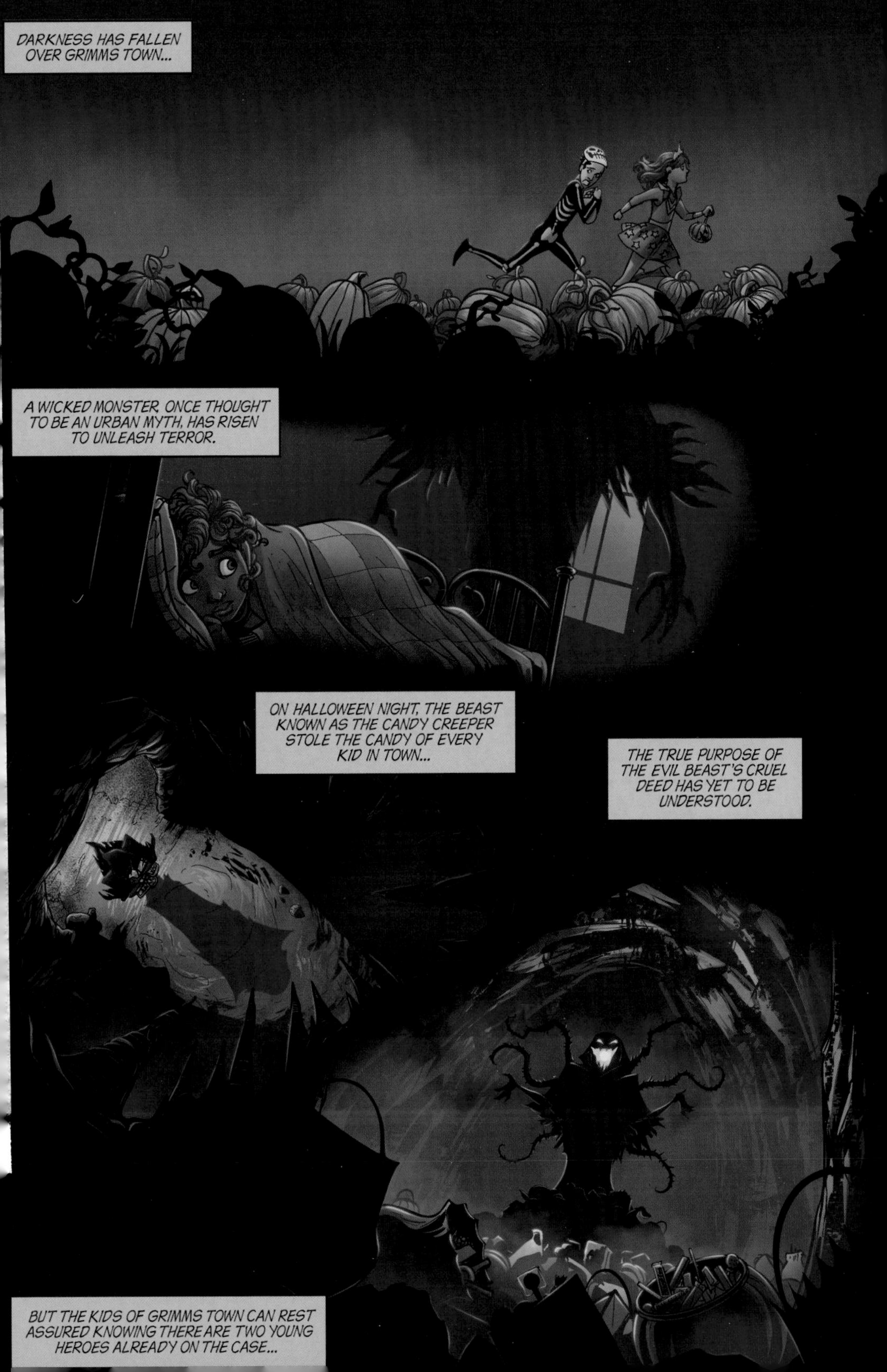
DARKNESS HAS FALLEN OVER GRIMMS TOWN...
A WICKED MONSTER, ONCE THOUGHT TO BE AN URBAN MYTH, HAS RISEN TO UNLEASH TERROR.
ON HALLOWEEN NIGHT, THE BEAST KNOWN AS THE CANDY CREEPER STOLE THE CANDY OF EVERY KID IN TOWN...
THE TRUE PURPOSE OF THE EVIL BEAST'S CRUEL DEED HAS YET TO BE UNDERSTOOD.
BUT THE KIDS OF GRIMMS TOWN CAN REST ASSURED KNOWING THERE ARE TWO YOUNG HEROES ALREADY ON THE CASE...

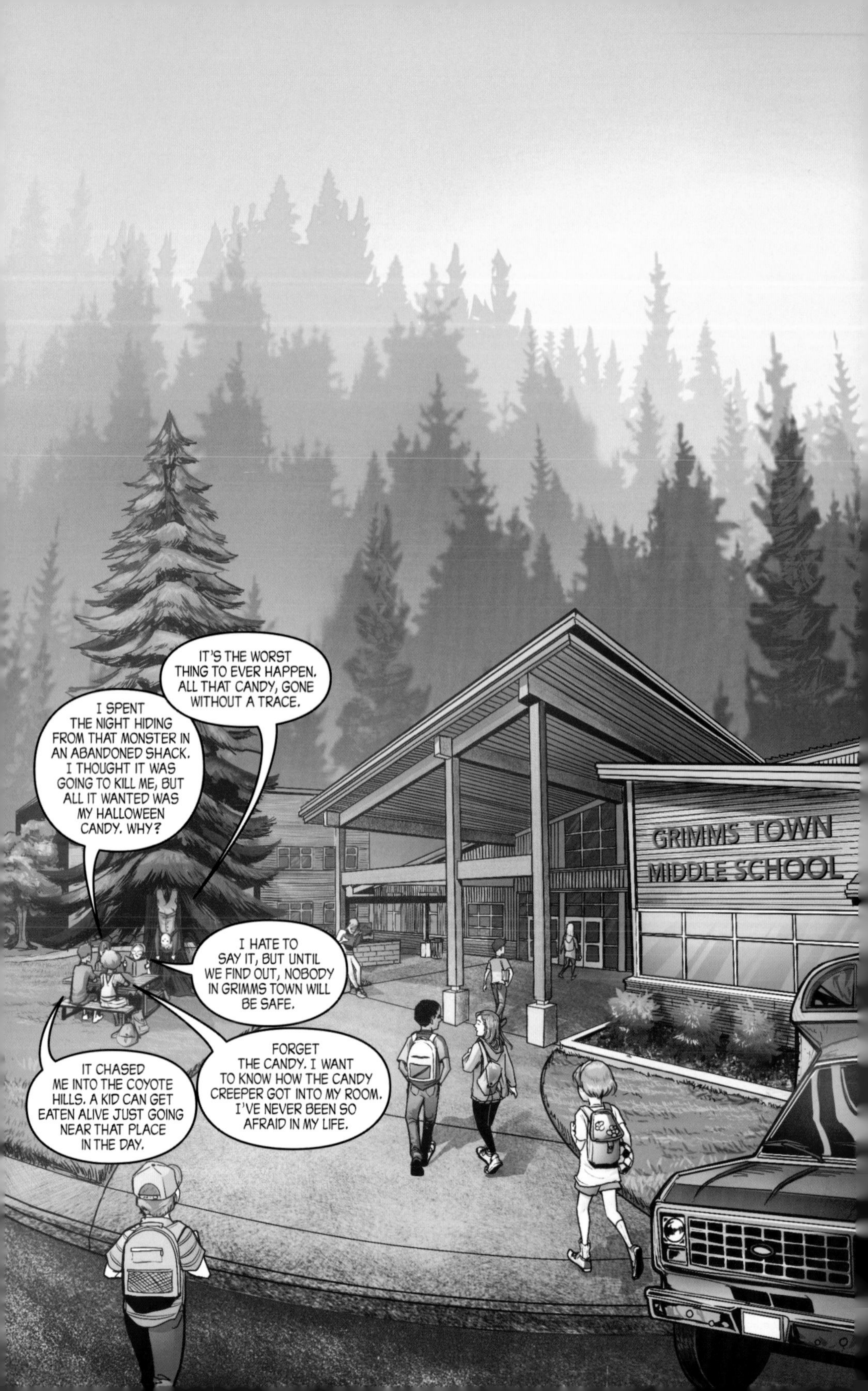
I SPENT THE NIGHT HIDING FROM THAT MONSTER IN AN ABANDONED SHACK. I THOUGHT IT WAS GOING TO KILL ME, BUT ALL IT WANTED WAS MY HALLOWEEN CANDY. WHY?
IT'S THE WORST THING TO EVER HAPPEN. ALL THAT CANDY, GONE WITHOUT A TRACE.
GRIMMS TOWN MIDDLE SCHOOL
I HATE TO SAY IT, BUT UNTIL WE FIND OUT, NOBODY IN GRIMMS TOWN WILL BE SAFE.
IT CHASED ME INTO THE COYOTE HILLS. A KID CAN GET EATEN ALIVE JUST GOING NEAR THAT PLACE IN THE DAY.
FORGET THE CANDY. I WANT TO KNOW HOW THE CANDY CREEPER GOT INTO MY ROOM. I'VE NEVER BEEN SO AFRAID IN MY LIFE.

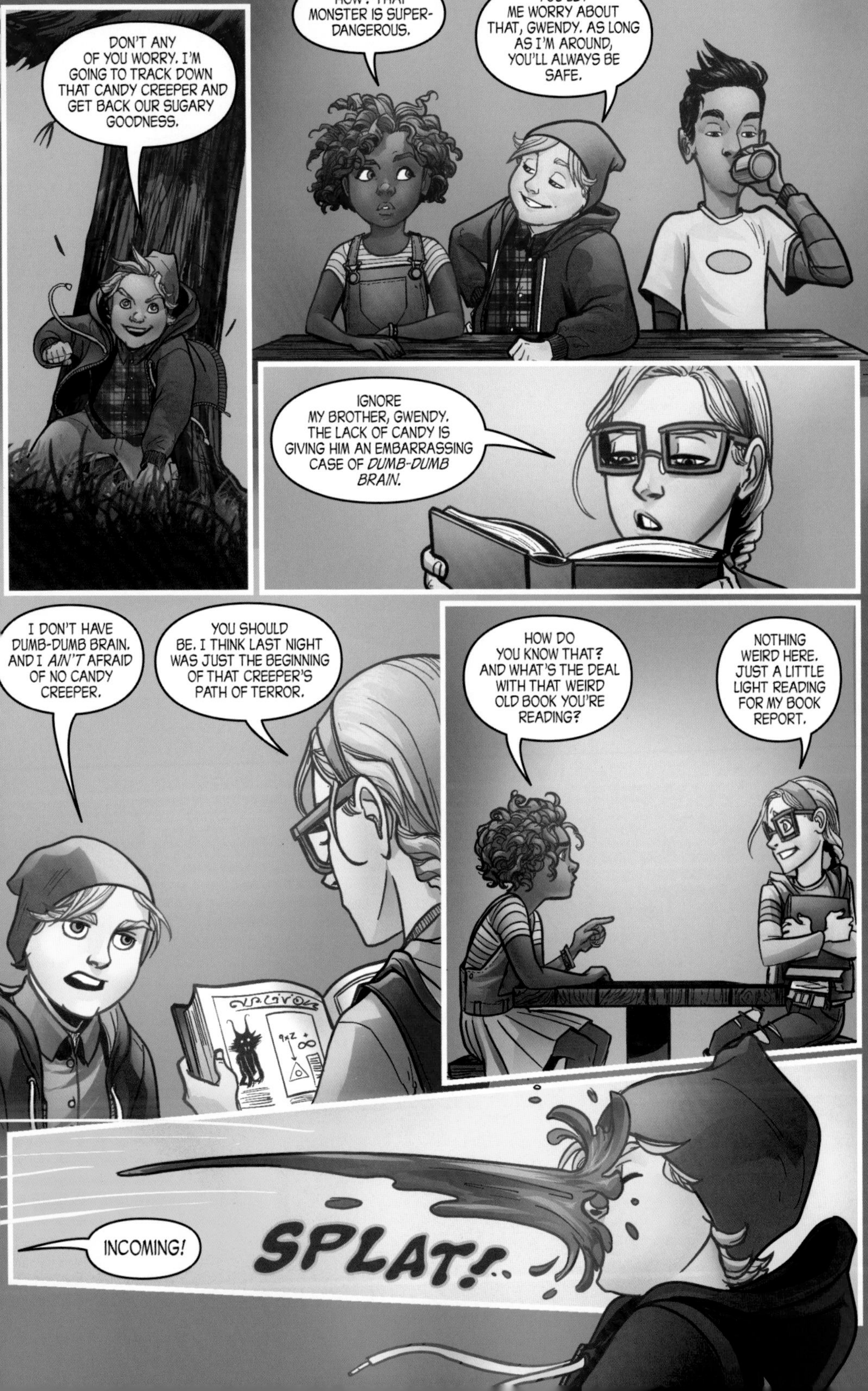
DON'T ANY OF YOU WORRY. I'M GOING TO TRACK DOWN THAT CANDY CREEPER AND GET BACK OUR SUGARY GOODNESS.
HOW? THAT MONSTER IS SUPER-DANGEROUS.
YOU LET ME WORRY ABOUT THAT, GWENDY. AS LONG AS I'M AROUND, YOU'LL ALWAYS BE SAFE.
IGNORE MY BROTHER, GWENDY. THE LACK OF CANDY IS GIVING HIM AN EMBARRASSING CASE OF *DUMB-DUMB BRAIN.*
I DON'T HAVE DUMB-DUMB BRAIN. AND I *AIN'T* AFRAID OF NO CANDY CREEPER.
YOU SHOULD BE. I THINK LAST NIGHT WAS JUST THE BEGINNING OF THAT CREEPER'S PATH OF TERROR.
HOW DO YOU KNOW THAT? AND WHAT'S THE DEAL WITH THAT WEIRD OLD BOOK YOU'RE READING?
NOTHING WEIRD HERE. JUST A LITTLE LIGHT READING FOR MY BOOK REPORT.
INCOMING!
SPLAT!

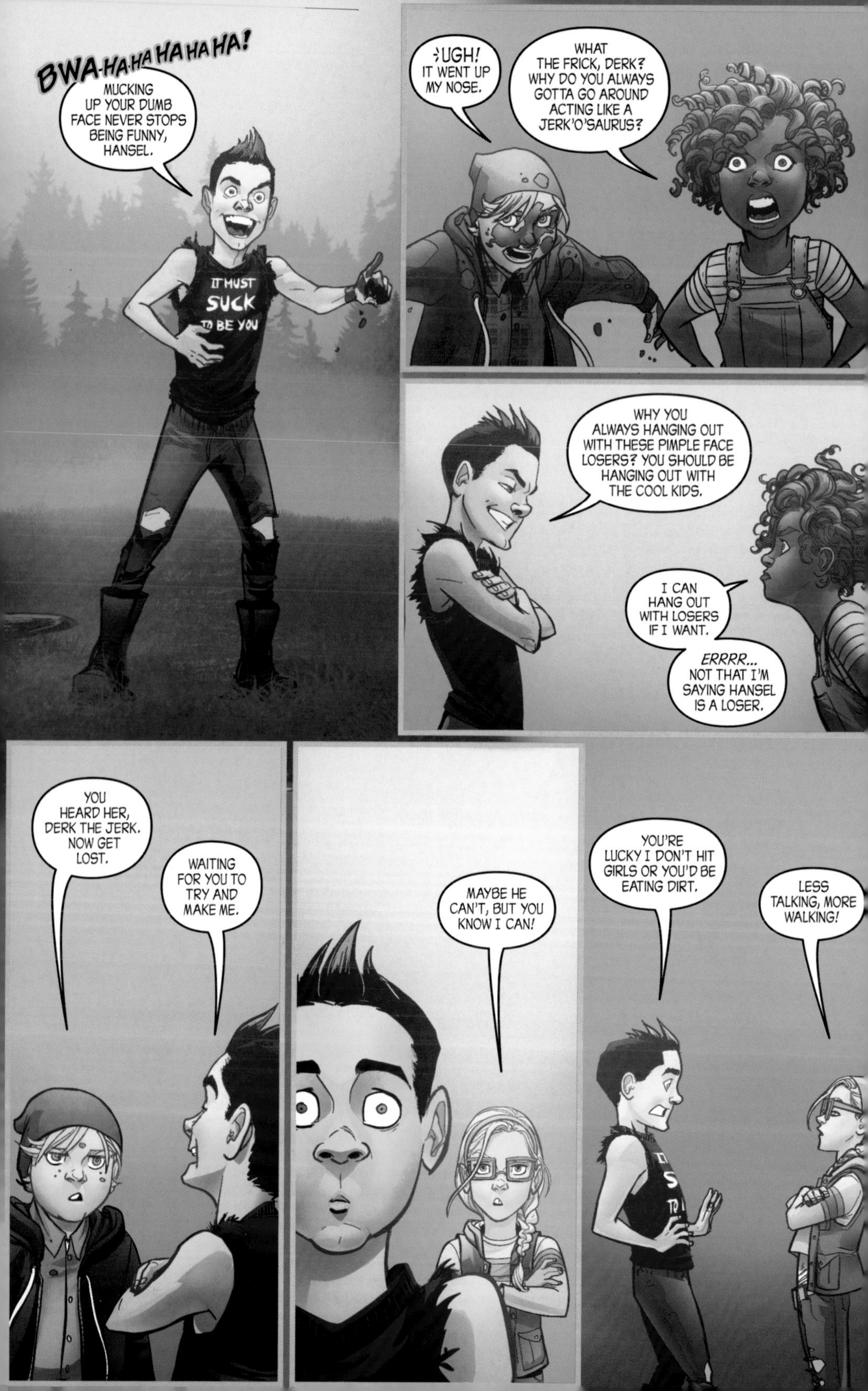
BWA-HA-HA HA HA HA!
MUCKING UP YOUR DUMB FACE NEVER STOPS BEING FUNNY, HANSEL.
IT MUST SUCK TO BE YOU
UGH! IT WENT UP MY NOSE.
WHAT THE FRICK, DERK? WHY DO YOU ALWAYS GOTTA GO AROUND ACTING LIKE A JERK'O'SAURUS?
WHY YOU ALWAYS HANGING OUT WITH THESE PIMPLE FACE LOSERS? YOU SHOULD BE HANGING OUT WITH THE COOL KIDS.
I CAN HANG OUT WITH LOSERS IF I WANT.
ERRRR... NOT THAT I'M SAYING HANSEL IS A LOSER.
YOU HEARD HER, DERK THE JERK. NOW GET LOST.
WAITING FOR YOU TO TRY AND MAKE ME.
MAYBE HE CAN'T, BUT YOU KNOW I CAN!
YOU'RE LUCKY I DON'T HIT GIRLS OR YOU'D BE EATING DIRT.
LESS TALKING, MORE WALKING!

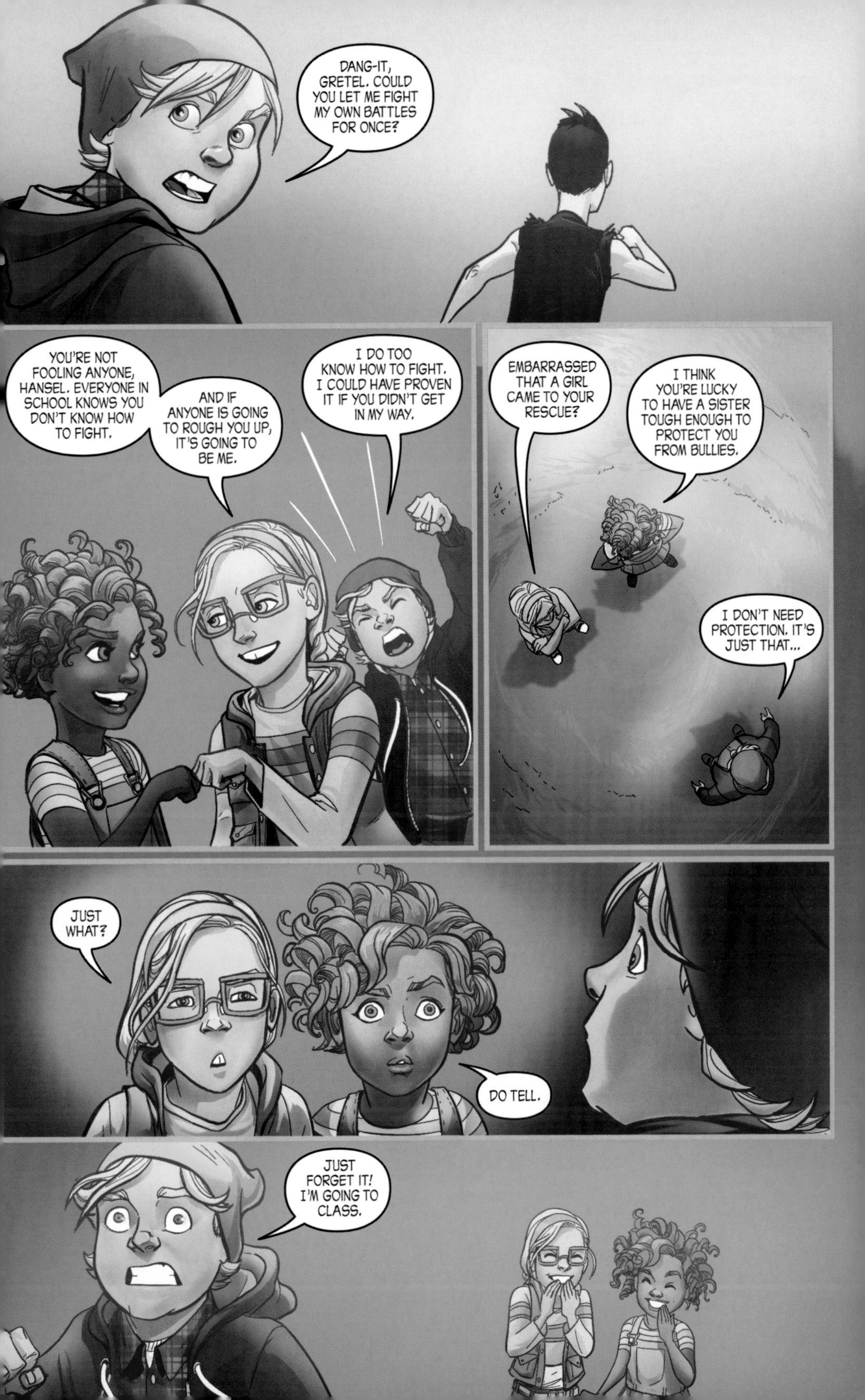
DANG-IT, GRETEL. COULD YOU LET ME FIGHT MY OWN BATTLES FOR ONCE?
YOU'RE NOT FOOLING ANYONE, HANSEL. EVERYONE IN SCHOOL KNOWS YOU DON'T KNOW HOW TO FIGHT.
AND IF ANYONE IS GOING TO ROUGH YOU UP, IT'S GOING TO BE ME.
I DO TOO KNOW HOW TO FIGHT. I COULD HAVE PROVEN IT IF YOU DIDN'T GET IN MY WAY.
EMBARRASSED THAT A GIRL CAME TO YOUR RESCUE?
I THINK YOU'RE LUCKY TO HAVE A SISTER TOUGH ENOUGH TO PROTECT YOU FROM BULLIES.
I DON'T NEED PROTECTION. IT'S JUST THAT...
JUST WHAT?
DO TELL.
JUST FORGET IT! I'M GOING TO CLASS.

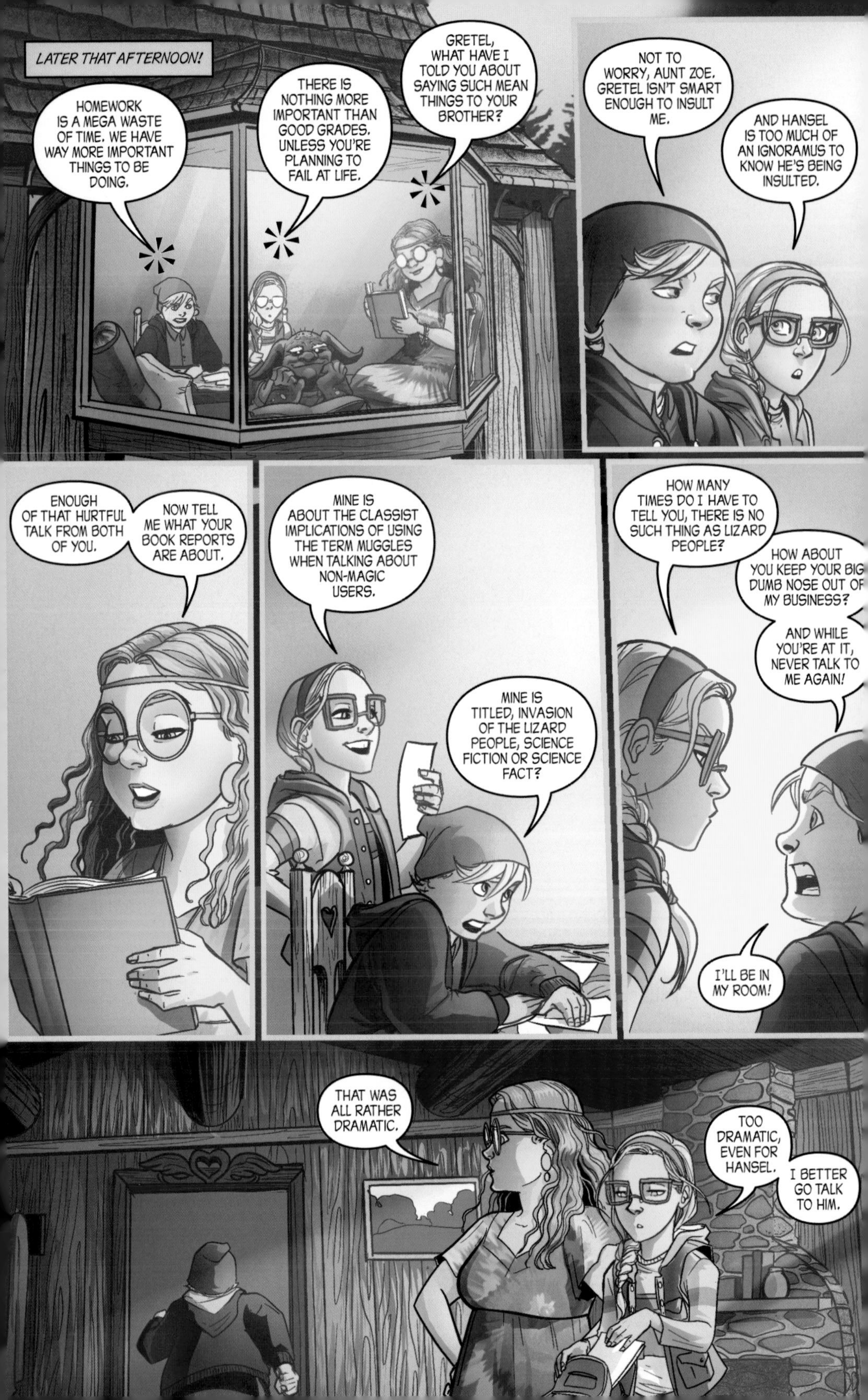
LATER THAT AFTERNOON!
HOMEWORK IS A MEGA WASTE OF TIME. WE HAVE WAY MORE IMPORTANT THINGS TO BE DOING.
THERE IS NOTHING MORE IMPORTANT THAN GOOD GRADES. UNLESS YOU'RE PLANNING TO FAIL AT LIFE.
GRETEL, WHAT HAVE I TOLD YOU ABOUT SAYING SUCH MEAN THINGS TO YOUR BROTHER?
NOT TO WORRY, AUNT ZOE. GRETEL ISN'T SMART ENOUGH TO INSULT ME.
AND HANSEL IS TOO MUCH OF AN IGNORAMUS TO KNOW HE'S BEING INSULTED.
ENOUGH OF THAT HURTFUL TALK FROM BOTH OF YOU.
NOW TELL ME WHAT YOUR BOOK REPORTS ARE ABOUT.
MINE IS ABOUT THE CLASSIST IMPLICATIONS OF USING THE TERM MUGGLES WHEN TALKING ABOUT NON-MAGIC USERS.
MINE IS TITLED, INVASION OF THE LIZARD PEOPLE, SCIENCE FICTION OR SCIENCE FACT?
HOW MANY TIMES DO I HAVE TO TELL YOU, THERE IS NO SUCH THING AS LIZARD PEOPLE?
HOW ABOUT YOU KEEP YOUR BIG DUMB NOSE OUT OF MY BUSINESS?
AND WHILE YOU'RE AT IT, NEVER TALK TO ME AGAIN!
I'LL BE IN MY ROOM!
THAT WAS ALL RATHER DRAMATIC.
TOO DRAMATIC, EVEN FOR HANSEL.
I BETTER GO TALK TO HIM.

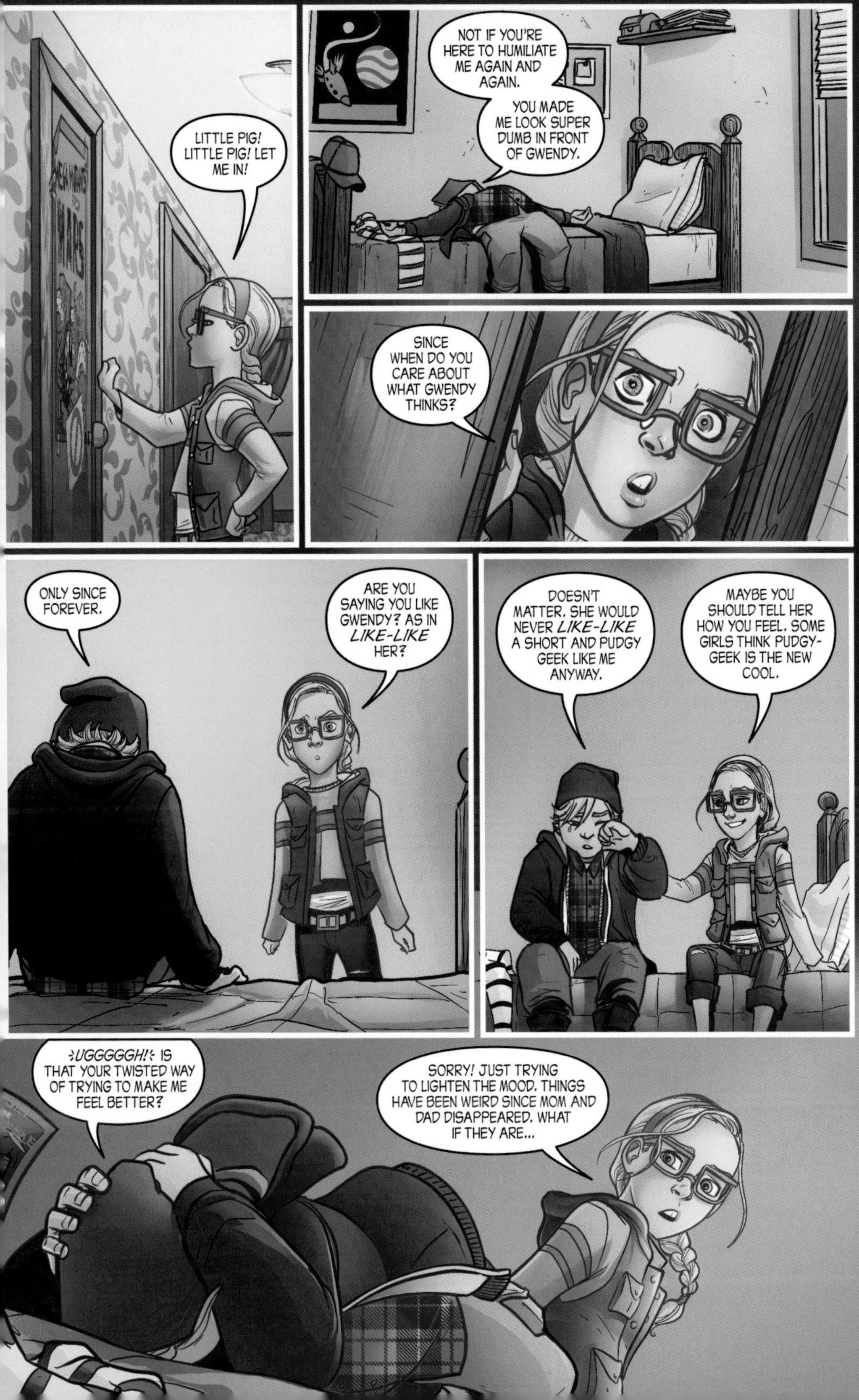
LITTLE PIG! LITTLE PIG! LET ME IN!
NOT IF YOU'RE HERE TO HUMILIATE ME AGAIN AND AGAIN.
YOU MADE ME LOOK SUPER DUMB IN FRONT OF GWENDY.
SINCE WHEN DO YOU CARE ABOUT WHAT GWENDY THINKS?
ONLY SINCE FOREVER.
ARE YOU SAYING YOU LIKE GWENDY? AS IN *LIKE-LIKE* HER?
DOESN'T MATTER. SHE WOULD NEVER *LIKE-LIKE* A SHORT AND PUDGY GEEK LIKE ME ANYWAY.
MAYBE YOU SHOULD TELL HER HOW YOU FEEL. SOME GIRLS THINK PUDGY-GEEK IS THE NEW COOL.
UGGGGGH! IS THAT YOUR TWISTED WAY OF TRYING TO MAKE ME FEEL BETTER?
SORRY! JUST TRYING TO LIGHTEN THE MOOD. THINGS HAVE BEEN WEIRD SINCE MOM AND DAD DISAPPEARED. WHAT IF THEY ARE...

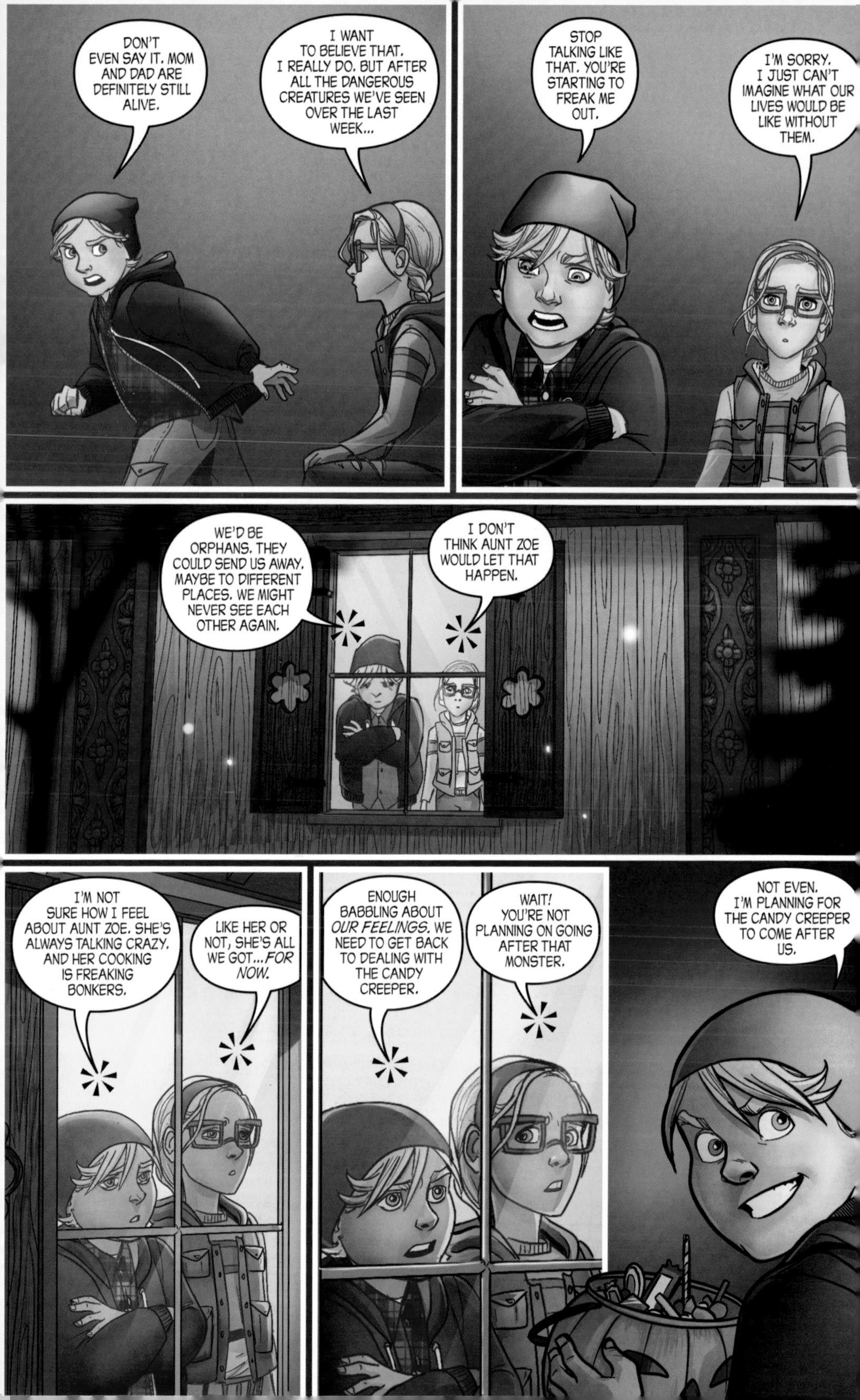

DON'T EVEN SAY IT. MOM AND DAD ARE DEFINITELY STILL ALIVE.
I WANT TO BELIEVE THAT. I REALLY DO. BUT AFTER ALL THE DANGEROUS CREATURES WE'VE SEEN OVER THE LAST WEEK...
STOP TALKING LIKE THAT. YOU'RE STARTING TO FREAK ME OUT.
I'M SORRY. I JUST CAN'T IMAGINE WHAT OUR LIVES WOULD BE LIKE WITHOUT THEM.
WE'D BE ORPHANS. THEY COULD SEND US AWAY. MAYBE TO DIFFERENT PLACES. WE MIGHT NEVER SEE EACH OTHER AGAIN.
I DON'T THINK AUNT ZOE WOULD LET THAT HAPPEN.
I'M NOT SURE HOW I FEEL ABOUT AUNT ZOE. SHE'S ALWAYS TALKING CRAZY. AND HER COOKING IS FREAKING BONKERS.
LIKE HER OR NOT, SHE'S ALL WE GOT...*FOR NOW.*
ENOUGH BABBLING ABOUT *OUR FEELINGS.* WE NEED TO GET BACK TO DEALING WITH THE CANDY CREEPER.
WAIT! YOU'RE NOT PLANNING ON GOING AFTER THAT MONSTER.
NOT EVEN. I'M PLANNING FOR THE CANDY CREEPER TO COME AFTER US.

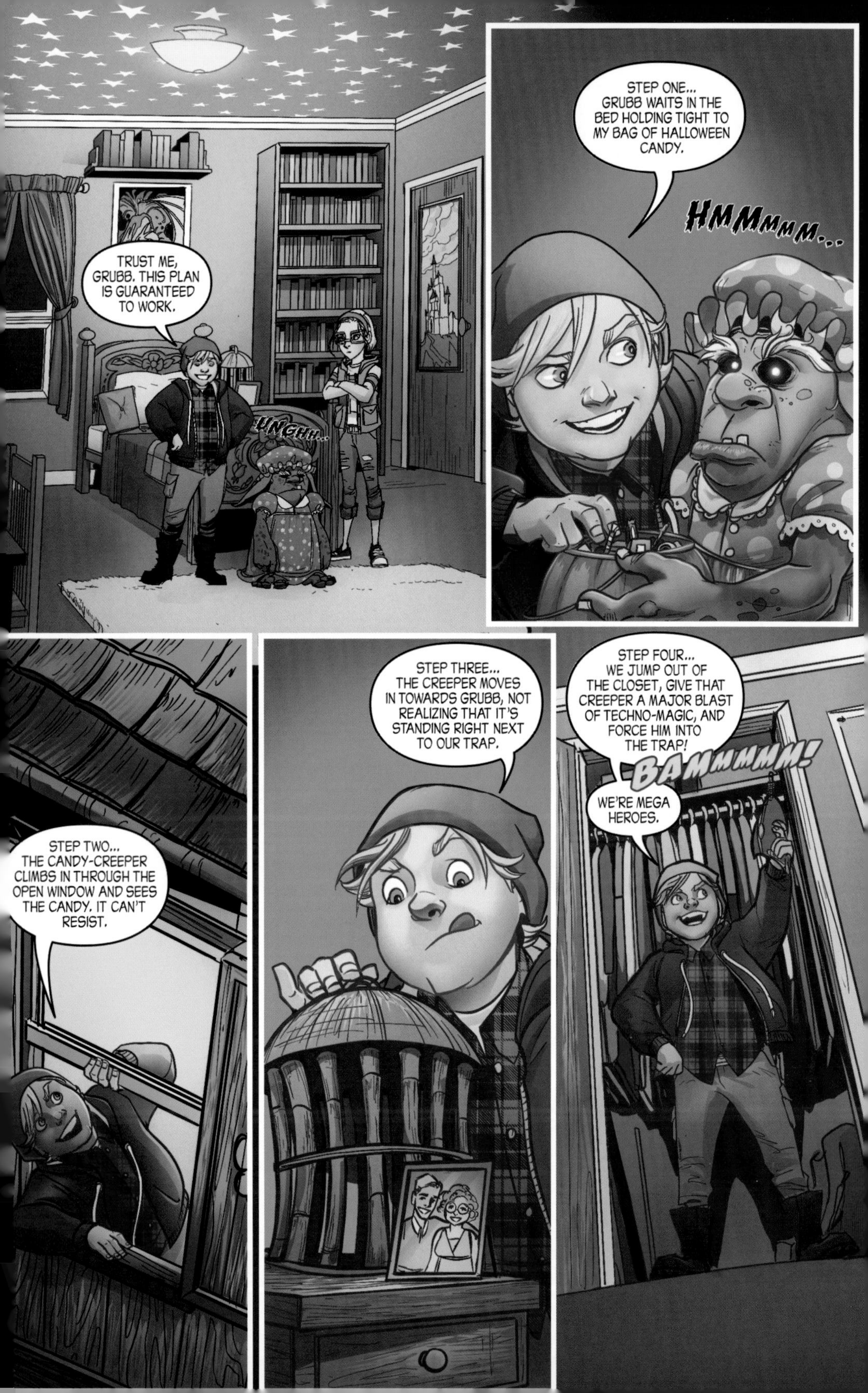
TRUST ME, GRUBB. THIS PLAN IS GUARANTEED TO WORK.
UNGH...
STEP ONE... GRUBB WAITS IN THE BED HOLDING TIGHT TO MY BAG OF HALLOWEEN CANDY.
HMMMMM...
STEP TWO... THE CANDY-CREEPER CLIMBS IN THROUGH THE OPEN WINDOW AND SEES THE CANDY. IT CAN'T RESIST.
STEP THREE... THE CREEPER MOVES IN TOWARDS GRUBB, NOT REALIZING THAT IT'S STANDING RIGHT NEXT TO OUR TRAP.
STEP FOUR... WE JUMP OUT OF THE CLOSET, GIVE THAT CREEPER A MAJOR BLAST OF TECHNO-MAGIC, AND FORCE HIM INTO THE TRAP!
BAMMMMM!
WE'RE MEGA HEROES.

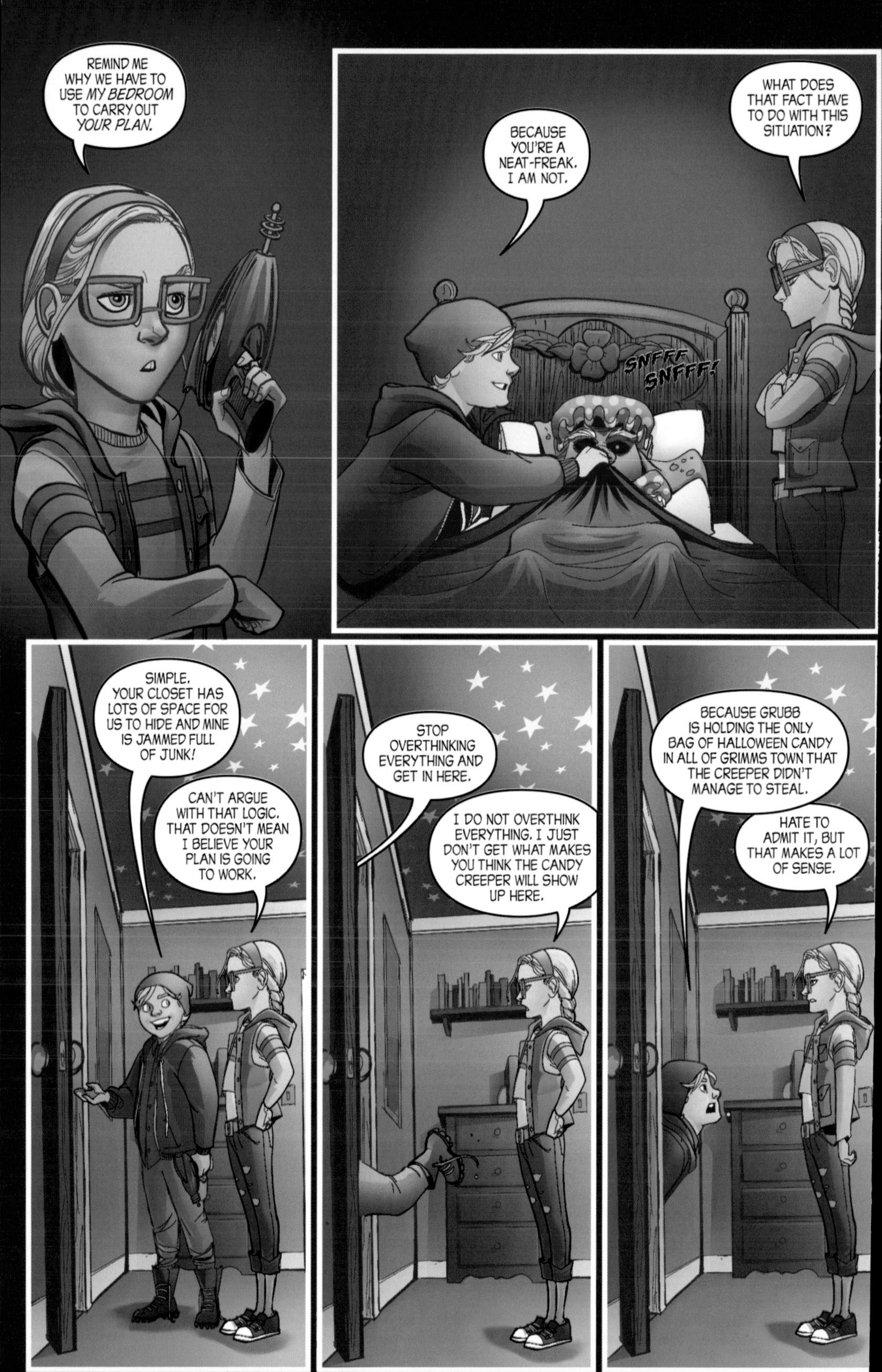
REMIND ME WHY WE HAVE TO USE *MY BEDROOM* TO CARRY OUT *YOUR PLAN.*
BECAUSE YOU'RE A NEAT-FREAK. I AM NOT.
WHAT DOES THAT FACT HAVE TO DO WITH THIS SITUATION?
SNFFF SNFFF!
SIMPLE. YOUR CLOSET HAS LOTS OF SPACE FOR US TO HIDE AND MINE IS JAMMED FULL OF JUNK!
CAN'T ARGUE WITH THAT LOGIC. THAT DOESN'T MEAN I BELIEVE YOUR PLAN IS GOING TO WORK.
STOP OVERTHINKING EVERYTHING AND GET IN HERE.
I DO NOT OVERTHINK EVERYTHING. I JUST DON'T GET WHAT MAKES YOU THINK THE CANDY CREEPER WILL SHOW UP HERE.
BECAUSE GRUBB IS HOLDING THE ONLY BAG OF HALLOWEEN CANDY IN ALL OF GRIMMS TOWN THAT THE CREEPER DIDN'T MANAGE TO STEAL.
HATE TO ADMIT IT, BUT THAT MAKES A LOT OF SENSE.

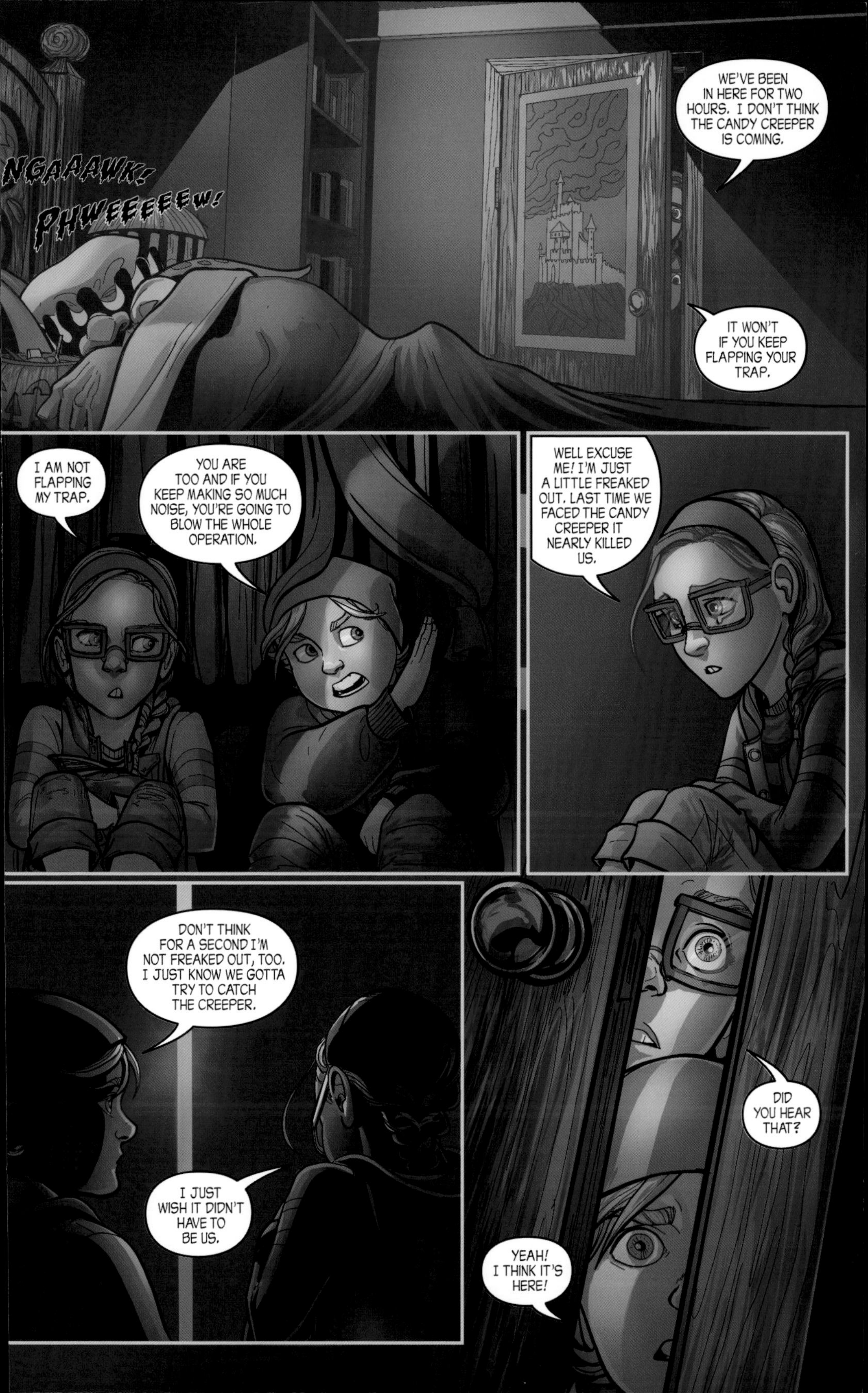
NGAAAWK!
PHWEEEEEEW!
WE'VE BEEN IN HERE FOR TWO HOURS. I DON'T THINK THE CANDY CREEPER IS COMING.
IT WON'T IF YOU KEEP FLAPPING YOUR TRAP.
I AM NOT FLAPPING MY TRAP.
YOU ARE TOO AND IF YOU KEEP MAKING SO MUCH NOISE, YOU'RE GOING TO BLOW THE WHOLE OPERATION.
WELL EXCUSE ME! I'M JUST A LITTLE FREAKED OUT. LAST TIME WE FACED THE CANDY CREEPER IT NEARLY KILLED US.
DON'T THINK FOR A SECOND I'M NOT FREAKED OUT, TOO. I JUST KNOW WE GOTTA TRY TO CATCH THE CREEPER.
I JUST WISH IT DIDN'T HAVE TO BE US.
DID YOU HEAR THAT?
YEAH! I THINK IT'S HERE!

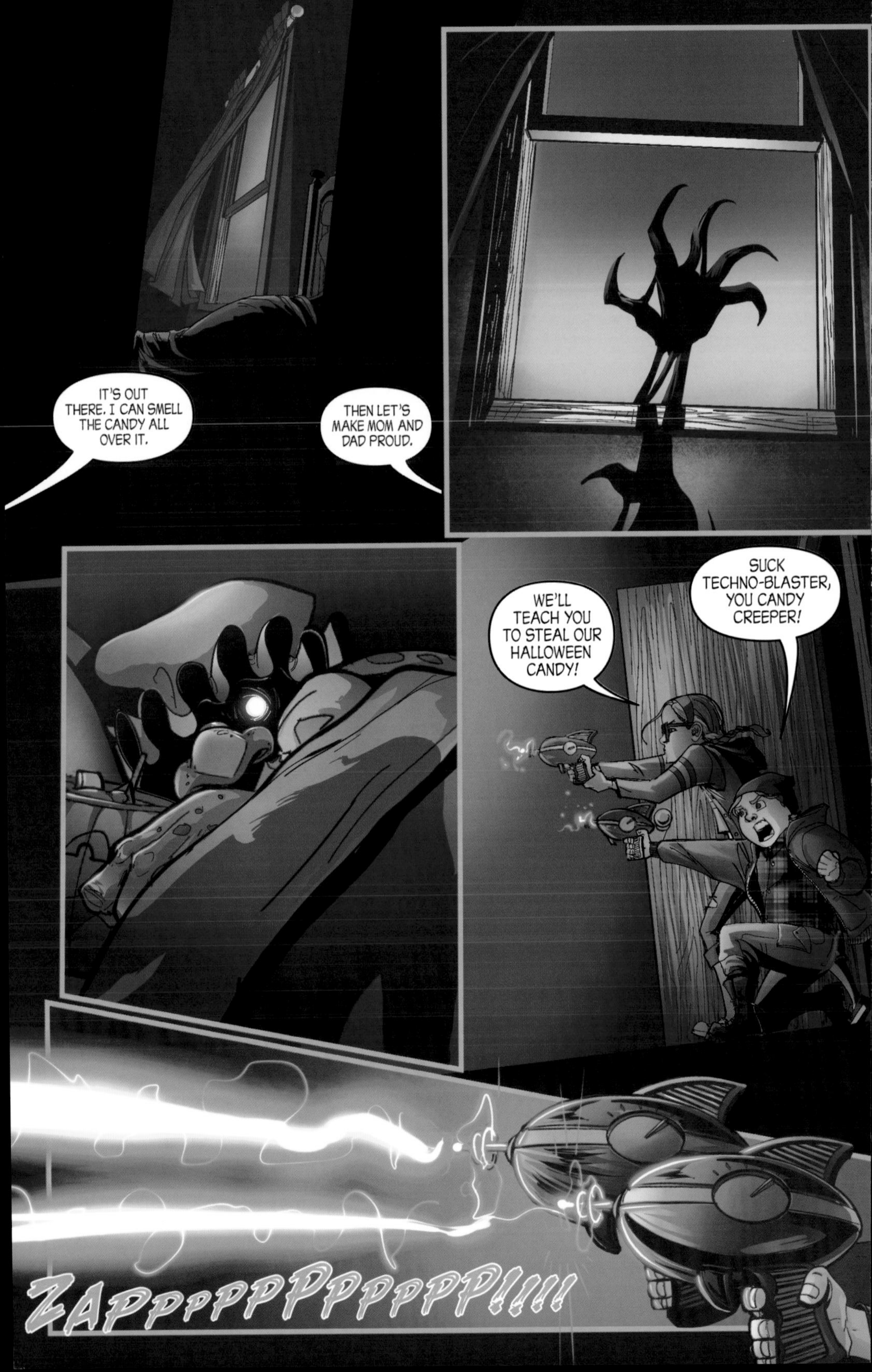
IT'S OUT THERE. I CAN SMELL THE CANDY ALL OVER IT.
THEN LET'S MAKE MOM AND DAD PROUD.
WE'LL TEACH YOU TO STEAL OUR HALLOWEEN CANDY!
SUCK TECHNO-BLASTER, YOU CANDY CREEPER!
ZAPppppPPppppPP!!!!

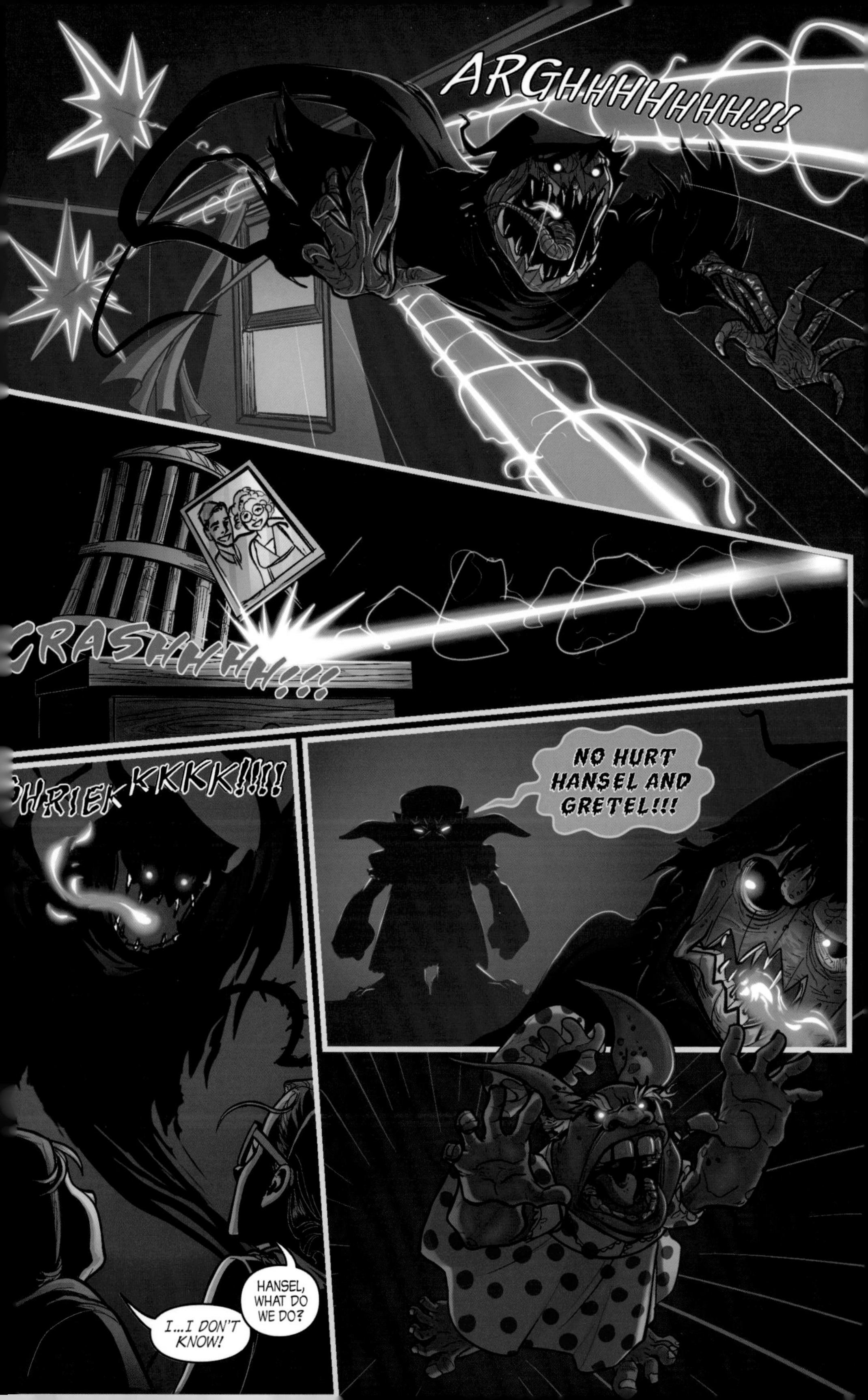
ARGHHHHHHHH!!!!
CRASHHHHH!!!!
SHRIEKKKKK!!!!
NO HURT HANSEL AND GRETEL!!!
HANSEL, WHAT DO WE DO?
I...I DON'T KNOW!

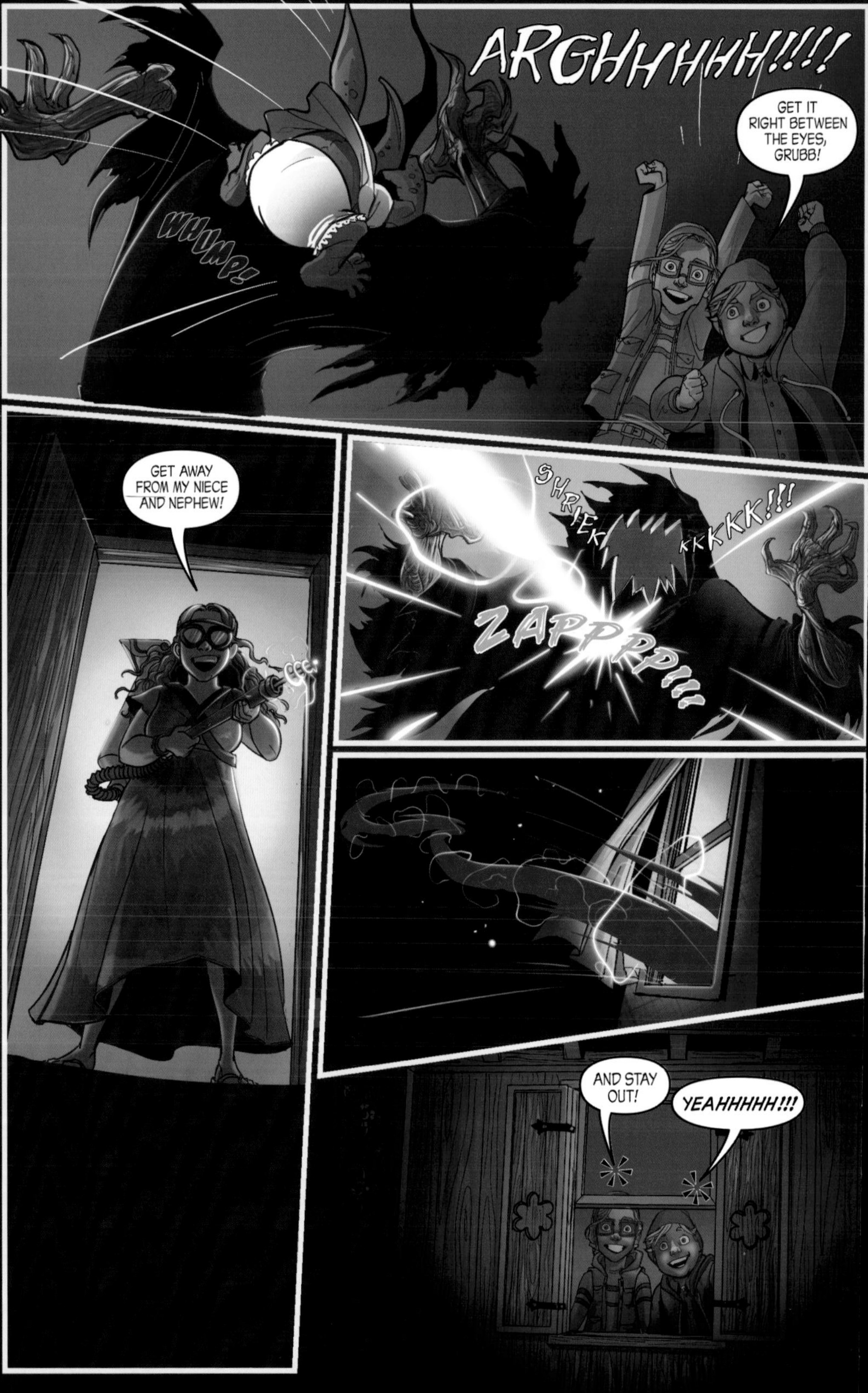
ARGHHHHH!!!!
GET IT RIGHT BETWEEN THE EYES, GRUBB!
WHUMP!
GET AWAY FROM MY NIECE AND NEPHEW!
SHRIEKKKKKK!!!
ZAPPPPP!!!
AND STAY OUT!
YEAHHHHH!!!

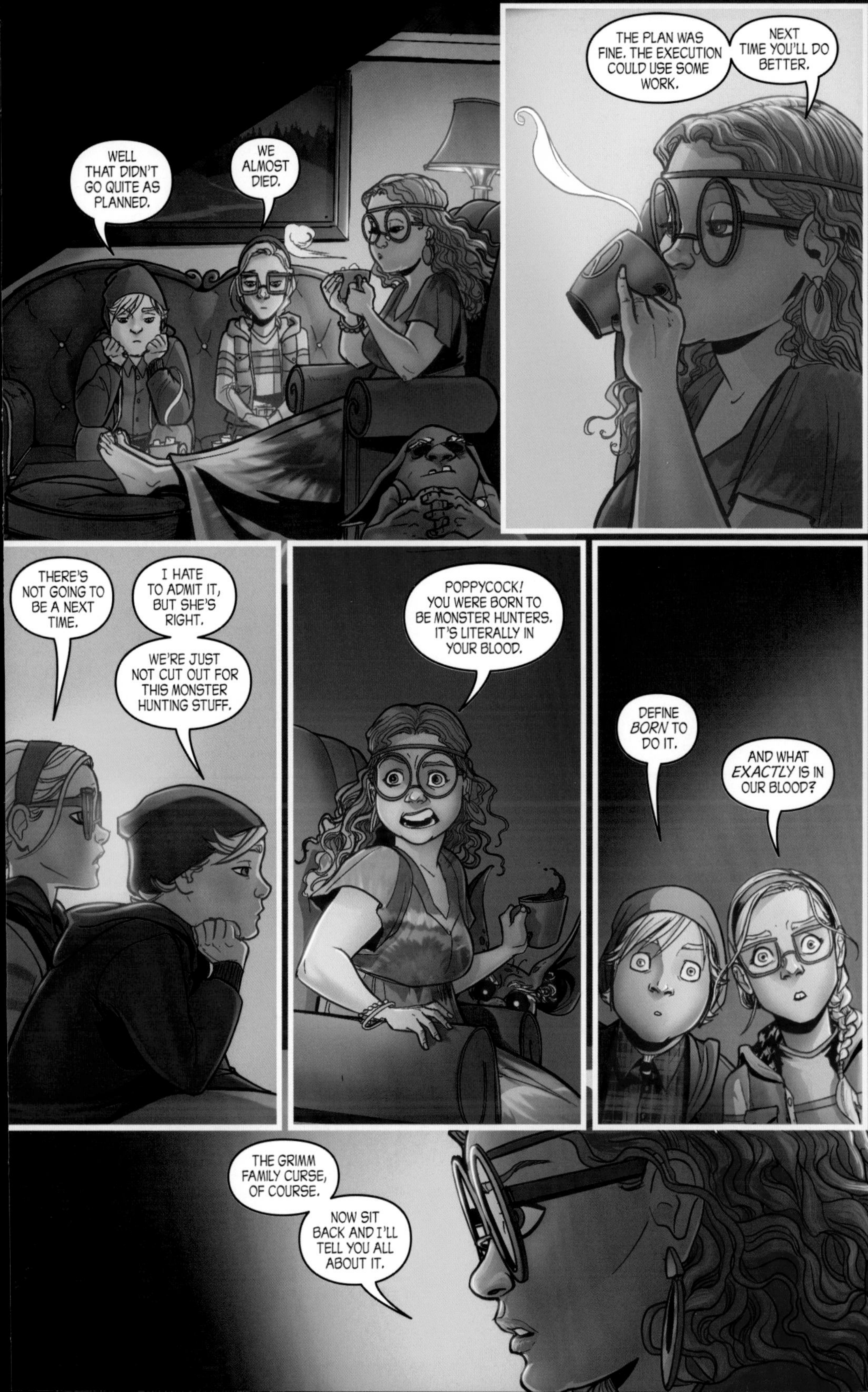
WELL THAT DIDN'T GO QUITE AS PLANNED.
WE ALMOST DIED.
THE PLAN WAS FINE. THE EXECUTION COULD USE SOME WORK.
NEXT TIME YOU'LL DO BETTER.
THERE'S NOT GOING TO BE A NEXT TIME.
I HATE TO ADMIT IT, BUT SHE'S RIGHT.
WE'RE JUST NOT CUT OUT FOR THIS MONSTER HUNTING STUFF.
POPPYCOCK! YOU WERE BORN TO BE MONSTER HUNTERS. IT'S LITERALLY IN YOUR BLOOD.
DEFINE *BORN* TO DO IT.
AND WHAT *EXACTLY* IS IN OUR BLOOD?
THE GRIMM FAMILY CURSE, OF COURSE.
NOW SIT BACK AND I'LL TELL YOU ALL ABOUT IT.

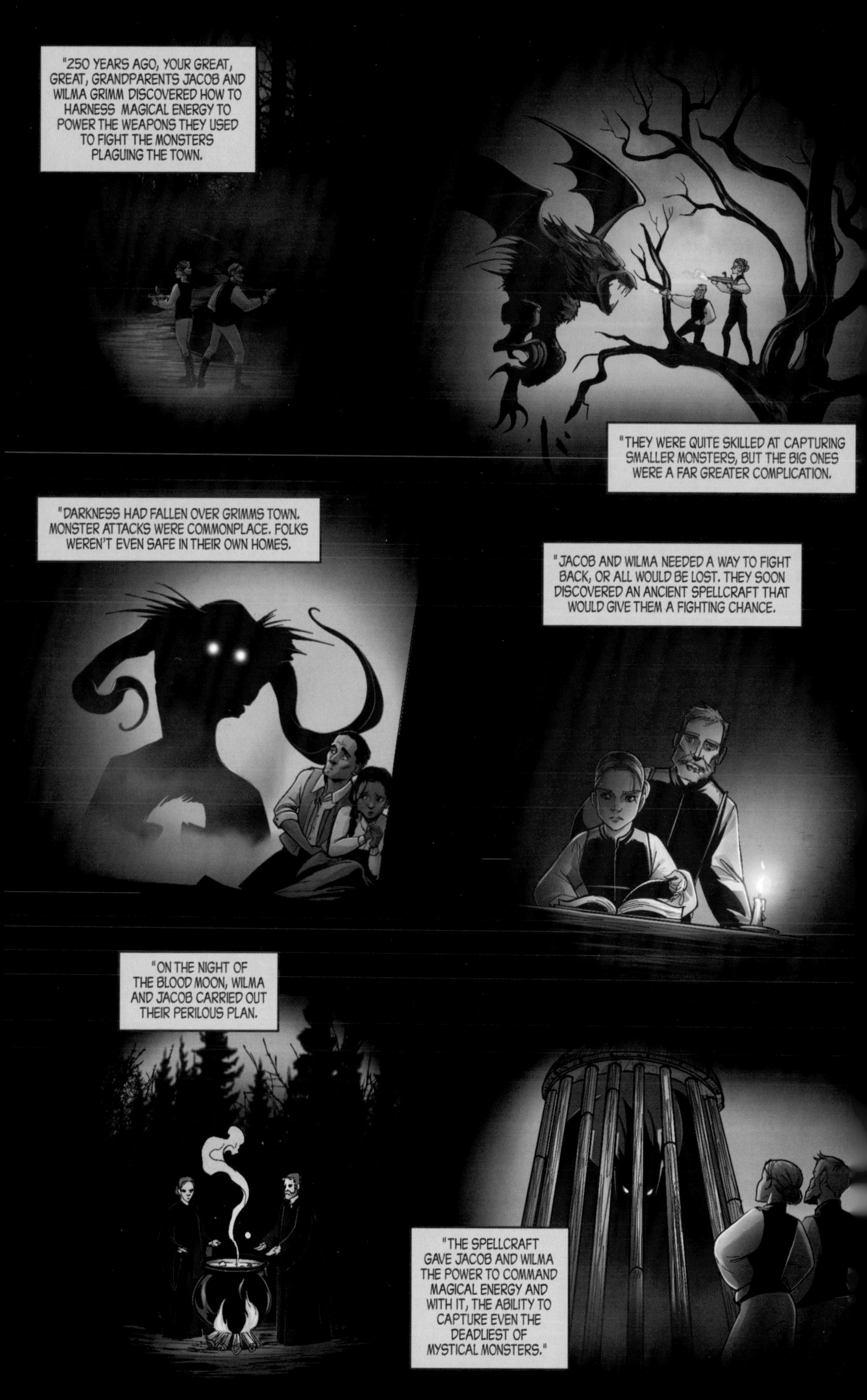
"250 YEARS AGO, YOUR GREAT, GREAT, GRANDPARENTS JACOB AND WILMA GRIMM DISCOVERED HOW TO HARNESS MAGICAL ENERGY TO POWER THE WEAPONS THEY USED TO FIGHT THE MONSTERS PLAGUING THE TOWN.
"THEY WERE QUITE SKILLED AT CAPTURING SMALLER MONSTERS, BUT THE BIG ONES WERE A FAR GREATER COMPLICATION.
"DARKNESS HAD FALLEN OVER GRIMMS TOWN. MONSTER ATTACKS WERE COMMONPLACE. FOLKS WEREN'T EVEN SAFE IN THEIR OWN HOMES.
"JACOB AND WILMA NEEDED A WAY TO FIGHT BACK, OR ALL WOULD BE LOST. THEY SOON DISCOVERED AN ANCIENT SPELLCRAFT THAT WOULD GIVE THEM A FIGHTING CHANCE.
"ON THE NIGHT OF THE BLOOD MOON, WILMA AND JACOB CARRIED OUT THEIR PERILOUS PLAN.
"THE SPELLCRAFT GAVE JACOB AND WILMA THE POWER TO COMMAND MAGICAL ENERGY AND WITH IT, THE ABILITY TO CAPTURE EVEN THE DEADLIEST OF MYSTICAL MONSTERS."

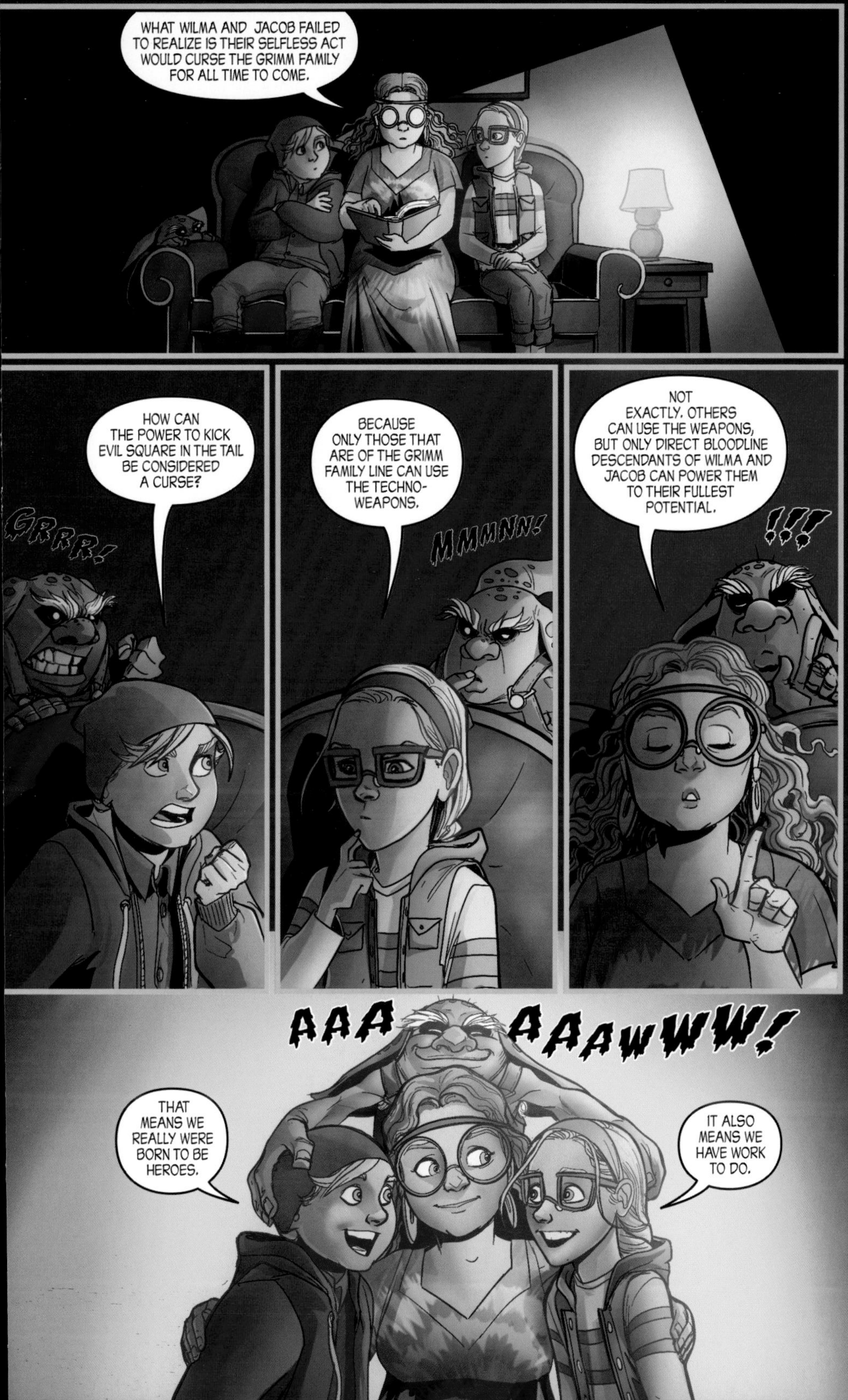
WHAT WILMA AND JACOB FAILED TO REALIZE IS THEIR SELFLESS ACT WOULD CURSE THE GRIMM FAMILY FOR ALL TIME TO COME.
HOW CAN THE POWER TO KICK EVIL SQUARE IN THE TAIL BE CONSIDERED A CURSE?
GRRRR!
BECAUSE ONLY THOSE THAT ARE OF THE GRIMM FAMILY LINE CAN USE THE TECHNO-WEAPONS.
MMMNN!
NOT EXACTLY. OTHERS CAN USE THE WEAPONS, BUT ONLY DIRECT BLOODLINE DESCENDANTS OF WILMA AND JACOB CAN POWER THEM TO THEIR FULLEST POTENTIAL.
!!!
AAA AAAAWWW!
THAT MEANS WE REALLY WERE BORN TO BE HEROES.
IT ALSO MEANS WE HAVE WORK TO DO.

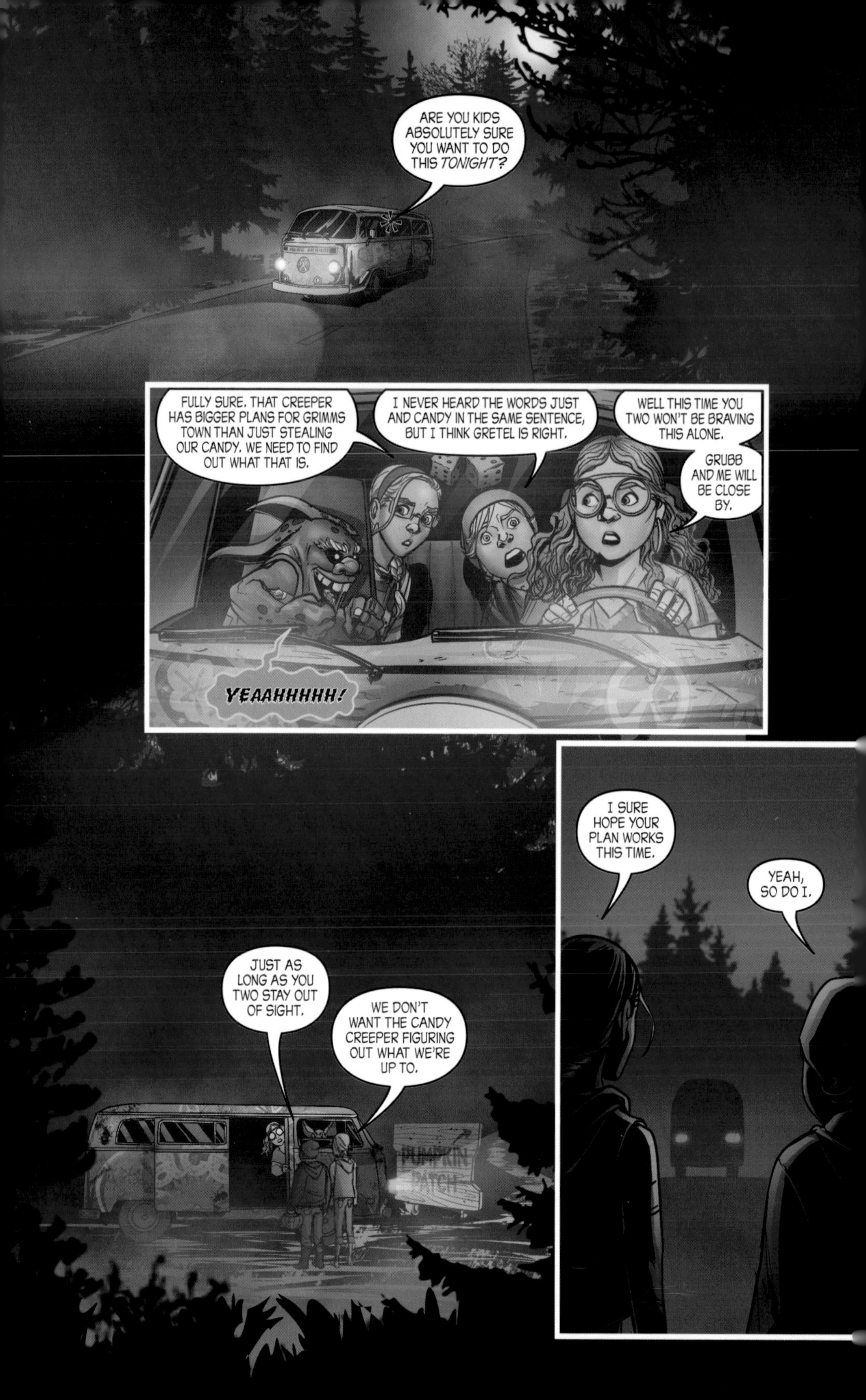
ARE YOU KIDS ABSOLUTELY SURE YOU WANT TO DO THIS *TONIGHT*?
FULLY SURE. THAT CREEPER HAS BIGGER PLANS FOR GRIMMS TOWN THAN JUST STEALING OUR CANDY. WE NEED TO FIND OUT WHAT THAT IS.
I NEVER HEARD THE WORDS JUST AND CANDY IN THE SAME SENTENCE, BUT I THINK GRETEL IS RIGHT.
WELL THIS TIME YOU TWO WON'T BE BRAVING THIS ALONE.
GRUBB AND ME WILL BE CLOSE BY.
YEAAHHHHH!
JUST AS LONG AS YOU TWO STAY OUT OF SIGHT.
WE DON'T WANT THE CANDY CREEPER FIGURING OUT WHAT WE'RE UP TO.
PUMPKIN PATCH
I SURE HOPE YOUR PLAN WORKS THIS TIME.
YEAH, SO DO I.

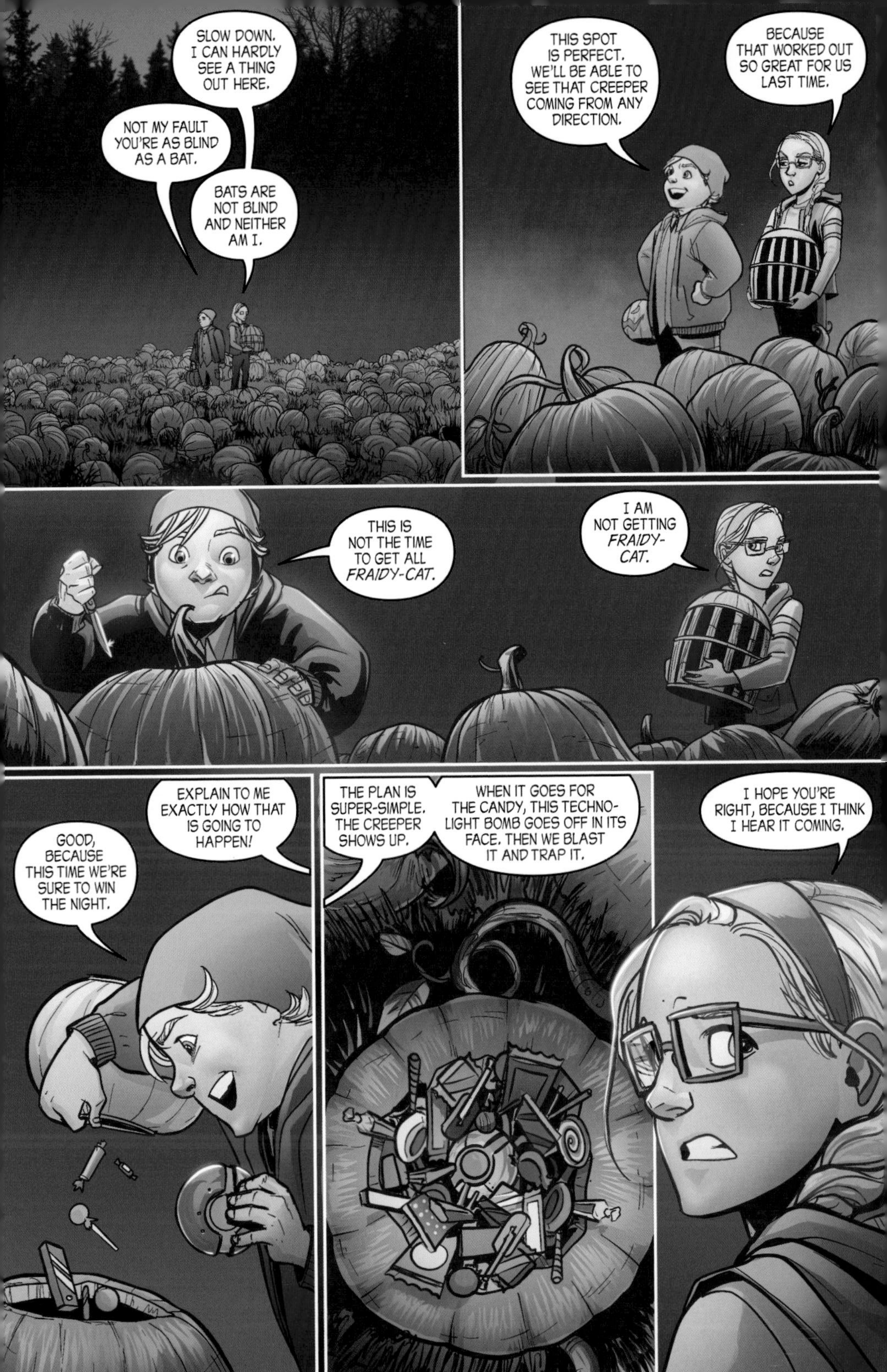
SLOW DOWN. I CAN HARDLY SEE A THING OUT HERE.
NOT MY FAULT YOU'RE AS BLIND AS A BAT.
BATS ARE NOT BLIND AND NEITHER AM I.
THIS SPOT IS PERFECT. WE'LL BE ABLE TO SEE THAT CREEPER COMING FROM ANY DIRECTION.
BECAUSE THAT WORKED OUT SO GREAT FOR US LAST TIME.
THIS IS NOT THE TIME TO GET ALL *FRAIDY-CAT*.
I AM NOT GETTING *FRAIDY-CAT*.
GOOD, BECAUSE THIS TIME WE'RE SURE TO WIN THE NIGHT.
EXPLAIN TO ME EXACTLY HOW THAT IS GOING TO HAPPEN!
THE PLAN IS SUPER-SIMPLE. THE CREEPER SHOWS UP.
WHEN IT GOES FOR THE CANDY, THIS TECHNO-LIGHT BOMB GOES OFF IN ITS FACE. THEN WE BLAST IT AND TRAP IT.
I HOPE YOU'RE RIGHT, BECAUSE I THINK I HEAR IT COMING.

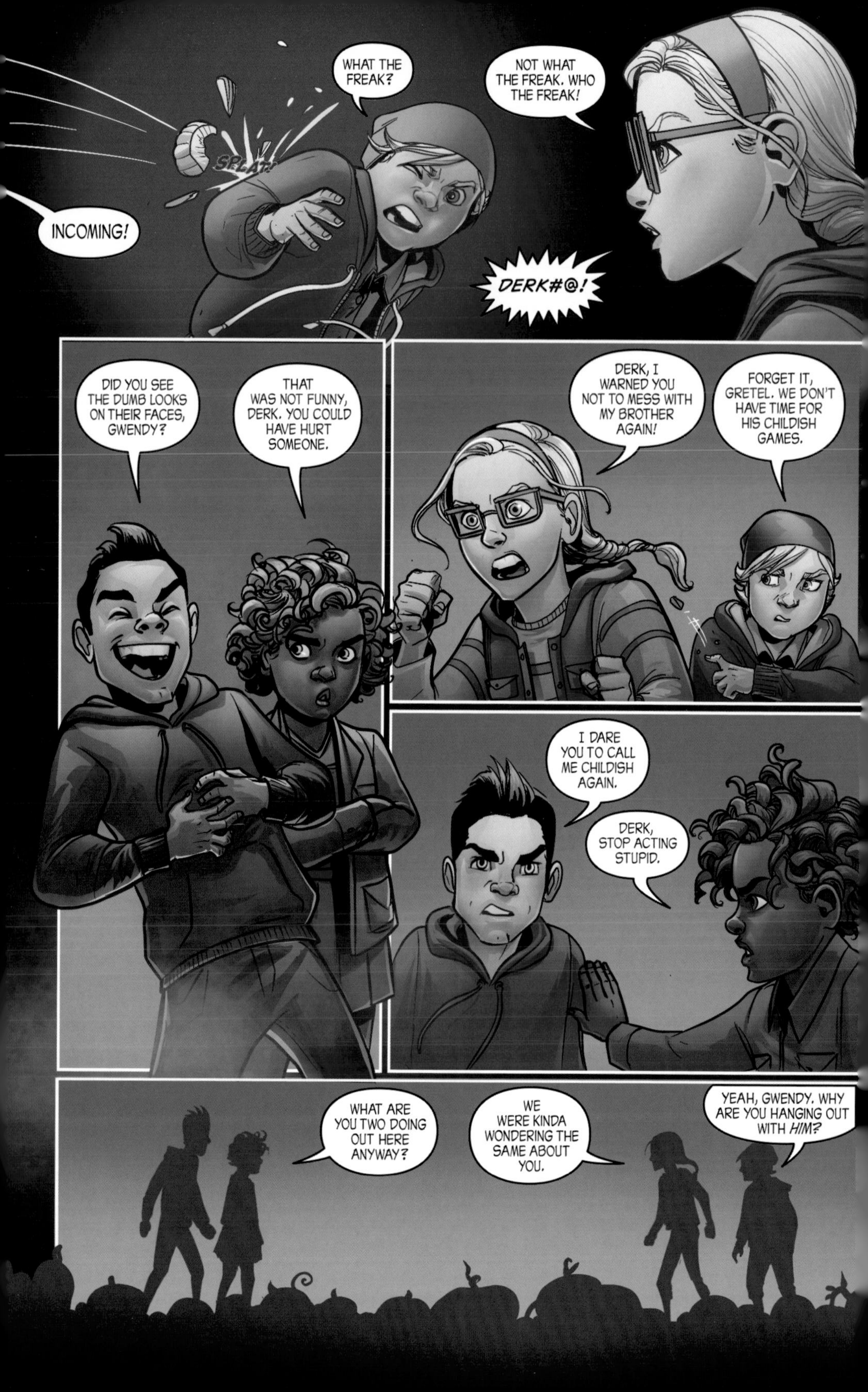
WHAT THE FREAK?
NOT WHAT THE FREAK. WHO THE FREAK!
SPLAT!
INCOMING!
DERK#@!
DID YOU SEE THE DUMB LOOKS ON THEIR FACES, GWENDY?
THAT WAS NOT FUNNY, DERK. YOU COULD HAVE HURT SOMEONE.
DERK, I WARNED YOU NOT TO MESS WITH MY BROTHER AGAIN!
FORGET IT, GRETEL. WE DON'T HAVE TIME FOR HIS CHILDISH GAMES.
I DARE YOU TO CALL ME CHILDISH AGAIN.
DERK, STOP ACTING STUPID.
WHAT ARE YOU TWO DOING OUT HERE ANYWAY?
WE WERE KINDA WONDERING THE SAME ABOUT YOU.
YEAH, GWENDY. WHY ARE YOU HANGING OUT WITH *HIM*?

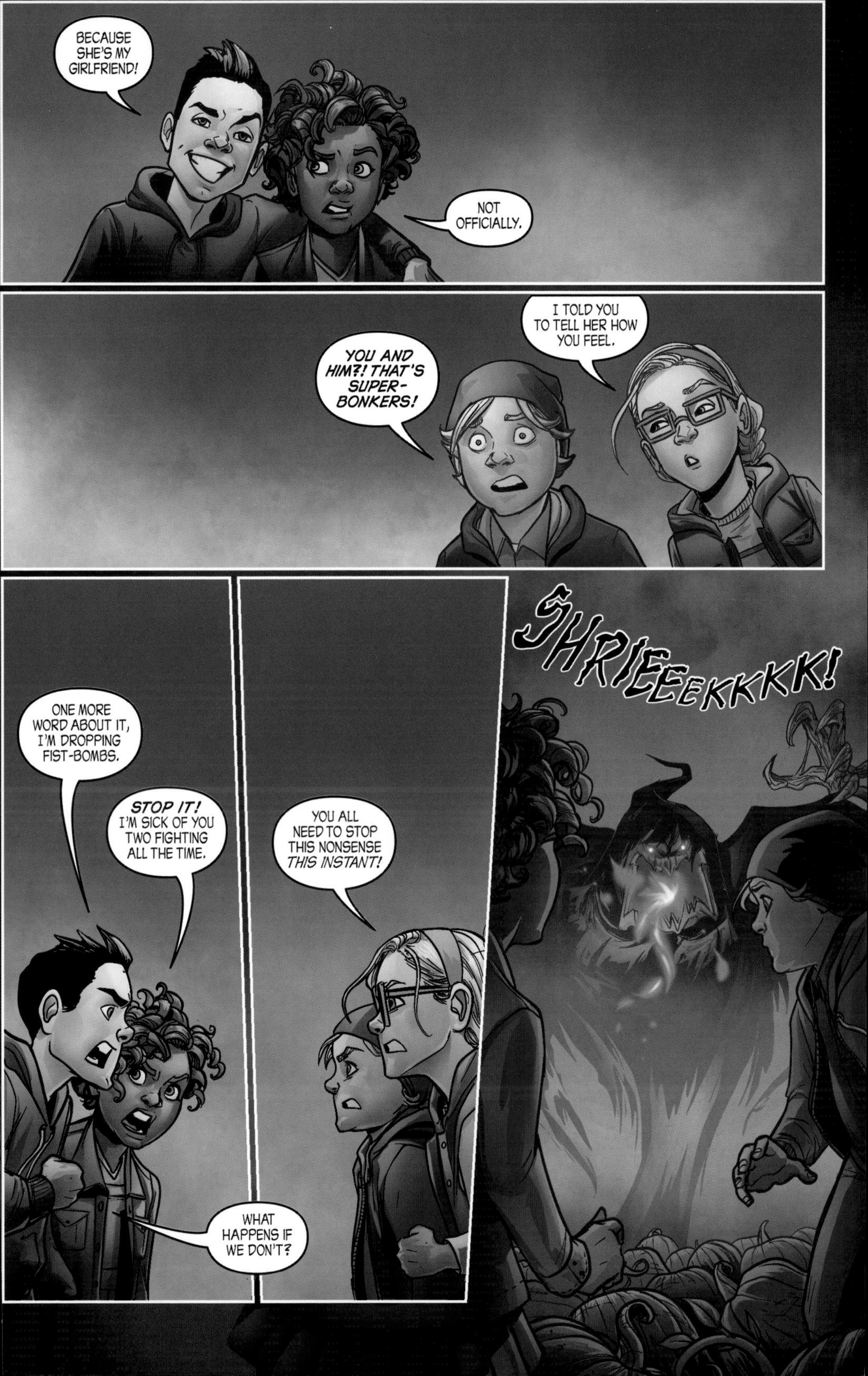
BECAUSE SHE'S MY GIRLFRIEND!
NOT OFFICIALLY.
YOU AND HIM?! THAT'S SUPER-BONKERS!
I TOLD YOU TO TELL HER HOW YOU FEEL.
ONE MORE WORD ABOUT IT, I'M DROPPING FIST-BOMBS.
STOP IT! I'M SICK OF YOU TWO FIGHTING ALL THE TIME.
YOU ALL NEED TO STOP THIS NONSENSE THIS INSTANT!
WHAT HAPPENS IF WE DON'T?
SHRIEEEKKKK!

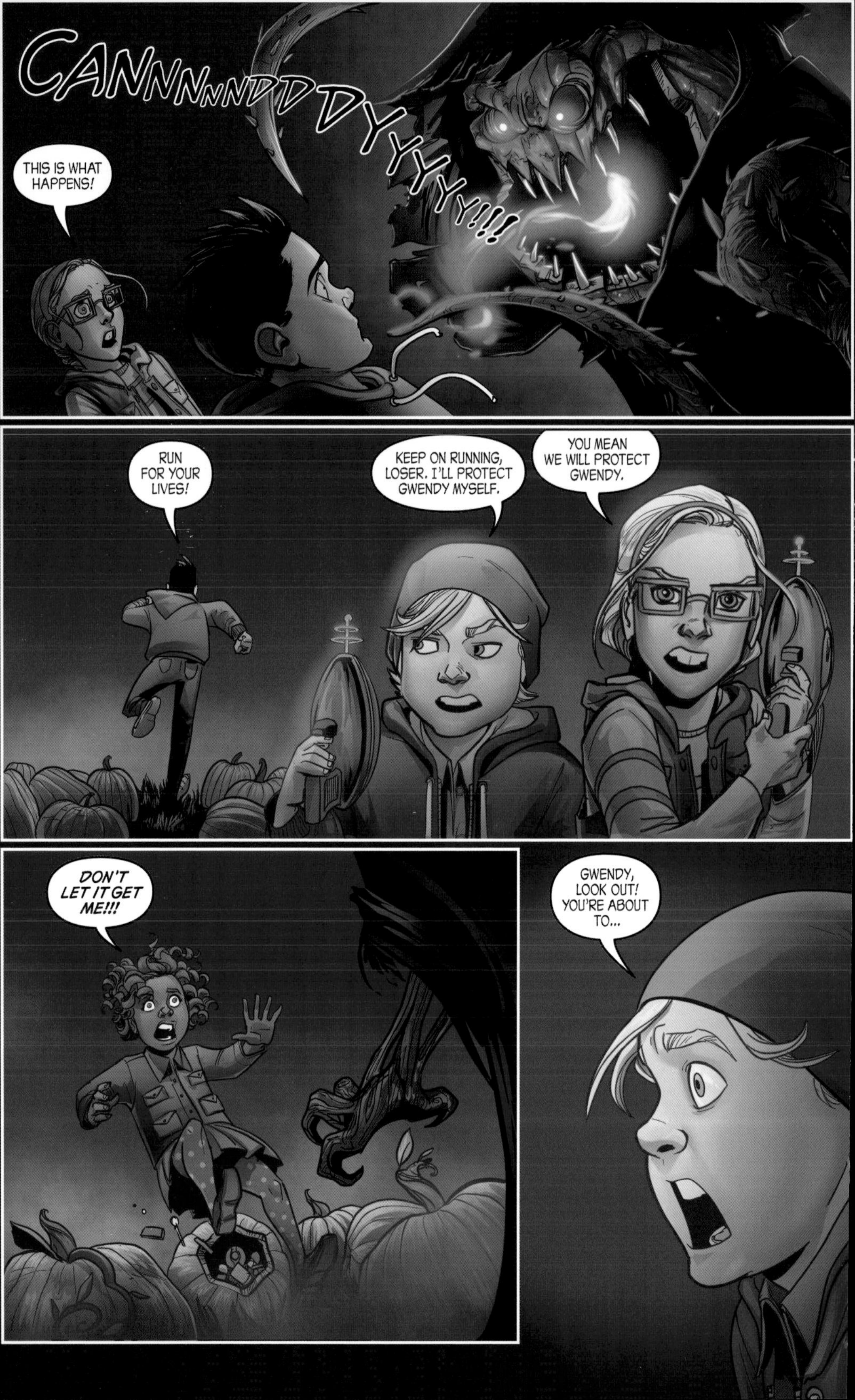
CANNNNNDDDYYYYY!!!
THIS IS WHAT HAPPENS!
RUN FOR YOUR LIVES!
KEEP ON RUNNING, LOSER. I'LL PROTECT GWENDY MYSELF.
YOU MEAN WE WILL PROTECT GWENDY.
DON'T LET IT GET ME!!!
GWENDY, LOOK OUT! YOU'RE ABOUT TO...

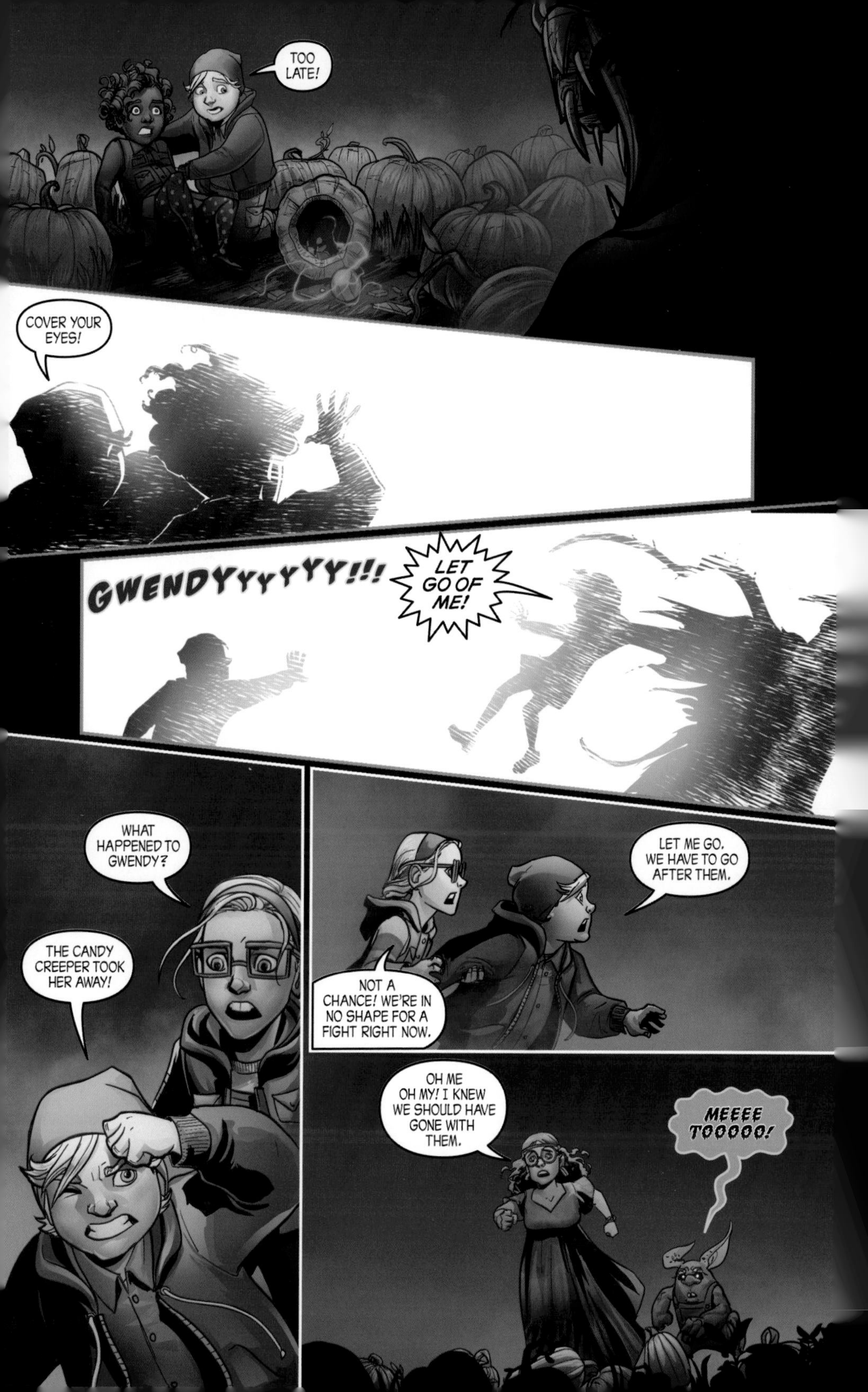
TOO LATE!
COVER YOUR EYES!
GWENDYYYYYY!!!
LET GO OF ME!
WHAT HAPPENED TO GWENDY?
THE CANDY CREEPER TOOK HER AWAY!
LET ME GO. WE HAVE TO GO AFTER THEM.
NOT A CHANCE! WE'RE IN NO SHAPE FOR A FIGHT RIGHT NOW.
OH ME OH MY! I KNEW WE SHOULD HAVE GONE WITH THEM.
MEEEE TOOOOO!

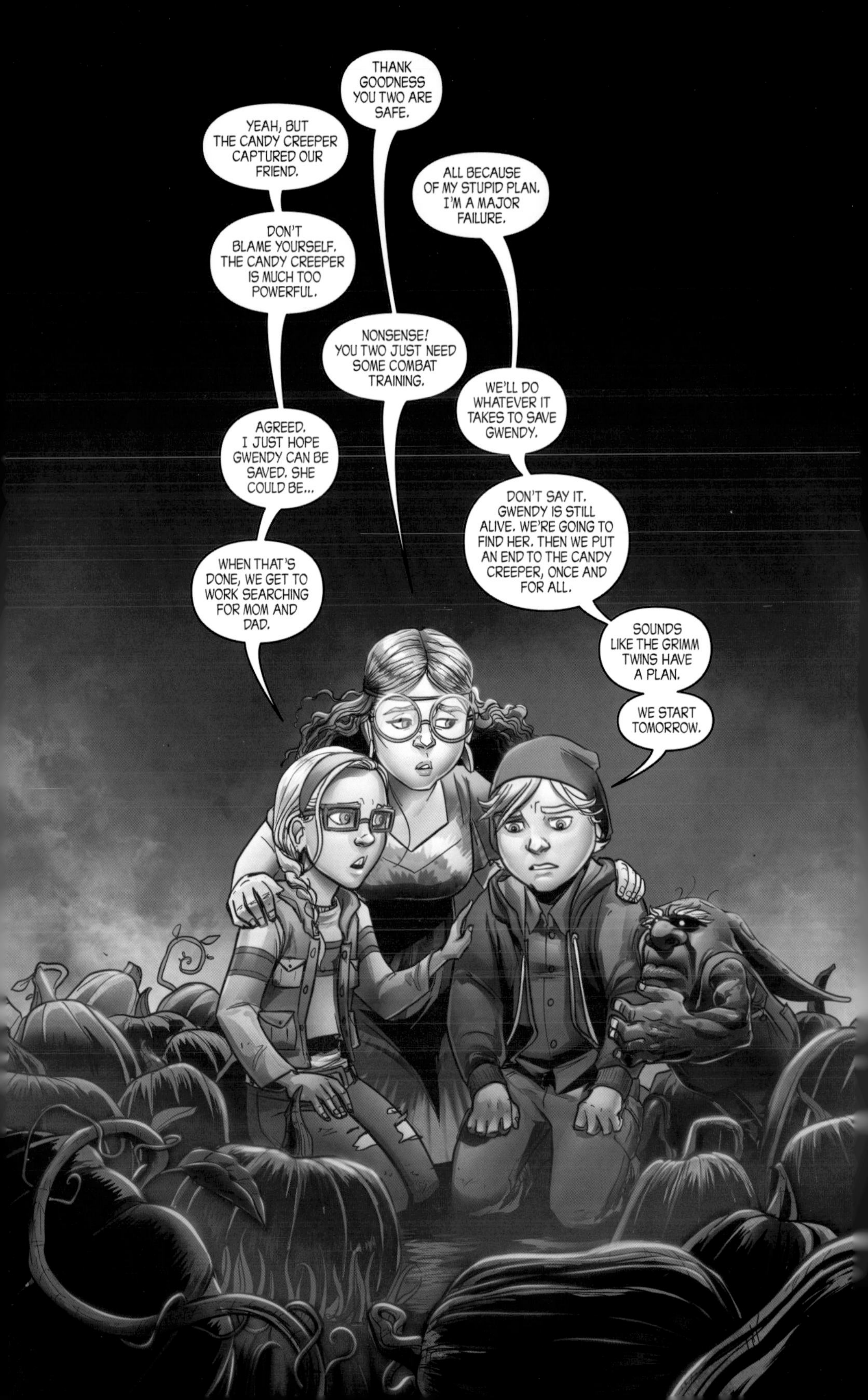
THANK GOODNESS YOU TWO ARE SAFE.
YEAH, BUT THE CANDY CREEPER CAPTURED OUR FRIEND.
ALL BECAUSE OF MY STUPID PLAN. I'M A MAJOR FAILURE.
DON'T BLAME YOURSELF. THE CANDY CREEPER IS MUCH TOO POWERFUL.
NONSENSE! YOU TWO JUST NEED SOME COMBAT TRAINING.
WE'LL DO WHATEVER IT TAKES TO SAVE GWENDY.
AGREED. I JUST HOPE GWENDY CAN BE SAVED. SHE COULD BE...
DON'T SAY IT. GWENDY IS STILL ALIVE. WE'RE GOING TO FIND HER. THEN WE PUT AN END TO THE CANDY CREEPER, ONCE AND FOR ALL.
WHEN THAT'S DONE, WE GET TO WORK SEARCHING FOR MOM AND DAD.
SOUNDS LIKE THE GRIMM TWINS HAVE A PLAN.
WE START TOMORROW.

CHAPTER 4

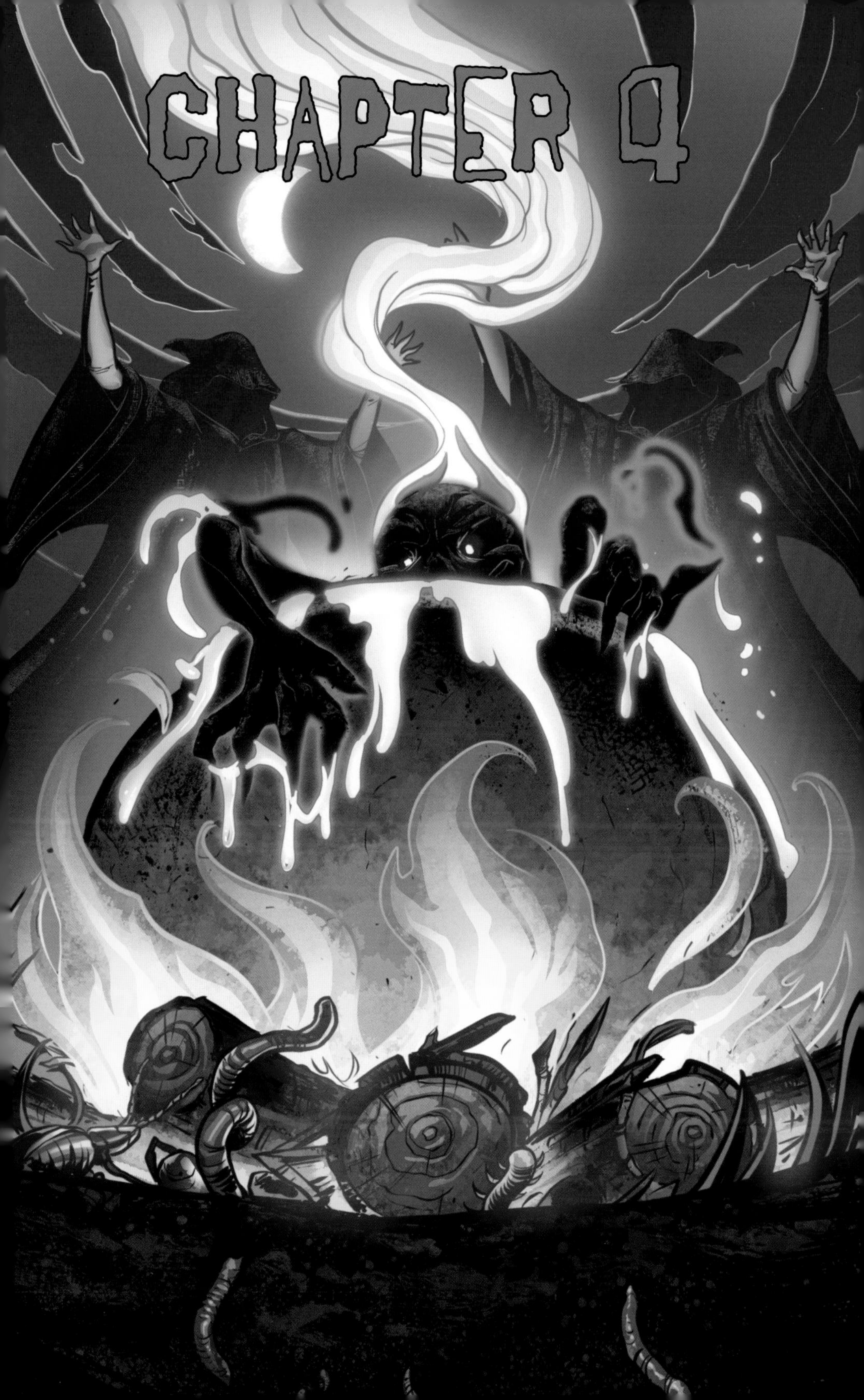

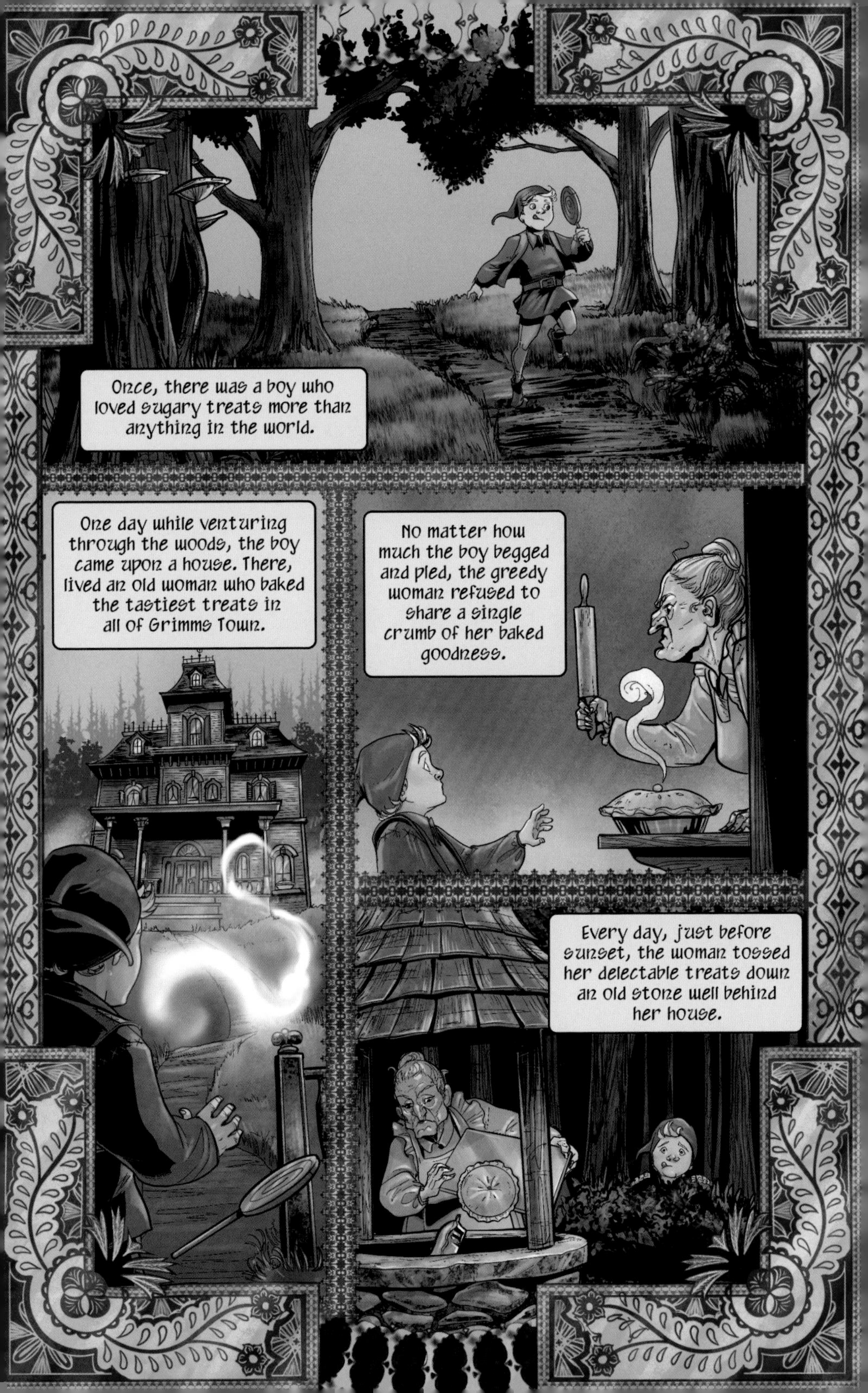
Once, there was a boy who loved sugary treats more than anything in the world.
One day while venturing through the woods, the boy came upon a house. There, lived an old woman who baked the tastiest treats in all of Grimms Town.
No matter how much the boy begged and pled, the greedy woman refused to share a single crumb of her baked goodness.
Every day, just before sunset, the woman tossed her delectable treats down an old stone well behind her house.

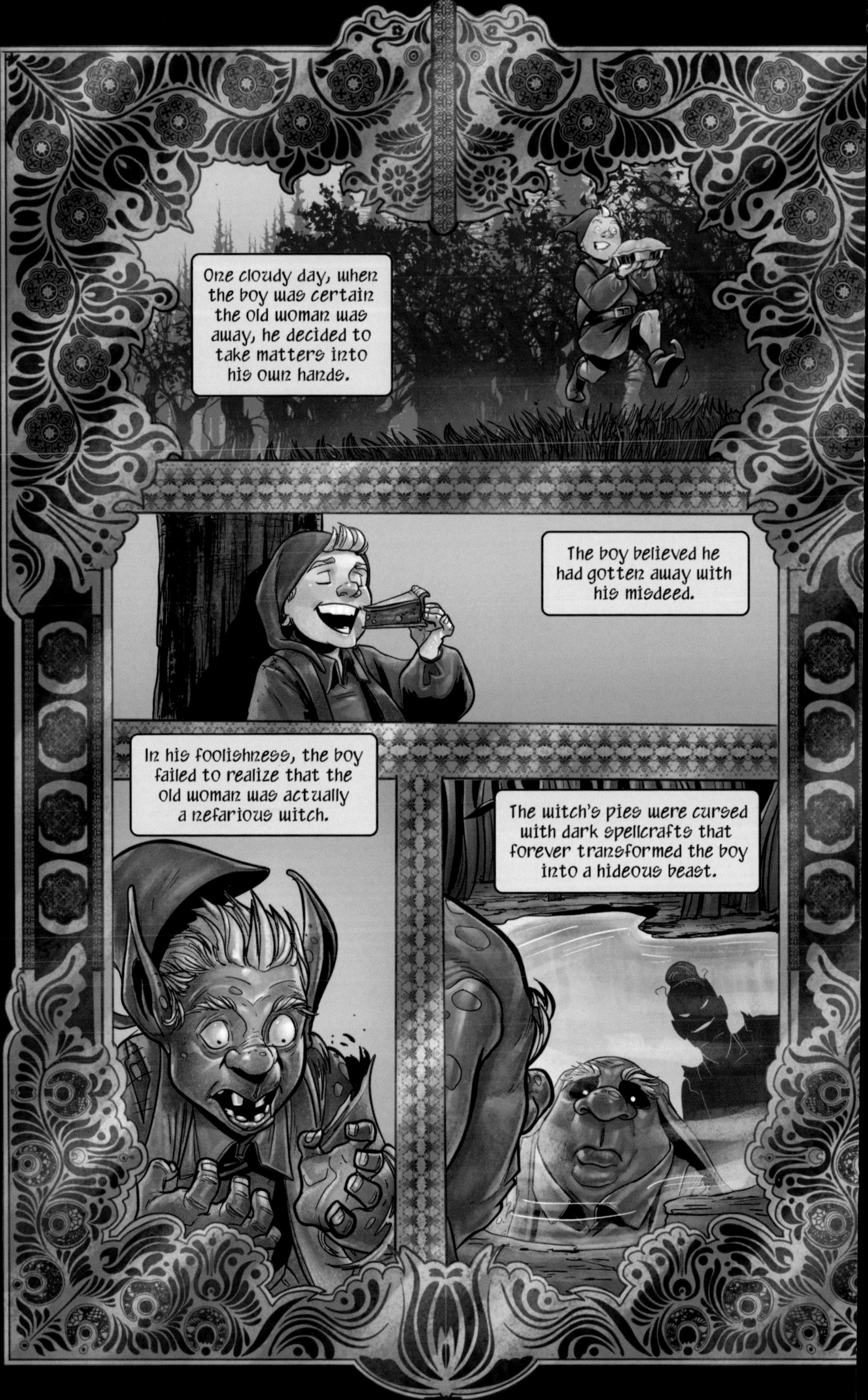
One cloudy day, when the boy was certain the old woman was away, he decided to take matters into his own hands.
The boy believed he had gotten away with his misdeed.
In his foolishness, the boy failed to realize that the old woman was actually a nefarious witch.
The witch's pies were cursed with dark spellcrafts that forever transformed the boy into a hideous beast.

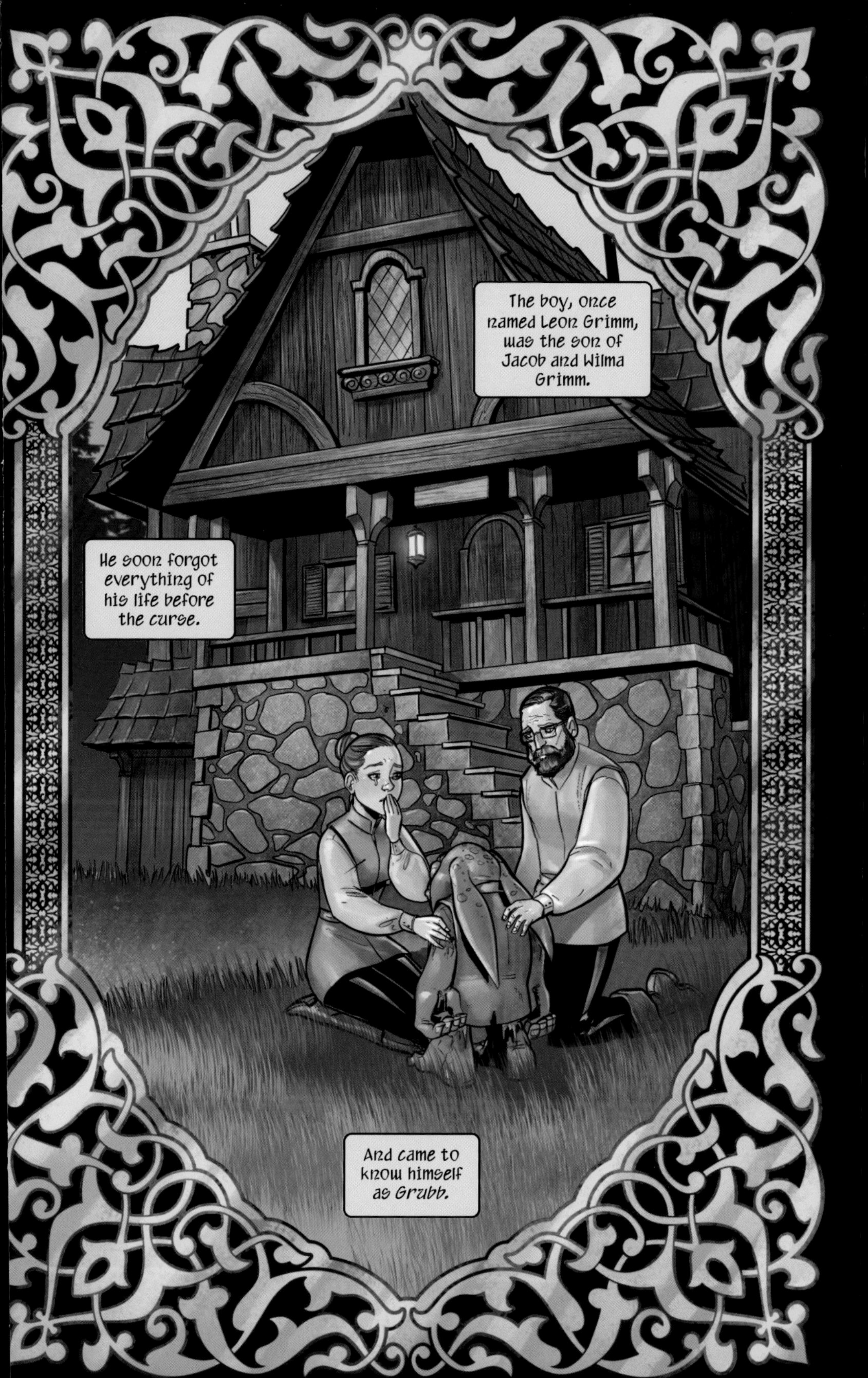
The boy, once named Leon Grimm, was the son of Jacob and Wilma Grimm.
He soon forgot everything of his life before the curse.
And came to know himself as *Grubb.*

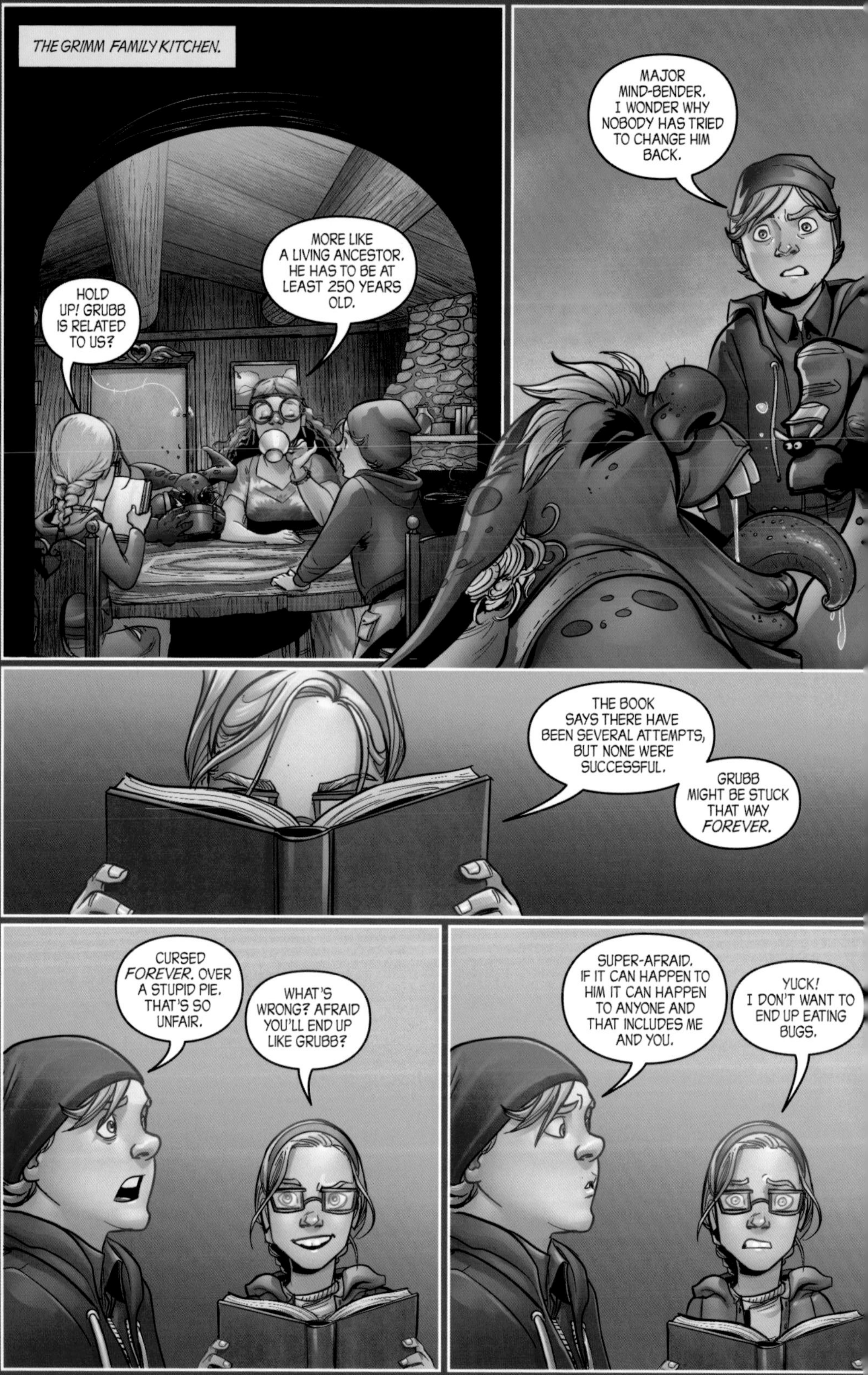
THE GRIMM FAMILY KITCHEN.
HOLD UP! GRUBB IS RELATED TO US?
MORE LIKE A LIVING ANCESTOR. HE HAS TO BE AT LEAST 250 YEARS OLD.
MAJOR MIND-BENDER. I WONDER WHY NOBODY HAS TRIED TO CHANGE HIM BACK.
THE BOOK SAYS THERE HAVE BEEN SEVERAL ATTEMPTS, BUT NONE WERE SUCCESSFUL.
GRUBB MIGHT BE STUCK THAT WAY *FOREVER*.
CURSED *FOREVER*. OVER A STUPID PIE. THAT'S SO UNFAIR.
WHAT'S WRONG? AFRAID YOU'LL END UP LIKE GRUBB?
SUPER-AFRAID. IF IT CAN HAPPEN TO HIM IT CAN HAPPEN TO ANYONE AND THAT INCLUDES ME AND YOU.
YUCK! I DON'T WANT TO END UP EATING BUGS.

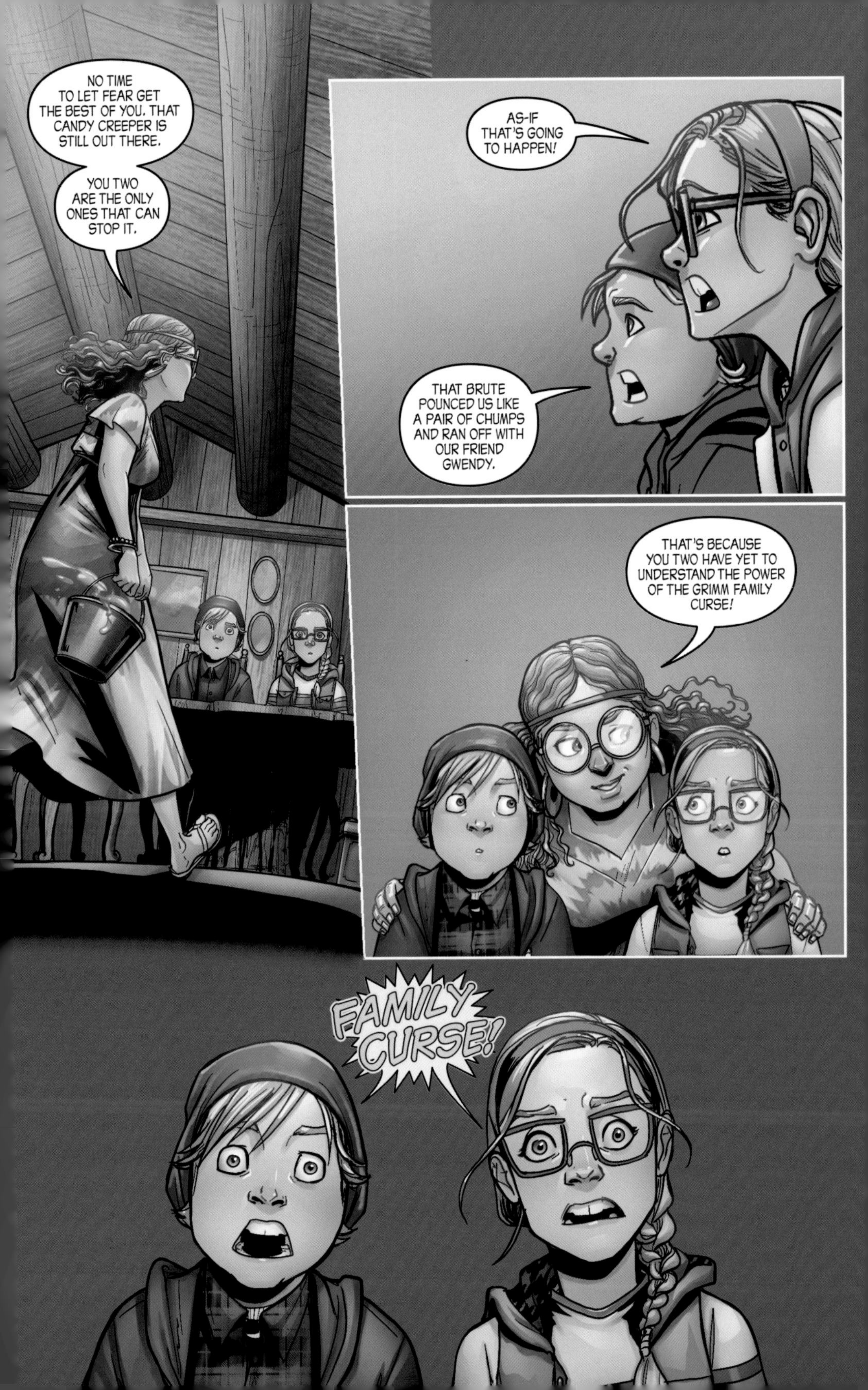
NO TIME TO LET FEAR GET THE BEST OF YOU. THAT CANDY CREEPER IS STILL OUT THERE.
YOU TWO ARE THE ONLY ONES THAT CAN STOP IT.
AS-IF THAT'S GOING TO HAPPEN!
THAT BRUTE POUNCED US LIKE A PAIR OF CHUMPS AND RAN OFF WITH OUR FRIEND GWENDY.
THAT'S BECAUSE YOU TWO HAVE YET TO UNDERSTAND THE POWER OF THE GRIMM FAMILY CURSE!
FAMILY CURSE!

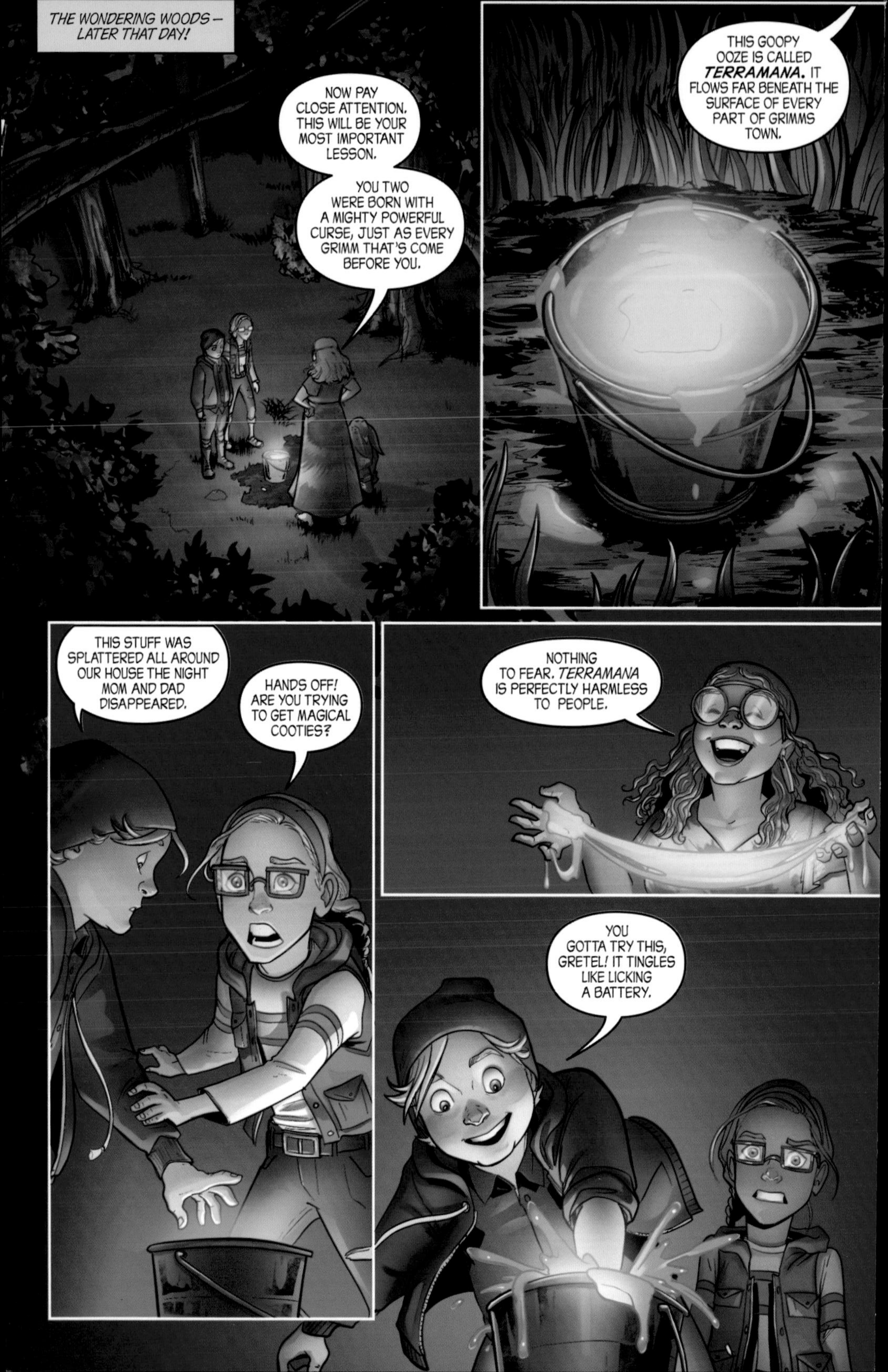
THE WONDERING WOODS — LATER THAT DAY!
NOW PAY CLOSE ATTENTION. THIS WILL BE YOUR MOST IMPORTANT LESSON.
YOU TWO WERE BORN WITH A MIGHTY POWERFUL CURSE, JUST AS EVERY GRIMM THAT'S COME BEFORE YOU.
THIS GOOPY OOZE IS CALLED **TERRAMANA.** IT FLOWS FAR BENEATH THE SURFACE OF EVERY PART OF GRIMMS TOWN.
THIS STUFF WAS SPLATTERED ALL AROUND OUR HOUSE THE NIGHT MOM AND DAD DISAPPEARED.
HANDS OFF! ARE YOU TRYING TO GET MAGICAL COOTIES?
NOTHING TO FEAR. *TERRAMANA* IS PERFECTLY HARMLESS TO PEOPLE.
YOU GOTTA TRY THIS, GRETEL! IT TINGLES LIKE LICKING A BATTERY.

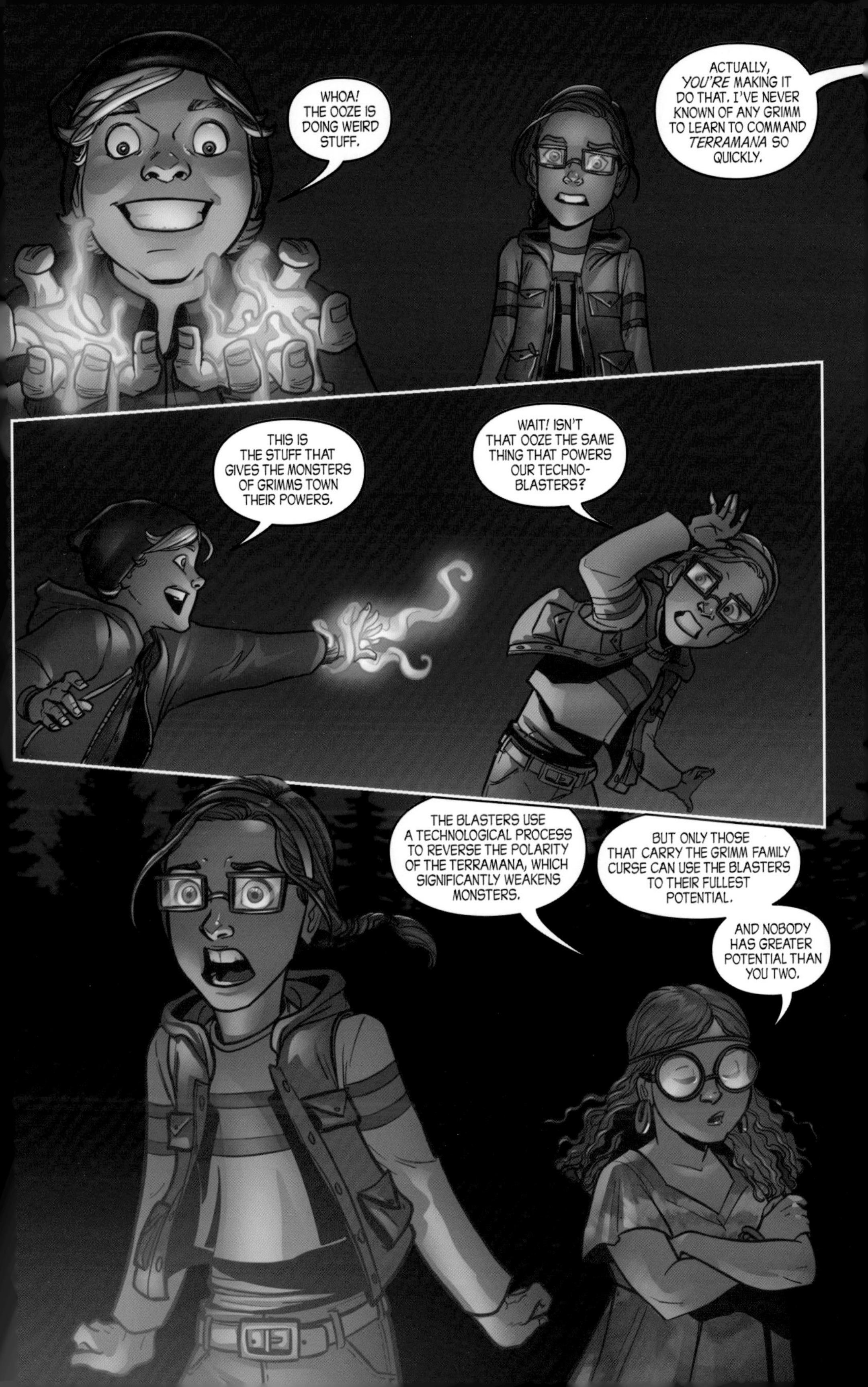
WHOA! THE OOZE IS DOING WEIRD STUFF.
ACTUALLY, *YOU'RE* MAKING IT DO THAT. I'VE NEVER KNOWN OF ANY GRIMM TO LEARN TO COMMAND *TERRAMANA* SO QUICKLY.
THIS IS THE STUFF THAT GIVES THE MONSTERS OF GRIMMS TOWN THEIR POWERS.
WAIT! ISN'T THAT OOZE THE SAME THING THAT POWERS OUR TECHNO-BLASTERS?
THE BLASTERS USE A TECHNOLOGICAL PROCESS TO REVERSE THE POLARITY OF THE TERRAMANA, WHICH SIGNIFICANTLY WEAKENS MONSTERS.
BUT ONLY THOSE THAT CARRY THE GRIMM FAMILY CURSE CAN USE THE BLASTERS TO THEIR FULLEST POTENTIAL.
AND NOBODY HAS GREATER POTENTIAL THAN YOU TWO.

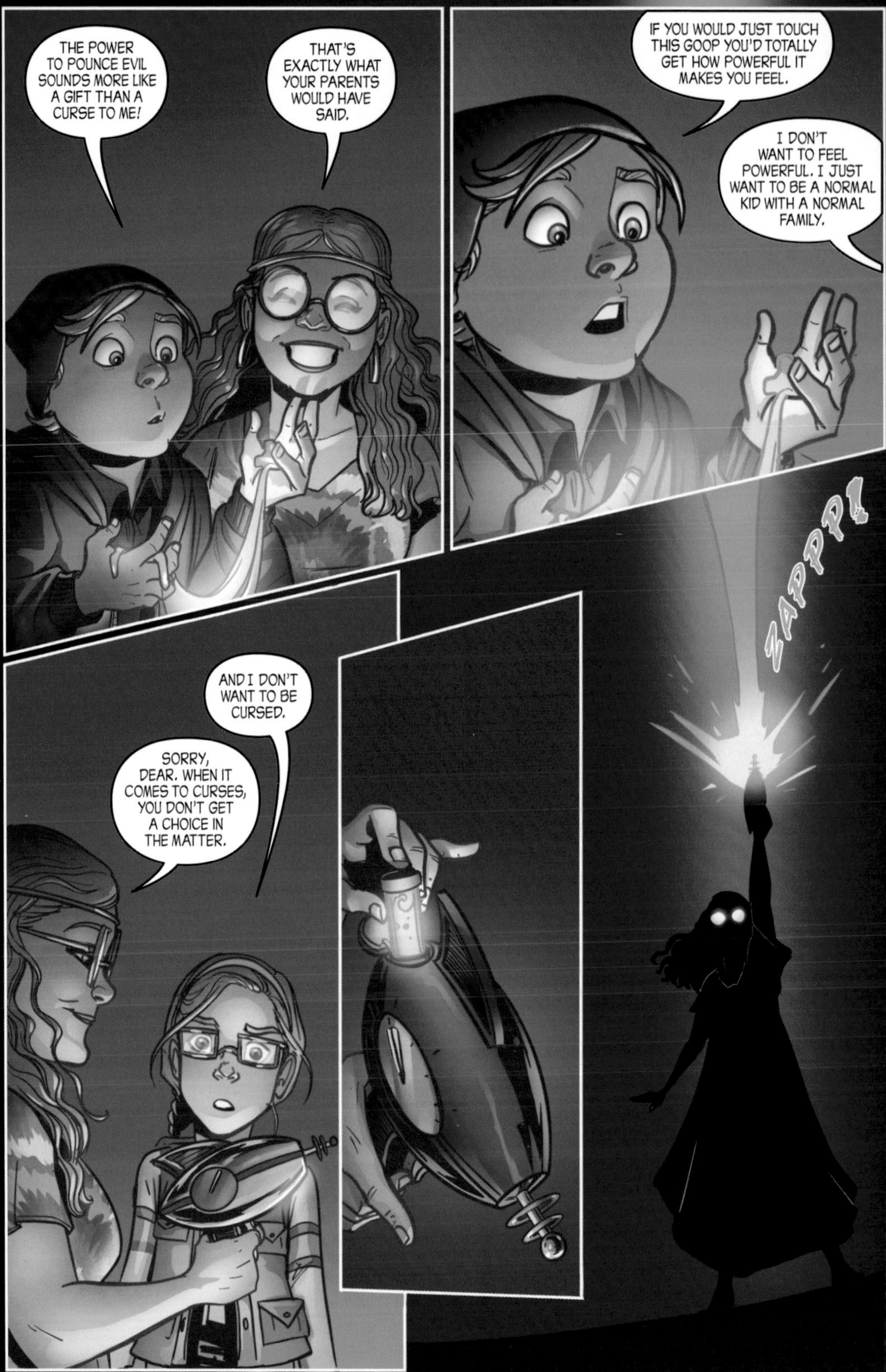
THE POWER TO POUNCE EVIL SOUNDS MORE LIKE A GIFT THAN A CURSE TO ME!
THAT'S EXACTLY WHAT YOUR PARENTS WOULD HAVE SAID.
IF YOU WOULD JUST TOUCH THIS GOOP YOU'D TOTALLY GET HOW POWERFUL IT MAKES YOU FEEL.
I DON'T WANT TO FEEL POWERFUL. I JUST WANT TO BE A NORMAL KID WITH A NORMAL FAMILY.
AND I DON'T WANT TO BE CURSED.
SORRY, DEAR. WHEN IT COMES TO CURSES, YOU DON'T GET A CHOICE IN THE MATTER.
ZAPPP!

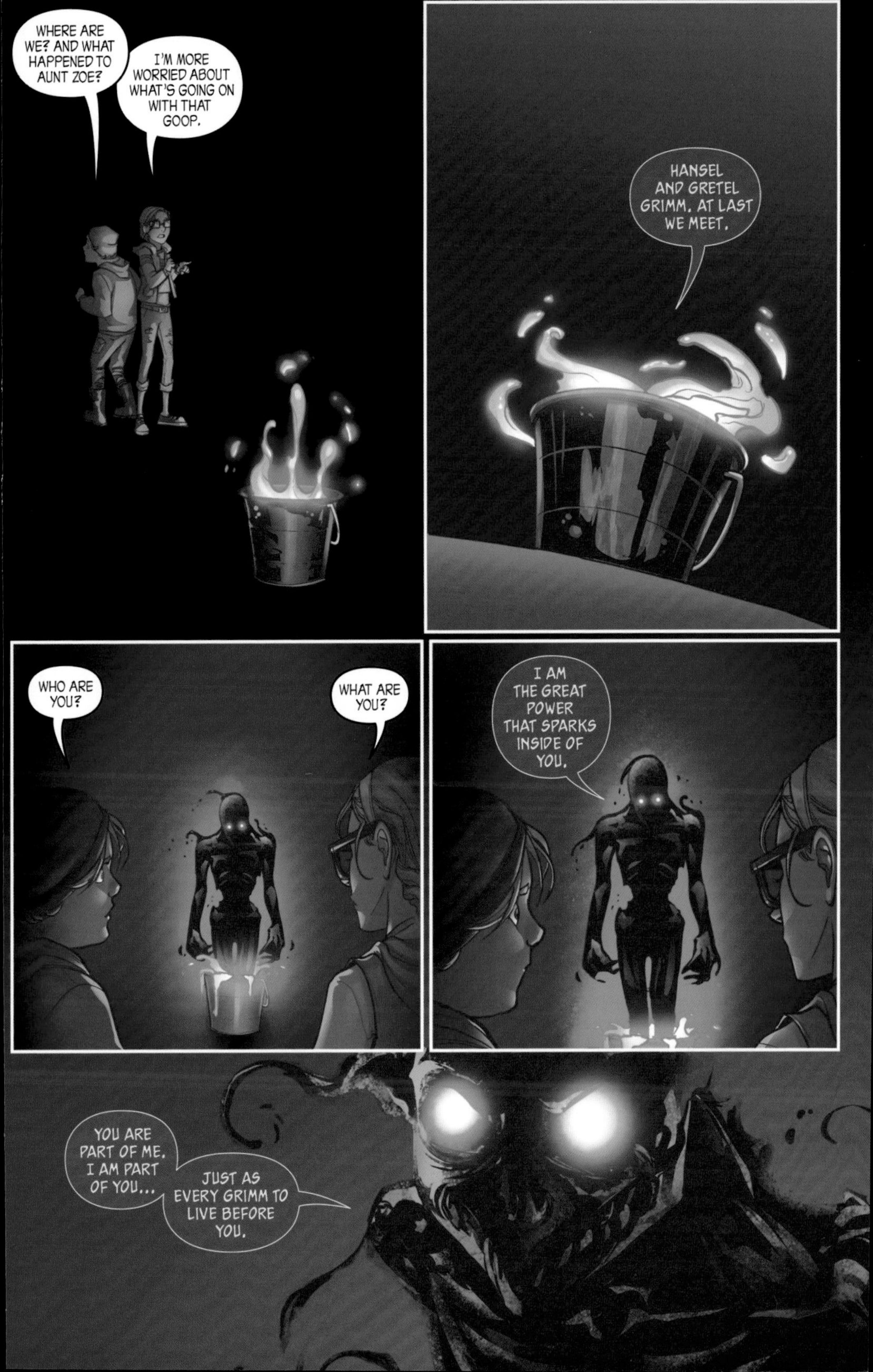

WHERE ARE WE? AND WHAT HAPPENED TO AUNT ZOE?
I'M MORE WORRIED ABOUT WHAT'S GOING ON WITH THAT GOOP.
HANSEL AND GRETEL GRIMM. AT LAST WE MEET.
WHO ARE YOU?
WHAT ARE YOU?
I AM THE GREAT POWER THAT SPARKS INSIDE OF YOU.
YOU ARE PART OF ME. I AM PART OF YOU...
JUST AS EVERY GRIMM TO LIVE BEFORE YOU.

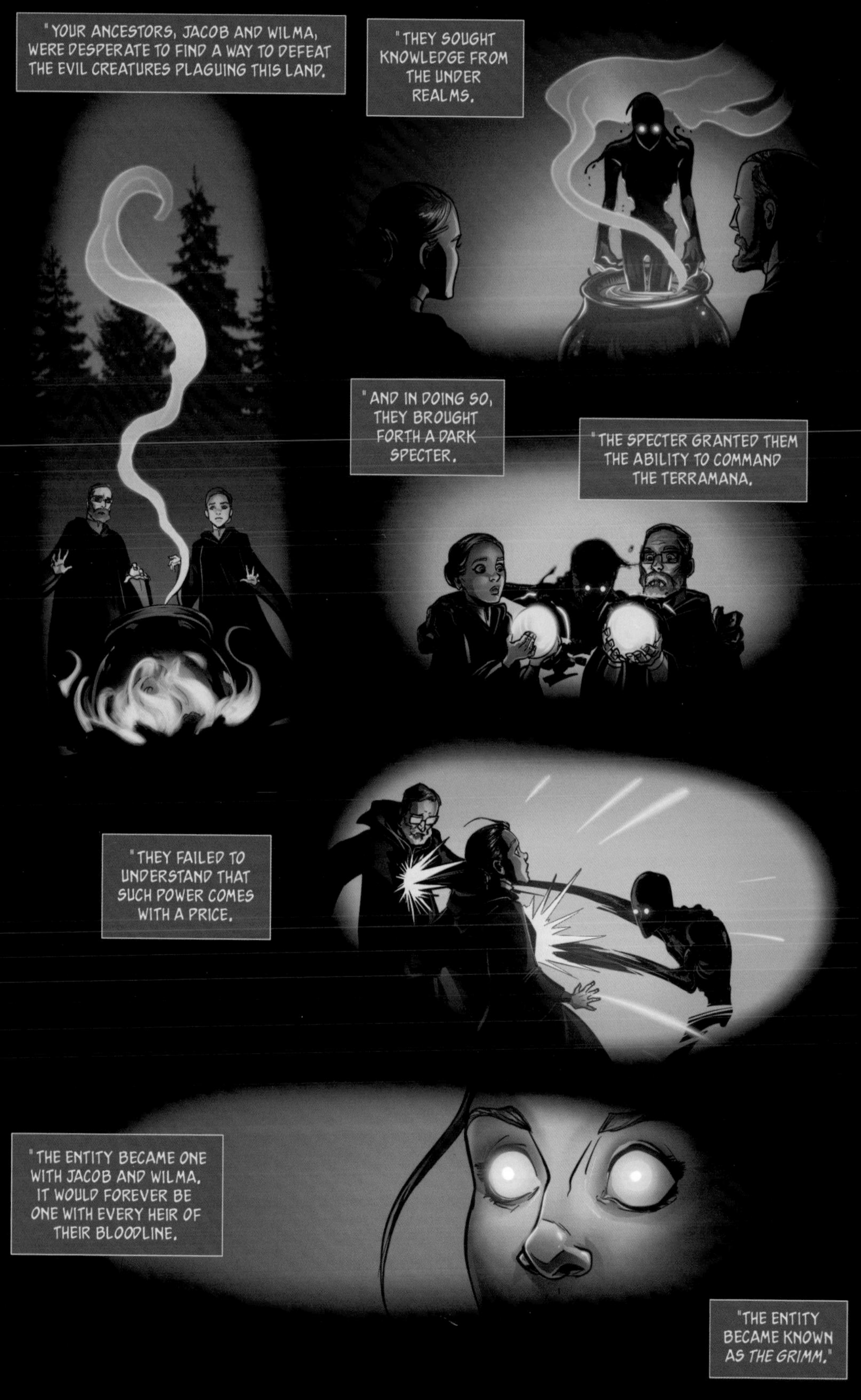
"YOUR ANCESTORS, JACOB AND WILMA, WERE DESPERATE TO FIND A WAY TO DEFEAT THE EVIL CREATURES PLAGUING THIS LAND.
"THEY SOUGHT KNOWLEDGE FROM THE UNDER REALMS.
"AND IN DOING SO, THEY BROUGHT FORTH A DARK SPECTER.
"THE SPECTER GRANTED THEM THE ABILITY TO COMMAND THE TERRAMANA.
"THEY FAILED TO UNDERSTAND THAT SUCH POWER COMES WITH A PRICE.
"THE ENTITY BECAME ONE WITH JACOB AND WILMA. IT WOULD FOREVER BE ONE WITH EVERY HEIR OF THEIR BLOODLINE.
"THE ENTITY BECAME KNOWN AS *THE GRIMM*."

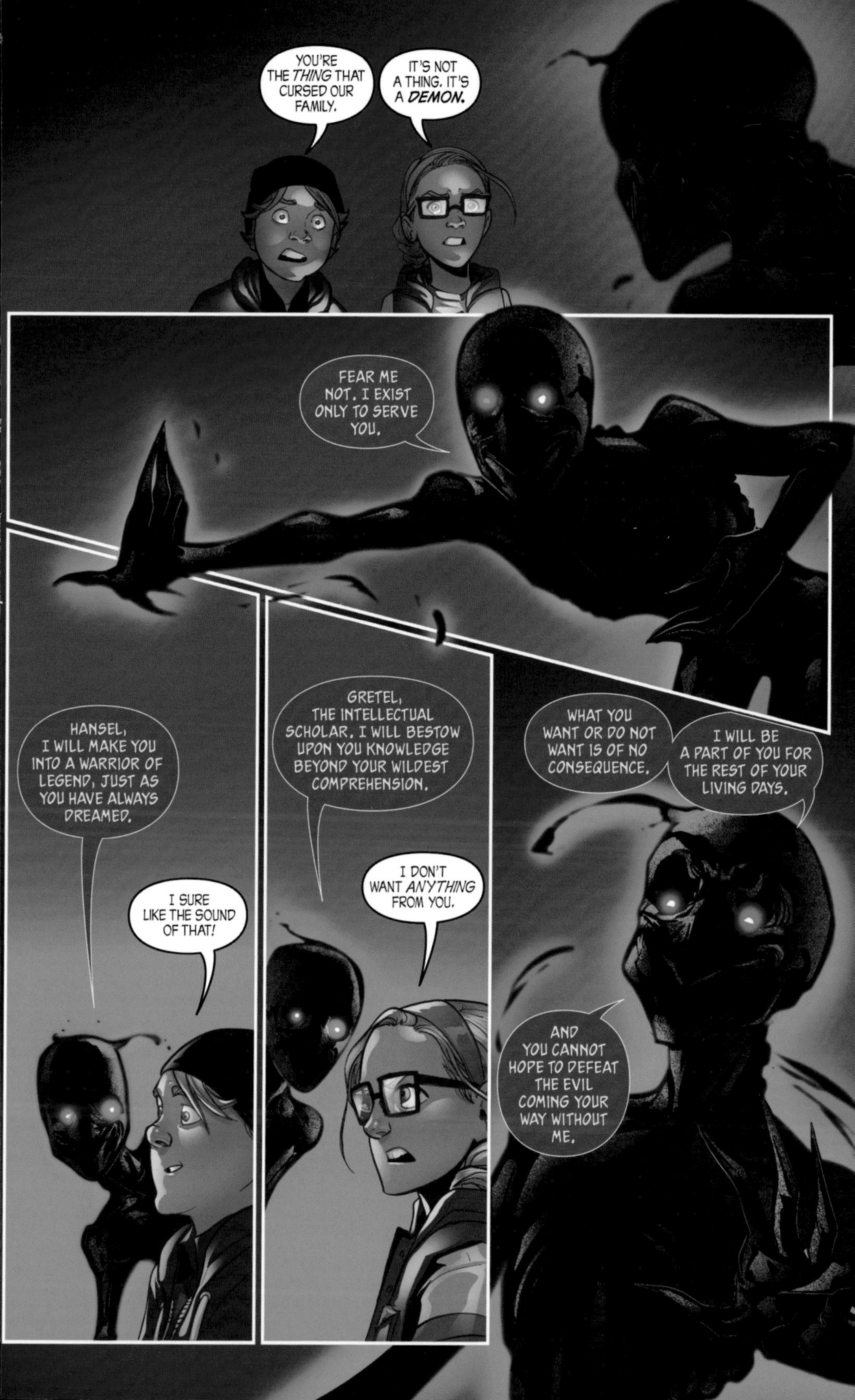
YOU'RE THE *THING* THAT CURSED OUR FAMILY.
IT'S NOT A THING. IT'S A ***DEMON.***
FEAR ME NOT. I EXIST ONLY TO SERVE YOU.
HANSEL, I WILL MAKE YOU INTO A WARRIOR OF LEGEND, JUST AS YOU HAVE ALWAYS DREAMED.
I SURE LIKE THE SOUND OF THAT!
GRETEL, THE INTELLECTUAL SCHOLAR. I WILL BESTOW UPON YOU KNOWLEDGE BEYOND YOUR WILDEST COMPREHENSION.
I DON'T WANT *ANYTHING* FROM YOU.
WHAT YOU WANT OR DO NOT WANT IS OF NO CONSEQUENCE.
I WILL BE A PART OF YOU FOR THE REST OF YOUR LIVING DAYS.
AND YOU CANNOT HOPE TO DEFEAT THE EVIL COMING YOUR WAY WITHOUT ME.

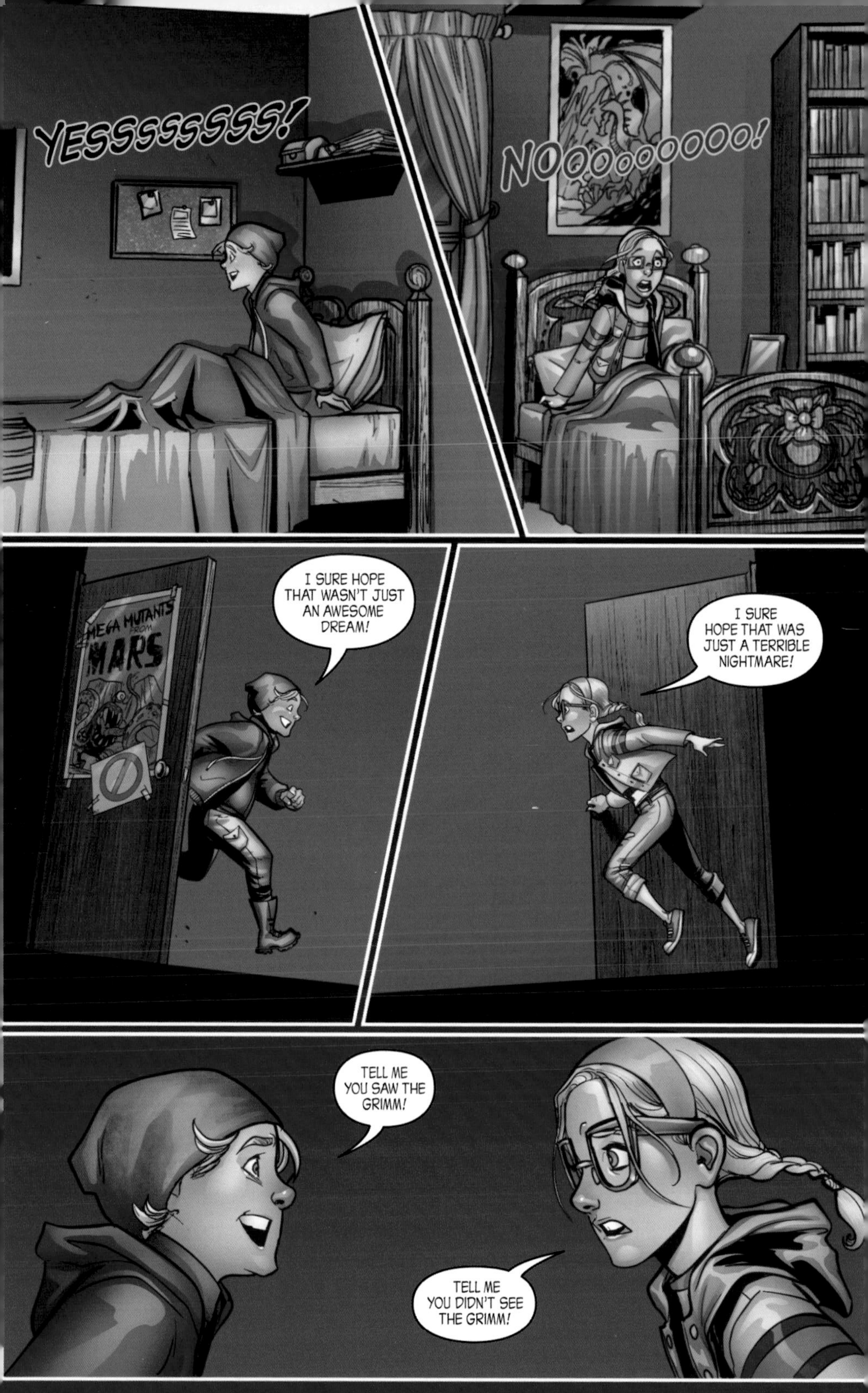
YESSSSSSSS!
NOOooooooo!
I SURE HOPE THAT WASN'T JUST AN AWESOME DREAM!
MEGA MUTANTS FROM MARS
I SURE HOPE THAT WAS JUST A TERRIBLE NIGHTMARE!
TELL ME YOU SAW THE GRIMM!
TELL ME YOU DIDN'T SEE THE GRIMM!

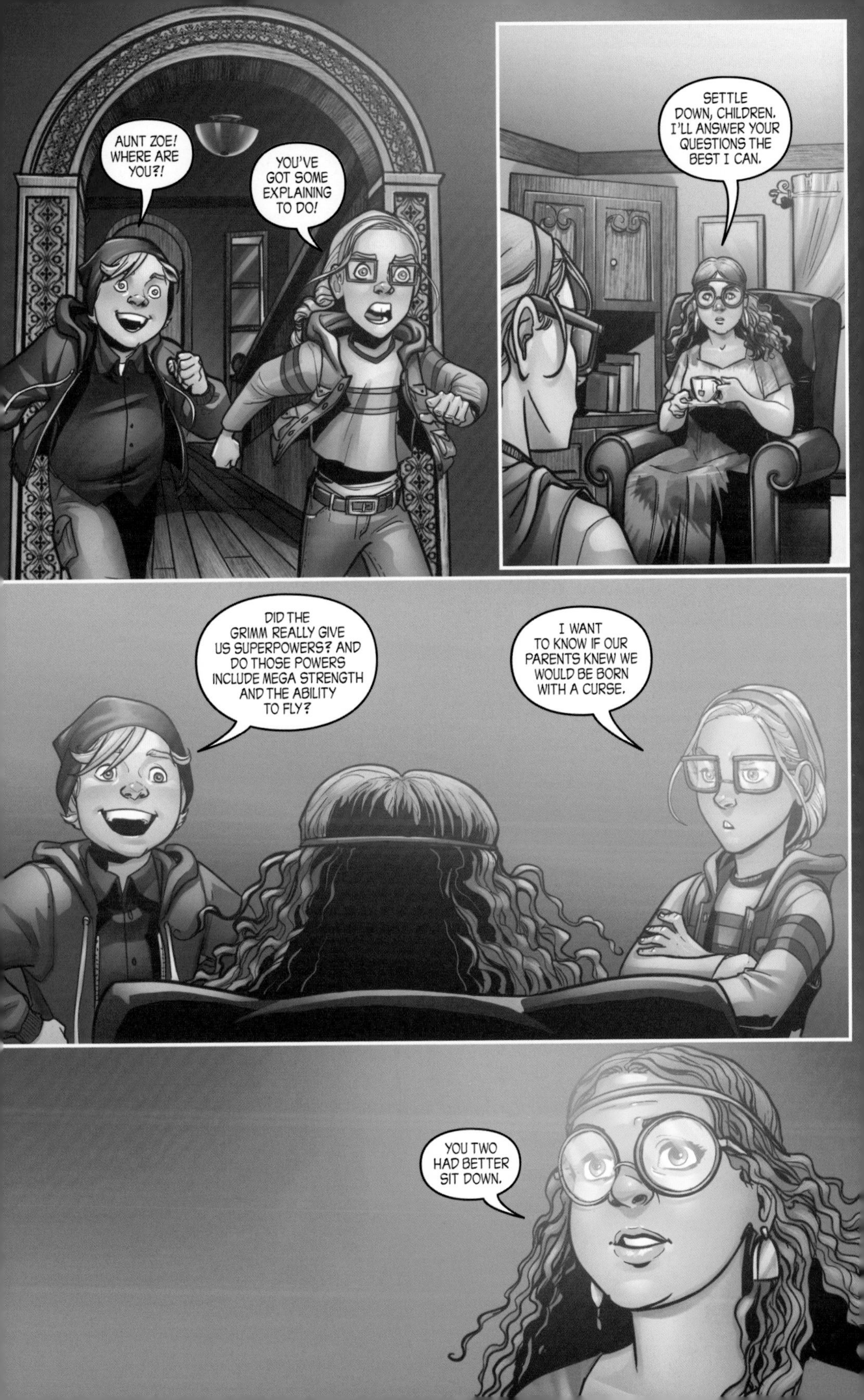
AUNT ZOE! WHERE ARE YOU?!
YOU'VE GOT SOME EXPLAINING TO DO!
SETTLE DOWN, CHILDREN. I'LL ANSWER YOUR QUESTIONS THE BEST I CAN.
DID THE GRIMM REALLY GIVE US SUPERPOWERS? AND DO THOSE POWERS INCLUDE MEGA STRENGTH AND THE ABILITY TO FLY?
I WANT TO KNOW IF OUR PARENTS KNEW WE WOULD BE BORN WITH A CURSE.
YOU TWO HAD BETTER SIT DOWN.

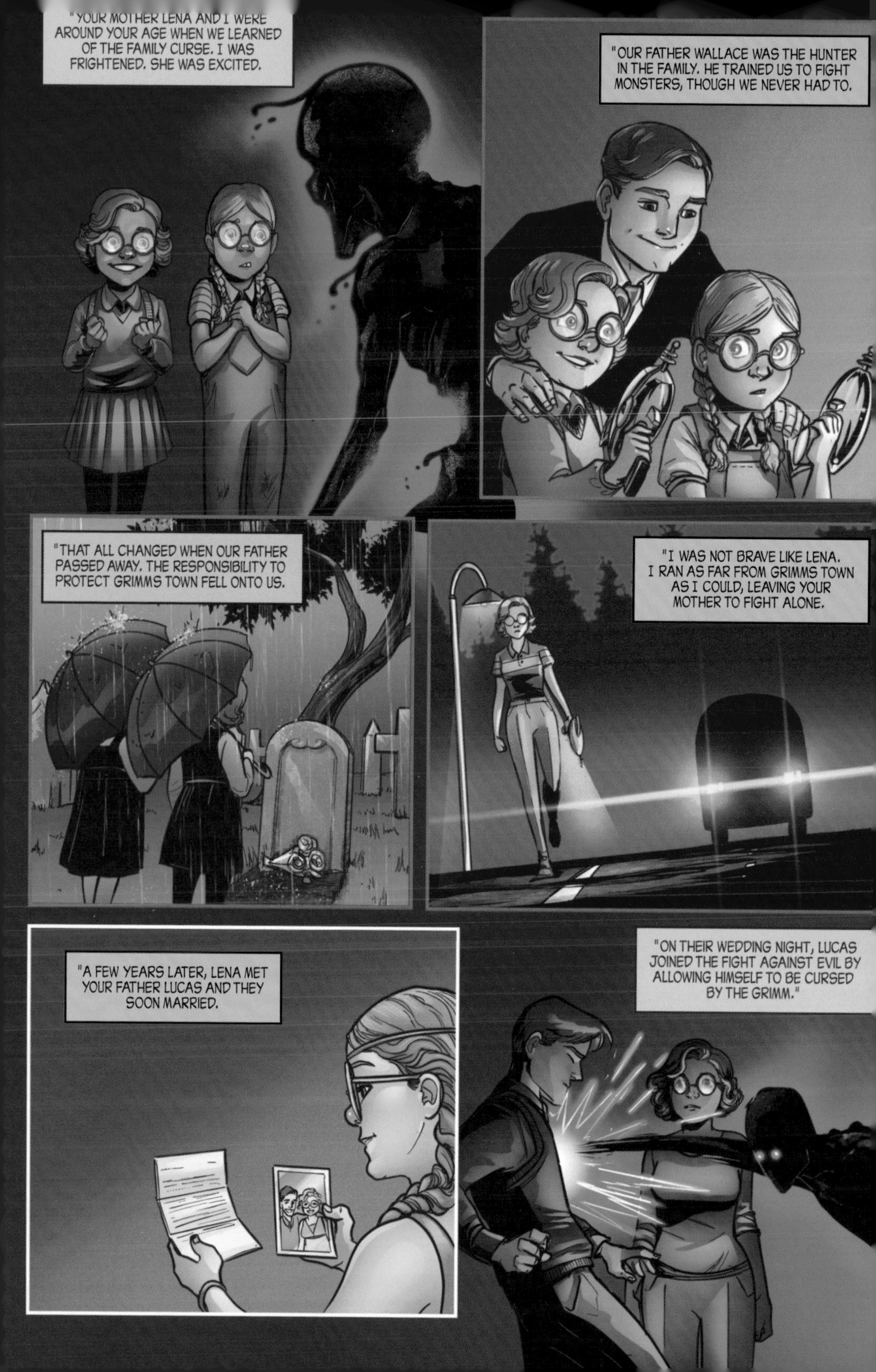
"YOUR MOTHER LENA AND I WERE AROUND YOUR AGE WHEN WE LEARNED OF THE FAMILY CURSE. I WAS FRIGHTENED. SHE WAS EXCITED.
"OUR FATHER WALLACE WAS THE HUNTER IN THE FAMILY. HE TRAINED US TO FIGHT MONSTERS, THOUGH WE NEVER HAD TO.
"THAT ALL CHANGED WHEN OUR FATHER PASSED AWAY. THE RESPONSIBILITY TO PROTECT GRIMMS TOWN FELL ONTO US.
"I WAS NOT BRAVE LIKE LENA. I RAN AS FAR FROM GRIMMS TOWN AS I COULD, LEAVING YOUR MOTHER TO FIGHT ALONE.
"A FEW YEARS LATER, LENA MET YOUR FATHER LUCAS AND THEY SOON MARRIED.
"ON THEIR WEDDING NIGHT, LUCAS JOINED THE FIGHT AGAINST EVIL BY ALLOWING HIMSELF TO BE CURSED BY THE GRIMM."

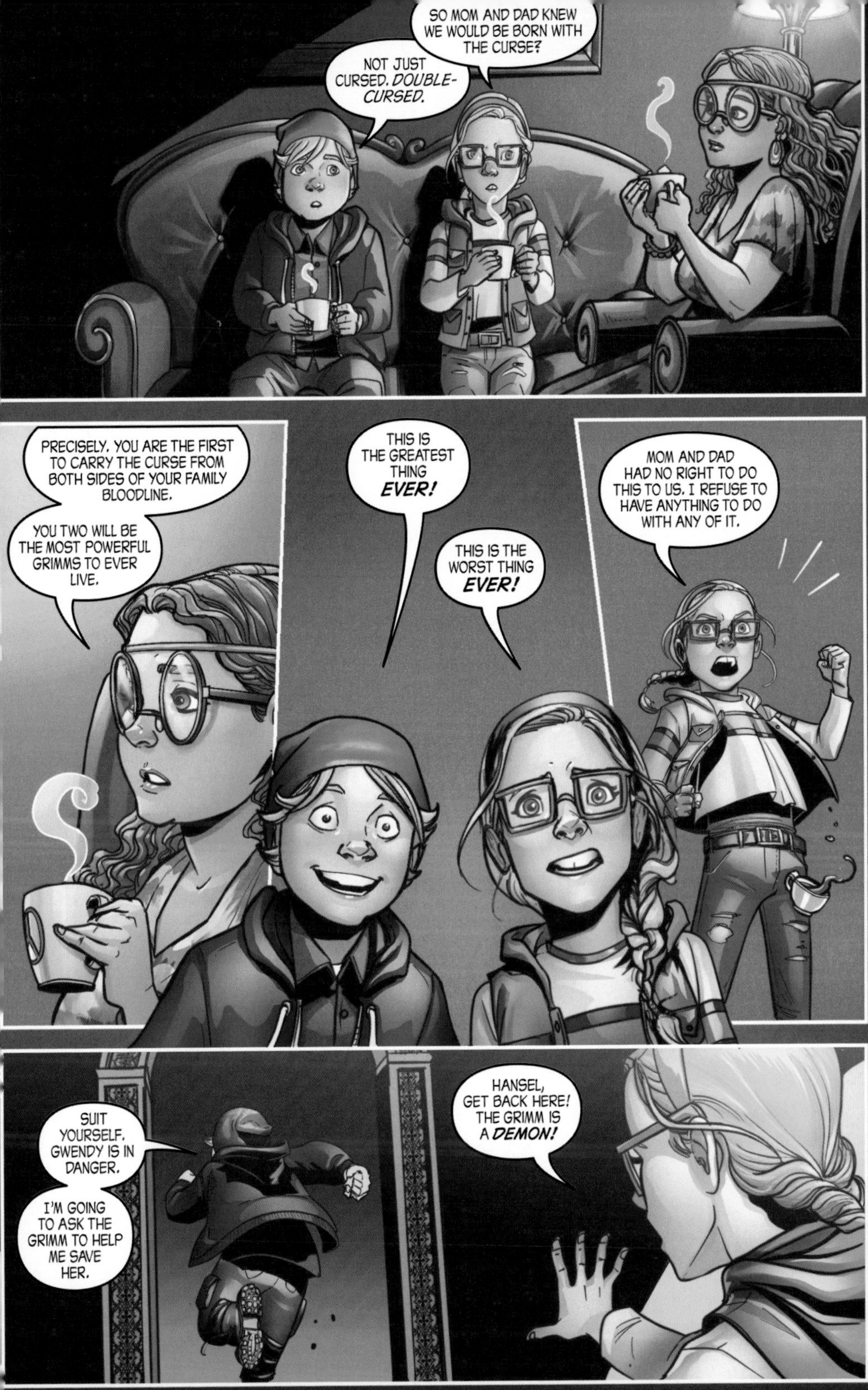
SO MOM AND DAD KNEW WE WOULD BE BORN WITH THE CURSE?
NOT JUST CURSED. *DOUBLE-CURSED.*
PRECISELY. YOU ARE THE FIRST TO CARRY THE CURSE FROM BOTH SIDES OF YOUR FAMILY BLOODLINE.
YOU TWO WILL BE THE MOST POWERFUL GRIMMS TO EVER LIVE.
THIS IS THE GREATEST THING ***EVER!***
THIS IS THE WORST THING ***EVER!***
MOM AND DAD HAD NO RIGHT TO DO THIS TO US. I REFUSE TO HAVE ANYTHING TO DO WITH ANY OF IT.
SUIT YOURSELF. GWENDY IS IN DANGER.
I'M GOING TO ASK THE GRIMM TO HELP ME SAVE HER.
HANSEL, GET BACK HERE! THE GRIMM IS A ***DEMON!***

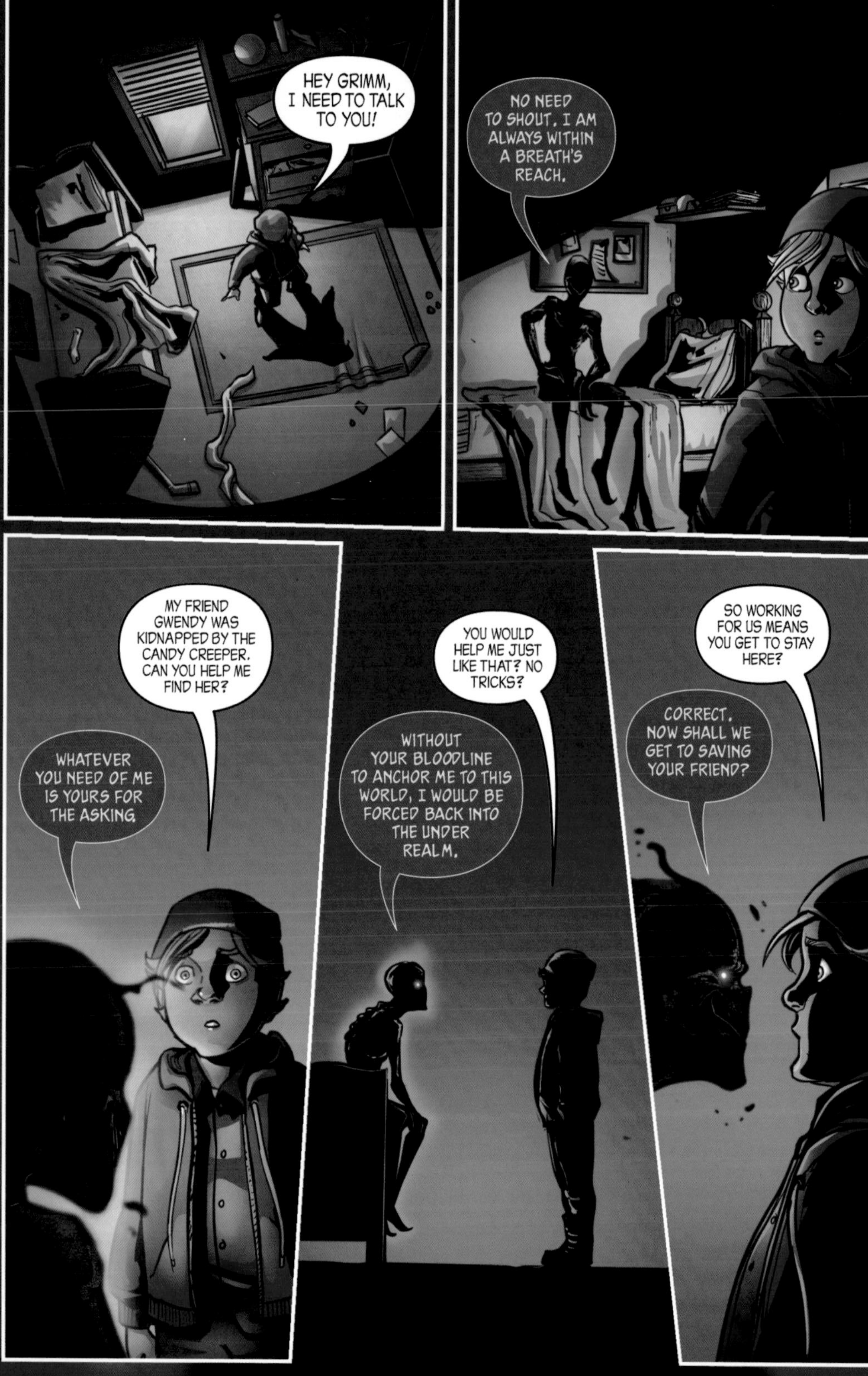
HEY GRIMM, I NEED TO TALK TO YOU!
NO NEED TO SHOUT. I AM ALWAYS WITHIN A BREATH'S REACH.
MY FRIEND GWENDY WAS KIDNAPPED BY THE CANDY CREEPER. CAN YOU HELP ME FIND HER?
WHATEVER YOU NEED OF ME IS YOURS FOR THE ASKING.
YOU WOULD HELP ME JUST LIKE THAT? NO TRICKS?
WITHOUT YOUR BLOODLINE TO ANCHOR ME TO THIS WORLD, I WOULD BE FORCED BACK INTO THE UNDER REALM.
SO WORKING FOR US MEANS YOU GET TO STAY HERE?
CORRECT. NOW SHALL WE GET TO SAVING YOUR FRIEND?

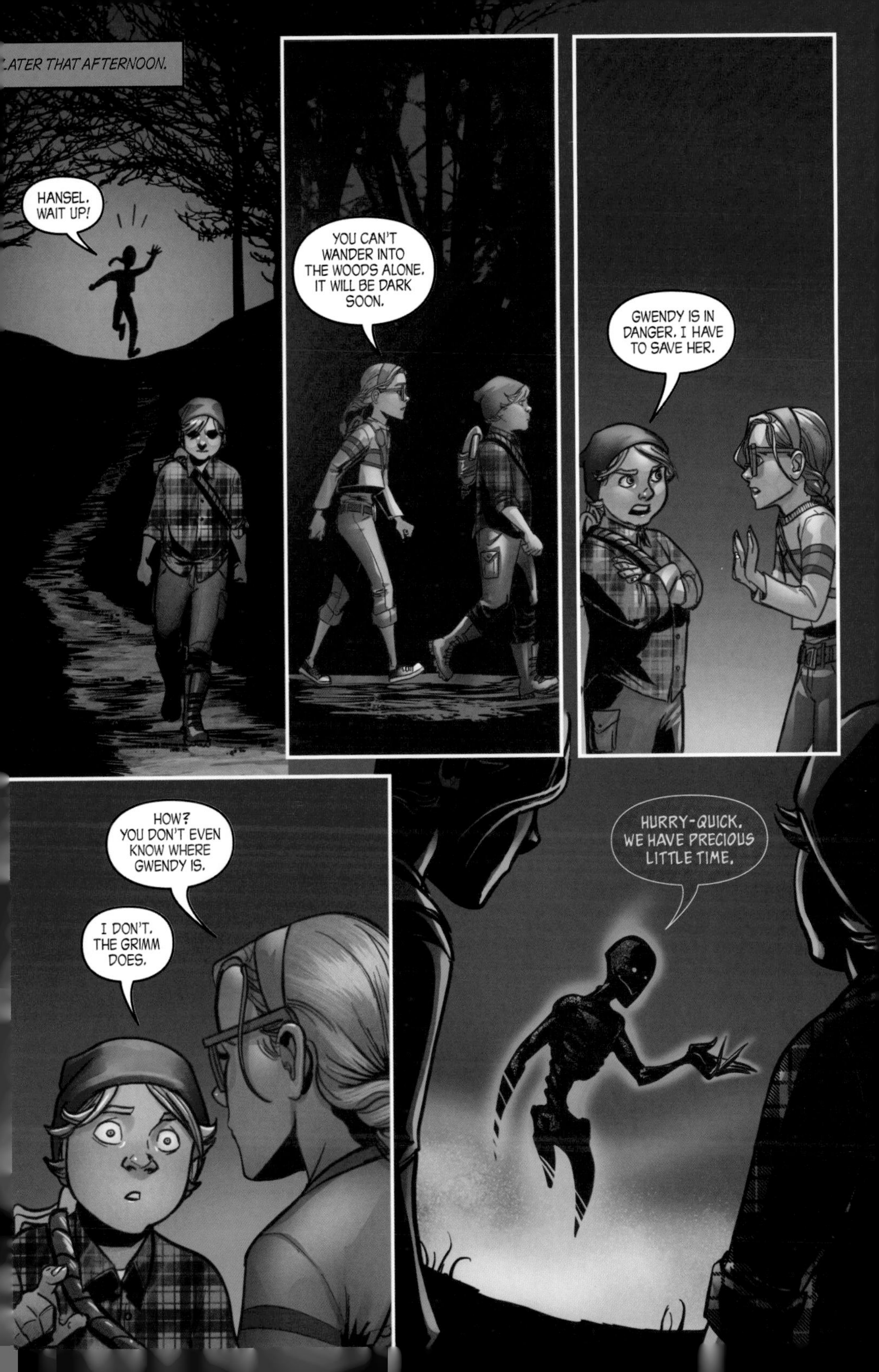
LATER THAT AFTERNOON.
HANSEL. WAIT UP!
YOU CAN'T WANDER INTO THE WOODS ALONE. IT WILL BE DARK SOON.
GWENDY IS IN DANGER. I HAVE TO SAVE HER.
HOW? YOU DON'T EVEN KNOW WHERE GWENDY IS.
I DON'T. THE GRIMM DOES.
HURRY-QUICK. WE HAVE PRECIOUS LITTLE TIME.

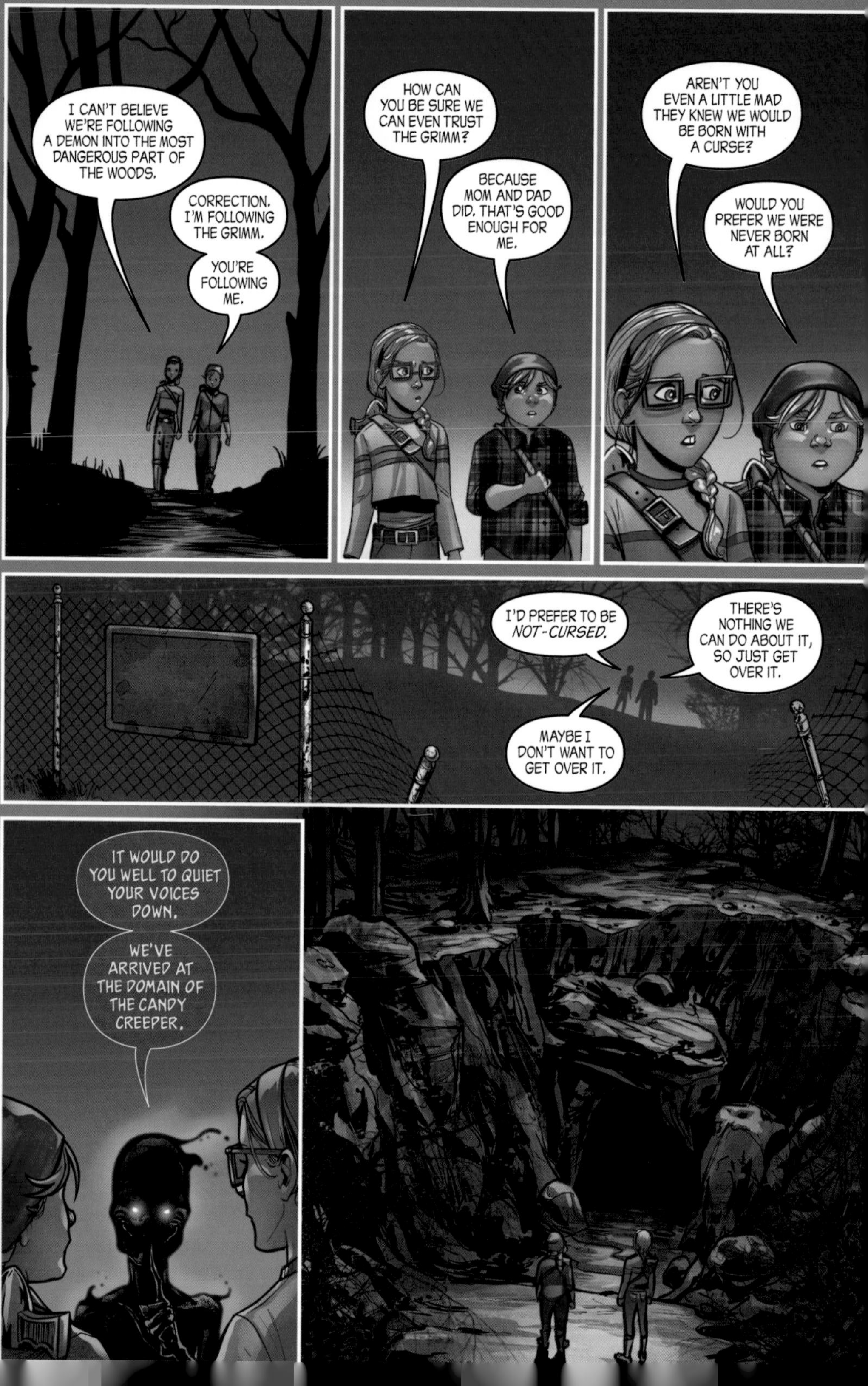
I CAN'T BELIEVE WE'RE FOLLOWING A DEMON INTO THE MOST DANGEROUS PART OF THE WOODS.
CORRECTION. I'M FOLLOWING THE GRIMM.
YOU'RE FOLLOWING ME.
HOW CAN YOU BE SURE WE CAN EVEN TRUST THE GRIMM?
BECAUSE MOM AND DAD DID. THAT'S GOOD ENOUGH FOR ME.
AREN'T YOU EVEN A LITTLE MAD THEY KNEW WE WOULD BE BORN WITH A CURSE?
WOULD YOU PREFER WE WERE NEVER BORN AT ALL?
I'D PREFER TO BE *NOT-CURSED.*
THERE'S NOTHING WE CAN DO ABOUT IT, SO JUST GET OVER IT.
MAYBE I DON'T WANT TO GET OVER IT.
IT WOULD DO YOU WELL TO QUIET YOUR VOICES DOWN.
WE'VE ARRIVED AT THE DOMAIN OF THE CANDY CREEPER.

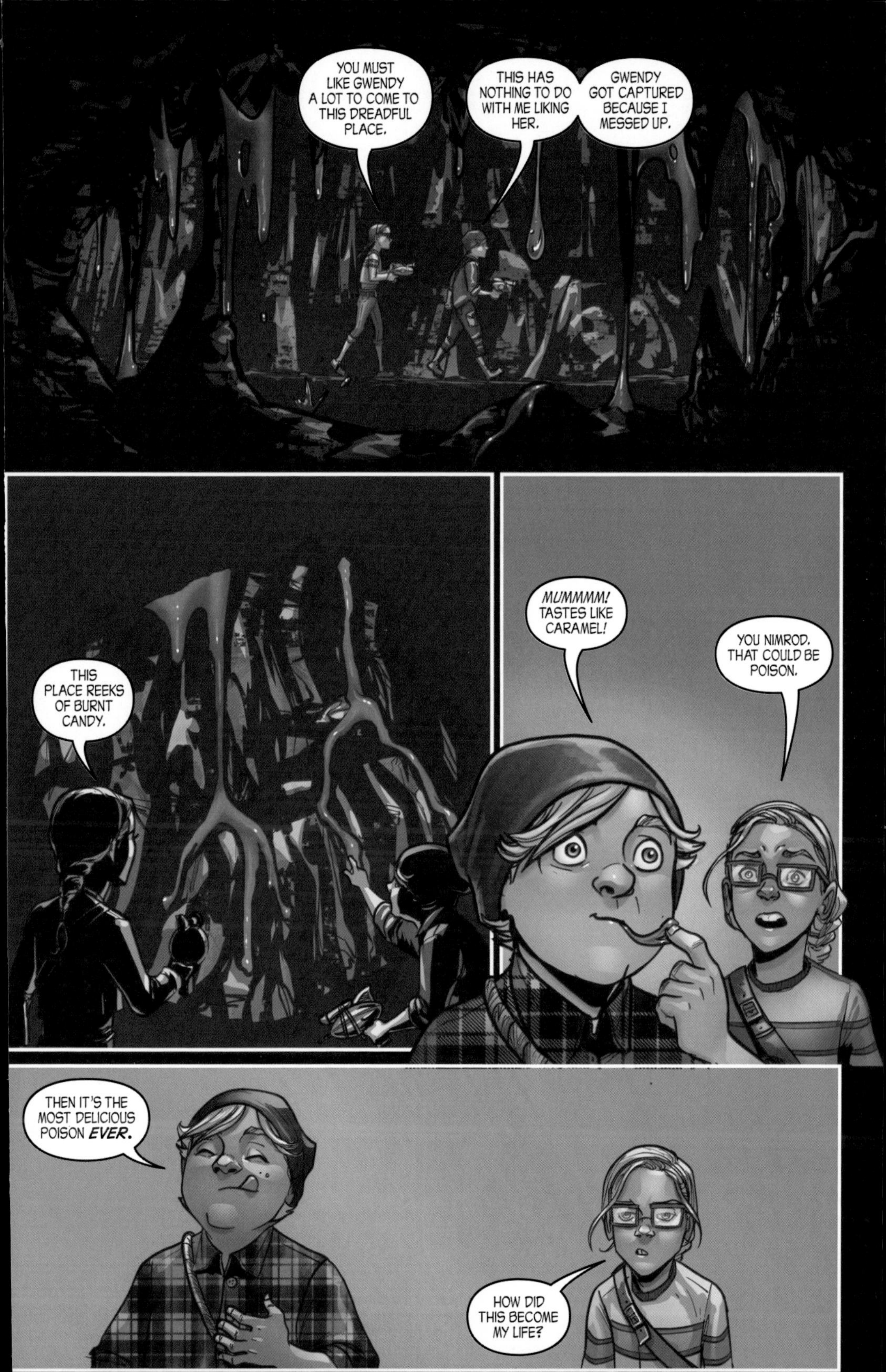
YOU MUST LIKE GWENDY A LOT TO COME TO THIS DREADFUL PLACE.
THIS HAS NOTHING TO DO WITH ME LIKING HER.
GWENDY GOT CAPTURED BECAUSE I MESSED UP.
THIS PLACE REEKS OF BURNT CANDY.
MUMMMM! TASTES LIKE CARAMEL!
YOU NIMROD. THAT COULD BE POISON.
THEN IT'S THE MOST DELICIOUS POISON ***EVER.***
HOW DID THIS BECOME MY LIFE?

ITS NESTING CHAMBER. THIS IS WORSE THAN I THOUGHT.

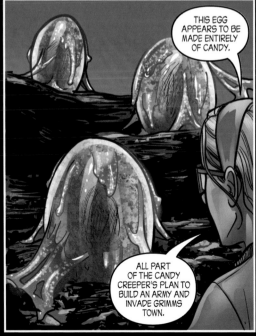

THIS EGG APPEARS TO BE MADE ENTIRELY OF CANDY.

ALL PART OF THE CANDY CREEPER'S PLAN TO BUILD AN ARMY AND INVADE GRIMMS TOWN.

AND ALL THESE PEOPLE WILL BE HOST BODIES FOR WHATEVER IS INSIDE THOSE EGGS.

I THINK FOR ONCE, YOU MAY ACTUALLY BE RIGHT.

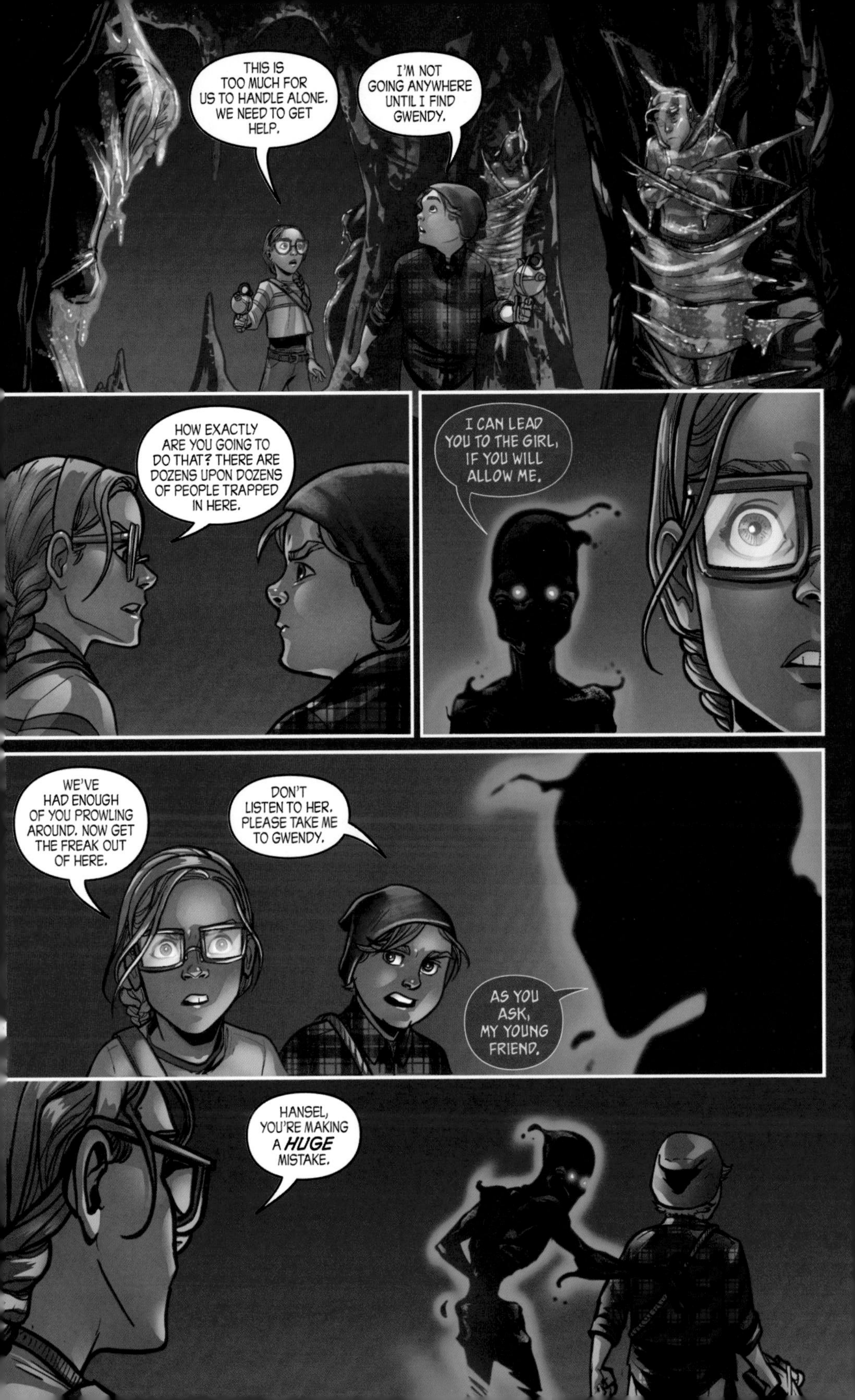
THIS IS TOO MUCH FOR US TO HANDLE ALONE. WE NEED TO GET HELP.
I'M NOT GOING ANYWHERE UNTIL I FIND GWENDY.
HOW EXACTLY ARE YOU GOING TO DO THAT? THERE ARE DOZENS UPON DOZENS OF PEOPLE TRAPPED IN HERE.
I CAN LEAD YOU TO THE GIRL, IF YOU WILL ALLOW ME.
WE'VE HAD ENOUGH OF YOU PROWLING AROUND. NOW GET THE FREAK OUT OF HERE.
DON'T LISTEN TO HER. PLEASE TAKE ME TO GWENDY.
AS YOU ASK, MY YOUNG FRIEND.
HANSEL, YOU'RE MAKING A ***HUGE*** MISTAKE.

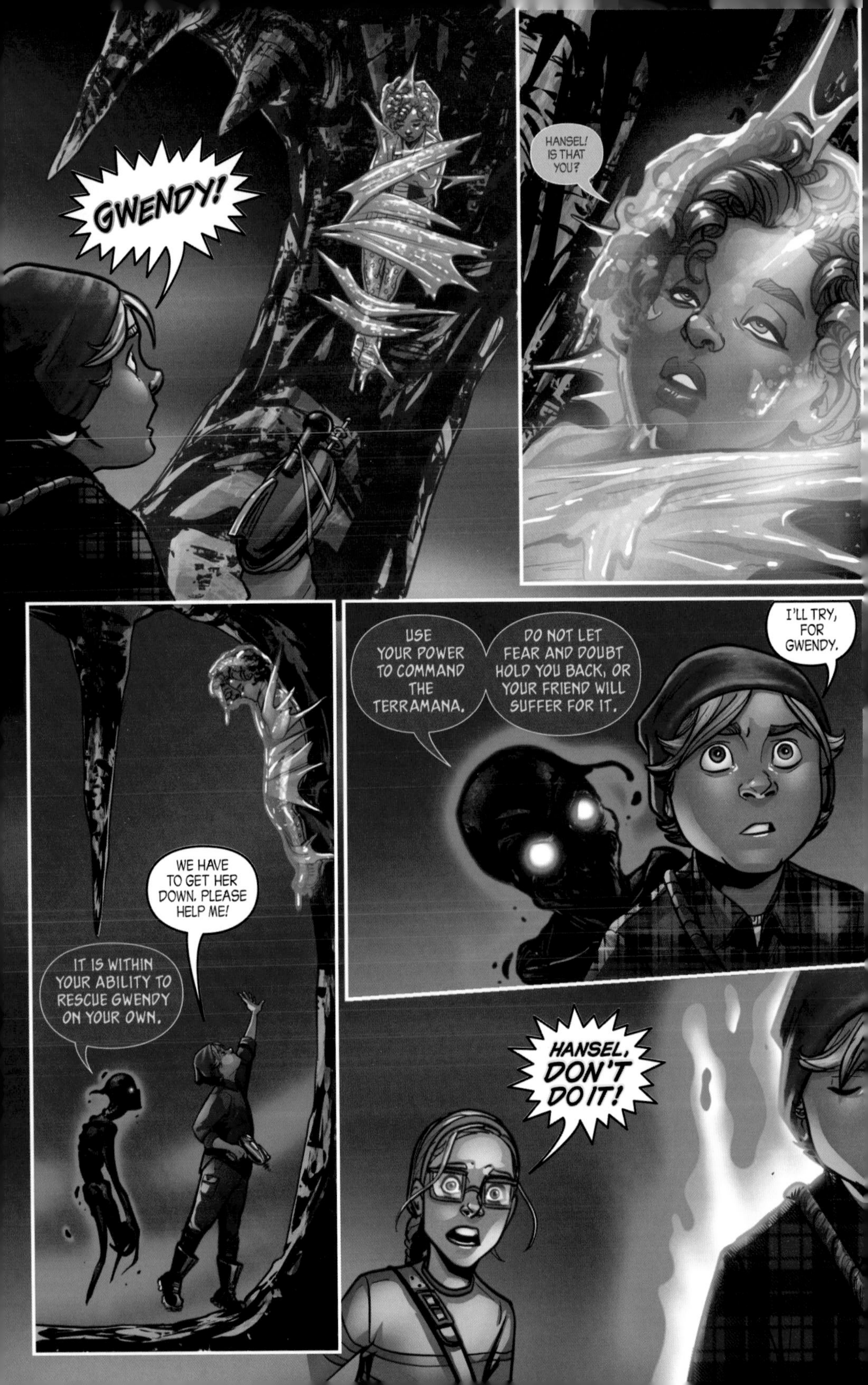
GWENDY!
HANSEL! IS THAT YOU?
WE HAVE TO GET HER DOWN. PLEASE HELP ME!
IT IS WITHIN YOUR ABILITY TO RESCUE GWENDY ON YOUR OWN.
USE YOUR POWER TO COMMAND THE TERRAMANA.
DO NOT LET FEAR AND DOUBT HOLD YOU BACK, OR YOUR FRIEND WILL SUFFER FOR IT.
I'LL TRY, FOR GWENDY.
HANSEL, DON'T DO IT!

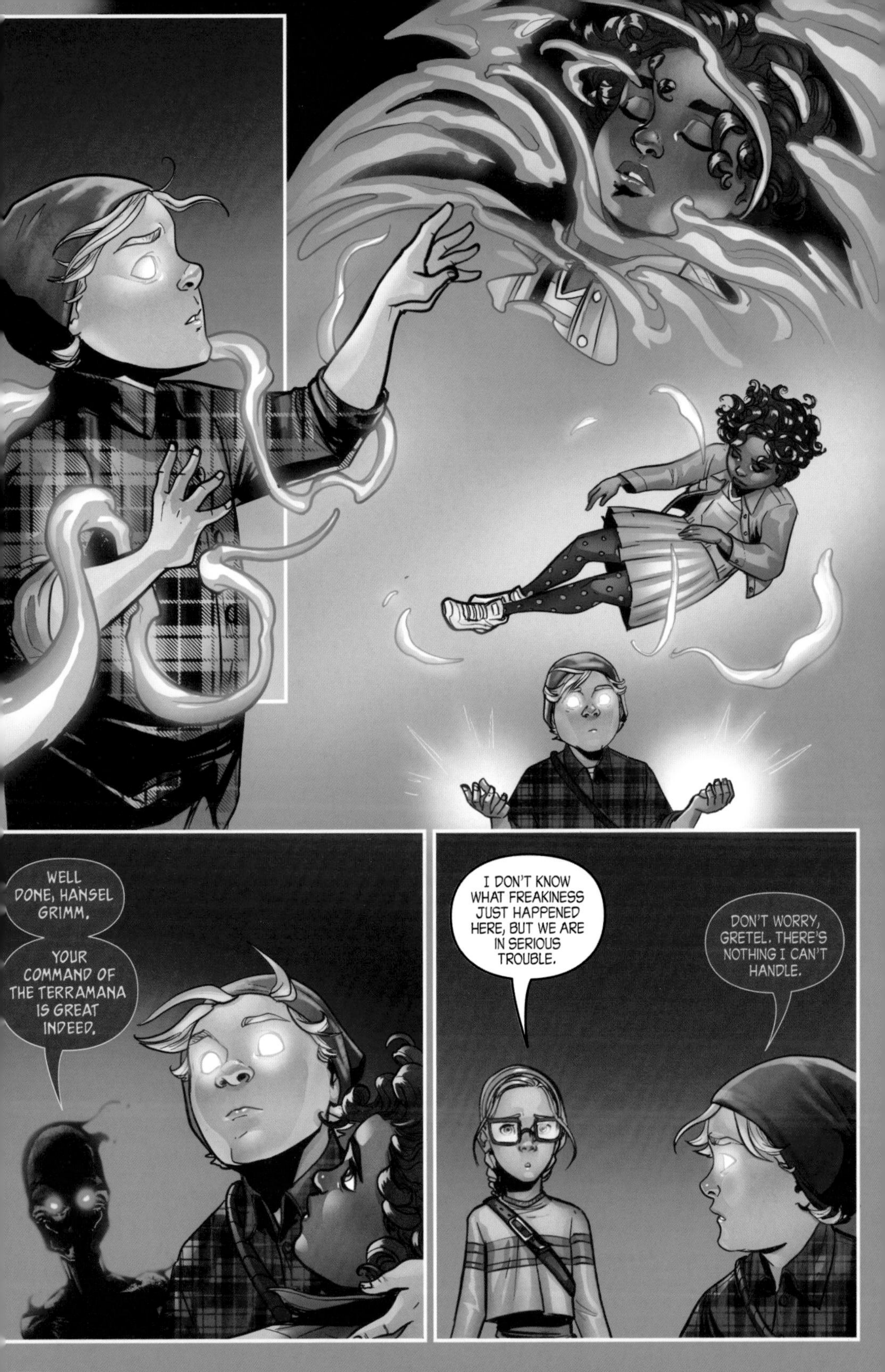
WELL DONE, HANSEL GRIMM.
YOUR COMMAND OF THE TERRAMANA IS GREAT INDEED.
I DON'T KNOW WHAT FREAKINESS JUST HAPPENED HERE, BUT WE ARE IN SERIOUS TROUBLE.
DON'T WORRY, GRETEL. THERE'S NOTHING I CAN'T HANDLE.

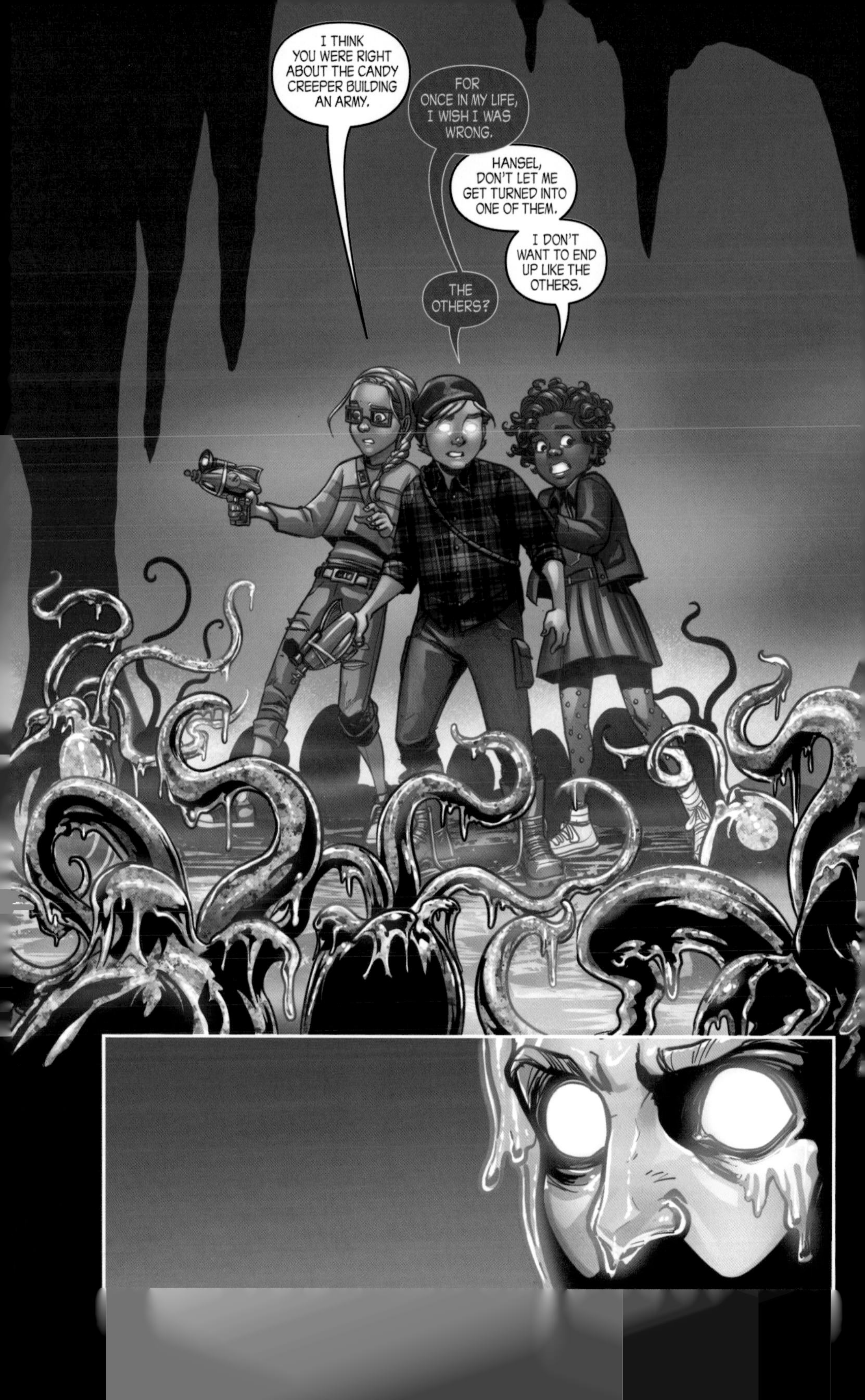
I THINK YOU WERE RIGHT ABOUT THE CANDY CREEPER BUILDING AN ARMY.
FOR ONCE IN MY LIFE, I WISH I WAS WRONG.
HANSEL, DON'T LET ME GET TURNED INTO ONE OF THEM.
I DON'T WANT TO END UP LIKE THE OTHERS.
THE OTHERS?

CHAPTER 5

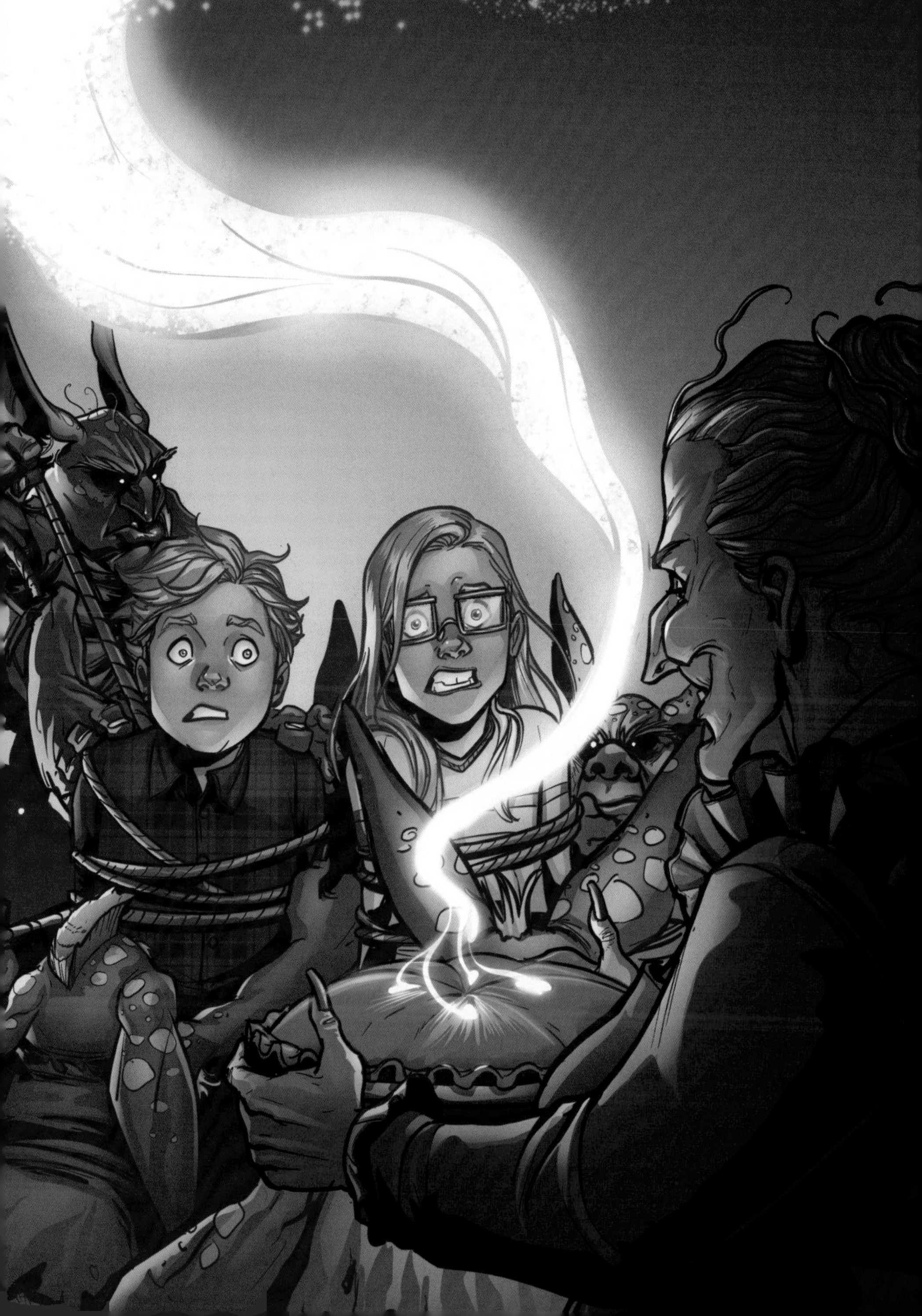

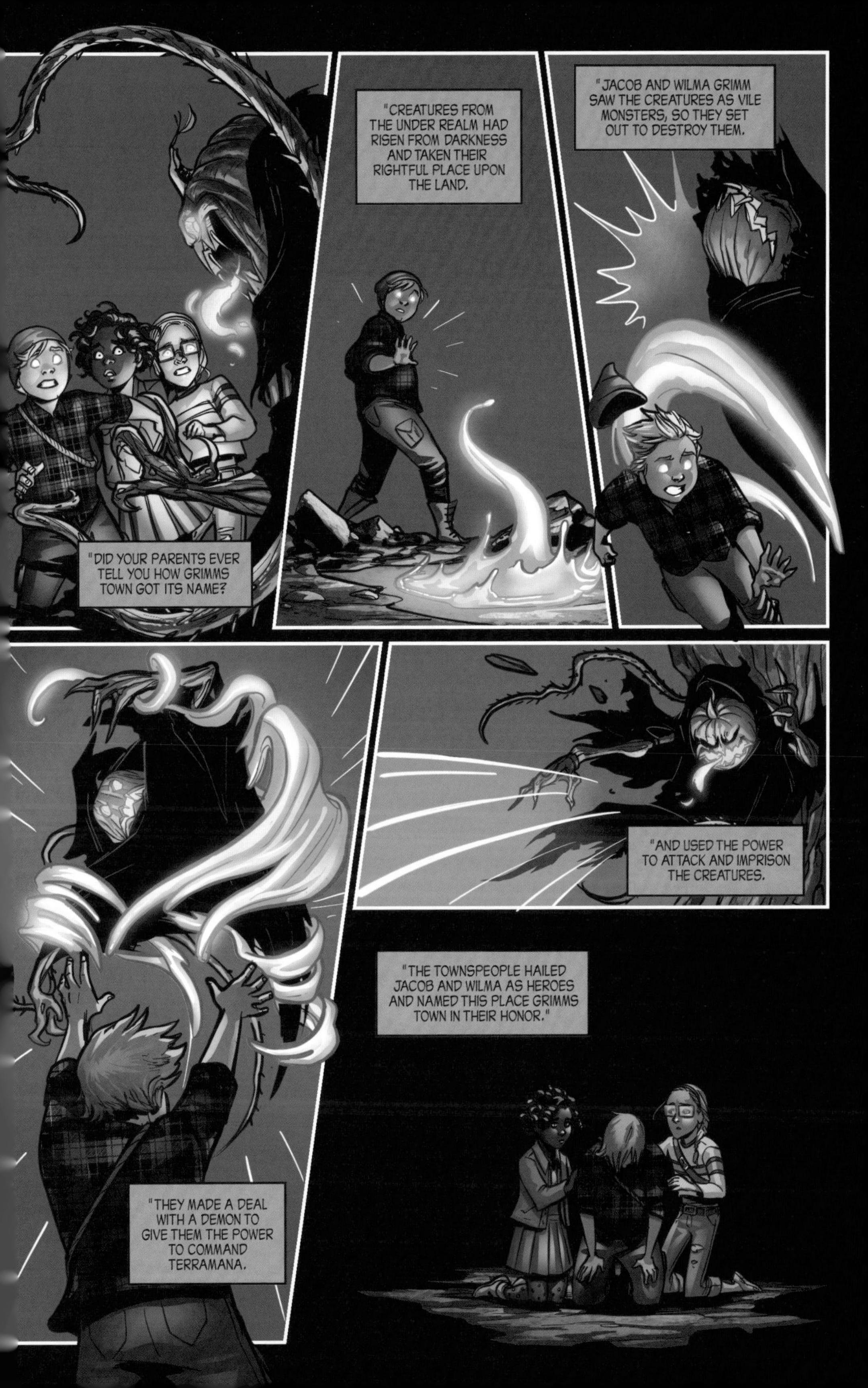
"DID YOUR PARENTS EVER TELL YOU HOW GRIMMS TOWN GOT ITS NAME?
"CREATURES FROM THE UNDER REALM HAD RISEN FROM DARKNESS AND TAKEN THEIR RIGHTFUL PLACE UPON THE LAND.
"JACOB AND WILMA GRIMM SAW THE CREATURES AS VILE MONSTERS, SO THEY SET OUT TO DESTROY THEM.
"THEY MADE A DEAL WITH A DEMON TO GIVE THEM THE POWER TO COMMAND TERRAMANA.
"AND USED THE POWER TO ATTACK AND IMPRISON THE CREATURES.
"THE TOWNSPEOPLE HAILED JACOB AND WILMA AS HEROES AND NAMED THIS PLACE GRIMMS TOWN IN THEIR HONOR."

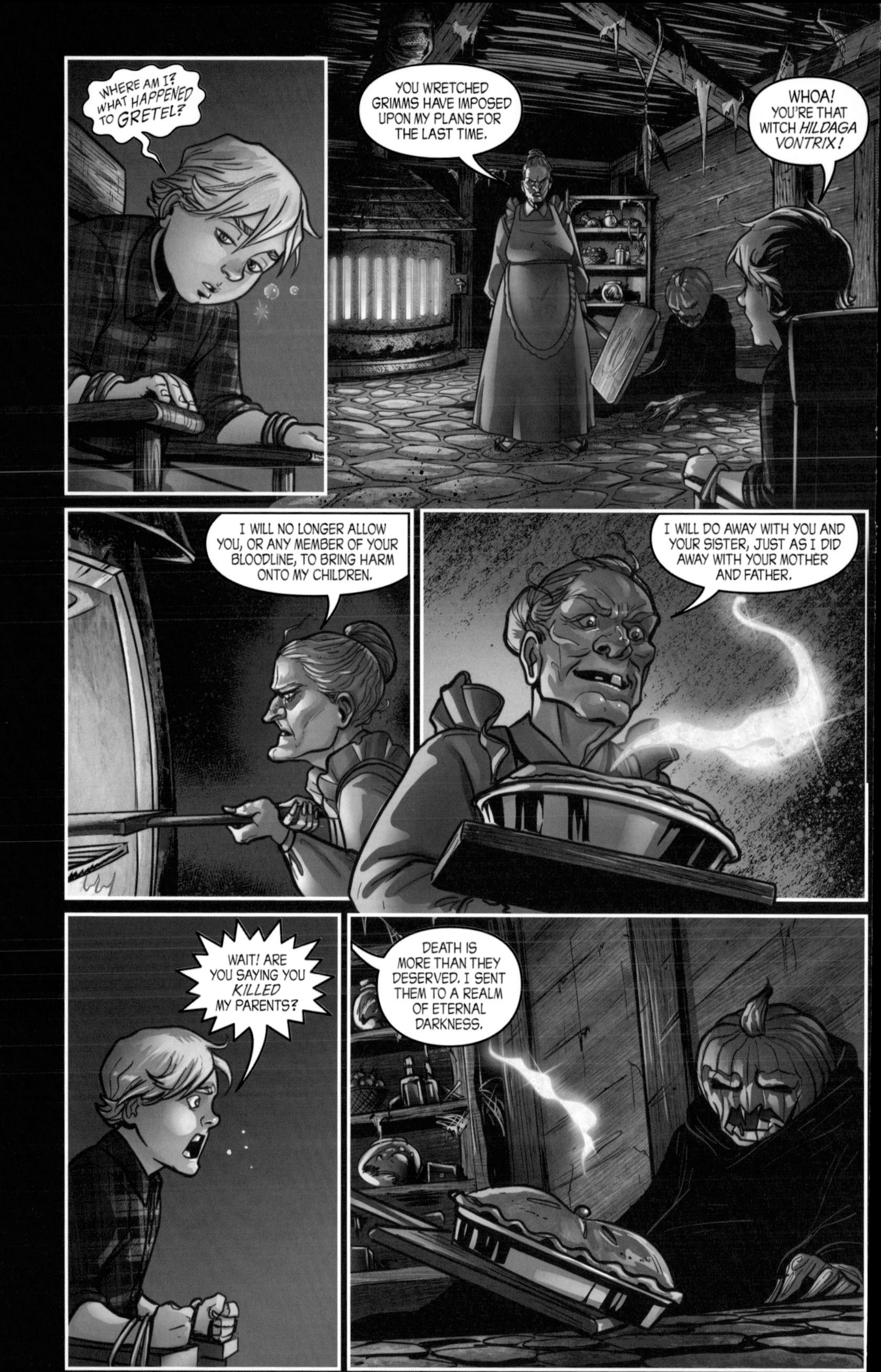
WHERE AM I? WHAT HAPPENED TO GRETEL?
YOU WRETCHED GRIMMS HAVE IMPOSED UPON MY PLANS FOR THE LAST TIME.
WHOA! YOU'RE THAT WITCH HILDAGA VONTRIX!
I WILL NO LONGER ALLOW YOU, OR ANY MEMBER OF YOUR BLOODLINE, TO BRING HARM ONTO MY CHILDREN.
I WILL DO AWAY WITH YOU AND YOUR SISTER, JUST AS I DID AWAY WITH YOUR MOTHER AND FATHER.
WAIT! ARE YOU SAYING YOU KILLED MY PARENTS?
DEATH IS MORE THAN THEY DESERVED. I SENT THEM TO A REALM OF ETERNAL DARKNESS.

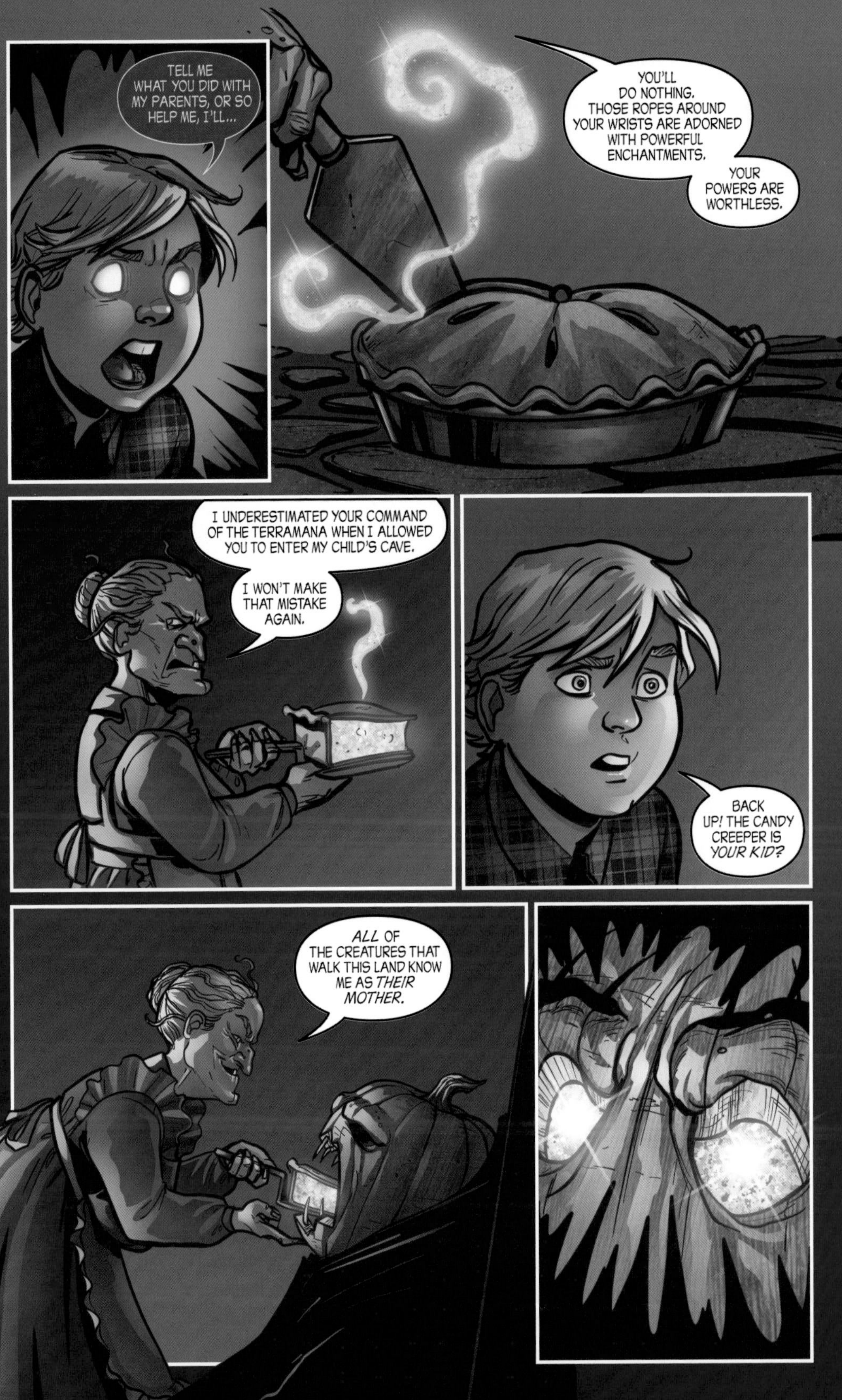
TELL ME WHAT YOU DID WITH MY PARENTS, OR SO HELP ME, I'LL...
YOU'LL DO NOTHING. THOSE ROPES AROUND YOUR WRISTS ARE ADORNED WITH POWERFUL ENCHANTMENTS.
YOUR POWERS ARE WORTHLESS.
I UNDERESTIMATED YOUR COMMAND OF THE TERRAMANA WHEN I ALLOWED YOU TO ENTER MY CHILD'S CAVE.
I WON'T MAKE THAT MISTAKE AGAIN.
BACK UP! THE CANDY CREEPER IS *YOUR KID?*
ALL OF THE CREATURES THAT WALK THIS LAND KNOW ME AS *THEIR MOTHER.*

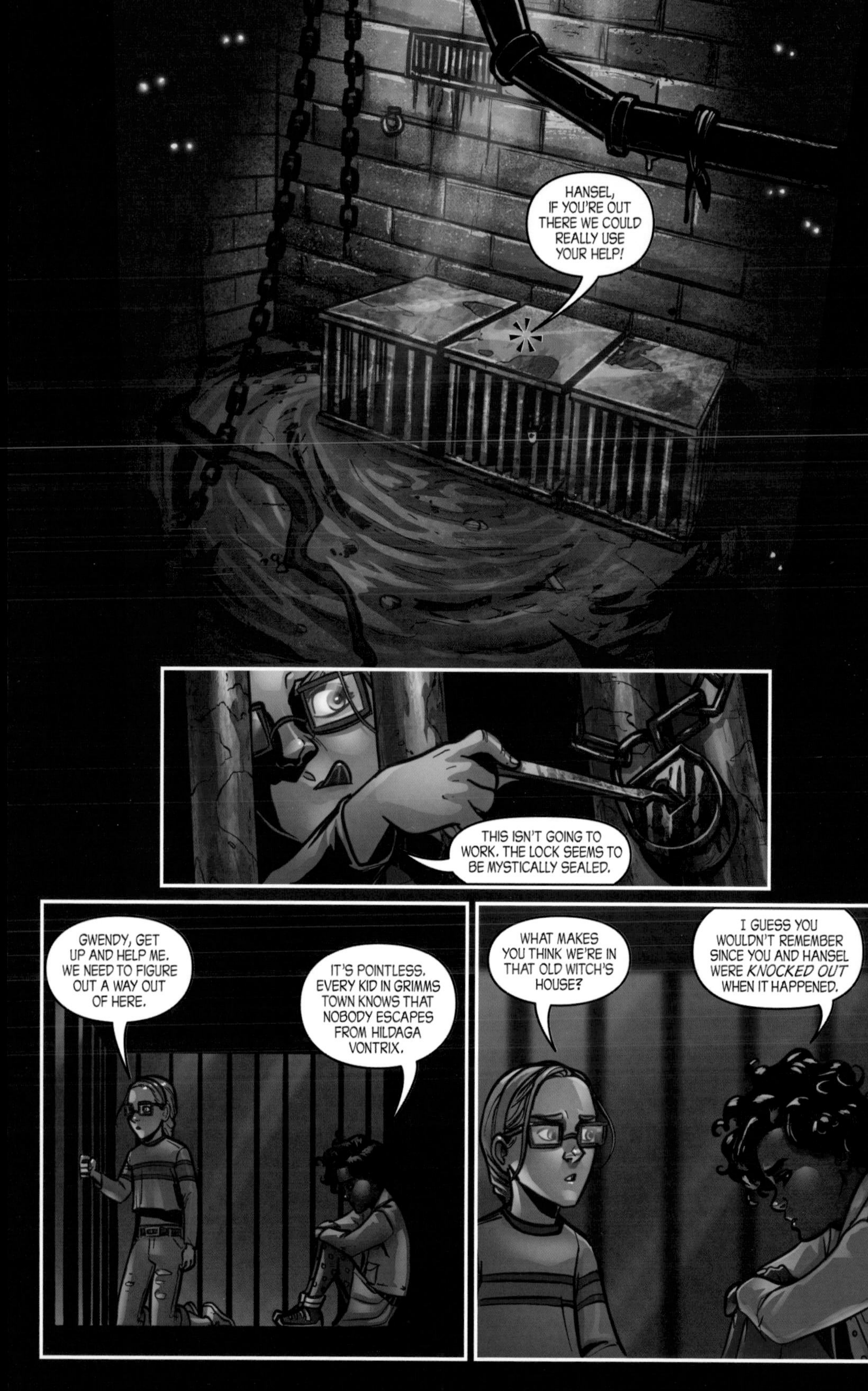
HANSEL, IF YOU'RE OUT THERE WE COULD REALLY USE YOUR HELP!
THIS ISN'T GOING TO WORK. THE LOCK SEEMS TO BE MYSTICALLY SEALED.
GWENDY, GET UP AND HELP ME. WE NEED TO FIGURE OUT A WAY OUT OF HERE.
IT'S POINTLESS. EVERY KID IN GRIMMS TOWN KNOWS THAT NOBODY ESCAPES FROM HILDAGA VONTRIX.
WHAT MAKES YOU THINK WE'RE IN THAT OLD WITCH'S HOUSE?
I GUESS YOU WOULDN'T REMEMBER SINCE YOU AND HANSEL WERE *KNOCKED OUT* WHEN IT HAPPENED.

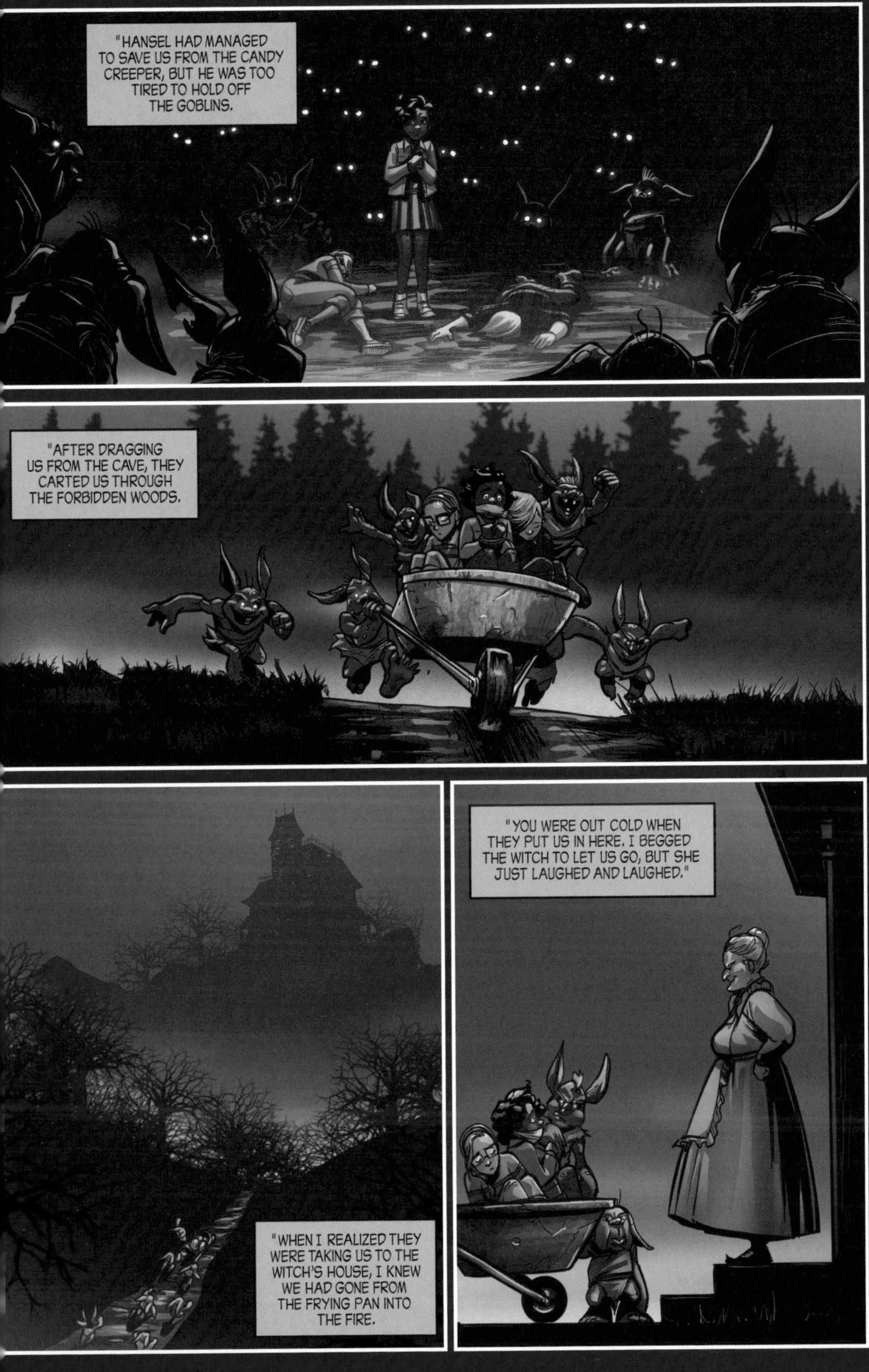
"HANSEL HAD MANAGED TO SAVE US FROM THE CANDY CREEPER, BUT HE WAS TOO TIRED TO HOLD OFF THE GOBLINS.
"AFTER DRAGGING US FROM THE CAVE, THEY CARTED US THROUGH THE FORBIDDEN WOODS.
"WHEN I REALIZED THEY WERE TAKING US TO THE WITCH'S HOUSE, I KNEW WE HAD GONE FROM THE FRYING PAN INTO THE FIRE.
"YOU WERE OUT COLD WHEN THEY PUT US IN HERE. I BEGGED THE WITCH TO LET US GO, BUT SHE JUST LAUGHED AND LAUGHED."

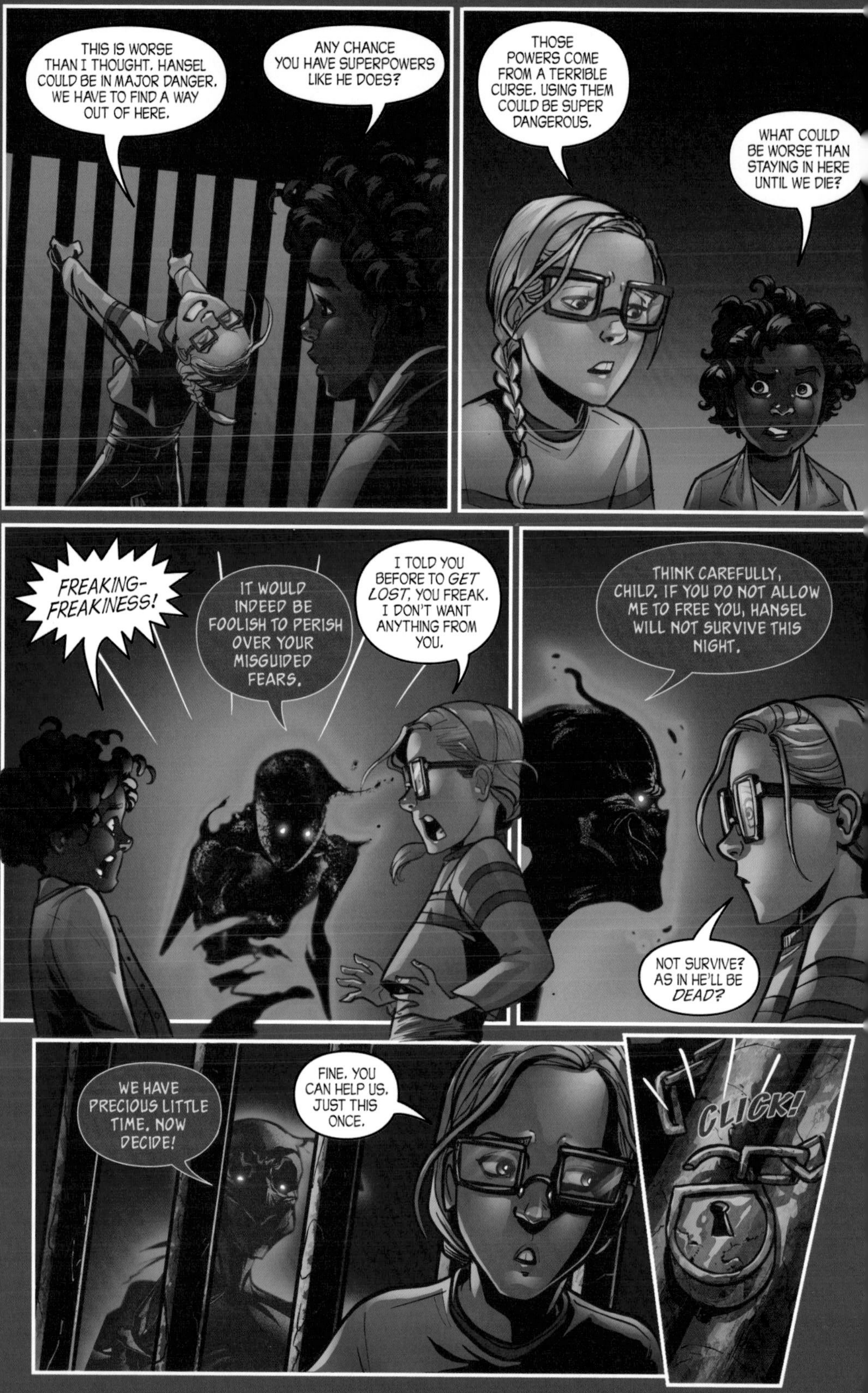
THIS IS WORSE THAN I THOUGHT. HANSEL COULD BE IN MAJOR DANGER. WE HAVE TO FIND A WAY OUT OF HERE.
ANY CHANCE YOU HAVE SUPERPOWERS LIKE HE DOES?
THOSE POWERS COME FROM A TERRIBLE CURSE. USING THEM COULD BE SUPER DANGEROUS.
WHAT COULD BE WORSE THAN STAYING IN HERE UNTIL WE DIE?
FREAKING-FREAKINESS!
IT WOULD INDEED BE FOOLISH TO PERISH OVER YOUR MISGUIDED FEARS.
I TOLD YOU BEFORE TO *GET LOST*, YOU FREAK. I DON'T WANT ANYTHING FROM YOU.
THINK CAREFULLY, CHILD. IF YOU DO NOT ALLOW ME TO FREE YOU, HANSEL WILL NOT SURVIVE THIS NIGHT.
NOT SURVIVE? AS IN HE'LL BE *DEAD*?
WE HAVE PRECIOUS LITTLE TIME. NOW DECIDE!
FINE. YOU CAN HELP US. JUST THIS ONCE.
CLICK!

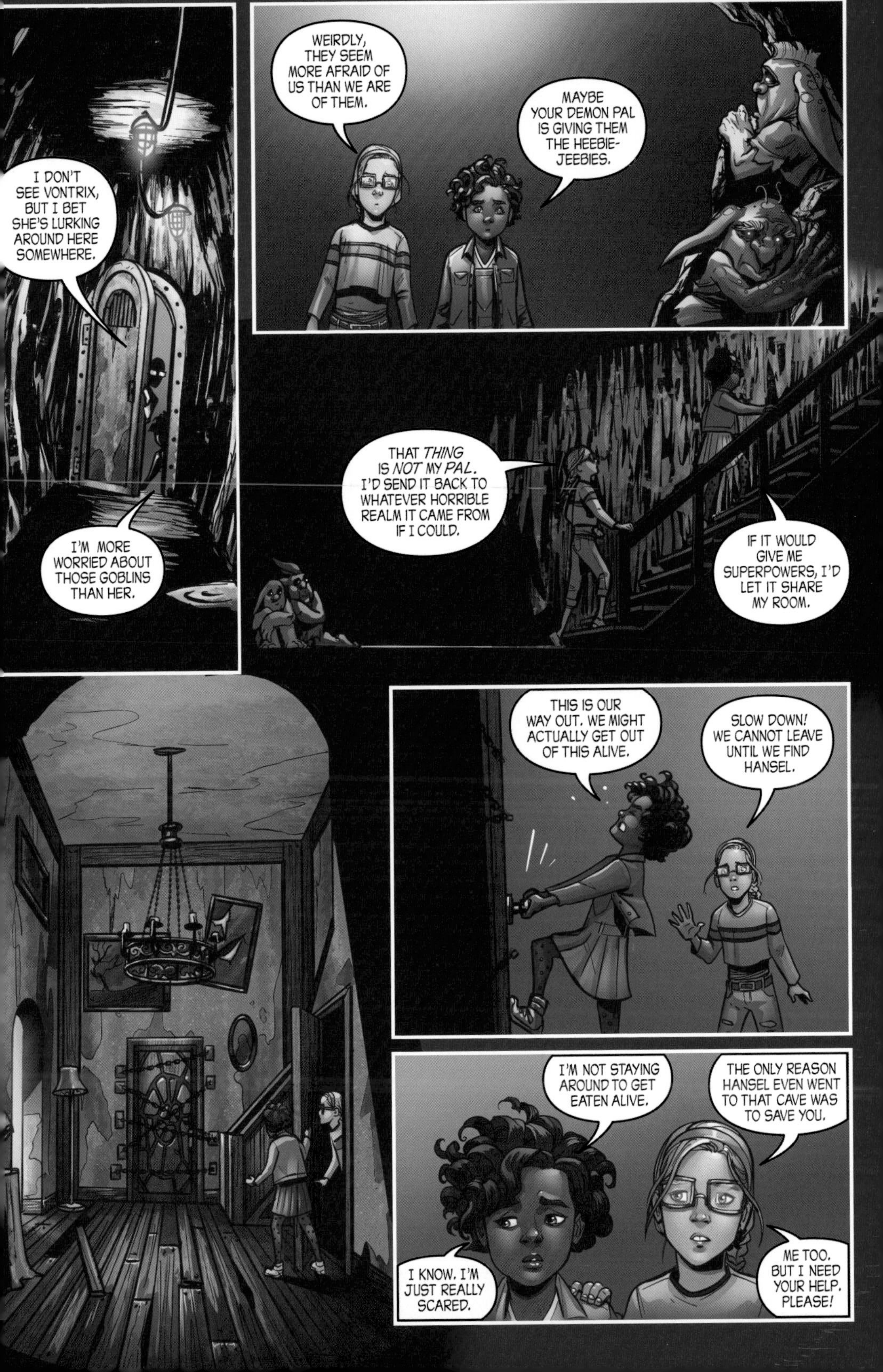
I DON'T SEE VONTRIX, BUT I BET SHE'S LURKING AROUND HERE SOMEWHERE.
I'M MORE WORRIED ABOUT THOSE GOBLINS THAN HER.
WEIRDLY, THEY SEEM MORE AFRAID OF US THAN WE ARE OF THEM.
MAYBE YOUR DEMON PAL IS GIVING THEM THE HEEBIE-JEEBIES.
THAT *THING* IS *NOT MY PAL*. I'D SEND IT BACK TO WHATEVER HORRIBLE REALM IT CAME FROM IF I COULD.
IF IT WOULD GIVE ME SUPERPOWERS, I'D LET IT SHARE MY ROOM.
THIS IS OUR WAY OUT. WE MIGHT ACTUALLY GET OUT OF THIS ALIVE.
SLOW DOWN! WE CANNOT LEAVE UNTIL WE FIND HANSEL.
I'M NOT STAYING AROUND TO GET EATEN ALIVE.
THE ONLY REASON HANSEL EVEN WENT TO THAT CAVE WAS TO SAVE YOU.
I KNOW. I'M JUST REALLY SCARED.
ME TOO. BUT I NEED YOUR HELP. PLEASE!

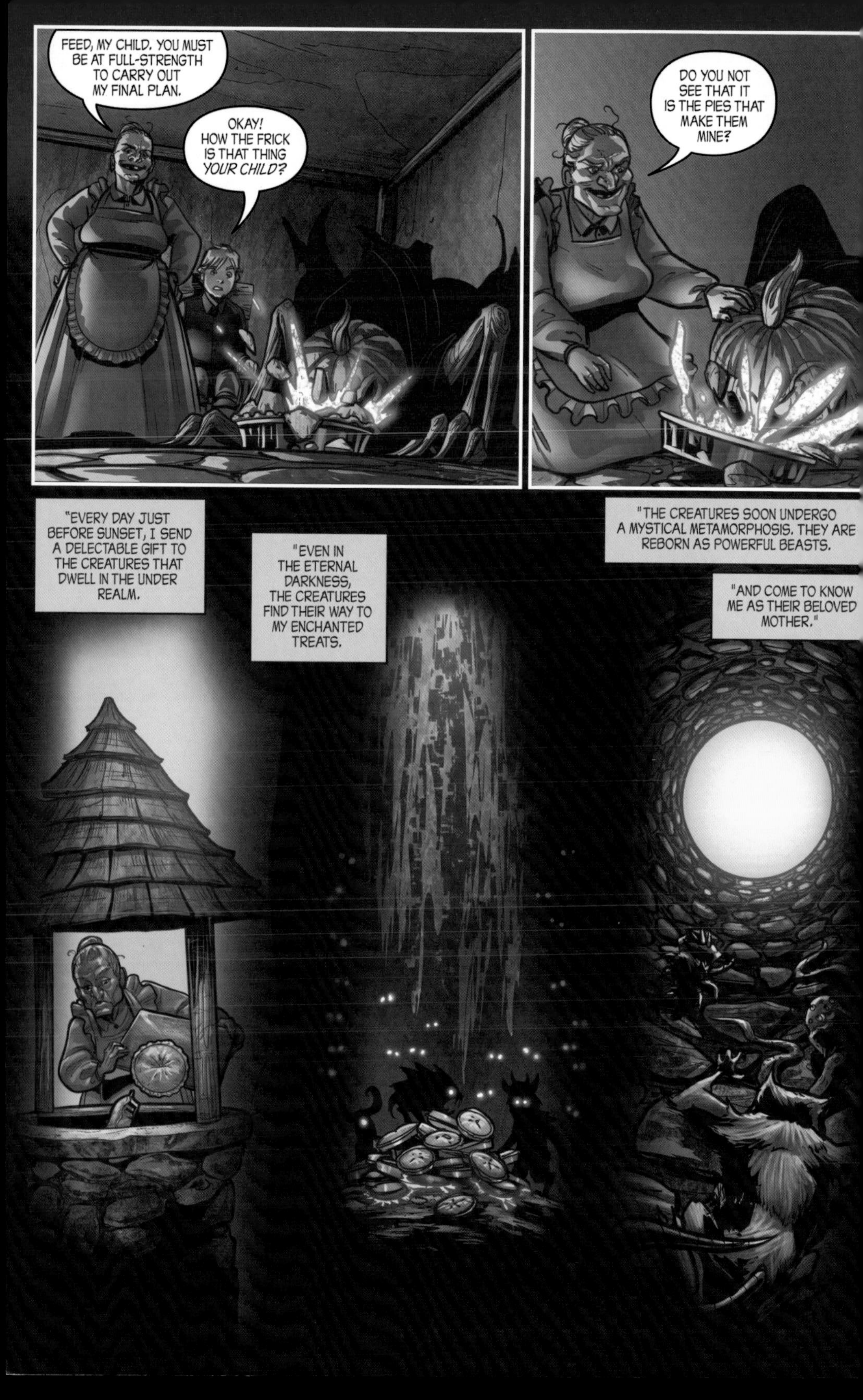
FEED, MY CHILD. YOU MUST BE AT FULL-STRENGTH TO CARRY OUT MY FINAL PLAN.
OKAY! HOW THE FRICK IS THAT THING *YOUR CHILD?*
DO YOU NOT SEE THAT IT IS THE PIES THAT MAKE THEM MINE?
"EVERY DAY JUST BEFORE SUNSET, I SEND A DELECTABLE GIFT TO THE CREATURES THAT DWELL IN THE UNDER REALM.
"EVEN IN THE ETERNAL DARKNESS, THE CREATURES FIND THEIR WAY TO MY ENCHANTED TREATS.
"THE CREATURES SOON UNDERGO A MYSTICAL METAMORPHOSIS. THEY ARE REBORN AS POWERFUL BEASTS.
"AND COME TO KNOW ME AS THEIR BELOVED MOTHER."

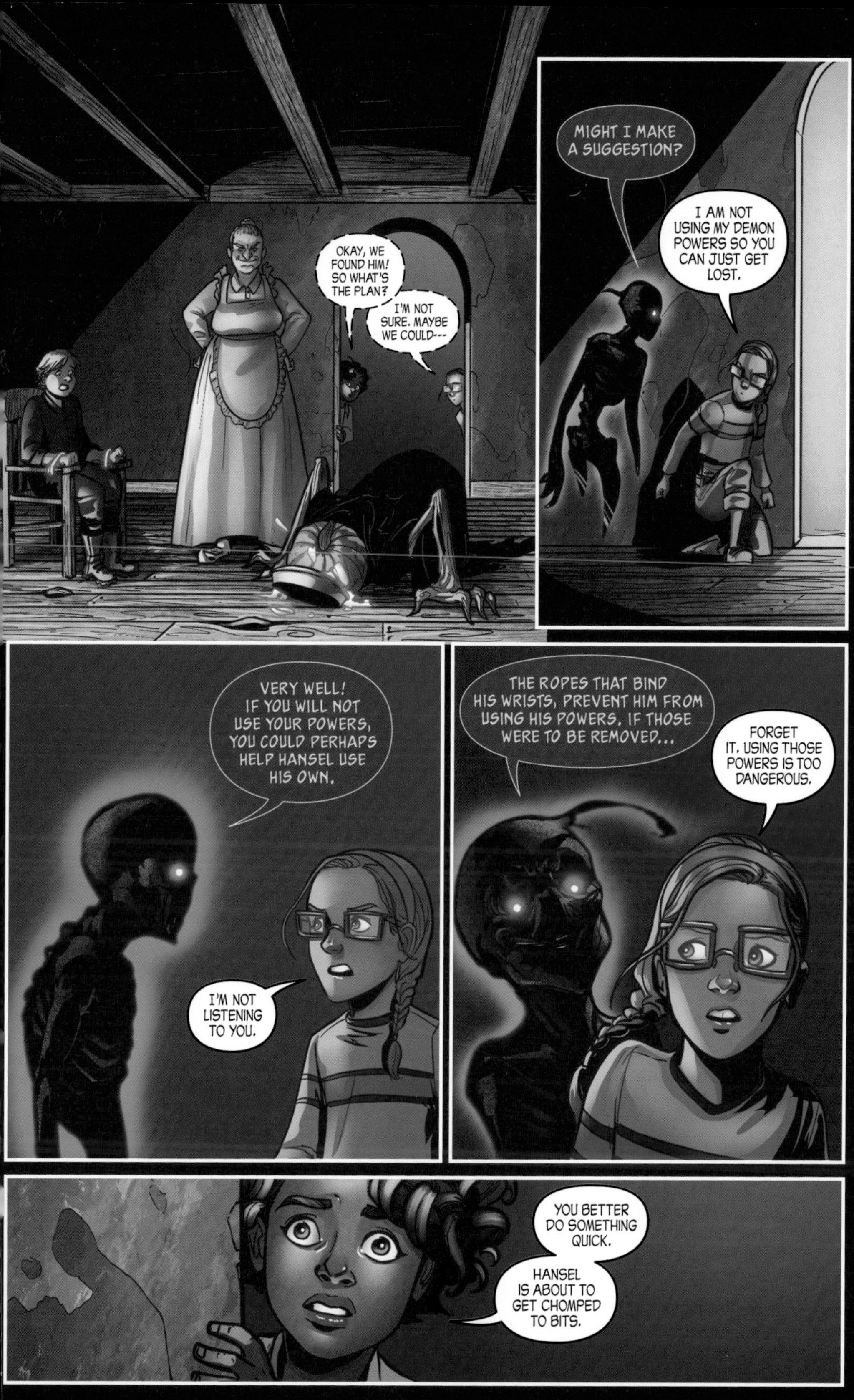
OKAY, WE FOUND HIM! SO WHAT'S THE PLAN?
I'M NOT SURE. MAYBE WE COULD---
MIGHT I MAKE A SUGGESTION?
I AM NOT USING MY DEMON POWERS SO YOU CAN JUST GET LOST.
VERY WELL! IF YOU WILL NOT USE YOUR POWERS, YOU COULD PERHAPS HELP HANSEL USE HIS OWN.
I'M NOT LISTENING TO YOU.
THE ROPES THAT BIND HIS WRISTS, PREVENT HIM FROM USING HIS POWERS. IF THOSE WERE TO BE REMOVED...
FORGET IT. USING THOSE POWERS IS TOO DANGEROUS.
YOU BETTER DO SOMETHING QUICK.
HANSEL IS ABOUT TO GET CHOMPED TO BITS.

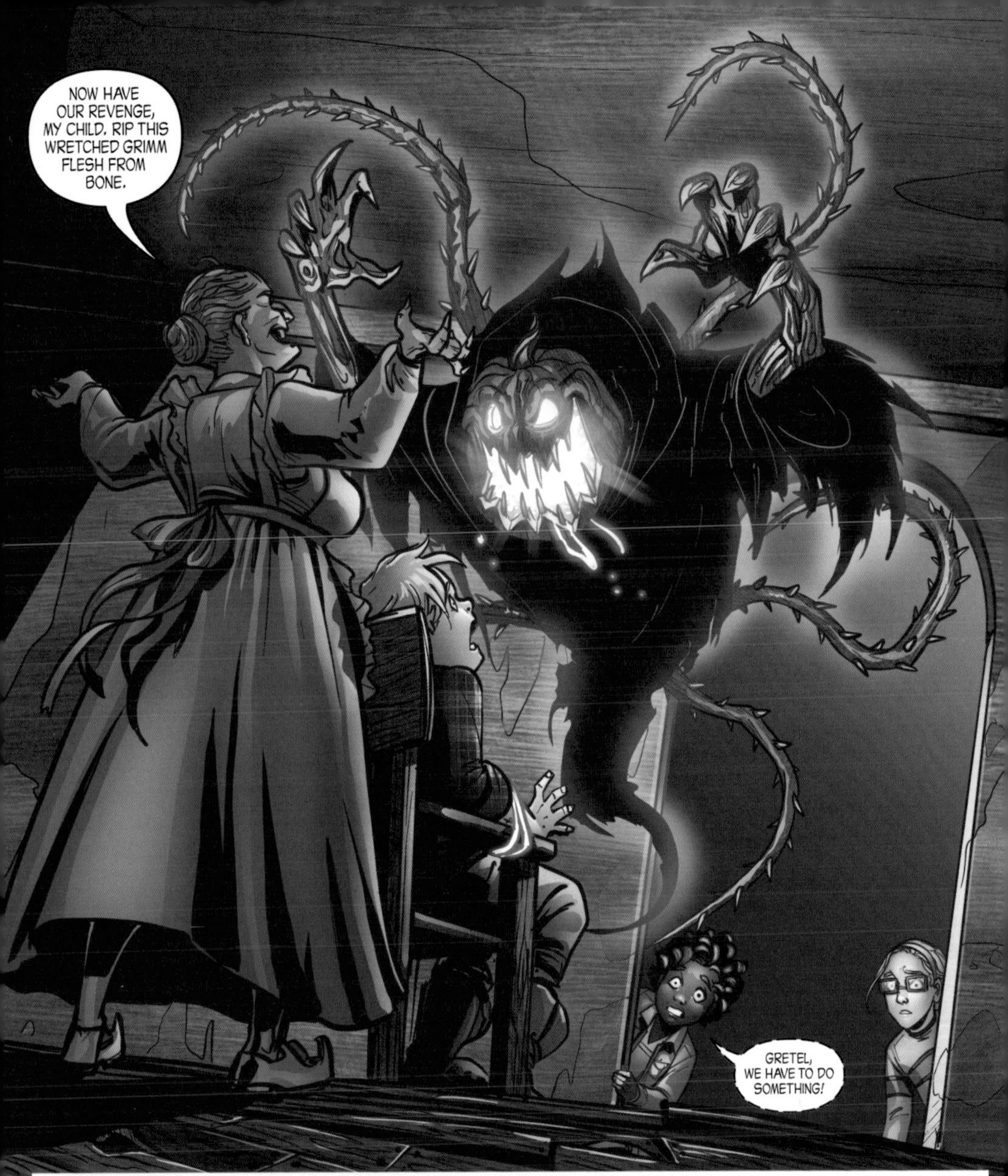
NOW HAVE OUR REVENGE, MY CHILD. RIP THIS WRETCHED GRIMM FLESH FROM BONE.
GRETEL, WE HAVE TO DO SOMETHING!
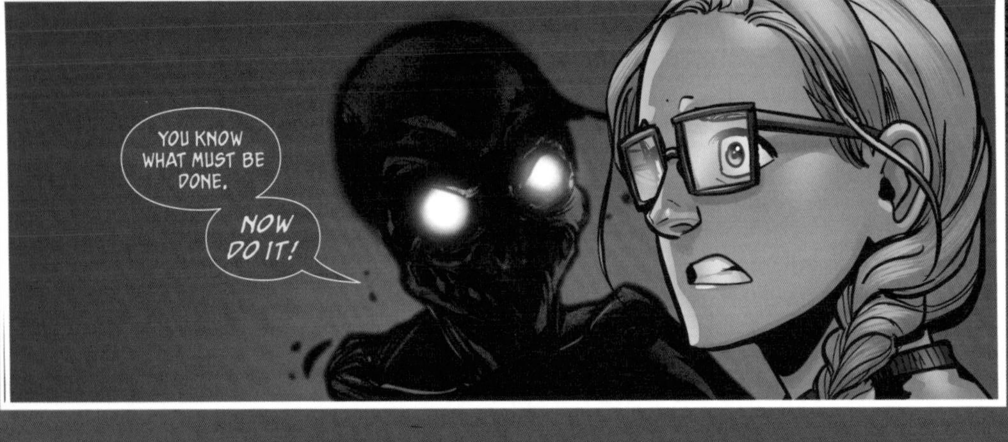
YOU KNOW WHAT MUST BE DONE.
NOW DO IT!

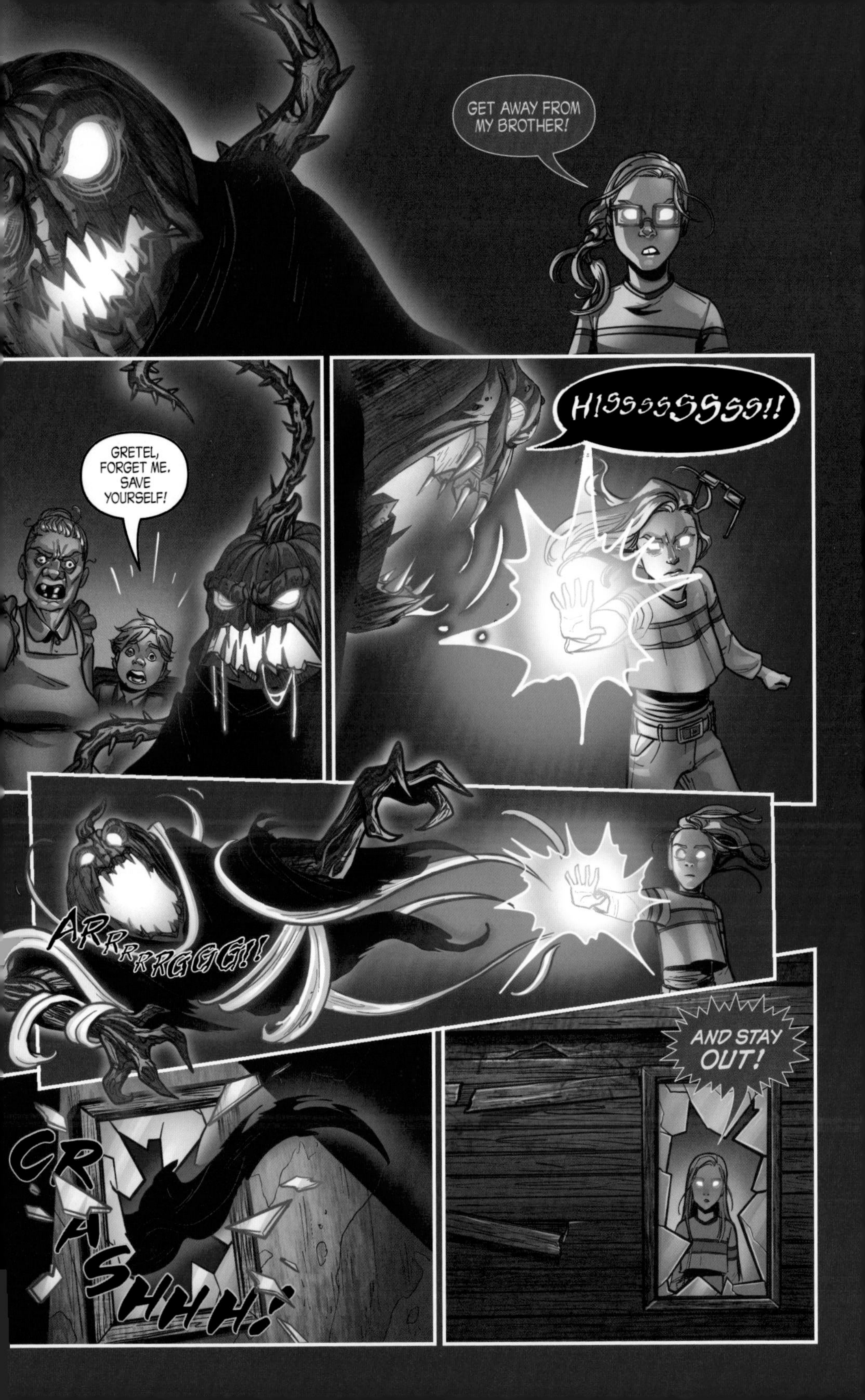
GET AWAY FROM MY BROTHER!
GRETEL, FORGET ME. SAVE YOURSELF!
HISSSSSSSSS!!
ARRRRRGGGG!!
GRASHHHH!
AND STAY OUT!

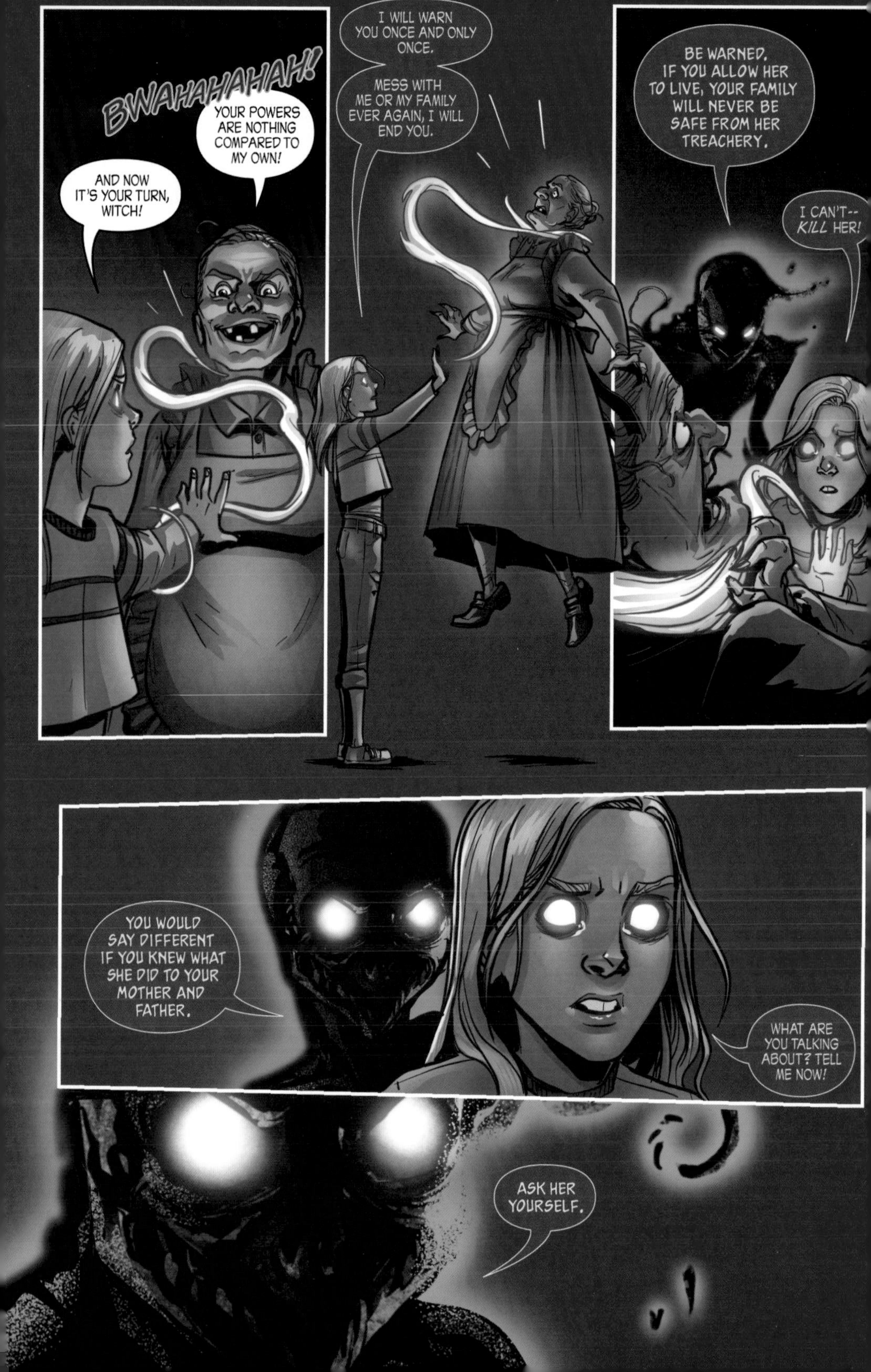
BWAHAHAHAH!
YOUR POWERS ARE NOTHING COMPARED TO MY OWN!
AND NOW IT'S YOUR TURN, WITCH!
I WILL WARN YOU ONCE AND ONLY ONCE.
MESS WITH ME OR MY FAMILY EVER AGAIN, I WILL END YOU.
BE WARNED. IF YOU ALLOW HER TO LIVE, YOUR FAMILY WILL NEVER BE SAFE FROM HER TREACHERY.
I CAN'T-- KILL HER!
YOU WOULD SAY DIFFERENT IF YOU KNEW WHAT SHE DID TO YOUR MOTHER AND FATHER.
WHAT ARE YOU TALKING ABOUT? TELL ME NOW!
ASK HER YOURSELF.

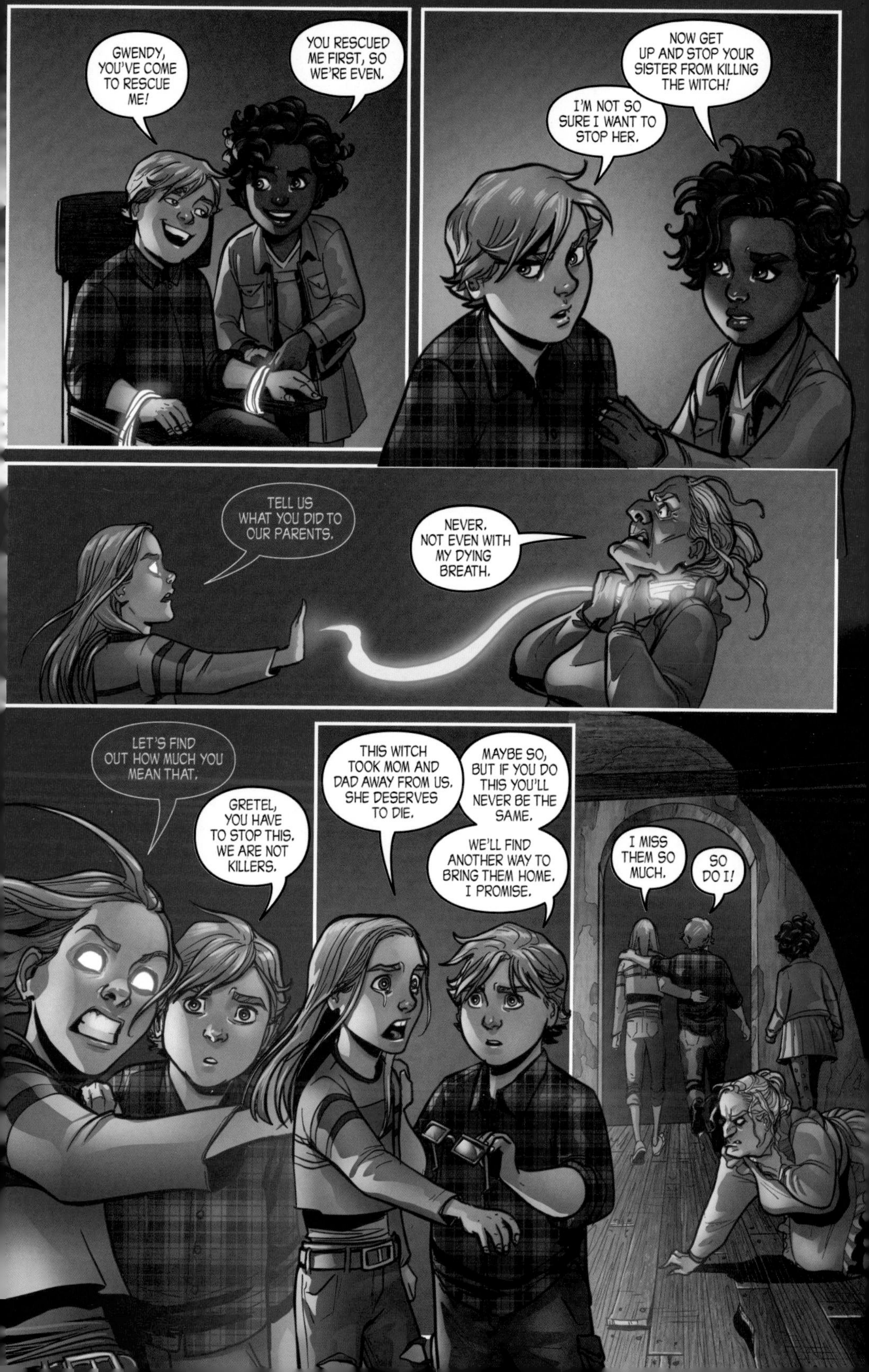
GWENDY, YOU'VE COME TO RESCUE ME!
YOU RESCUED ME FIRST, SO WE'RE EVEN.
I'M NOT SO SURE I WANT TO STOP HER.
NOW GET UP AND STOP YOUR SISTER FROM KILLING THE WITCH!
TELL US WHAT YOU DID TO OUR PARENTS.
NEVER. NOT EVEN WITH MY DYING BREATH.
LET'S FIND OUT HOW MUCH YOU MEAN THAT.
GRETEL, YOU HAVE TO STOP THIS. WE ARE NOT KILLERS.
THIS WITCH TOOK MOM AND DAD AWAY FROM US. SHE DESERVES TO DIE.
MAYBE SO, BUT IF YOU DO THIS YOU'LL NEVER BE THE SAME.
WE'LL FIND ANOTHER WAY TO BRING THEM HOME. I PROMISE.
I MISS THEM SO MUCH.
SO DO I!

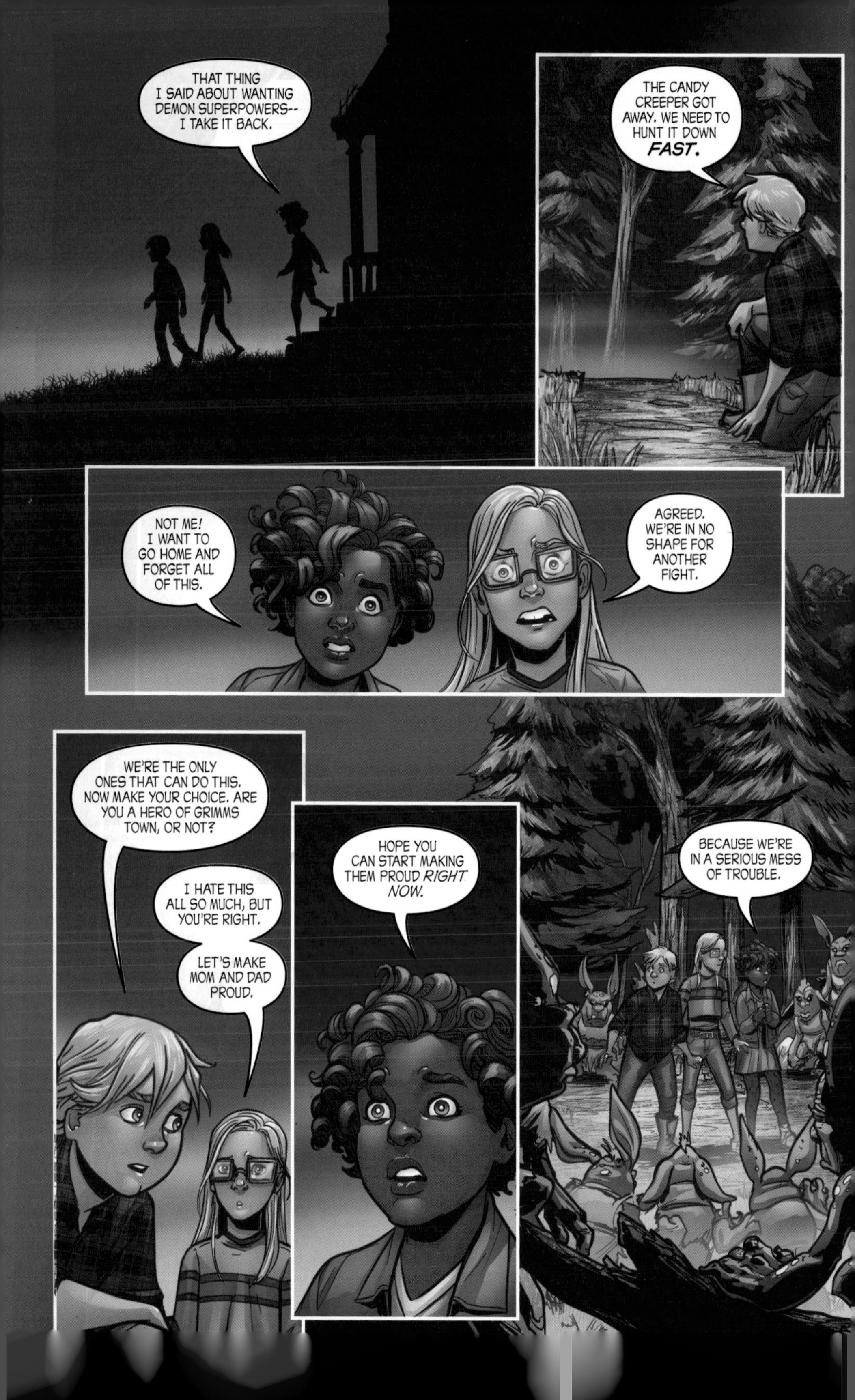
THAT THING I SAID ABOUT WANTING DEMON SUPERPOWERS-- I TAKE IT BACK.
THE CANDY CREEPER GOT AWAY. WE NEED TO HUNT IT DOWN *FAST*.
NOT ME! I WANT TO GO HOME AND FORGET ALL OF THIS.
AGREED. WE'RE IN NO SHAPE FOR ANOTHER FIGHT.
WE'RE THE ONLY ONES THAT CAN DO THIS. NOW MAKE YOUR CHOICE. ARE YOU A HERO OF GRIMMS TOWN, OR NOT?
I HATE THIS ALL SO MUCH, BUT YOU'RE RIGHT.
LET'S MAKE MOM AND DAD PROUD.
HOPE YOU CAN START MAKING THEM PROUD *RIGHT NOW.*
BECAUSE WE'RE IN A SERIOUS MESS OF TROUBLE.

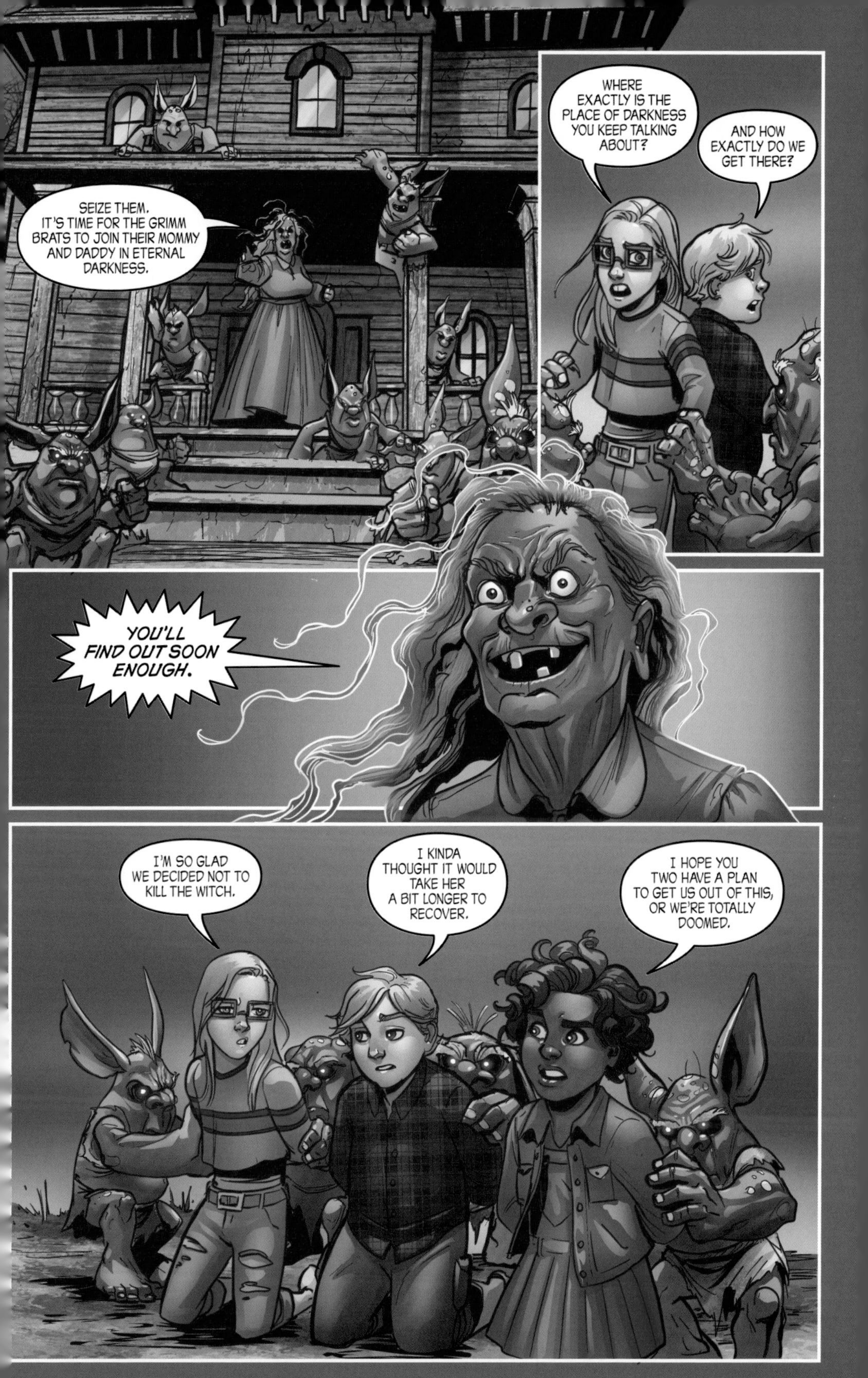
SEIZE THEM. IT'S TIME FOR THE GRIMM BRATS TO JOIN THEIR MOMMY AND DADDY IN ETERNAL DARKNESS.
WHERE EXACTLY IS THE PLACE OF DARKNESS YOU KEEP TALKING ABOUT?
AND HOW EXACTLY DO WE GET THERE?
YOU'LL FIND OUT SOON ENOUGH.
I'M SO GLAD WE DECIDED NOT TO KILL THE WITCH.
I KINDA THOUGHT IT WOULD TAKE HER A BIT LONGER TO RECOVER.
I HOPE YOU TWO HAVE A PLAN TO GET US OUT OF THIS, OR WE'RE TOTALLY DOOMED.

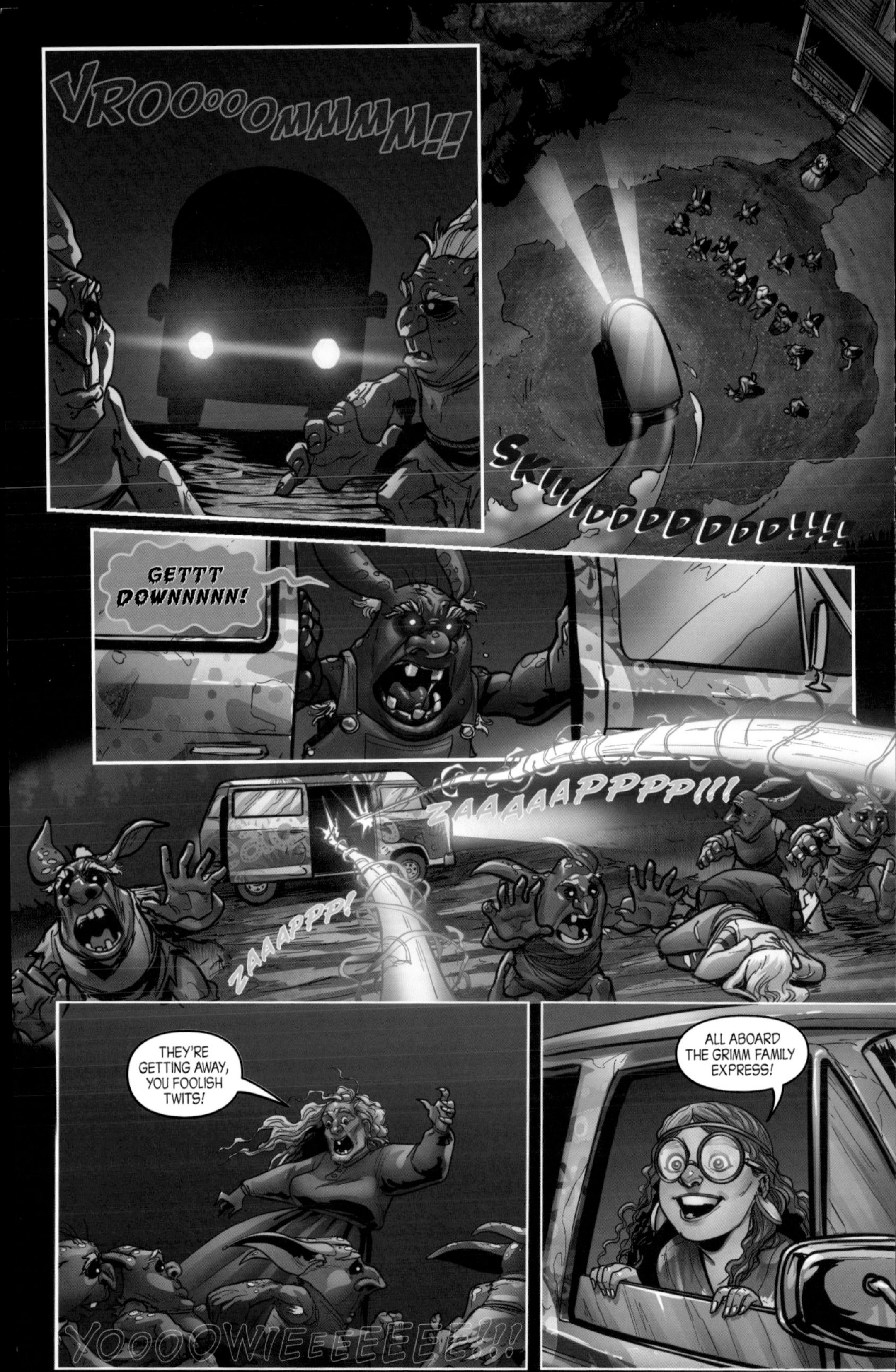
VROOoooOMMMMM!!
SKIIIIIDDDDDDDD!!!!
GETTT DOWNNNNN!
ZAAAAAPPPPP!!!
ZAAAPPPP!
THEY'RE GETTING AWAY, YOU FOOLISH TWITS!
YOOOOWIEEEEEEEE!!!
ALL ABOARD THE GRIMM FAMILY EXPRESS!

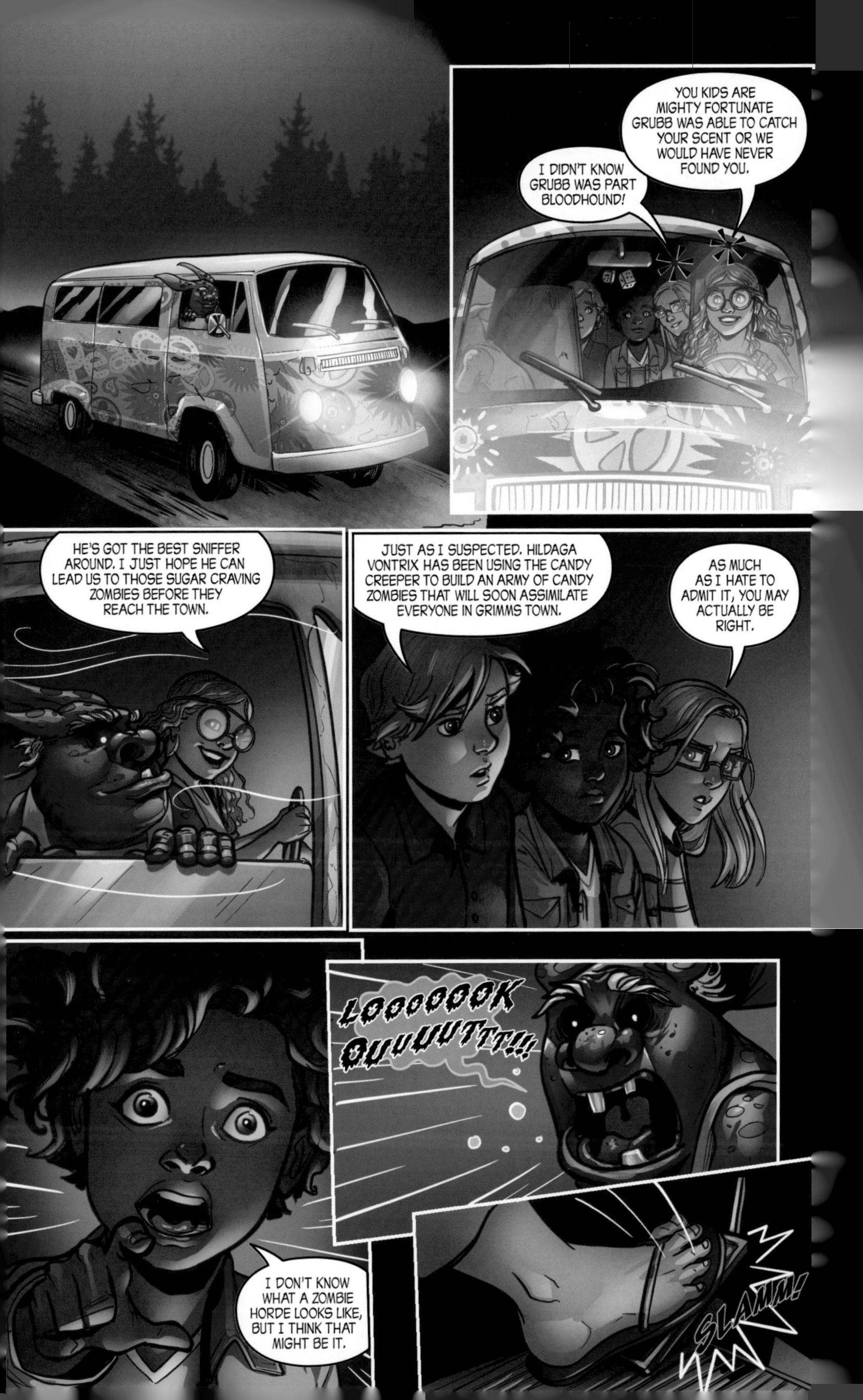
I DIDN'T KNOW GRUBB WAS PART BLOODHOUND!
YOU KIDS ARE MIGHTY FORTUNATE GRUBB WAS ABLE TO CATCH YOUR SCENT OR WE WOULD HAVE NEVER FOUND YOU.
HE'S GOT THE BEST SNIFFER AROUND. I JUST HOPE HE CAN LEAD US TO THOSE SUGAR CRAVING ZOMBIES BEFORE THEY REACH THE TOWN.
JUST AS I SUSPECTED. HILDAGA VONTRIX HAS BEEN USING THE CANDY CREEPER TO BUILD AN ARMY OF CANDY ZOMBIES THAT WILL SOON ASSIMILATE EVERYONE IN GRIMMS TOWN.
AS MUCH AS I HATE TO ADMIT IT, YOU MAY ACTUALLY BE RIGHT.
I DON'T KNOW WHAT A ZOMBIE HORDE LOOKS LIKE, BUT I THINK THAT MIGHT BE IT.
LOOOOOOK OUUUUTTT!!!
SLAMM!

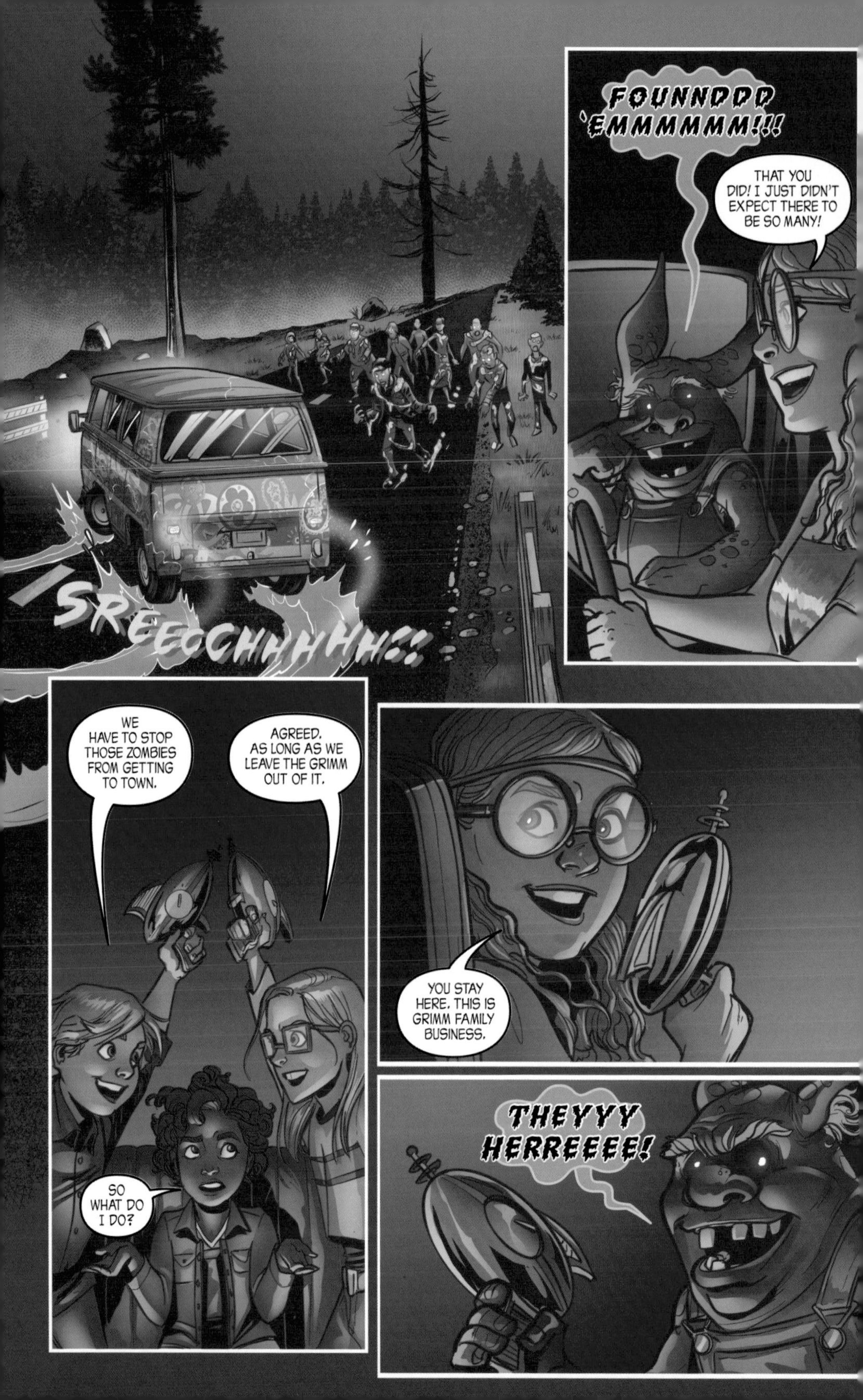
SREECCHHHHH!!
FOUNNDDD 'EMMMMMM!!!
THAT YOU DID! I JUST DIDN'T EXPECT THERE TO BE SO MANY!
WE HAVE TO STOP THOSE ZOMBIES FROM GETTING TO TOWN.
AGREED. AS LONG AS WE LEAVE THE GRIMM OUT OF IT.
SO WHAT DO I DO?
YOU STAY HERE. THIS IS GRIMM FAMILY BUSINESS.
THEYYY HERREEEE!

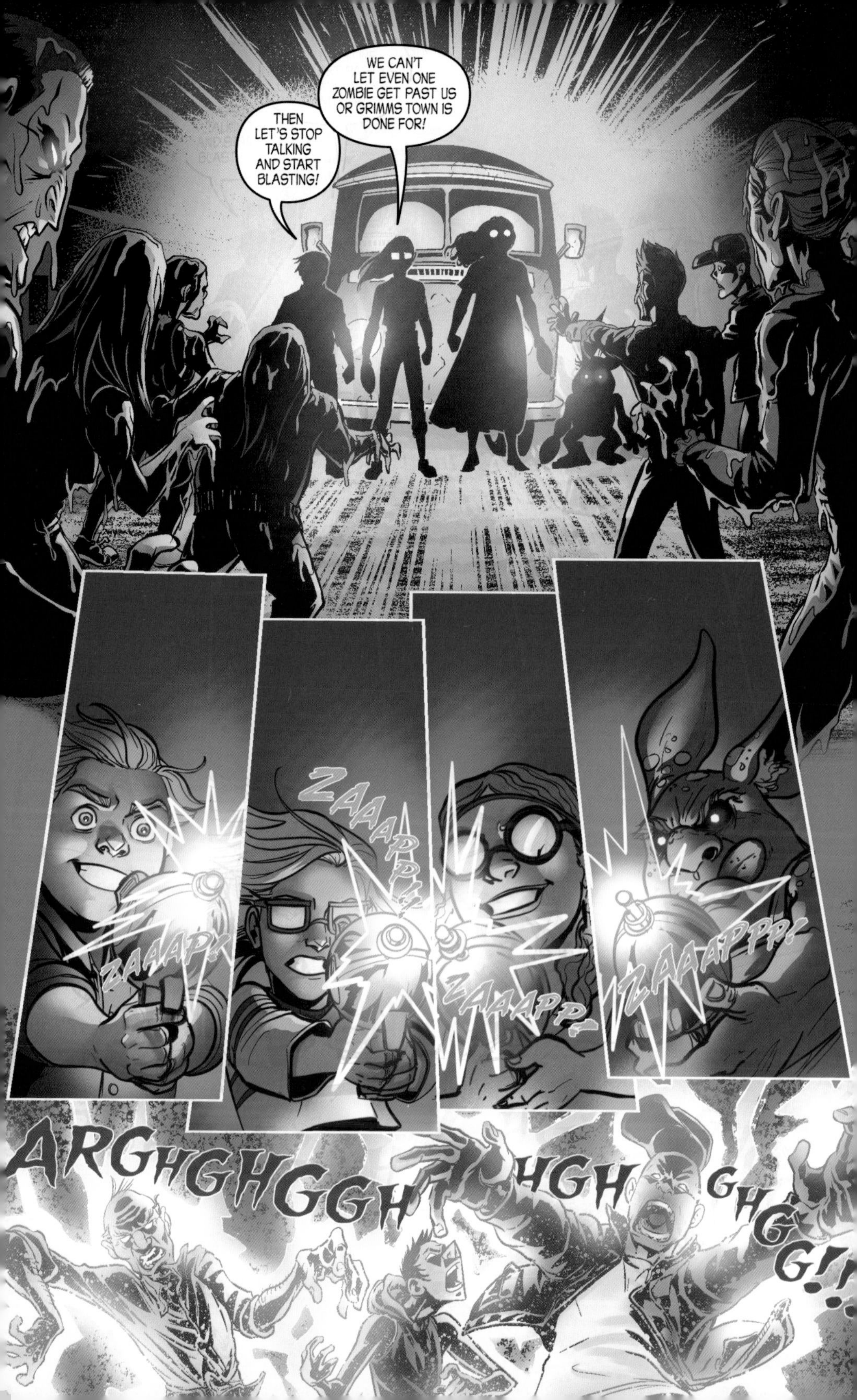
THEN LET'S STOP TALKING AND START BLASTING!
WE CAN'T LET EVEN ONE ZOMBIE GET PAST US OR GRIMMS TOWN IS DONE FOR!
ZAAAP!
ZAAAPP!!
ZAAAPP-
ZAAAPPP!
ARGHGHGGGH
HGH
GHGG!!

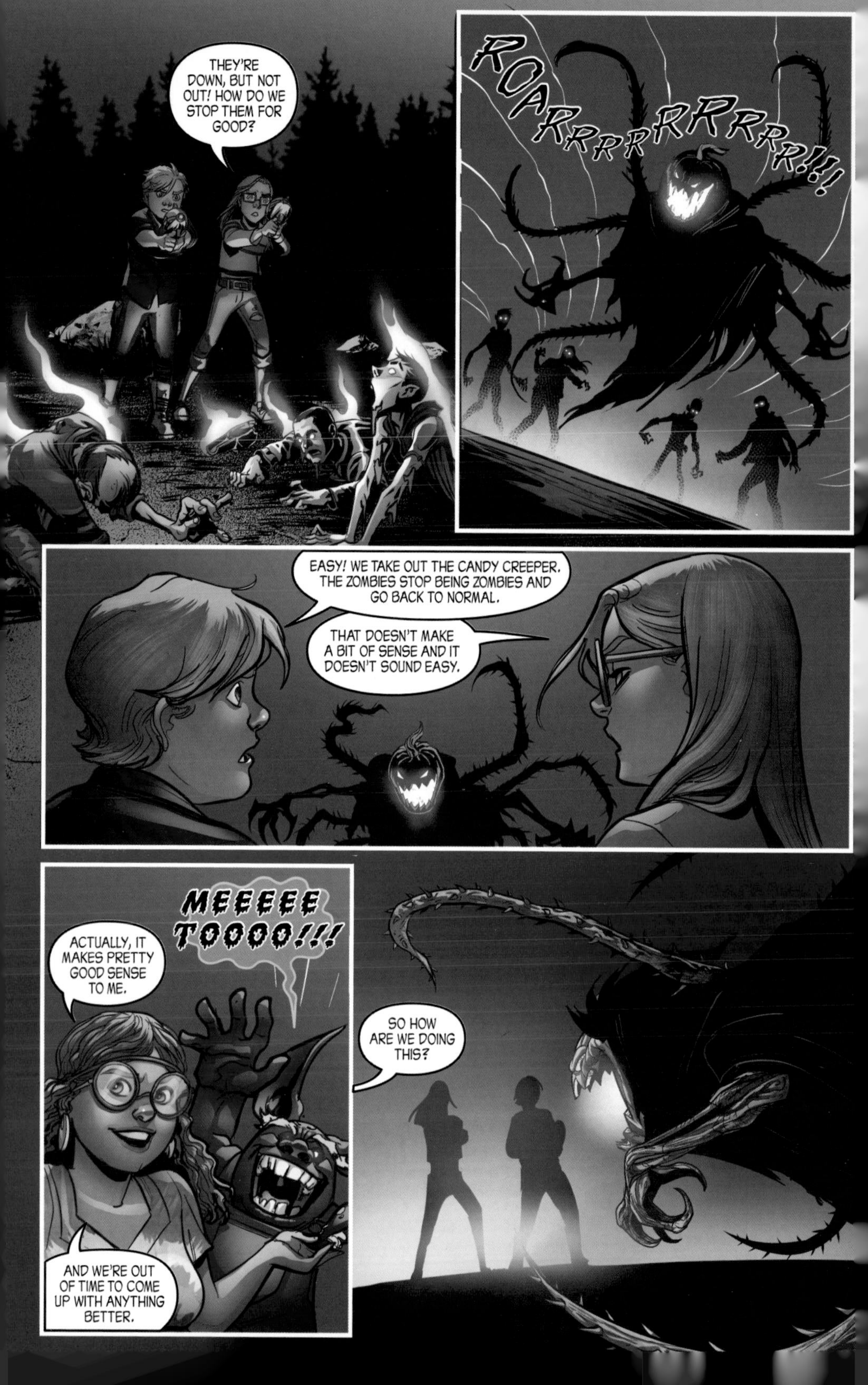
THEY'RE DOWN, BUT NOT OUT! HOW DO WE STOP THEM FOR GOOD?
ROARRRRRRRRRRRR!!!
EASY! WE TAKE OUT THE CANDY CREEPER. THE ZOMBIES STOP BEING ZOMBIES AND GO BACK TO NORMAL.
THAT DOESN'T MAKE A BIT OF SENSE AND IT DOESN'T SOUND EASY.
ACTUALLY, IT MAKES PRETTY GOOD SENSE TO ME.
MEEEEE TOOOO!!!
AND WE'RE OUT OF TIME TO COME UP WITH ANYTHING BETTER.
SO HOW ARE WE DOING THIS?

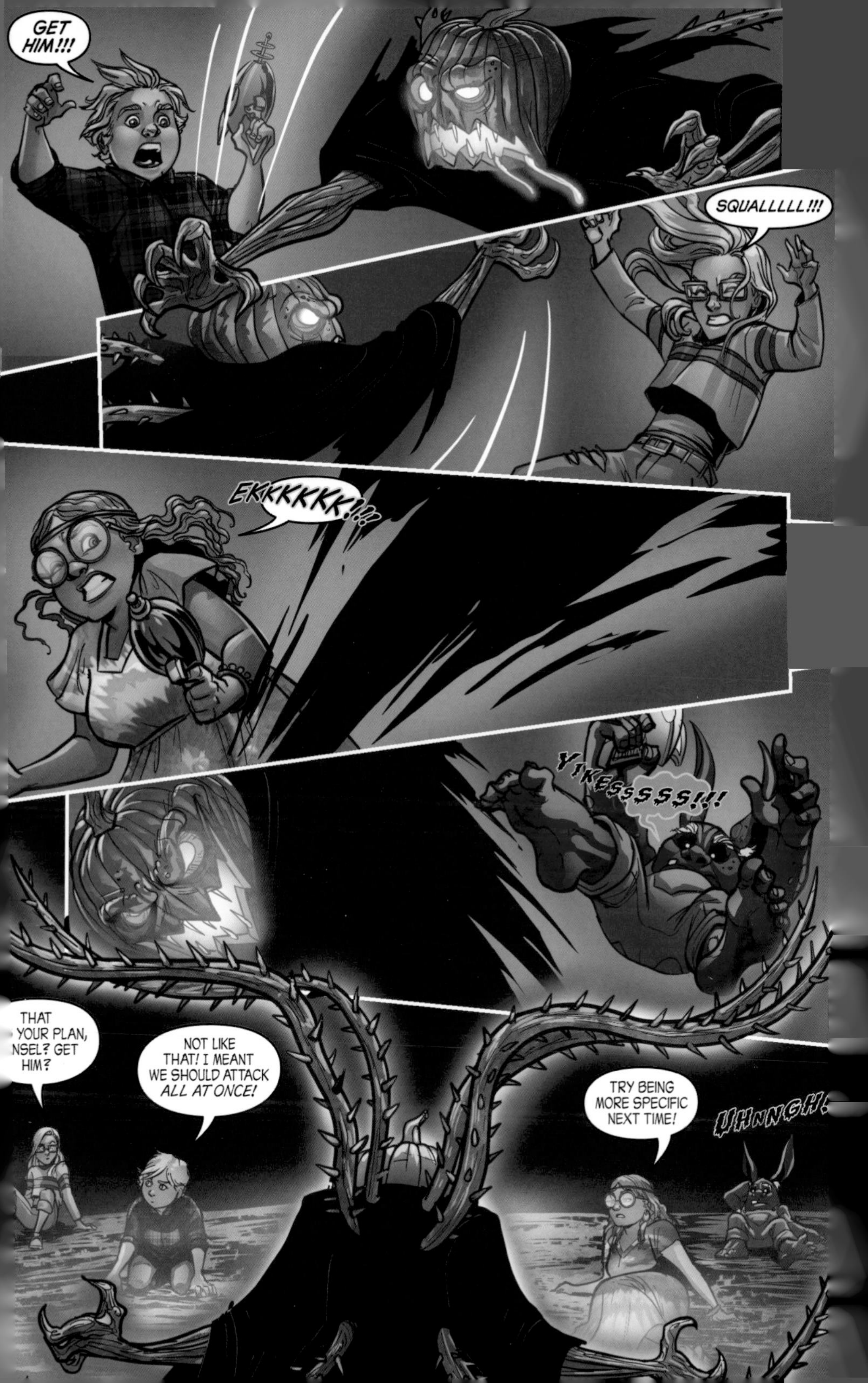
GET HIM!!!
SQUALLLLL!!!
EKKKKKK!!!
YIKESSSSSS!!!
THAT YOUR PLAN, NSEL? GET HIM?
NOT LIKE THAT! I MEANT WE SHOULD ATTACK *ALL AT ONCE!*
TRY BEING MORE SPECIFIC NEXT TIME!
UHNNGH!

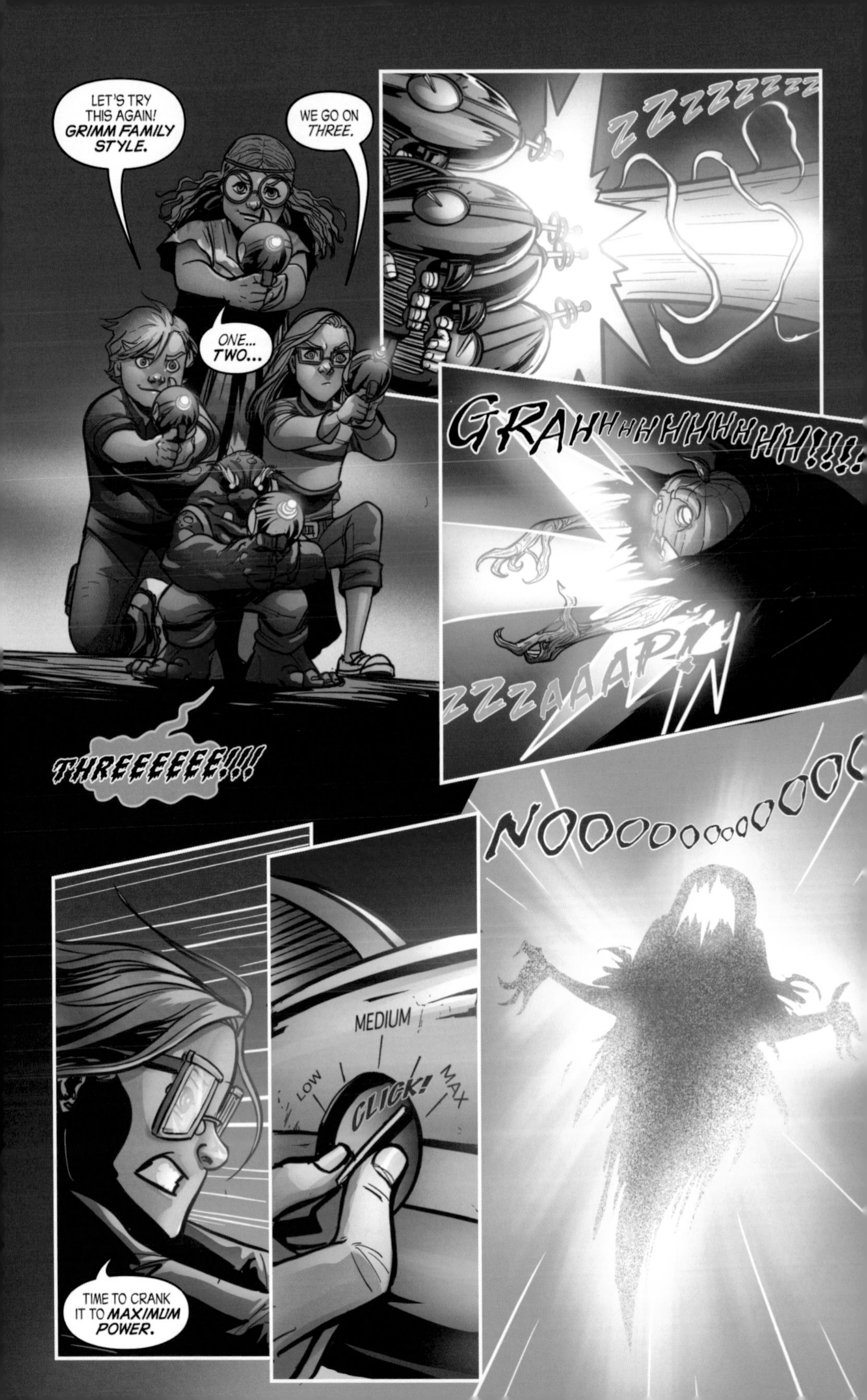

LET'S TRY THIS AGAIN! GRIMM FAMILY STYLE.
WE GO ON THREE.
ONE... TWO...
THREEEEEEE!!!
ZZZZZZZZZ
GRAHHHHHHHHHHH!!!!
ZZZAAAP!
TIME TO CRANK IT TO MAXIMUM POWER.
MEDIUM
LOW
MAX
CLICK!
NOOOOOOOOOOOO

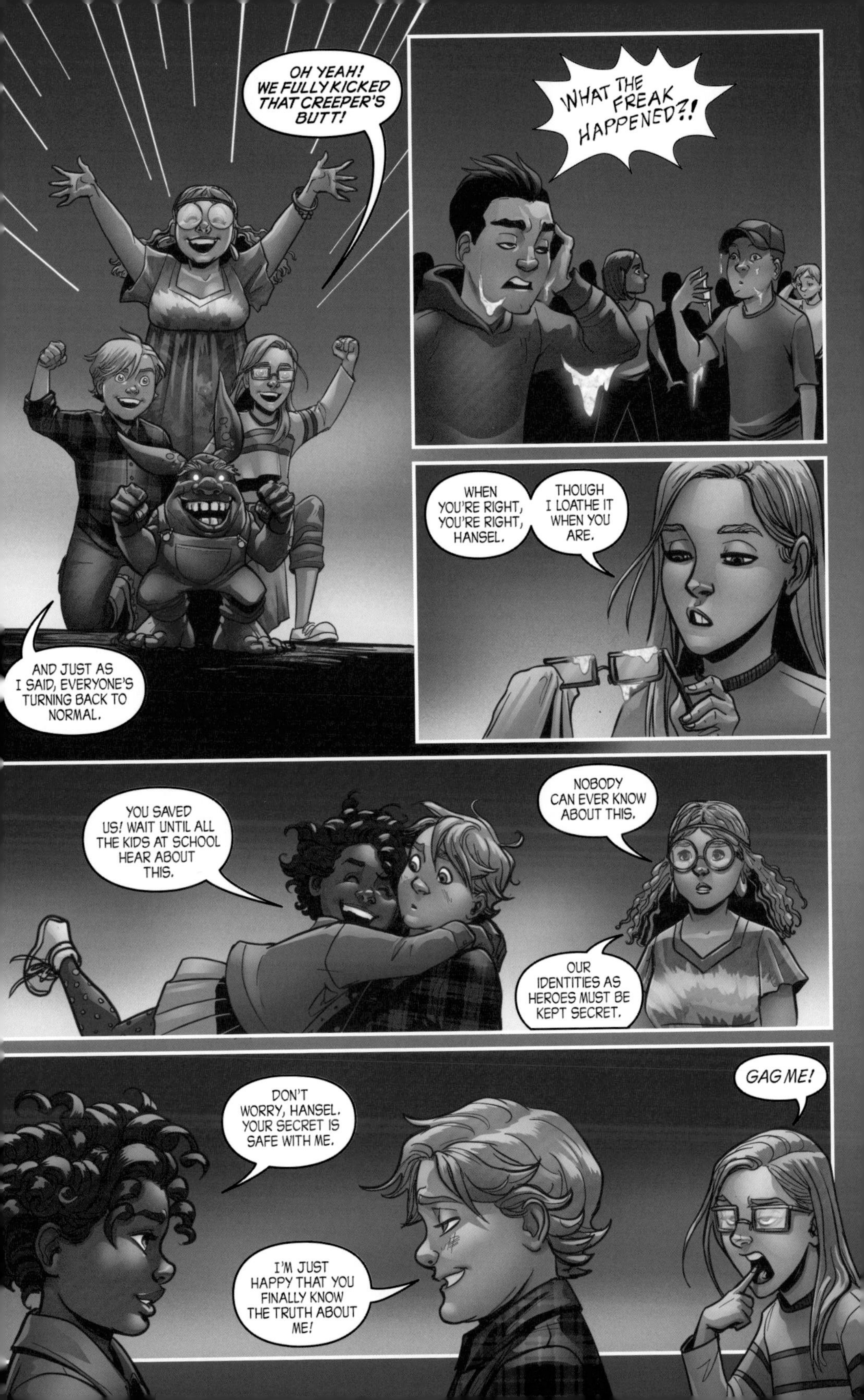
OH YEAH! WE FULLY KICKED THAT CREEPER'S BUTT!
AND JUST AS I SAID, EVERYONE'S TURNING BACK TO NORMAL.
WHAT THE FREAK HAPPENED?!
WHEN YOU'RE RIGHT, YOU'RE RIGHT, HANSEL.
THOUGH I LOATHE IT WHEN YOU ARE.
YOU SAVED US! WAIT UNTIL ALL THE KIDS AT SCHOOL HEAR ABOUT THIS.
NOBODY CAN EVER KNOW ABOUT THIS.
OUR IDENTITIES AS HEROES MUST BE KEPT SECRET.
DON'T WORRY, HANSEL. YOUR SECRET IS SAFE WITH ME.
I'M JUST HAPPY THAT YOU FINALLY KNOW THE TRUTH ABOUT ME!
GAG ME!

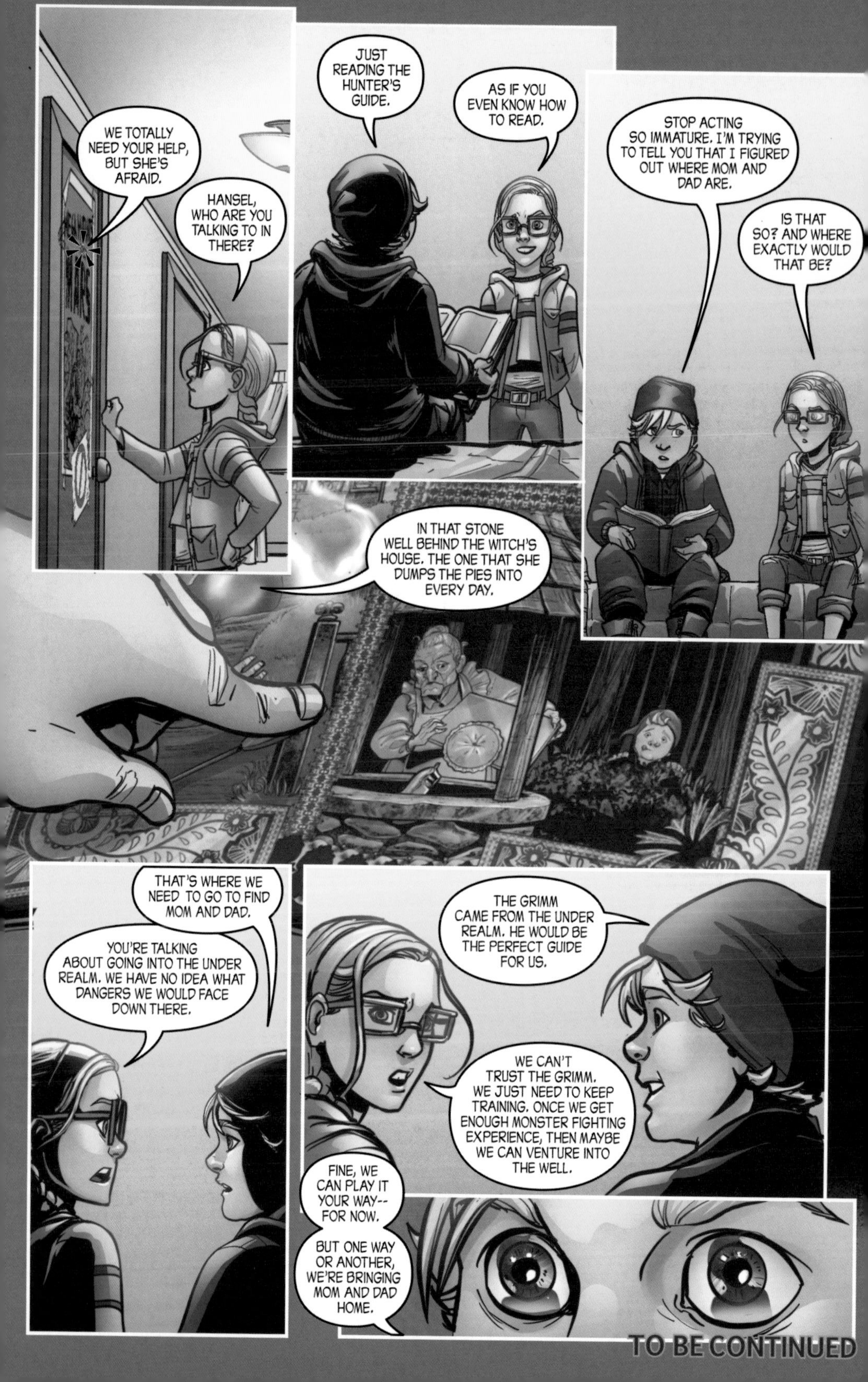
WE TOTALLY NEED YOUR HELP, BUT SHE'S AFRAID.
HANSEL, WHO ARE YOU TALKING TO IN THERE?
JUST READING THE HUNTER'S GUIDE.
AS IF YOU EVEN KNOW HOW TO READ.
STOP ACTING SO IMMATURE. I'M TRYING TO TELL YOU THAT I FIGURED OUT WHERE MOM AND DAD ARE.
IS THAT SO? AND WHERE EXACTLY WOULD THAT BE?
IN THAT STONE WELL BEHIND THE WITCH'S HOUSE. THE ONE THAT SHE DUMPS THE PIES INTO EVERY DAY.
THAT'S WHERE WE NEED TO GO TO FIND MOM AND DAD.
YOU'RE TALKING ABOUT GOING INTO THE UNDER REALM. WE HAVE NO IDEA WHAT DANGERS WE WOULD FACE DOWN THERE.
THE GRIMM CAME FROM THE UNDER REALM. HE WOULD BE THE PERFECT GUIDE FOR US.
WE CAN'T TRUST THE GRIMM. WE JUST NEED TO KEEP TRAINING. ONCE WE GET ENOUGH MONSTER FIGHTING EXPERIENCE, THEN MAYBE WE CAN VENTURE INTO THE WELL.
FINE, WE CAN PLAY IT YOUR WAY-- FOR NOW.
BUT ONE WAY OR ANOTHER, WE'RE BRINGING MOM AND DAD HOME.
TO BE CONTINUED

CREATOR BIOS

PHOTO BY KYLE CASSIDY

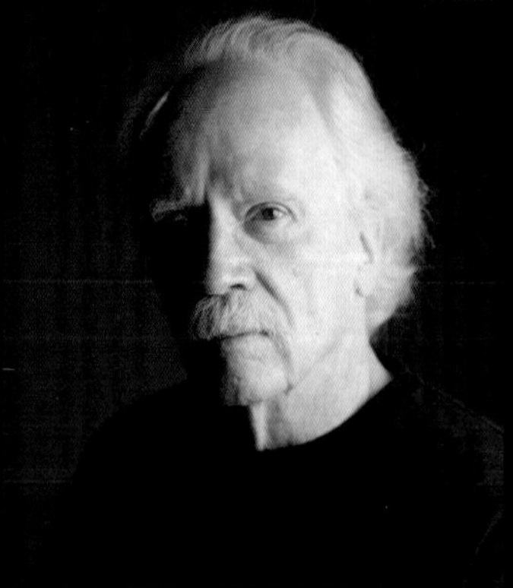

PHOTO BY DAN SANTONI

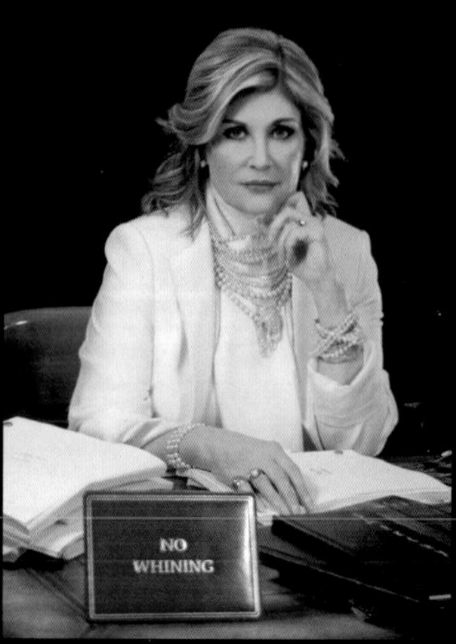
NO
WHINING

JOHN CARPENTER

John Carpenter's films are legendary: from the breakthrough ***Halloween*** (1978) to classics like ***Escape From New York, The Thing, Big Trouble In Little China*** and ***They Live***. His sci-fi love story, ***Starman***, earned Jeff Bridges a Best Actor Oscar nomination.

For the small screen, Carpenter directed the thriller ***Someone's Watching Me***, the acclaimed biographical mini-series, ***Elvis***, and the Showtime horror trilogy ***John Carpenter Presents Body Bags***. He also directed two episodes of Showtime's ***Masters Of Horror*** series.

He won the Cable Ace Award for writing the HBO movie, ***El Diablo***.

In the gaming world, he co-wrote the video game ***Fear 3*** for Warner Bros. Interactive.

In the world of comics, Carpenter co-wrote the BOOM! books ***Big Trouble in Little China*** with Eric Powell and the ***Old Man Jack*** series with Anthony Burch. He also co-wrote DC's ***Joker: Year Of The Villain*** with Burch. At Storm King Comics he is the co-creator of the award-winning series, ***John Carpenter's Asylum*** and the acclaimed annual anthology collection, ***John Carpenter's Tales for a HalloweeNight*** as well as ***John Carpenter's Tales of Science Fiction, John Carpenter Presents Storm Kids,*** and the upcoming ***John Carpenter's Night Terrors***.

SANDY KING

Writer, film and television producer and CEO of Storm King Productions.

With a background in art, photography and animation Sandy King's filmmaking career has included working with John Cassavetes, Francis Ford Coppola, Michael Mann, Walter Hill, John Hughes and John Carpenter.

She has produced films ranging from public service announcements on Hunger Awareness to a documentary on astronaut/teacher Christa McAuliffe for CNN, and major theatrical hits like ***They Live*** and ***John Carpenter's Vampires***. More recently, she directed and produced the John Carpenter Live Tour film and produced the horror/thriller, ***Crones***, for BlumHouse/Amazon.

New challenges interest and excite her.

The world of comic books is no exception. King is the first woman founder of a comic publishing house.

Through Storm King Comics, she has created and written the award-winning ***Asylum*** series, the multiple award-winning ***Tales for a Halloween Night*** anthologies, the monthly, ***John Carpenter's Tales of Science Fiction***, and the graphic novel line, ***Night Terrors***. In December 2019, King launched the new comics line, ***Storm Kids***, offering comics for ages 4 to 18 years old.

NEO EDMUND began his creative career appearing on numerous TV shows, most notably 100+ episodes of **Mighty Morphin Power Rangers**, as well as **The Walking Dead**, and **Buffy The Vampire Slayer.** He is also a USA Today best-selling author, a screenwriter, and comic book writer. His most recent works include the bestselling novel series **The Red Riding Alpha Huntress Chronicles,** numerous **Power Rangers** novels for Hasbro, and a new series of YA comics titled **The Grimms Town Terror Tales**. He has written for companies including Hasbro, Storm King, Penguin, Random House, Saban, History Channel, Discovery Channel, Animal Planet, Spike TV, & JumpStart Interactive.

RENAE DELIZ is a professional comic book artist, whose projects include the Eisner Nominated **The Legend of Wonder Woman**, and the NYT Bestseller **The Last Unicorn**, as well as managed the community charity project **Womanthology**, which celebrated and highlighted the great and diverse female creative talent in the comic book industry.

Born in Alaska and raised on the west coast, she now lives in Portland, Maine, with her four children, where she works at home.

JANICE CHIANG is a comic pioneer as one of the first female letterers in the industry. From hand-lettering to digital, she has forged the way for countless female comic artists. Janice works with publishers old (Marvel) and new (DC's Ringo Award-winning **Supergirls**). Comics Alliance honored Chiang as Outstanding Letterer of 2016 and ComicBook.com gave her the 2017 Golden Issue Award for Lettering. In May 2017, Chiang was featured as one of 13 women who have been making comics since before the internet on the blog Women Write About Comics. With her kind and forthright nature, Janice has built a loyal family within the comic community.

Another spooky tale from Storm King Comics...

Oh no! Who's been stealing fruit from all the gardens in Arbordale? Was it the prankster Chester Chipmunk? Or maybe Baby Fang? Accusations fly until someone suggests that maybe it was the Ghost of Bunnyburrow Manor! Neighbors have claimed to have seen it flying around, but are ghosts even real? And if they are, why would they be stealing fruit? Stanley Squirrel offers to lead an expedition into the house to see if it really is haunted and find out just what's been going on. But as the gang creeps around the house looking for answers, what they find isn't what any of them were expecting!